A
KNOCK
AT THE
DOOR

A KNOCK AT THE DOOR

T. W. ELLIS

SPHERE

First published in Great Britain in 2020 by Sphere

1 3 5 7 9 10 8 6 4 2

A CIP catalogue record for this book
is available from the British Library.

Hardback ISBN 978-0-7515-7593-4
Trade paperback ISBN 978-0-7515-7594-1

Typeset in Sabon by M Rules
Printed and bound in Great Britain by
Clays Ltd, Elcograf S.p.A.

Papers used by Sphere are from well-managed forests
and other responsible sources.

Sphere
An imprint of
Little, Brown Book Group
Carmelite House
50 Victoria Embankment
London EC4Y 0DZ

An Hachette UK Company
www.hachette.co.uk

www.littlebrown.co.uk

For Marjorie

A knock at the door can change everything. If it's expected, maybe not so much. But if you don't expect it, what then? There's that moment of surprise, perhaps even alarm, that demands your attention. Who just shows up unannounced these days? It's a summons that can't be ignored. A question that must be answered. Are they bringing good news or bad? Do they have something for you or do they want something from you?

Are they friend or are they foe?

Everywhere is busy in Rome at the height of the summer tourist season. This espresso bar was no exception. Tucked away in the Old City, it was small and cramped with bare stone walls, a domed ceiling, and only marginally less hot than it was outside. The huge coffee machine saw to that, pumping out a dragon's breath of steam and heat every few seconds. Fans thrummed overhead and did little more than stir the soupy humidity. I didn't really mind it. I liked the sheen I had to my skin, the glow. I had been in Italy for a few weeks and had somewhat acclimatised. I liked wearing shorts and sandals every day. I liked wearing my oversized sunglasses and floppy-brimmed hat. I felt in disguise. Another person almost. No longer a clueless New Yorker but a pseudo-European. I had been travelling for so long most people I met couldn't guess where I was born, but returning was inevitable because I was broke. Although in the process I had become cultured, tanned, worldly, and most of all bored as hell.

I'd grown up on the move and now I was a grown-up and restless.

Reckless, too. But I had a plan.

I had already made so many bad decisions I think I had lost the ability to recognise one in the making.

In he walked.

There was such an effortlessness to his gait that his footsteps seemed weightless. He was tanned from the Italian sun and his fair hair bleached blonder. I knew he wasn't a native because of his shoes. No Italian man would wear such severe lace-ups in the summer heat.

I watched him from the little round table where I was sat in the corner. Which wasn't a great distance away given the espresso bar was tiny. There were only a few tables for sitting at because most of the customers ordered an espresso, drank it while stood at the bar for usually no longer than a minute, then left. The bar itself was stainless steel, wiped down by the baristas every few minutes so that it always gleamed.

I found such places intimidating at first because they weren't the relaxed coffee shops I was used to back home but now I couldn't think of anywhere better to sit and people watch. My table was messy with my bag, my guidebook, the memoir I was struggling to read, my journal, my hat, my sunglasses. The glass of water and espresso cup had to compete for the leftover space.

I'd like to think there was something cute in this chaos.

His Italian was clumsy if I were to be generous and laughable if I wanted to be cruel. He tried, though. He only resorted to English because the barista took pity on him and cut short the indignity.

That's when I first saw him smile.

There was a sweet self-consciousness to it that was immediately ingratiating, as if he had no idea how handsome he was, how beautiful he looked when smiling.

2

Of course he did. He would have to be a fool not to know, but the power of his smile was in creating the illusion of obliviousness.

Maybe he practised.

Yes, I was a cynic.

Either way, I didn't care. I was already attracted to him and because the only other table in the bar was next to me, I had positioned my own chair so as to be closer to the one he would inevitably take before he had even turned round to look for a seat.

By that point, of course, I had my head in my book.

It was one of those achingly serious journeys of self-discovery, personal growth and womanhood.

I wanted such a journey myself, but so far no sale.

He took his time crossing the short space between the bar and the table. Maybe he felt awkward at the potential intrusion into my personal space given how close the chairs were set.

Fearing he might be a little shy and sip his coffee at the bar like a local, I glanced up and provided him with a shy smile of reassurance.

He relaxed and set his drink down on the table next to mine and then knocked it with a knee as he sat down. Coffee spilled from his cup and formed a small but steaming dark puddle on the table.

He exhaled. 'That was smooth.'

'Don't be too hard on yourself,' I told him. 'Those legs of yours are too long for these little tables.'

'They seemed taller at a distance.'

He went to stand again in the search for napkins but I took some tissues from my bag.

'Here,' I said.

He thanked me and took them, soaking up the spillage as

best he could, shaking his head to himself as if this was an unforgiveable error on his part.

'You're a lifesaver.'

'You don't know how much I'm going to charge you for the tissues yet.'

He smiled and offered his hand. 'I'm Leo.'

I took it. 'Jem.'

He already knew I was from the US too, so he said, 'What brings you to Rome?'

'That's a long story.'

'An interesting story?'

'I'm not so sure about that but maybe you'll be able to tell me by the end.'

He said, 'So you're willing to tell that story to a stranger?'

'Are we really strangers?'

He smiled again. 'Not any more.'

8:01 a.m.

The first thing I remember about that day is Leo gliding through the kitchen, trailing a scent of shower gel and shampoo in his wake. Clean, robust notes. He won't put on cologne until he's ready to leave. He's looking for something and humming to himself, providing a sweet if out-of-tune soundtrack to my preparations.

He finds what he's searching for – cufflinks he left by the sink as he slurped a hurried cup of coffee, hair still wet and uncombed – and passes behind me on his way back out.

'Doesn't really make any sense,' he says, peering over my shoulder.

I know what he's trying to do and I refuse to take the bait.

'If you say so then it must be true,' I reply, my tone as innocent as a fat little cherub.

He makes a sound of dissatisfaction. A gruff, throaty growl because he doesn't get to have his fun with me. He's in too much of a hurry to hang around here on a lost cause.

He's gone just as swiftly as he entered yet I know he'll be

distracted as he continues to get ready, conceiving and scheming little ways to take revenge. Ours is an endless game of one-upmanship fought hard with passion and verve. Kind of like a duel but a gentle one – playing not fighting – and there can be no loser because it's too much fun simply to play.

I smile to myself, both pleased at winning this little exchange and curiously excited in anticipation of his inevitable counter when he returns. I remind myself not to be too smug because I'm holding one of our good samurai knives and I really don't want to slice off a finger by mistake. I need to concentrate on the task at hand, which is halving a fat avocado, turning it around in my palm to circle the stone. I separate the two halves with a disproportionate degree of satisfaction because there are few things more satisfying than slicing an avocado in half and finding that it's not just ripe but perfect. People say they can tell just by squeezing one, but if that power does exist, I don't possess it. In fact, it could only ever be an estimate of ripeness at best and doesn't account for the possibility of bruising or oxidisation. In that way, slicing one open is a lottery. You have to commit to playing to know if you've won or lost.

In this instance, I've hit the jackpot.

There's not a single dark speck. Not a hint of oxidisation. The flesh is soft all the way through but not squishy. When I chop at the stone with the knife and twist and tug, it plops out without effort. My stomach cheers me on from the sidelines with rumbles of encouragement.

I'm going as fast as I can, I assure it.

Leo must have a sixth sense for timing, or he was sneakily waiting outside the kitchen for this exact moment to make his reappearance.

'It really doesn't make any sense,' he tells me again, this time not gliding by but stopping next to me as he fixes his tie into a well-practised full Windsor knot. His tone is firmer now, resolute, because whereas before he was making a passing observation, now he's all set to make a point.

I honour his presence with a glance in his direction. 'Are you looking for something else or are you just here to tease me?'

'If I were here to tease you I wouldn't be knotting this tie,' he says with a wry smile. 'I would be ripping it off.'

I place the knife down and swivel on the spot so my back is against the worktop, which I grip hard in both hands.

'Then why don't you?' I say, voice hushed and meaningful and my gaze boring into his own. 'I'm yours for the taking.'

Blood rushes to colour his cheeks as he stammers an incomprehensible response before roaring in frustration.

'What's wrong, honey?' I ask.

He points a finger at me. '*You*,' he snarls with a smile. 'You're what's wrong.'

I flutter my eyelashes. 'Whatever could you mean?'

His mouth hangs open for a moment but he says nothing further. Instead, he taps his watch with that same rigid finger and backs away, beaten again.

There's a chill to the morning air as I step outside to the greenhouse and inspect the tomato plants. There's more than a dozen, all tall and bushy thanks to the greenhouse's warm embrace and my diligent watering. Now in the first throes of winter they're yellowing in the tragedy of the perennials. Soon, they'll all be dead. They're all grown from seeds planted at the start of spring. Each seed saved from last year's harvest and lovingly germinated indoors until the shoots grew strong enough to be taken outside. No pesticides. No chemicals whatsoever. The tomatoes may be a little on the small side as a result, but they're one hundred per cent organic and utterly delicious. You've never really tasted a tomato until you've tasted one you've grown yourself.

It takes a few minutes to dig through foliage to find the ripest fruits to pick, and, when I have a fist's worth, I return to the kitchen to give them a quick rinse. A couple of seconds under the tap is all they need. Like I said: organic.

I heat a few drops of cold-pressed virgin coconut oil – organic too, obviously – in a stainless-steel skillet before swiping in the avocado chunks from the chopping board. A couple of minutes later I add the tomatoes after halving them. Himalayan salt, chilli flakes and freshly ground pepper follow. The scent is divine.

I try to be healthy, but what's the point in living for ever if you can't eat bread along the way? I saw off a couple of doorstop-thick slices from the crusty loaf I picked up at the farmer's market yesterday. It's sourdough, wholewheat, and sprinkled with all kinds of seeds. Soft and crunchy at the same time.

Leo is back in the kitchen for one last try to even the score. I almost feel guilty that I'm winning so handily thanks to his pressing need to be out of the door in a few minutes. Well, almost guilty.

He gives up any pretence of looking for something and gets straight to the point he's failed to make twice already.

He gestures at my breakfast. 'This is what I'm talking about. Avocado and tomato. They're both technically fruits, right? And you're going to put them on toast. Which means you're going to eat fruit ... on toast. How does that make any kind of sense?'

'It's delicious and you know it.'

'Hamburger ice cream might be a taste sensation but I'm never going to try it.'

I sigh. An exaggeratedly sympathetic sigh with plenty of disappointment wrapped up in there too.

'Is that really the best you can do?'

He grunts. 'Well, you kinda killed my groove the first time. And the second.'

'If something's easy is it even worth doing?'

He leans in to kiss me on the neck. 'I do what I have to do to get your attention.'

'If you want my attention,' I whisper into his ear, 'you know exactly what to do.'

'*Jemima Talhoffer*,' he says in his very best stern schoolmaster tone, 'I'm not doing *that*.'

'When exactly did you become so boring?'

'In case you've forgotten, your loving husband needs to be on a plane very soon.' He smiles a smile that could melt glaciers. 'Also, because you clearly have forgotten, I was always boring. You just didn't care before.'

'Yeah,' I say in return. 'Because you'd do that when I asked you to.'

'I had more time in those days. Have you seen my cufflinks?'

'You're wearing them.'

He glances down. Shakes his head. '*Duh.*'

I shoo him out of the kitchen, saying, 'Don't you dare miss that flight, mister.' Then, I shout after him: 'You need to keep me in the manner to which I've grown accustomed.'

He calls back with some retort but I've already switched on the radio for some musical accompaniment while I finish preparing breakfast and sit down at the kitchen table to devour my creation.

The table is too big for just the two of us but so is the rest of the house. It has more rooms than Leo and I could ever need, which is the point. When we bought the property we did so with the idea – the *intention* – of filling up that extra space. We spent months hunting for the perfect town, the perfect school, the perfect neighbourhood, the perfect street, and the perfect home. We spent so long getting everything right we didn't stop for a second to think that everything would go wrong before it even started.

My fruit on toast is delicious, yet somehow it's utterly unsatisfying and I can't finish it. I don't want to finish this one small plate of food on a table large enough to hold many plates.

Leo says, 'I'm almost set and I even have a whole minute spare with which to lavish you with affection.'

I don't hear him at first because my mind has drifted to that dark place, so familiar it's almost routine, and it takes an extra moment for his words to reach me. They drag me back out of that void. I don't know how long I dwelt there. It felt like a few seconds but it could have been so much longer.

I stand and face him so he can draw me into an embrace. He's now fragrant with cologne, warm and strong.

He glances down at my unfinished breakfast. 'You're not hungry?'

I shake my head. 'I'm not as hungry as I thought.'

He gives me a look I know too well. 'Did you sleep okay?'

An innocent question asked in an innocent tone and yet there are so many questions within that one single question it would take all morning to answer them all. It's not just how did I sleep, but did I sleep enough? Did I have nightmares? Am I tired? Am I feeling okay? Is how I slept going to affect my day? My mood? Do I feel down as a result? Am I so down I will go back to bed? Will I cry all afternoon? Will I make a phone call begging him to come home because I can't make it through the day without him? Will he then speed home to find me perfectly fine because my mood has flipped once more? Am I going to explode into a rage over nothing at all because I simply have to let out all the negative thoughts? Can I be saved? Will I drive him away with this awful, cruel disease?

All those questions and more can be boiled down into one, which is what he's really asking:

Can he still love me?

I smile. I'm so good at smiling sometimes even I forget they're not real. 'Slept like a baby.'

He smiles back, relieved. He can carry on loving me a little longer.

I have a whole host of metaphors to hide the truth: slept like a baby, like a log, like the dead, like an Egyptian mummy, like a drunk, like a regular person . . .

He reaches across me to scoop up the half-finished slice of toast. 'Don't mind if I do then.' He takes a huge bite and is loud as he chews because despite his earlier claim of having time, he's anxious not to miss his flight. 'You're right,' he says. 'It really is delicious.'

I nod in agreement. I can't bring myself to offer a smug retort. I'll get no satisfaction from I-told-you-so.

'I'll call you when I land,' Leo says and moves in for a good-bye kiss, something passionate and lingering.

We bump teeth.

We laugh.

I say, 'If that isn't a sign to get moving then I don't know what is.'

He rubs his incisors with a finger. 'Let's try again.'

We kiss with more success this time, his hands on my hips and mine holding his shoulders. He's always been a good kisser and even now after all these years still makes the effort, yet I realise my eyes are open before we finish.

He doesn't notice.

As he steps back he says, 'How do I look?'

He twirls on the spot like a ballerina, only a clumsy one.

'Absolutely, incredibly, demonstrably . . . passable.'

He frowns but he knows I'm joking. He doesn't need me to tell him he's handsome in his suit – far too handsome – and I feel a rush of jealousy at the inevitable attention he will draw. When we were first dating I would find it amusing to catch women checking him out when he had absolutely no idea. It made me feel good about myself, about being with him. That seems a long time ago. Now, I worry he might start noticing, he might start checking out those young fertile creatures in return.

I notice the time. 'You gotta move, bud.'

He notices too. 'Whoa, yes I do.'

He grabs his suitcase and I follow him to the door. I hug myself against the chill while I watch him climb into his car.

'Bye,' he calls from behind the wheel.

I wave at him while he pulls out of the driveway and he looks back at me in the wing mirror. There's something in his eyes I can't quite read.

Sadness?

Regret?

I keep my hand up until he's driven out of sight.

Five minutes later, there's a knock at the door.

Nothing will ever be the same again.

8:18 a.m.

In those few minutes between Leo's departure and the knock at the door I return to the kitchen to clean up but find myself sat back at the table, tired and heavy. Pale sunlight streams through the window above the sink and bathes my face. Refracted through the glass pane, that light is bright and warm and in this moment it's almost possible to convince myself this is all I need. This husband, this life, this house.

I should be grateful for everything I have, not angry for what I don't.

The house around me is staggering in its beauty. Or, it will be when it's finished. A grand old thing fallen into disrepair that I've been renovating since the day we moved in. It started out as a hobby and a passion project and then somewhere along the way became a kind of medication. But drugs lose their effectiveness over time, don't they? We build up a tolerance, a resistance. Eventually, they stop working altogether.

Now, the house is an excuse for isolation, a reason to absent myself from the world. There's never any time to meet an acquaintance for coffee because there's always a skirting board to replace. There's never a weekend free to take a little vacation because I've paint arriving at the hardware store for the study. Nothing ever gets finished. Every room is a work-in-progress.

We both know what's really going on but this has been a long, slow process. For all his endless perfections, Leo never figured he would have to deal with my problems. He doesn't know how to, and since I've become so very good at faking it, most of the time there's no need for him to do so. I'm so used to hiding my anxiety that he has no idea how stressful I find it simply going to get groceries. He doesn't know I sometimes stop my car before I reach the house so I can scream or cry to reset myself before pulling up with a big smile. I keep eye drops in the glove compartment, wet wipes and makeup. I'm not sure if he's worked out that if I didn't have to leave the house to teach my class, I probably wouldn't at all.

The way I see it is that we have a finite capacity for dealing with stress. It doesn't matter if that capacity is overfilled by one huge trauma or lots of little ones.

Once we're over it then we're in trouble.

After that point, we can't cope.

Leo's a good man and this Jem is not the Jem he signed up for, not the Jem he married, the Jem to whom he planned to spend the rest of his life as husband. We're both suffering, and it's unfair on him that I'm suffering more, that I need so much more than him. He's still Leo. He's still the exact same Leo I fell for, who I said 'yes' to without a second of hesitation. He hasn't changed one single bit. My biggest fear is that one day he'll realise he doesn't recognise me, that he doesn't know me. I'm doing everything I can to wear the mask of the me he wants, not the me I am.

Ours is the only house on the end of the single-lane of

asphalt. The previous owners told me that there had been a plan to build more houses, to make a little suburb. It was all a scam, apparently. Some elaborate tax fraud scheme by the developers. I've never looked into it so I'm not entirely sure it's true. I don't care. The house is isolated, which is what I wanted then, because I wanted peace, I wanted space for the children to play. This Jem is so grateful for that Jem's thinking, because this Jem couldn't deal with neighbours, couldn't fake all those smiles, all that small talk.

How are you today?

Awful, how are you?

Uh, I'm, uh . . .

If you go left at the intersection there's a long stretch of highway that leads to the interstate. I've been that way maybe half a dozen times in the five years we've been here. Leo has travelled the world twice over in the same time I've covered twenty square miles. I've become the ultimate homebody. I make endless excuses. I tell him things like, 'Everything I need is right here,' and it's been for ever since he's tried to get me out of the county. He's long since given up trying to get me to go travelling with him, to join him on one of his many business trips.

Leo knows what I'm doing with the house – or not doing – of course. He doesn't say anything but it would be pointless if he did. What could he even say? I'd just deny it, rationalising my actions so well I'd end up believing my own lies.

He wants the house finished because he's desperate for me to try new things. New things are not all they're cracked up to be in my experience. There is safety in familiarity. There is sanity in routine. I need both.

Which is the only reason I still work. Thankfully, I work for myself so there's no boss to answer to, no one to fire me for not fulfilling my obligations.

Thinking of work reminds me I need a shower. I'm still sweaty and dishevelled from the early morning class I taught, but I don't stink – I hope I don't stink – and after an hour of intense bending and stretching I am always exhausted. The uneducated think yoga is easy, but when you do it right, you feel it in a way that no other workout can match. You can feel it for days. Not just in your legs or your arms or whatever you're working on, but everywhere. Every muscle. Every sinew. I'm merciless with my pupils. I'm a monster. I delight in that role and they take my class because that's what they need me to be for them. And it is a role. That monster isn't me. It's me in a scary mask. I feel sorry for those who take my class and then have to rush off to the office or back home to make breakfast for a brood of screaming kids.

With Leo gone, our house is devastatingly silent.

Then the knock at the door destroys that quiet.

A firm knock from a strong hand.

I'm quick to answer because I think it's going to be Leo. I don't for a second consider it might be anyone else. If I did, I would stay at the kitchen table, not moving, not breathing. I can't answer the door to strangers. I don't even remember the last time I tried.

As I hurry along the hallway, I picture Leo with his heart beating fast, cheeks a little flushed having dashed back because he's forgotten his passport or his currency or some letter or document or purchase order. It's a loud knock because he thinks I'll be in the shower and I won't hear otherwise. That's why he didn't call ahead. He's left the car running so he doesn't have his house keys on his person. They're dangling from the steering column.

I'm shaking my head as I make my way into the hallway, smiling to myself because I can't quite understand how Leo

16

can be both so switched on, so clever, and yet so forgetful and disorganised. He's a walking contradiction and I adore him all the more for it.

There's a second knock, harder than the first. Leo's thumping the door with the meaty part of his fist.

'All right, Mister Sommelier,' I call. 'I'm coming, I'm coming . . .'

I make a series of orgasmic moans that grow increasingly louder as I draw closer to the door because I'm feeling silly and I want him to smile, despite the obvious stress he must be feeling at forgetting whatever it is he's forgotten.

'*I'm coming,*' I cry out as I turn the handle and pull the door open to reveal not Leo but two serious individuals in dark suits.

One man. One woman.

The fresh organic tomatoes I picked earlier weren't as red as my resulting face.

My mouth is a desert. My throat is stripped raw by sand.

'I'm, uh . . .'

'Coming?' the serious man asks.

'Sorry,' I manage to utter, forcing air up through my constricted windpipe. 'I'm sorry . . . about that. I thought you were someone else.'

The serious woman reaches a hand beneath her jacket and withdraws a leather folding wallet that she flips open in an effortless gesture. She's done the exact same motion a thousand times at least, I'm sure. I glimpse a holstered gun.

'I'm Agent Wilks,' she proclaims in a strong, assured voice. 'With me is Special Agent Messer. We need to speak with you about your husband, Mrs Talhoffer. May we come inside?'

8:19 a.m.

I stare at the shiny FBI badge. There's a little photograph of Wilks accompanying it. Serious face, just like in real life.

She looks to be somewhere in her late forties with an intense expression and a short, neat haircut. Blonde hair. Green eyes. Messer is a big guy, a decade younger, with a square face and short black hair. He's a little paler too, a little more pruned and scrubbed. Just about young enough to use a moisturiser without it being an attack on his masculinity.

I'm a decent, law-abiding citizen with nothing to hide but I'm still embarrassed. Humiliated. I don't want to let these two people inside my home, yet they're FBI agents. I can't say no, can I? It doesn't even cross my mind to ask for more details first. I'm immediately subservient, immediately inferior to their badges, their authority.

I can't quite look them in the eye as I nod and say, 'Okay.'

I hold the door open for them and they walk in with the same kind of robotic gait. I imagine they take classes for everything, even walking.

'Go through, please,' I say.

I'm confused more than anything else.

Why would the FBI need to talk to me about Leo?

The good thing about feeling so embarrassed is that it completely overrides my anxiety. Just like that, I'm cured. If only temporarily.

I follow them through the hallway and into the living area where they turn round to face me. My embarrassment is starting to fade because with every passing second I'm growing more curious as to why they're here.

They stand side by side, with their serious expressions and their serious suits. Messer is tall and wide and intimidating for it, but Wilks has an absolute confidence that makes me just as uneasy. I guess she is the more senior because she's the older of the two. I don't know enough about the FBI to know whether these two would be partners or if there is some hierarchy. For once I regret not watching more television.

'You just missed him,' I say. 'He left only a few minutes ago.'

Wilks says, 'Why don't we sit down?'

I shrug. 'Sure.'

I take a seat on the arm of the chair closest to me while Wilks and Messer take the sofa next to them. It's a three-seater so there's plenty of room. Neither sits back. Neither relaxes. This is something severe.

'Mrs Talhoffer—'

'Jem, please,' I insist. 'I don't even know why I took Leo's last name when I hate it so much. Hate's probably too strong a word, but I—'

Wilks makes a polite nod of acquiescence. 'Jem, I'm hoping you can assist us with an ongoing investigation involving a money-laundering ring we've been trying to expose for some time now.'

My eyebrows have never been such perfect arches. 'Money-laundering ring? I don't even know how money is laundered in the first place let alone anything about a ring.' I think of something. I don't know where I know this from, but I say, 'Wouldn't that be the jurisdiction of the Treasury? Shouldn't it be the Secret Service investigating?'

Messer answers the question: 'The Secret Service covers counterfeiting. Money laundering is under the jurisdiction of the FBI. We wouldn't be here otherwise.'

His tone is steering into condescension by the end and evidently that isn't part of the game plan because Wilks shoots him a brief look of admonishment.

'What has money laundering got to do with Leo?'

Wilks says, 'Mrs Talhoffer – sorry, Jem – we believe that a criminal enterprise has been using your husband's wine merchant business to clean drug money. Which is, as I'm sure you can appreciate, a very serious matter. So, it's important that you answer our questions as thoroughly as you can. Do you understand what I've told you so far?'

I understand the words yet I can't quite believe what I'm hearing. 'Drug money . . . ?'

Wilks nods.

'Leo's business?'

Wilks nods.

'A criminal enterprise using Leo to clean drug money? So, you mean a cartel? A drug cartel? I can't believe it. I don't believe it. He would never do that. I'm telling you, never.'

My voice rises with each word.

Wilks leans closer. 'We don't believe your husband is involved willingly, which is why we're talking to you now in advance of Mr Talhoffer. We have reason to think he is being coerced into working for this organisation.'

'They're forcing him? How? Why?' I'm shaking my head. 'How could they possibly coerce Leo into working for them?'

Wilks and Messer are looking at me like it's obvious.

It takes me a moment to realise it is obvious.

'Me?'

'Leo is trying to do what he thinks is best,' Wilks explains, 'to protect you.'

Messer is a little less subtle. 'If he doesn't do what they want they'll send people to kill you. And we're not talking by way of a nice clean bullet to the head. These are ruthless people. Awful people. The worst of the worst.'

The room is so heavy with silence I feel like it might collapse and entomb me. I don't know what to say, so I say, 'I don't know what to say.'

Wilks does her best to look sympathetic. 'We appreciate it's a lot to take in.'

'No offence, but you really can't appreciate how much this is to take in.' I look down at my hands wringing in my lap. 'I'm just starting my day and you come by and drop this bomb on me. I haven't even showered yet.'

Wilks and Messer are silent as they let me work through my shock. Something occurs to me.

'Did you wait for Leo to leave before coming to see me?'

For an instant they look like guilty schoolchildren caught throwing stones or stealing treats.

I say, 'How long have you been spying on us?'

'We waited at the intersection,' Wilks answers. 'Once we saw Leo pass, we gave it a minute and came here. We haven't been spying on you, Jem.' She smiles. 'We really don't have the resources.'

I guess the smile is part of a softly-softly strategy but there is nothing gentle about what I'm being told and I don't return it.

'Is Leo in danger?'

'No,' is Wilks' quick reply. 'He's of a rare value to the criminal organisation he—'

'Why can't you just call it a cartel?'

'Leo is an essential part of their organisation thanks to his business. He's perfectly safe, and we want to keep it that way. Which is why we've come to see you first.'

Messer adds: 'We don't want to approach Leo in case he's under observation.'

'You're saying the cartel has people watching him?'

'We're saying that it's a possibility.'

'Then they would be watching here, the house, wouldn't they?'

Wilks is shaking her head before I'm finished. 'There's no need for them to do that. They know where he lives, where you live, which is enough. When he's away from here, when he's working for them, that's when they would pay closer attention.'

'How can you possibly know that?'

'It's what we do,' Wilks says with the kind of unshakable confidence I've never come close to feeling myself. 'We know how this kind of criminal organisation – how this kind of cartel – operates. Please trust us on that.'

I'm not sure exactly when it's happened during this conversation but I've slipped off the arm of the chair and into it proper. Slipped is perhaps too generous a term. I've fallen. I've collapsed.

'You promise me that nothing is going to happen to Leo?'

Wilks is resolute: 'I swear it.'

'Okay,' I breathe, nodding. 'Okay. What do you need to know from me? Not that I know how I can possibly help when I didn't know any of this until a few minutes ago.'

Messer takes over. 'We believe that the last time Leo was in Rome he met with the European representative of the cartel.

22

We believe this representative gave Leo information: accounts, codes, businesses all around the world. Fronts, Jem. Cartel fronts. We believe that Leo was given access to their global financial infrastructure. That kind of information could expedite our progress by years. I don't want to stray into hyperbole but we're talking about enough evidence to bring down the entire cartel.'

'Why would they trust him with so much information?'

'Because he's already proved himself to them,' Wilks explains. 'For a long time he's been washing money through his business. A few thousand here, a hundred thousand there. He's reliable. He's consistent. More than that: he's whiter than white in all the ways they're dirty.'

'And,' Messer adds, 'they have the perfect leverage in you. Leo can't betray them. He can't say no.'

'I don't know anything about that information,' I say. 'I wish I did.'

'We don't expect you to, but perhaps you might know where Leo is keeping it. They'll have given him an external hard drive, maybe a thumb drive. Something physical that can't be copied, that isn't attached to the internet. Leo would naturally be very protective of it. Maybe you've noticed him trying to hide something.'

I shrug. I shake my head. 'I don't pay enough attention to Leo's business to know if he brought back a few thumb sticks from Rome. How could I?'

Wilks and Messer exchange a look I can't read. Wilks' mouth opens to say something but no words come out because a phone rings from the kitchen. For a second I assume it's my cell that I've left on the table, next to my plate. But it's not. It's the house phone. It's an unfamiliar sound because almost no one ever calls it.

23

'I'd best get that,' I say, grateful for the excuse to leave the room, to take a break from all this sensory overload.

Wilks is unsure but nods and I stand up.

'If it's Leo,' she says, 'don't tell him about this conversation.'

My brow furrows.

'Until we're finished,' she adds. 'Please, for his sake.'

I give her a limp nod and make my way to the kitchen. It won't be Leo because he would call my cell. No one calls their own house any more, do they?

As if I haven't already got enough to process, now I'm wondering who could possibly be calling first thing in the morning?

The answer will change everything.

8:26 a.m.

I'm still dazed from what Wilks and Messer have told me when I reach the house phone on the kitchen wall. Like answering the door, picking up a phone is not something I'm good at. Usually I can check the number on my cell phone and not answer the call if I don't recognise the number, but my head is spinning so much from what Wilks and Messer have just told me that my brain is playing by a whole different rulebook and my problems are again taking a back seat.

Anxiety is a crippling condition with no outward symptoms. I look normal. I even act normal. I can hide my anxiety so well that few people have ever seen it. Confidence can be feigned. Calmness can be faked. A smile is a mask anyone can wear and I've always been so good at smiling.

Leo wants to understand. God knows he's tried to understand, but when even I can't explain how I'm feeling, let alone why I'm feeling like it, how could he possibly get it?

I don't get it.

I never used to be like this. If one day I had woken up like it, I could have fixed it because I would have known there was a problem. But that's how anxiety gets you. You don't see it coming. You don't know you have it until the damage is done and you're trapped in a downward spiral of negative thoughts and emotions that feed off one another in an endless cycle of misery.

At best, an observer thinks you've become moody, withdrawn, irritable, uncommunicative, even rude. They don't know there's something wrong inside because nothing's wrong on the outside.

I have a hard enough time getting through the morning without all this stuff about Leo and cartels to process, but for some inexplicable reason it helps my greater problems because I feel numb, a different person almost.

For once, answering the phone seems like no big deal.

That different person scoops up the receiver and says, 'Yeah?'

A slight silence before a man says, 'Mrs Talhoffer?'

It's a deep voice. A serious tone.

'Yeah,' I say, my mind still far away.

'Mrs Jemima Talhoffer?'

'There isn't a second Mrs Talhoffer here, I assure you. Who is this?'

The deep voice says, 'Mrs Talhoffer, I'm sorry to call you out of the blue but my name is Agent Carlson. I work for the Federal Bureau of Investigation and I need a couple of minutes to ask you a few questions about your husband, Leo. It's really important.'

I'm in no mood to have even a couple of minutes of my time wasted. 'Don't you people talk to one another?'

Carlson says, 'Sorry, what? I don't understand.'

'I've already had enough of FBI agents asking me about my husband and it's not even nine in the a.m.'

26

Again, Carlson says, 'Sorry, what?'

'Please, for the sake of my sanity and the US tax payer, learn how to coordinate your investigations. I'm sure you'll understand if I'm a little short of patience considering the morning I'm having. There's only so much a girl can take.'

'Mrs Talhoffer, I'm afraid I—'

'What is it with you people insisting on that level of formality? Call me Jem, for the love of all that is good in this world. Write it on a Post-it. Stick it in the file. Let all the other agents know. While you're at it you can add that I don't even like Jemima. In short: Call. Me. Jem.'

'Jem,' Carlson says, 'I don't understand what you're telling me.'

'Have another coffee, Carlson, because you need it. What I'm telling you is that I have two of your colleagues in my living room right at this very moment asking me questions about Leo, his business, criminal organisations, information on memory sticks. You know, all the things you're about to ask me, and I'm not going to waste my breath repeating everything to you now. Wait for the report or give your fellow agents a call later or whatever it is you would normally do in this situation.'

A silence, then: 'You have two FBI agents in your home? Right now?'

'That's what I just said. A woman and a man. Wilks and Messer.'

There's another silence and I can hear myself, what I've just said, and I feel guilty for my abruptness, my rudeness. This isn't me.

'I'm sorry,' I say to Carlson. 'I'm not in a good place right now and all this about Leo is a lot to take in and I shouldn't have been so curt with you. I'm really very sorry.'

Is there a word a woman says more than sorry?

27

Carlson's tone becomes grave. 'Listen to me very carefully, Jem. I'm the only FBI agent interested in your husband's affairs.'

I echo Carlson's earlier words: 'Sorry, what?'

'This is my case, Jem. No one else is involved at this stage. It's still very early days. Still preliminary enquiries. I'm on my own.'

I have so many things to ask yet all I can utter is, 'But Wilks and Messer ... '

'Whoever that man and that woman say they are they're not with the Bureau.'

My heart is beating so fast it's making my whole body tremble.

Carlson continues: 'The only people who know what you've told me would be myself, your husband, and Leo's business associates.'

I'm cold. I'm so cold.

'They have badges,' I say.

'Jem,' Carlson begins, 'any identification they've shown you is bogus. As I said: there are no other agents privy to what I'm doing. Jem, whoever those people say they are, they're lying.'

8:29 a.m.

Wilks and Messer aren't FBI agents.

Then who are they?

I've answered my own question before I've finished asking about it. As Carlson said, there's only so many people who know what Leo's been doing.

Wilks and Messer are Leo's business associates.

Cartel.

If he doesn't do what they want they'll send people to kill you.

'I really don't want to scare you,' Carlson says, 'but you need to get out of there immediately.'

Too late for that, I want to say.

I'm already terrified but I'm only half-listening because I realise Wilks is in the kitchen with me.

I've been so focused on what Carlson's been telling me that I failed to hear her approach.

'You're in a lot of danger, Jem,' Carlson says in my ear while my gaze is locked on Wilks nearing me. 'Hang up the phone and get out of the house. Call the Bureau as soon as you're safe

29

and I'll come get you. Wherever you are, I'll come to you. I'll make sure you're safe, I swear. But now, Jem, you need to run. You need to get out right now. You need—'

'That's okay, Mom,' I say, trying to push the fear from my face. 'I'll call you back later. Gotta go.'

I somehow manage to hang the receiver back in place on its cradle without it falling from my shaking fingers.

'Is everything okay?' Wilks asks in her stern, deadpan tone.

I don't know how long she was in the kitchen. I don't know how much she heard.

Wilks is close to me now and the wall is behind me. I have nowhere to go.

I'm trapped.

I think about the gun in the holster under her jacket. It's still there because it's not in her hands. They're empty at her sides.

For how long?

But despite the implicit threat of her presence she's not aggressive. She must not have heard anything concrete. She only heard me, what I said. She doesn't know who was on the phone. She can't know what Carlson told me.

Messer's words echo in my mind: *Enough evidence to bring down the entire cartel.*

That's why they're here, that's why they're asking me questions, I realise. They want the information Leo has on them. They *need* the information. I don't understand why but something must have changed.

Carlson, of course. They've realised someone is on to them, to Leo. They want the information back before it can be used against them. I don't get why they're coming to me instead of Leo but that doesn't matter right now, does it? I need to get out of here like Carlson said. Answers can wait.

I force myself to look normal. Thankfully, that's one thing

I know without a doubt I can do well. Like I said: a smile is a mask anyone can wear. But you can't understand how tiring it is to smile when you don't feel it, when you feel the exact opposite. It's exhausting, but I'm so well-practised at it, I can do it now and I know it will work.

I smile and shake my head and roll my eyes as if I was lost in a moment, a dilemma.

'My mother . . . ' I say.

Wilks seems to soften with the words, reassured. Convinced. She has no reason to doubt me. As far as Wilks is concerned, I'm still valuable. I'm still ignorant. I'm still no threat.

'We have a difficult relationship,' I continue, somehow, the words spilling out of my mouth with an amazing degree of coherence I didn't realise I was capable of manifesting. 'She . . . Look, you don't want to hear about our mother–daughter issues, do you?'

Wilks says, 'I'm afraid we have more pressing matters.'

I tilt my palms up. 'I understand. Frankly, I'd prefer to talk about Leo and money laundering than I would my dear mamma.'

Wilks' lips turn up a little in an imitation of a smile. She's not a people person, and in that understanding I also realise that the cartel has sent a certain kind of person to take care of this problem. The kind of people who aren't used to making friendly faces. The kind of people who aren't even capable of faking it.

The worst of the worst, by Messer's own admission.

I swallow. My throat is dry again. I gesture to the doorway, to the living room, to Messer. 'Shall we continue?'

Wilks nods. 'We'll try not to take up too much more of your time.'

'There's no rush,' I tell her. 'I'm happy to help.'

It's amazing how easy the lies keep flowing when you're scared for your life.

She shuffles on ahead of me and when we're in the hallway I see that Messer is standing in the living area, looking this way. His expression is concerned, questioning. I don't see the look Wilks gives him but Messer relaxes and sits back down.

When Wilks is almost through the threshold, I say, 'I'm going to use the restroom,' as I begin ascending the stairs.

Wilks stops. Turns back. 'You don't have a downstairs bathroom?'

'Cistern is on the fritz,' I say with a casual air, not looking back because I'm not convinced the bluff will survive the scrutiny of eye contact. A welcome side effect is that it seems to reinforce the lie, because why would I feel the need to convince someone if it were true?

When I reach the top of the stairs I dare to glance back down and catch Wilks' back heading for the living area. She's bought it.

My heart is hammering now. A flight of stairs is no physical challenge for me but combined with all the adrenalin coursing through my system, making it up to the landing has taken its toll. I'm trying so hard not to release the fear building inside of me my whole body feels ready to explode.

Still, I've bought myself some time, some breathing room.

But what do I do now?

8:32 a.m.

Going upstairs feels like an instant mistake. I've created distance from Wilks and Messer but I have to fight off the feeling of despair that I've trapped myself and made things even more difficult and even more dangerous. I had no choice. There's nothing I could have said that would plausibly explain me leaving the house as Carlson implored me to do. Wilks and Messer would have seen through anything I had said as justification. Claiming I needed some fresh air while swiping my car keys from the bowl by the door was never going to work.

I have no plan, but I need to think of one.

Fast.

I figure I have a couple of minutes to formulate a course of action. If Wilks isn't yet on to me – and if she is, she wouldn't have let me go upstairs – then there's no reason for them to think I'm doing anything up here but peeing. Worse, I do need to pee. That's going to have to wait. I can't afford to burn what little time I have.

I'm in my yoga gear. Should I change into something more

practical? Like what? I don't know. My thoughts are racing at a hundred miles an hour. No time to change, and what's the point? My only priority right now is to get out of this house.

But how?

The building is two storeys, and despite a decent level of fitness and strength, I'm no climber. If I try and scale a drainpipe I'm going to fall and could break my neck or at best turn my ankle. Which might as well be the same thing once Wilks and Messer realise what I'm doing. I wouldn't be able to outrun them hobbling on one foot, let alone a bullet.

The garage, I realise. That's only one storey. I can get out on to the garage roof, then lower myself down. It won't be easy, but it's possible. It's doable.

First, though, I ease the bathroom door open, making as little noise as I can, then rush to the sink and turn on a tap. I make sure to give the door a bit of a slam after I've left. I don't imagine the sound of running water will fool Wilks or Messer long when they come to investigate but it might give me a few extra seconds and I have an awful premonition every single second is going to count.

The home office overlooks the garage so that's where I go next, padding with slow steps along the landing on the balls of my bare feet in an effort to remain silent. I know where the floorboards creak so I avoid them. We don't keep doors closed in this house – bathrooms excluded – so I slip into the office without having to risk squeaky hinges. If I get out of this mess, I'm going to drown every hinge in grease.

If ...

The office is for both of us yet it's only Leo who uses it with any kind of regularity. I can run my business from a couple of spreadsheets and email so I work from my laptop anywhere in the house that takes my fancy. Often, I'll do so outside on the porch. Because the office has become Leo's domain it's disorganised. Not messy, but cluttered. There are too many things on the desk. Too many box files on the shelves. Too many little succulents and cacti on the windowsill.

He names them all. Five minutes ago, I still thought it was cute that he had a parade of plants on the sill, all christened after his favourite seventies folk rock artists: Steely, Jefferson, Jethro, Ambrosia ... Now, they form a barrier of prickly alarms threatening to slow me down, or potentially announce my escape. I hesitate with indecision. Clamber over them and risk knocking one off or take the time to move them all out of the way?

Damn you, Leo. Damn your cuteness.

I push the door to but I don't shut it. I want it to block noise, not make more. Then I wheel Leo's big office chair from under the desk and across the carpet so it sits beneath the sill. I undo the catch and heave the sash. It takes some effort. I feel my shoulders contract. I have to push, hard. The window opens but it squawks, painted wood against painted wood, in a sudden release of tension.

It's loud. It's so loud.

I daren't move. I stand immobile, in fear, listening for the inevitable sound of hard soles stamping on the stairs, Wilks and Messer dashing up in response.

Nothing. I hear nothing.

Which means they heard nothing too. For this moment, I'm safe. For this moment only, I'm safe.

I climb up on to the chair. It's more precarious than I imagined with its four wheels, but the carpet is thick. Too much friction slowing those wheels down. Thank goodness we didn't go for wooden flooring throughout. I could have been doomed by red oak.

Gripping the back of the chair in one hand for support I stretch one leg out of the window. I'm glad I haven't showered. I'm glad I'm still in my yoga attire and not dressed and ready for the day. I couldn't be this limber in jeans.

I look out on to the roof, the barrier I need to cross, but to where?

There are no other buildings in sight. No neighbours to run to for safety. The house sits alone on the end of the road. There are trees everywhere: in front of the house, behind the house, on both sides of the house. We bought it for its isolation and serenity, and now both have turned against me.

I try not to think about that impending problem because I'm still in the house. What comes afterwards can get in line.

My bare sole finds roof tiles. They're cold and hard and unstable. I'm shaking as I apply pressure, searching for sure footing, scared the tiles will collapse underfoot and a cascade of slate will slide off the roof and shatter in a black waterfall on the driveway.

I'm not going to find the stability I'm looking for, I soon realise. No roof is going to provide the perfect exit. I need to commit, to risk it, because I have no choice. I shift my weight and breathe a sigh of relief when the tiles stay put beneath my toes. I grip the window frame and pull as I push off with the foot on the chair.

The chair rolls away from me and I watch with horror, half-way through the window, precarious and immobile, as the chair creeps towards a bookcase that Leo never bothered to secure to the wall, a bookcase heavy with books and files and boxes and any number of things that Leo has crammed on there, all ready and waiting to fall off when the chair bumps into it.

But the chair stops well before. I could kiss that carpet.

I go to withdraw my trailing leg and realise I didn't keep it high enough because the hem of my yoga pants is attached to one of the cacti's needles. Damn you, Jethro.

I raise my leg in the hope gravity will help me out and little Jethro will come free yet no such luck. The little shit is too spiky and too light. I can't prise him free because both my hands are occupied as I maintain a fierce grip on the window frame. I haven't been contorted like this for long but already I can feel the burn building in my muscles, already I'm starting to tremble. I never realised how heavy one leg could quickly become.

With no other option presenting itself I draw my leg towards me, slowly – so slowly – through the window with a cactus dangling from my ankle.

Don't drop, Jethro, please don't drop.

When I have my left leg and foot and cactus all through the open window, I'm able to free up one hand and give Jethro's pot a gentle tug. He comes free, pulling Lycra fibres with him, and I set him back down on the sill.

I'm sweating so hard now that there's a drop at the end of my nose. I swipe it away.

In movies, every American teen has climbed out of a window and on to a roof, or the other way round, but I never did. It's scary off the ground with nothing solid beneath your feet, with nothing secure to hold on to. I don't know how I'm going to traverse the slope once I release the window frame. Years of yoga mean I can perform some pretty crazy feats of balance, yet out here, on an incline, with precarious tiles underfoot, I'll lose my balance in seconds after standing and tumble off the roof moments later.

That's the key, I realise: don't stand up.

I shift my ass from the frame and on to the slate. I brace with my legs. I let go with my hands.

I don't move.

37

I'm stable. Well, as stable as I can hope. I plant my palms on the roof either side of my hips and shuffle like a beetle. The slate clinks beneath me but isn't loud. Progress is slow but as long as the tiles don't come free under me I can maintain a semblance of control.

I don't know how long it takes because time seems to have lost all meaning – or perhaps I'm too stressed, too scared, to keep track. I'm not sure if it's only been seconds or whole minutes. In either case I need to be fast. I need to be off this roof before Wilks and Messer realise what I'm doing. While I'm up here I'm just as trapped as if I was with them inside the living room.

I make it down the incline to the guttering that separates this section of roof from the garage roof. I'm now only about ten feet off the ground but it seems dizzyingly high. Still plenty high enough to break my skull if I fall headfirst, but I've found a rhythm. I feel as good as I can be shuffling down my roof to avoid cartel killers. I'm not going to fall, I tell myself.

I cross the guttering on to the garage roof. I've crossed a threshold both real and metaphorical.

I can do this because I have to do this.

The roof has other ideas and a tile comes loose underfoot. Maybe I pressed down too hard. Maybe I moved too fast, too eagerly. That instance of self-belief was self-destruction.

The tile slides along the sloped roof. At first at a slow speed, but one that doesn't slow, doesn't halt.

It takes all my strength and balance to maintain my position, and I can only watch as it reaches the edge, then tips over.

I have a moment's fantasy that soft flowerbeds will cushion the tile and it will remain intact.

An instance of horrible, awful silence.

The tile shatters.

8:36 a.m.

The time for stealth has passed. Now, I need speed.

I shuffle faster across the roof, slate tiles clinking and rattling, working my way to the far side, the east wall of the garage where the trash cans stand against it. They're metal, corrugated steel, so I'm thinking they'll hold my weight when I lower myself down on to one or more.

To get there I need to climb over the central peak of the garage roof, which means switching to my hands and knees and then scrambling up the slope. It's so much easier than descending with my beetle-shuffle but I'm moving faster, with more desperation.

Tiles feel unsecure beneath me and move as though the whole roof is going to slide off and take me with it.

It's only seconds before I've reached the east wall and yet each long second is pure terror. I peer down at the shiny trash cans. They're maybe three feet tall, so I guess I can just reach them when my arms are extended.

I hope.

I turn away from the edge and, on my hands and knees, inch backwards until my feet are off the roof, and then my shins follow, then my left knee. Then my right.

I'm trying to control my breathing but there's too much fear, too much adrenalin. I'm exhaling and inhaling at such speed it's more like a pant.

The guttering and the tiles jab into my abdomen, which is taking the weight of my dangling lower body. My elbows and palms are pressed hard against the roof yet I can feel myself sliding backwards regardless. There's nothing to hold on to and I'm not strong enough to fight gravity tugging at me. I'm not sure how I would work my way backwards off the roof without risking slipping.

Gravity is beating me, little by little.

It hurts, a lot. Slate tiles may look lovely but they are digging into me, scratching me. I'm sure the adrenalin is mitigating much of the pain I would otherwise feel.

My breaths are quick and shallow as my elbows, now in line with my shoulders, reach the guttering and the vast majority of me is dangling off the roof. I'm stretching with my toes but I still haven't found the trash cans. I can turn my head but I can't look down and see how far I have to go because my body is in the way.

For all I know, Wilks and Messer are standing right beneath me.

I don't know what to do, whether to keep trying to lower myself and risk losing control of my descent or make a controlled drop now while I still can. Either way, I can't remain hanging off the garage roof for much longer. There are two killers in my house, and even if there weren't I don't have the strength to stay like this.

I'm trying to go as fast as I can but progress is painfully slow.

I don't want to make more noise than I have already and I don't want to drop and turn my ankle, or worse.

I risk slipping to lower myself a little further, hopeful the trash cans are just inches beneath my feet.

They're not.

I'm starting to lose control. The pain in my fingertips from the pressure I'm applying is intensifying, soon to become agony. I'm going to fall any moment. I have to let go.

I do.

I drop.

It doesn't even last a second, or a half-second. Almost as soon as I let go steel clangs beneath my feet. Despite expecting it, despite wanting it, I'm not ready. I can't react.

The can's lid crumples, deforming yet momentarily holding my weight. I slip straight off and hit the ground, landing on my hip. I grimace. It hurts, but I'm not hurt. Not injured. I scramble to my feet, aware of the noise the smashed tile made, the noise the trash can made, the noise I made.

I expect Wilks and Messer to appear, guns in hand, at any moment. I can't hear them, though. Maybe, just maybe, the tile smashing didn't alert them. The living area is at the rear of the house after all, and it's a big house, larger than Leo and I need, bought to be filled. A waste of money but that size has helped me here.

What now?

Trees everywhere, but I can't run off into the forest, can I? Close to the house, the trees are not as dense, but the undergrowth is thick. I'll have to flatten an obvious trail through it. Maybe Wilks and Messer can run faster than me but I don't for a second think they can run as far, for as long. As fit as they may be, I work out seven days a week. It's my job to be fit. Stamina is no good when you have bare feet, however, and

41

I'll shred my soles trying to run along a forest floor, or put a thick twig right through my foot. No thanks. They make hiking shoes for a reason.

I still don't know how much time has passed since I started up the stairs but I know I've been longer than any normal trip to the bathroom. Wilks or Messer or both must be investigating by now. Maybe knocking on the door. Maybe asking me in a loud voice if everything is okay, growing concerned when I don't answer, getting ready to kick the door down but trying the handle and realising it isn't locked.

I pause for a second to get my breath back, to think, to realise my cell phone is still on the kitchen table.

Stupid, stupid Jem.

No, it's not my fault. I was so scared in that moment when I saw Wilks was with me that I wasn't thinking I might need it a few minutes later. I was only trying to survive. No point worrying about that now, especially when I have another, greater problem: my car is on the driveway yet the keys are in the house. They're sat in a bowl right next to the front door inside a house with two cartel killers.

A sound. Muted, but aggressive.

A shout, perhaps.

Wilks or Messer calling for assistance after finding the bathroom empty and the tap running.

I make my way along the side of the garage. At the corner, I peek round to look at the front of the house. There's maybe twenty feet from my position to the front door. On the driveway is my beloved Prius. Behind it is a black SUV, an Explorer – that must belong to Wilks and Messer. It looks like the kind of thing the FBI – or those pretending to be them – would use. It's an intimidating vehicle. They must have driven slowly to the house, otherwise I'm sure I would have heard this monster pulling up.

I peek through the window in the minuscule hope that the keys have been left in the ignition, but of course Wilks and Messer aren't stupid or lazy enough to do so. I creep up to the house, hoping I can get inside the front door, grab my car keys from the nearby bowl, and be out before they have any idea what's happening.

That's no longer viable because I can hear Wilks' voice, loud and coarse, shouting, 'No, of course she hasn't.'

A response to some question I wasn't close enough to hear Messer shout.

Wilks sounds like she's at the top of the stairs.

Messer says, 'They're by the door so she's not gone anywhere.'

He's in the hallway, only a few feet away from where I'm hiding, only an inch or so of walnut door between us.

'Then what is she—' Wilks begins to say, then: 'I can feel a draught. A window's open.'

I have mere seconds before Messer comes rushing out.

I don't know what to do, where to go. I don't have anywhere to go.

The big SUV.

I hurry over to it, lie on my stomach, and shuffle beneath.

The front door bangs open.

Messer charges outside.

8:40 a.m.

I'm facing the house. I made sure to turn round before I crawled beneath the Explorer. My view is interrupted by the Prius but I can still see the open door, the step, and Messer's polished black shoes. They look like solid, decent footwear. I can see the lower portion of his trousers, charcoal grey. For a few seconds he doesn't move and I picture him looking at the vehicles to reassure himself they're both still there. He takes a step forward, then another. He's looking into the distance, checking I'm not sprinting down the road, or maybe into the woodland flanking both sides of the road and surrounding the house.

He shouts back to Wilks: 'Nothing. She's not out here.'

I'm not sure what I'm going to do next. Without knowing their next move I'm too frightened to do anything.

Please, give me an opportunity.

Wilks joins Messer.

'There's a window open upstairs. I think she climbed out on to the roof. She must have done. She's nowhere else inside.'

'You're kidding me,' Messer replies. 'What's she trying to do?'

A pause, during which I guess Wilks shrugs. 'The window's facing front,' she says. 'But maybe she scrambled over. Stay, I'll circle round back. She might—'

'Look,' Messer interrupts. 'A tile's missing. There, it fell off.'

I watch their feet and lower legs head towards the smashed tile. They stop. Think.

Messer says, 'Why's she running?'

Wilks says, 'She knows.'

'But how—'

'Phone call. Has to be.'

'Leo?'

'Maybe.'

Messer says, 'Go. If she's out back she won't have gone far barefoot. I'll keep eyes on the front.'

Wilks hurries off, not circling around the building but going back inside via the front door to cut through the house. Messer stays behind as they've discussed. I can't tell what he's doing – I can still only see a sliver of him – but I can't do anything, go anywhere, with him right there. The second I'm out from under the SUV, he'll see me.

All I can do is wait, hope. Pray.

I squeeze my eyes shut.

Please, let me get out of this. I don't want to die.

Amen.

Nothing's different. I've probably left it a little late in life to turn to religion.

Messer stalks about. I can only see him from the shin down. It's frustrating not being able to see what he's doing but I suppose I should be grateful. If I can't see him he can't see me.

How long will that last?

Wilks calls for him and he goes back inside.

At last, I'm alone again.

Now what?

This is a step-by-step process. All I'm trying to do is make it through to the next step, the next moment where I can get my breath back and collect my thoughts. My face is damp with perspiration from crossing the roof and the perpetual fear of discovery.

What have you gotten yourself into, Leo? You should have told me. We could have worked it out. We could have—

I have an idea. I don't know where it came from but it's the only one I have. In the absence of any other, it's the best idea.

I crawl out from under the SUV. Stand. There are bits of gravel embedded in my skin and I ignore them. I don't care.

I dash back to the house. Barefoot, I'm as good as silent. This time I can't hear Wilks and Messer – they must be out back – and I slip inside.

I'm so full of adrenalin, so overflowing with fear, I'm shaking. I can hardly breathe. I grab my keys from the bowl by the door, then stop. Look back.

The SUV is blocking the Prius.

I place the keys back into the bowl. I don't want to be parted from them but Wilks and Messer know they should be there. If they notice they're gone they'll know I'm nearby. It takes a huge effort of will to release the keys, to deny myself the option of speeding away from here in a car, yet I have to let them go. There's no choice.

I can hear Wilks and Messer shouting to each other, but I can't decipher the words. They're checking something out behind the house. Maybe a helpful fox or deer has wandered by, disturbing undergrowth, fooling them.

There's a door off the entrance hall that leads inside the garage. I ease it open and close it carefully behind me. The soft click of the brass catch seems as loud as a ringing bell.

It's gloomy, yet I don't reach for the light switch. There's just enough daylight creeping around the edges of the motorised door for me to see and I know my way around the space blind-folded. This is my domain. I put up the metal shelving units. I hung the tools off the wire rack. Leo can spend hours up in his office, working on whatever he needs to work on. I can spend all weekend in the garage if he doesn't come and drag me out, working on furniture, making candles, building art out of trash. If I'm not busy, I'm thinking. If I'm thinking, I'm going to end up thinking of things that only make unhappy. I'm not religious but this is my temple. Here, I find peace.

I'm not after power tools or wax or even a hefty table leg. I'm not going to fight my way out of this mess. As well as being my workshop, the garage stores our mountain bikes. We have his and hers colours, blue and pink – not because we're that pathetic but because we find a certain kind of childish humour in the thought that other people will assume that about us. I think it was Leo's idea: let them think we're that kind of couple. It'll be hilarious.

I take my bike from its hook, place it carefully down so it doesn't make any noise, then activate the bypass for the garage door's motor and heave the door open. Doing so is loud, so loud, but it can't be helped and Wilks and Messer should be far enough away around the back of the house not to hear it.

I'm a fast pedaller and the mountain bike is a lightweight engineering marvel, yet there's no way on earth I'm going to outrun an Explorer even with a head start. Maybe I'd make it to the intersection, maybe further, but how long before they run me off the road? Town is at least a ten-minute drive away.

Instead of getting on the bike and pedalling for my life, I wheel it round the side of the garage to where the trash cans stand. I position the bike against the garage wall and move the trash cans to hide it. I can't disguise it completely but I can make sure that no one can see it without getting close. Certainly, anyone at the front of the house looking back will have their line of sight blocked. That's all I need. It's a temporary distraction, not a solution to my predicament. With a little luck it could be enough.

Then, I wait.

I hunker down behind the trash cans and try to control my breathing. It won't take long, I'm sure, and it doesn't.

It's Messer.

'Oh shit,' he calls from the driveway.

He's seen the open garage door.

'*Oh shit*,' he shouts.

He's seen Leo's mountain bike and the empty space next to it where mine should be hanging.

'Hey,' he calls to Wilks, 'get over here. Right now.'

Wilks' rushing footsteps are obvious to me.

'What's going on?' she asks as she draws closer to Messer.

'A bike's missing.'

'Clever girl,' Wilks says with a degree of respect. 'She duked us. Stay here. She's not going to have got far. I don't care how fast she is.'

'I should come too,' Messer protests.

'No, stay put. Maybe she gets down the road and hides in the trees. Waits for us to burn past and comes back for her car.'

Not a bad idea. Wish I had thought of it myself.

Messer must agree with the logic because he says, 'Go.'

Seconds later the big SUV comes to life. Tyres screech as Wilks throws it into a fast three-point before the engine roars and I catch a glimpse of the vehicle as it speeds along the road. A wisp of rubber smoke swirls in the air.

Now I just need to get Messer away from the front of the

house so I can get in and get those keys. Yes, I may run into Wilks in the Explorer, but I'll deal with that possibility when it materialises.

One killer down, one to go.

8:46 a.m.

I've never paid a huge amount of attention to geography but I know my local area well enough. It's maybe half a mile to the intersection, then right, or east, and another five miles until the outskirts of town. Which is a modest place named Cornwall with a population not much north of a thousand. I'm sure in ye olde days they would have called it a village. Realtors no doubt use terms like 'unspoiled' and 'rustic', 'peaceful' and 'character-ful', when trying to sell properties here. Leo found it, way back, when we were first looking for a town outside of New York City. Neither of us needed to commute but we wanted to stay close enough that heading into Manhattan wasn't a huge excursion. And Leo needed to have access to La Guardia and JFK.

There's a lot of these kind of towns upstate. Young Jem would have found them insufferable. She would have torn her hair out with boredom, gone mad with frustration. This Jem, however – *me* – is exactly where she needs to be at this point in her life.

If only I had neighbours ... I could run to the next house,

bang on the door, scream for help. Maybe they're not home but *someone* would be at one of the houses on the street. Someone would hear me. Someone would help.

I'm listening hard in an attempt to decipher what Messer is doing. Since Wilks left in the Explorer, I haven't heard Messer at all. I don't know if he's still on the driveway or if he's gone back into the house. I realise I can't just wait it out to be certain because at some point Wilks is going to come back, having failed to catch up with me. They won't have to hunt too hard to find the pink mountain bike hidden behind the trash cans and understand I'm still here, playing the most intense game of hide and seek imaginable. I never liked it as a kid.

I'm liking it a whole lot less as an adult.

I creep alongside the garage, down the side of the house, heading to the back of the property. I just can't risk sticking my head around the front, not if there's even a slim chance Messer is still there.

I take my time, staying quiet, and reach my rows of tall tomato plants on the patio, standing proud for their mamma.

The back door is open. In their hurry, Wilks and Messer didn't close it. Good. That's one less thing I have to worry about. I duck low under the kitchen window and approach the door, listening hard for Messer, but I hear no heavy footsteps, no signs he's close.

Maybe he's there, maybe he's lying in wait for me.

Could be a trap, couldn't it? He's hiding, waiting for me to make a mistake and reveal myself.

No choice. Got to risk it.

I peer through the open doorway, seeing glimpses of the living area and the kitchen, but no Messer. He must still be out front, waiting by my Prius in case I had indeed escaped by bike only to double back as Wilks suggested.

Not good. Not good at all.

With his attention elsewhere, I feel reasonably confident I can get to my keys but they're no use to me with Messer on guard duty next to my only means of escape.

I remember something: my phone is on the kitchen table and the kitchen is close.

Yes.

I can call the cops, the local police department's office. I know the chief, Rusty. She'll be here in a heartbeat, backup in tow. As far as I know there are only a handful of troopers, but they're close, and in such a quiet, boring town the chances of them being busy on an important callout are minimal. I feel a rush of relief with a potential end to this nightmare mere feet away.

I can't wait to hear the beautiful sound of screeching sirens.

I take a few fast steps on the balls of my feet into the kitchen – and that brief moment of relief is dashed because my phone isn't on the table where I left it. Wilks or Messer must have taken it.

I should have expected that and yet I'm still devastated.

Hopelessness begins to suffocate me. I can't see a way out of this. All I'm doing is delaying the inevitable. I'm destined to lose this game of hide and seek whatever I do.

I feel like holding my hands up and walking out front to give myself up to Messer and whatever fate awaits me. I'm not strong enough for this. I've been fooling myself since I hung up the phone on Carlson. My eyes moisten. I just want to stop, to breathe, to lie down. I'd give anything to be able to sleep.

Why can't this be over?

A phone rings. Not the house phone or my generic default ringtone or the cute one I've set to Leo's number. Must be Messer's ringer. It's coming from the front of the house.

The sound ends as he answers it.

I hear him say, 'Yeah?'

He's coming closer. He steps into the house to take the call. 'What?'

I see his shadow on the hallway wall. Dark and looming. 'You're kidding me?'

Wilks is telling him she hasn't found me, that I couldn't have made it as far as she's driven in the short time I had for a head start, that it's another trick.

'If she's still here, I'll find her,' Messer says with such determination, such resolve, I have no doubt he will.

I have no other option.

I run.

8:50 a.m.

The back lawn is cold underfoot, still damp with dew. But soft against my bare soles. It feels heavenly to sprint across but I don't appreciate it in the moment. Only when I reach the edge of the lawn and cross into the woodland and my toes find rough earth and rock and plants and debris do I realise how good I had it. And isn't that always the way? We only truly appreciate something when it's no more.

I'm not sure at what point Messer saw me but I'm in the treeline before I dare look back. The lawn is maybe one hundred feet in length so I'm hoping for at least that much of a head start.

Messer is already at the midpoint of the lawn.

Our gazes meet.

'*Stop*,' he yells.

I do the exact opposite. I power forward, away from Messer, away from my home. In seconds I'm grimacing, my feet already cut and scraped. Messer's wearing his good shoes. He won't have the same problem. If I thought I could outrun him, I'm realising that with every step I'm reducing my chances as I increase the likelihood of making myself lame.

He calls out nothing further behind me. Nothing he can say is going to make me comply and it's hard to run and shout at the same time, if not impossible. He's saving his energy for running, for chasing.

I don't know where to go beyond directly away from Messer. I seem to recall there's a road that cuts through this wood. Whether it's in the direction I'm running or not, I have no idea. I can't stop to think, to orientate myself.

I'm trying to look at the ground as I run, trying to see where I can run, where I need to avoid. It's perilous to do so. My balance falters when I'm not looking ahead, which is hard enough to maintain anyway at speed on an uneven surface. I use tree trunks to brace against, their overhanging branches for support.

Between looking ahead and looking down, I daren't glance back as well. I can't. I'm running so fast I know I'll fall if I do. I know Messer is not far. I feel him closing like a relentless bull, tearing up chunks of earth, smashing through undergrowth, knocking down trees.

I'm half his size, though. I'm more agile. That's got to count for something. I need to make it count.

I try to use the woods to my advantage, heading for where the trees are denser, the gaps between them narrow, the undergrowth thicker. I seek out protruding roots to hop over. Inclines to scramble up. Low branches to duck under.

I ran the New York City marathon once, many years back. I did it in a pretty good time too, yet now it feels a lifetime ago. I'm tiring fast covering this woodland obstacle course. I'm slowing. I don't know how much longer I can keep pushing myself. I'm starting to stumble more than run.

My lungs are on fire. I'm gasping for air, for relief.

Ahead, the trees start to thin. Is that asphalt I can see?

Yes, the road. A road. Any road.

Yellow paintwork flashes past.

'*Help*,' I shout, loud and clear, but only a wheezing croak emerges from my mouth.

Even had I been able to make enough noise, the car is moving too fast and I'm too far away. It's gone in seconds, from yellow flash to pale speck in the distance.

I keep going, slowing almost to a walk now, almost rebounding off the trees I reach out to put a palm on to because I have no strength.

The trees open up before me and I'm at the edge of the road surface. It's set higher than the ground, as any decent road should be, and it feels like a giant's step to climb in my fatigue. I glance both ways into the distance, hoping to see another car, but I'm terrified a black SUV will be heading this way.

No cars.

I peer into the trees. I can't see Messer. I don't know if I've lost him or if he's still coming.

I'm exhausted yet the last thing I want to do is remain stationary and give my pursuer more time to close the distance.

I look both ways along the road again. The asphalt is a straight line flanked by trees stretching off into the distance. I'm pacing about, unable to keep still with my pulse sky high from all the running. Sweat soaks my clothes and drips from my face.

'Come on,' I say to the empty road, 'come on.'

Each second I wait here I'm wasting my lead on Messer, I'm giving Wilks more time to head me off. But what alternative do I really have? I'm spent. My feet are shredded. I've no phone. No money. Nowhere to go.

I hear an engine, an exhaust.

There's a rush of relief that makes me feel lightheaded as I picture rescue, salvation. Then that relief becomes dread as I realise the sound is coming from the direction of the town, of my house. It could be the big SUV. It could be Wilks.

No, no, no, no . . .

I dash off the road, back into the treeline. I duck down into the undergrowth and hide, wait.

I don't want to look. I don't want to risk Wilks spotting me. With Messer behind me, I'll be trapped. But I need to look because maybe, just maybe, it's not Wilks. This could be my one chance to escape, because if I let this vehicle pass without trying to flag it down then the next one could indeed be driven by Wilks.

What should I do?

I picture Messer in the trees behind me. Determined. Relentless.

The noise of the vehicle grows louder, nearer.

Decision time.

I rise out of the undergrowth and step into the road, whatever my fate.

8:54 a.m.

Tyres squeal. Burnt rubber clouds. I don't have the energy to move out of the way and in that instant I realise I don't care. I'm too scared and too tired.

A bumper kisses my thighs, but no more. I almost collapse on to the hood. It's not the black SUV driven by Wilks but a dull red pickup.

The driver thumps the horn, hard.

'*What in the holy hell are you doing, lady?*'

'Please ...'

I can barely speak. I stumble around the wheel arch to the passenger's side, grab the door handle and pull. Nothing. At first I think I'm too weak to open the door, but it's locked.

The driver is a white-bearded man with a deep tan and deeper frown lines. 'Get away from my truck. What is this?'

I must look a state. I must look crazy.

'Please,' I say again. 'Help me.'

The driver is still in mild shock at almost running me down, still perplexed, but he recognises the desperation before him.

He can hear the terror in my voice. He hesitates for a moment only before he leans across and unlocks the door. I heave it open, clamber up on to the seat and pull the door shut behind me with the last of my energy.

'What is going on?' the driver asks me. 'Who are you?'

'Drive,' is all I can say in response.

He's shaking his head. 'That's what I was doing before you tried to kill yourself with my here vehicle.'

'Please,' I beg. 'Please.'

He frowns but says nothing and puts the truck back in drive.

We're in motion by the time Messer has made it out of the trees and on to the road behind us.

I turn in the seat to peer at him, to see what he's doing, if he's drawing his gun, but in seconds he's a dark spot in the distance, indiscernible.

I slump in the seat, panting, overwhelmed, but safe. Only now do I realise that there is a small dog in the footwell. A scruffy mutt with skinny legs and a pot belly. Teeth are bared at me and it's growling.

'Don't pay any mind to Merlin,' the driver says. 'He doesn't like nobody.'

I have a mild phobia of dogs after being bitten by one as a child yet right now it seems that phobia is cured. Merlin's angry growls, his bared teeth, bounce off me without effect. Perspective, my dad would have said, changes everything.

There's a silence. I suppose it's uneasy for the driver but it's perfect for me, calming. My heart rate is now slowing. The heightened state of stress I've been in for what seems like for ever is finally dissipating.

The driver keeps glancing at me, his furry white eyebrows narrowing. I don't blame him for his unease, for his curiosity. So far he doesn't have any idea who I am or why I'm in his truck.

Eventually, he says, 'Why don't you try telling me what's happened to you, yeah? Let's see if together we can't make it all right. How's that sound to you?'

It sounds like a great idea.

I try to tell him, to explain, but I can only answer with tears.

8:57 a.m.

The old man introduces himself as Trevor and waits with kindly patience while I release the build-up of so much stress and fear. Even at my very low points – of which there have been many – I've never been much of a crier out of worry of being seen as too emotional, too unstable, but I'm making up for it now. My eyes spill a constant flow of tears and my nose leaks an endless stream of mucus. At some point Trevor digs out a handkerchief from one of the pockets of his jeans and hands it over. At any other point in my life I would have curled up my lip at the mere suggestion of using someone else's handkerchief and here I am taking it without a second's consideration to stem what the sleeves of my yoga top cannot hope to slow.

It seems a long time before my sobs subside enough and I can finally speak. I tell him all about Wilks and Messer knocking at my door, Carlson's phone call, and running for my life. Trevor is a responsible driver and keeps his gaze on the road ahead for the most part. When he does glance my way, his expression is pinched with disbelief. I can't blame him for that. It sounds crazy just speaking the words out loud. Had I not been through it myself I doubt I would believe it.

But I don't tell him everything. I don't tell him that my husband seems to have been laundering money for a cartel. He doesn't need to know that, and until I've seen proof I refuse to believe it. Besides, Trevor's saved my life and he's helping me. I don't want to put him in danger by telling him something that could come back to haunt him at a later point. It's the least I can do for him.

He says, 'Sounds like you've had quite the morning.'

I nod. I wipe my eyes with the back of my hand because the handkerchief is now soaked.

I clear my throat to respond. 'Not exactly what you expect when you've only just had your avocado on toast.'

Trevor shoots me a look. 'Your what?'

'It's a fruit. It's ...' I make a dismissive gesture. 'Not important.'

Merlin is still growling at me. I don't think he's stopped for a second since I climbed into the truck.

'He'll do that all day long given half the chance,' Trevor explains, shaking his head. 'Then he'll tire himself out and go to sleep, dream about growling at you, then wake up and start the process all over again.'

'He's committed,' I say. 'I'll give him that.'

'That's one word for it. He just isn't a fan of people.'

'All people? What about you?'

Trevor is silent, composing his thoughts. 'I would say that, at best, he tolerates me. But only because I feed him.' Trevor smiles at me, showing crooked teeth and gaps between them and the smile is mischievous and warm at the same time. He says, 'What now? Where am I taking you?'

I shift on my seat. 'I need to go and speak to the police. I need to speak to Rusty.'

'The chief's a good woman,' Trevor says in an approving tone.

'Could you take me into town, to the police department? I know it's a lot to ask so I won't be offended if—'

'Of course I will take you,' he interrupts. 'This country may be going to hell in a handbasket but there are still some with integrity left.'

'Thank you. Thank you so much.'

'Day I turn my back on a lady in distress is the day I call myself a damn socialist.'

I wait for him to smile to let me know he's joking, only he's not.

'We'll take the back ways,' Trevor tells me, 'since we're already heading the wrong direction. We can take a nice long circular route and come at the town from the other side. That way, if they're expecting you to show up – which would be a fine guess considering that's exactly what you want to do – we'll sneak up on their flank. Fools will never see us coming.'

He has a sparkle in his eyes. He's pleased with this idea and so am I.

'Good thinking,' I say. 'Of course, we could just call the police if you had a phone like everyone else in the world.'

The sparkle is replaced by a glare.

'Never had one of them cellular devices and never will have one either. You want the government to keep track of every single moment of your life, that's your prerogative. Me, I like my freedom the old-fashioned way. We did pretty well as a civilisation before the invention of the personal communications device, did we not? You modern folk don't own your technology, you let it own you. Those phones tell you when to wake up, when to go to bed, you check your Bookface ninety times a day, you walk around with a GPS locator in your pocket and you pay for the privilege. Best of all you think you're the smart ones for doing so and I'm the crazy one for staying well clear.' He shakes his head. 'Don't make no sense to me.'

I'm not sure how to respond.

Trevor isn't done. 'But what do I know? I'm just an old man in a new world that I don't like too much and that new world doesn't like me either. So, screw the world.' He reaches a hand down to give Merlin a rough stroke. 'Ain't that right, buddy?'

Merlin just growls in response.

Trevor sticks to his plan, taking me on a mini-tour of the local area, along backroads and tracks I didn't even know existed, circling all the way to the other side of town without ever going near it. I'm getting nervous as we get closer. I can't shake the feeling that Wilks and Messer have everything figured out, that they are lying in wait to ambush us. Messer saw the truck, after all.

We've been driving in silence for a while. I'm so tired I could fall into a deep sleep at any moment. It's a constant fight to stay awake yet my mind is restless with so many unanswered questions. The memory of terror is constant, inescapable. I've never been so scared in my life. Anxiety means I'm constantly worried, always on edge, sometimes to the point of feeling like I'm going to die, but I've never before thought someone might murder me. It's such a powerful, base feeling, but until earlier utterly alien to me. My existence has been so safe, so uneventful, that I'm unprepared for this experience and these lingering sensations. I feel an exhaustion that is not only physical but mental, not only mental but emotional. I feel . . .

'Stop the truck.'

Trevor glances my way. 'I'm not sure we should really—'

'*Stop the truck.*'

Trevor needs no further convincing.

I have the door open before the tyres have stopped moving and throw up in the middle of the road.

I vomit several violent times, heaving and retching until my insides are an empty void, until ropes of spit and snot stretch from my nose and lips, until my eyes are full of moisture and my cheeks are drenched and the dark asphalt is splattered bright by the contents of my stomach.

I feel so much better.

Trevor leans across the cab to check I'm okay. I form a weak thumbs up to tell him not to worry. He peers past me and grunts.

'If that's what avocado looks like on the way back out then count me glad I've never tried it.'

9:14 a.m.

Trevor says, 'ETA eight minutes.'

I don't know what that means but a minute later when he says 'ETA seven minutes' I crack the code. 'Almost there' would have done fine, but I stay squashed half in the footwell, half on the seat, and let him do it his way. I'm so grateful for his help that he's my new favourite person in all the world.

Keeping low was my idea and I'm not sure it was the right one. I don't like the restricted view, I realise. I can see the upper floors of taller buildings flanking the road but that's it. I can't see ahead and I can't see the sidewalks. Of course, this means that anyone out there – Wilks and Messer in particular – can't see me in return. I'm hidden and I'm blind because of it.

I'm closer to Merlin than either of us wants me to be and his constant growling has taken on a deeper, angrier tone. I'm invading his personal space and it's no surprise that he doesn't like it one little bit.

I know how you feel, buddy, I had two cartel hitmen invade my personal space this morning.

'You sure you wanna do this?' Trevor asks.

I say, 'What choice do I have? I need to tell the police. I need help.'

Trevor shrugs. 'My cabin is out of the way up the creek. No one can come within a mile without me knowing about it. You'll be safe there.'

'That's sweet of you, Trevor. Thank you. But then what? I can't just hide out there indefinitely, can I? I need to get hold of Leo before he gets on that plane and I need to speak to Carlson again and find out what's going on, why the cartel is coming after Leo. Without a phone, I'm helpless. Worse, Leo is helpless. This is a matter for the police whatever else happens or doesn't happen. Leo's in danger and so am I. Rusty will know what to do, won't she?'

Trevor is not wholly convinced.

'You can get some rest,' he begins. 'Figure out your next move without pressure. You've been through hell so far today so you ain't thinking clear. In my experience that's when people make a bad call. Can you afford to make the wrong move?'

'At this moment Leo's on his way to the airport. Maybe he's there, maybe he's waiting to board his plane to Europe. I hope he's safe in the departure lounge and out of everyone's reach. If he's not then I have to speak to him and warn him. God, maybe they sent people after him too. They could be waiting at the airport for him.' My heart is beating faster and my breathing's quicker as I picture Leo taken by people like Wilks and Messer.

'Sounds like he should have been the one to warn you.'

I don't respond. Oh, Leo, what have you got yourself into? You should have told me. We could have found a solution before killers turned up at our home.

'ETA five minutes,' Trevor says. 'So far so good.'

I have described the black SUV driven by Wilks and Messer so Trevor knows what to look out for on the roads. I also gave him descriptions of the two of them, but to my surprise I found it hard to describe them. Is Wilks the older one or is that Messer? Are they both wearing charcoal suits or is Wilks' navy? Which one had dark hair and which was blonde?

'A man and a woman in suits,' Trevor summarised. 'Never trust a person in a suit.'

He's my eyes. He keeps me updated as he drives deeper into town, speaking with his teeth clenched together and his lips hardly moving in an extreme, but necessary, precaution. Slowly, my fears diminish. There's no sign of a black SUV blocking the road, waiting to ambush. No man and woman in suits with guns ready to fill the truck with bullet holes.

My back has been aching for a while as I keep hunkered down below the window line, contorted in the footwell.

'You want me to pull up right outside the police department?'

'Something in your tone tells me you don't recommend that course of action.'

He's still speaking with his crooked teeth clenched, doing his best ventriloquist impression that almost makes me smile despite the circumstances. 'I'm just thinking out loud here,' he says. 'But it's not like you have a million options at your disposal, is it? They know that. Could expect you to head to Rusty and they've had plenty of time to get there first, haven't they? Not that I expect they would open fire outside an outpost of law enforcement but in my opinion it don't do you any favours to underestimate your enemies.'

'Okay,' I say in return, 'stop half a block away. If it's clear I can walk the rest of the way, and make doubly sure. Stop half a block round the back, I mean.'

He nods. 'Was gonna.'

It's a quiet town. Quaint. There are handsome little bed and breakfasts, welcoming cafés and lots of little mom and pop stores. There's no concrete in sight. Every building looks as though it hasn't changed in more than a century. Trees on every street. There's lots of red brick and white-painted wood. Lots of decorative awnings. Everyone here appreciates its small-town charm and wants to keep it that way.

The diner on Main Street advertises the best apple pie in the state. I think the movie theatre is the second oldest in the country. It's an 'on the way' kind of town because despite its picturesque beauty it's not a place anyone goes out of their way to visit. There's more famous, more touristy towns in every direction. Real picture-postcard locations. And that suits us just fine, thank you very much.

Trevor drives slower as we near our destination. He's cautious. He's on constant lookout. I'm hoping that Wilks and Messer will be easy enough for him to spot in their suits. This isn't the kind of place where folks wear collared shirts and ties, loafers and single-breasted jackets. Wall Street is only eighty miles away yet it might as well be a thousand.

He stops the pickup outside Earnest's convenience store, which is on the road that runs behind the police precinct, and says, 'This is it.'

I take a deep breath.

'No rush,' he assures me. 'Go only when you're ready. I have all day if you need it.'

I shuffle up from my hiding spot, feeling every one of my fatigued muscles, my many aches and pains. Trevor sees my suffering.

'You don't have no shoes,' he says. 'Why did I only just notice?'

My feet are bare but they're covered in a crust of earth and dried blood. Kind of like the world's worst pair of socks.

'Take mine,' Trevor says, reaching down to untie his laces. 'Can't go anywhere like that.'

His generosity is touching but, 'You've got clown feet, Trevor. I won't be able to walk in those things. I'll fall over and crack my head open.'

He stops. Pouts a little.

'Listen,' I say, 'I can't thank you enough for what you've done for me so far. You've saved my life. That's not an exaggeration. I know in my soul I would be dead by now if you hadn't driven by when you did.'

He can't look at me, such is his embarrassment at receiving praise. I give him a half-hug with one arm and kiss him on the cheek. He goes a ketchup shade of red.

'Trevor,' I tease, 'you're blushing.'

'I am not,' he's quick to insist. 'It's just high blood pressure.'

I smile. He's sweet. 'I'd take your number but you don't have one.'

He responds with something like a grunt.

'Where's your cabin?' I ask. 'I'll bring you round some of my tomatoes once this is all over. They're delicious. Organic too.'

He huffs. 'Don't get me started on that hippy nonsense. This country was built with food grown the proper way. We didn't come over here to—'

'Your address, Trevor. Please.'

He tells me, then adds, 'I'll wait here for a while. Anything even feels wrong, you come running – hobbling – back. Okay? Promise me, Jem.'

I nod. 'Will do.' I take a deep breath and open the door. 'See you soon, Merlin.'

Merlin growls.

I take a breath. Just a short walk to safety, to Rusty.

I tell myself I can do this.

9:18 a.m.

Any right-minded individual prefers to start her day with a good cup of coffee and Rusty is no different. But just so long as that coffee is not your regular drip machine fare. No ma'am, Rusty has more refined tastes than that. Tastes she acquired at an early age. Her granddad had come back from the war after operations in Italy and, as well as a thousand stories, he returned with a little aluminium stove-top percolator. Rusty, who spent many summers at his house, watched every morning as he took the time to grind beans by hand until he had a fine black-brown powder that she would come to know in time as espresso.

He would put those grounds in the percolator and tell her, 'Now, the best part. We wait.'

She hadn't understood the value of waiting back then. Little Rusty was an impatient child, as most children are, and became bored in seconds. Patience is an acquired virtue, after all. Yet she wanted to make Grandpa proud and so sat with him each morning to watch the percolator.

When it finally hissed, he grinned, revealing his uneven jaw that had been broken in two by a German rifle stock long ago. He poured steaming coffee from the percolator into an enamel mug and took a noisy sip.

'Unbeatable,' he said, so happy and so content.

That first time Rusty looked on with eager eyes, waiting for her turn to taste this unbeatable black liquid. Her mouth watered in anticipation.

'Oh no, young lady, this is not for you.'

Rusty was not happy. All that patience she had displayed, all that expectation, for nothing.

'You're too young,' he insisted.

Well, she would show him, she decided. Having watched him step by step, she waited until he had gone outside to start the day's chores. Then Rusty set about emulating him. She ground the beans, which was really hard to do. She had to brace the grinder between her thighs and use both hands to wrench the handle round and round. With each rotation it grew quicker and easier until she had that fine espresso powder Grandpa had made. He had already washed out the percolator so she filled the base with water and filled the middle compartment with the grounds and screwed on the top and set it on the stove. She was too short to reach it so used a stool to make up the difference.

Then, she waited.

This time she didn't mind the wait. She didn't grow bored. She was excited and scared and couldn't wait to sip her creation.

She had made one hell of a mess with coffee beans on the floor and grounds scattered here and there and splashes and puddles of water everywhere else. She didn't notice any of it.

In time, the percolator hissed, announcing her success, her victory.

Grandpa had used a rag to take it from the stove and she did the same, dropping down from the stool and spilling some steaming coffee on the floor, almost scalding her tiny pink toes in the process. A narrow escape, and she made a concentrated effort to be more careful.

Grandpa's enamel mug was outside with Grandpa so she found another, set it down on the kitchen table and filled it to the brim with the coffee.

The steam moistened her face as she peered down at her creation. Her mouth watered so much she had to swallow away the saliva.

It was too hot to sip, she knew.

She waited.

Rusty wasn't sure how long it would take and grew impatient. She blew on the dark surface and watched the ripples and waves, and more steam rose into her face. She gripped the mug in both hands and brought it to her face, blowing the whole time.

The brim found her bottom lip and she tilted the mug and sipped her coffee.

She spat it back out.

Not because it was hot but because it was disgusting.

Forty years later, she won't touch anything else.

Which makes her wonder why Officer Sabrowski has set a cup of tasteless, soulless filter coffee on her desk. After one grimacing sip, she calls Sabrowski back into her office just so she can throw a pen at him.

To his credit, he's fast enough to duck.

'Are you trying to poison me, Officer?'

'Ma'am?'

'Do you want me to suffer?'

'Ma'am?'

'Do you really hate me so very much?'

'Ma'am?'

She uses both hands to gesture at the cup of pure insult on her desk.

Sabrowski takes a few seconds to understand. 'Sorry, boss. Must've given Zeke yours by mistake and you his.'

Rusty plants both meaty palms on her desk and leans forward. 'Then you'd best hurry to rectify this travesty before Zeke acquires tastes far beyond his lowly station.'

'What, now?'

She raises another pen, ready to throw at Sabrowski. 'Go get my coffee, limp dick.'

Sabrowski flinches in frightened anticipation, as if the pen might do some real damage, and reaches for the door.

'Take this abomination with you,' Rusty orders. 'Its very presence offends me.'

Sabrowski does as he's told, returning a couple of minutes later.

'Why are your hands empty, Officer?' Rusty asks. 'My thirst has become untenable and my patience stretched thinner than your thighs.'

Sabrowski says, 'Sorry, Rust, I was waylaid.'

'Now what does that mean?'

'We have a couple of people here to see you,' he explains. 'From the FBI.'

'It's too early in the morning for practical jokes, Officer. If I get up from my desk and see Zeke in a rented suit and his hair slicked down with bacon grease and acting like he's finally finished puberty I'm not going to be amused. That's foolery only fit for the afternoon and certainly won't be appreciated by this here under-caffeinated chief.'

Sabrowski pleads sincerity. 'I'm telling you, Rust, there are two severe individuals out there with badges who want to speak to you immediately.'

Rusty is not quite ready to believe this. In all her years as police chief she hasn't so much as had a call from the FBI let alone a couple of agents show up on her doorstep.

'They're real stone-faced, boss,' Sabrowski continues. 'You want me to tell them to come back in the afternoon when you'll appreciate their foolery?'

'Don't be an idiot every waking moment, Officer.' Rusty stands. 'Take a break every now and again. See how it feels. Maybe you'll like it.'

She rounds her desk and makes sure her belt is tight and her shirt tucked in.

Outside her office, Rusty sees a smartly dressed woman and man who don't belong. They're already looking her way, waiting. Sabrowski was right: these are a couple of serious people.

'I'm the chief,' Rusty says, nearing.

The woman makes the introductions. 'I'm Agent Wilks, this is Special Agent Messer. We'd like to talk to you about one of your residents.'

'And who in this here quiet town has come to the attention of the great and the good at the FBI?'

'A Mrs Jemima Talhoffer.'

Rusty purses her lips. 'Yoga Jem? She's quieter than a mute mouse. Whatever has she done?'

Wilks glances at Sabrowski and Zeke, both inching closer so they don't miss a word of this unprecedented conversation.

She says, 'Perhaps we could discuss this further in a more private setting?'

'Sure,' Rusty replies. 'You guys want something to drink?'

'Not for me,' Wilks says.

Messer shakes his head.

She steps aside and gestures for the two FBI agents to make their way to her office.

'This way, please. Make yourselves at home.'

She follows a step behind, pausing only to point at Sabrowski and mouth, *My coffee, now.*

9:23 a.m.

In the summer this town is beautiful and now, in the fall, it maintains that beauty, although there is a richness and maturity to its palette with rust-coloured leaves frosting the sidewalk and rooftops. The town is quiet because it's always quiet. I need that quietness. Without it I would have never been able to drive here for groceries. I don't like noise these days just like I don't like a lot of things. Today, though, this morning, I don't like the quiet. The lack of noise makes the town feel empty, threatening. It's only a short half-block to the police department's office but I can't shake the feeling I'm being watched. I'm hyperaware of all the windows around me – on my side of the street, on the opposite side, on ground level and on floors above – and how someone could be standing behind any one of them. They could see me yet I couldn't see them in return.

I feel like the whole town is my enemy.

I'm paranoid, I know, but I think I have every right to be given what has just happened.

Keep it together, Jem. You're almost there. Just get inside the precinct.

Inside, you're safe. Wilks and Messer can't get you in there.

Without the doping effect of adrenalin, the simple act of walking is painful. I'm hobbling more than walking. There are so many cuts and scrapes on the soles of my feet and I'm becoming more and more aware of each and every one of them. Running through the woods did more damage than I thought.

I catch a glimpse of my reflection in a store front. Man, I look like I've stepped straight out of the jungle after being lost there for a decade. It's almost comical how crazy my hair has become, how smeared my clothes are with dirt and blood and God knows what. I was worried earlier that I might stink after yoga but now I must reek.

Least of your worries, Jem.

In fact, it's not a worry at all. Not even a sliver of a worry. Funny how we can be so concerned with appearances so much of the time yet they're nothing close to a priority when it really comes down to it.

I near the police department. It's a low, square building. There's no signage on the back of the building to denote its purpose and to the unknowing it could serve all manner of purposes: an office, a bank, maybe even a place of worship.

I turn on the spot to look at Trevor. I'm not sure why, what I hope to see. Reassurance, probably. I just need to know he's still there.

He is. He gives me a slow nod and it's enough for me to turn back round and hobble the rest of the way to the end of the block. I circle around the building because there's no entrance round back that I can use.

I can no longer see Trevor and that's not good for my nerves but I'm so close now, to safety, that I keep stumbling along without slowing down, reaching the front of the building.

Parked in the lot is a black Explorer.

I don't hesitate for even a second. I retreat. I don't see Wilks or Messer but they must be inside or close.

I hurry back to Trevor, who sees me hobbling along the sidewalk and accelerates over to me to spare my feet.

'What's wrong?' he asks as I heave open the passenger door and climb back inside.

'They're there,' I say, panting, distraught. 'Wilks and Messer.'

'Outside the police building?'

'I only saw their vehicle out front. They might be inside. God, what am I going to do now?'

Trevor is confused. 'You think they're inside the police department?'

I nod. 'Yes. Yes, I do. Their SUV is in the lot, why else would it be there?' I'm shaking my head, angry at myself. 'We must have taken too long. We gave them too much time. They must have realised what we were planning to do. What am I going to do now?'

Trevor still has the look of confusion. 'The cartel folk are inside the precinct?'

'*Yes,*' I hiss, losing my temper. 'What's so hard to understand about that? They've beaten us here.'

Trevor is silent in thought with his lips pursed. He has grey eyes and they're looking at me questioningly.

My temper calms, and now I'm confused too.

I say, 'Why are they inside the police HQ?'

'Beats me,' he says. 'Now, I don't know a whole heap about forgeries, but to my mind I don't think that drug dealers could get fake FBI badges so good as to fool local law enforcement.'

'You're saying they don't just work for the cartel? You think they're agents on the take?'

He shrugs. 'Perhaps, but that's not really what I'm saying.'

I know what he's saying and I'm silent. I put my face in my hands for a moment.

'Please don't tell me I'm on the run from real FBI agents, Trevor. Oh God, please don't say that. That can't be right, can it?'

Trevor breathes a sympathetic sigh.

He says, 'I think you need to consider the possibility that perhaps you've had your wires crossed this whole time. Because even if a couple of badass enforcers working for a cartel could get access to the kind of forgeries that might trick Rusty, would they really risk it? Would they really stride into the lion's den and try and fool the lions if they didn't have to?'

I can't answer. The pain from my feet is forgotten because with every wise, sensible word Trevor is making me feel worse.

'But Carlson,' I say eventually. 'He said . . . he told me I was in danger. That those two didn't work for the Bureau. That's what he said. I swear that's what he said. He's the only agent working on the case, who knows about Leo. I didn't mishear him, Trevor. I'm not making it up.'

'I believe you,' Trevor responds in a soft voice. 'I'm sure he told you exactly that.'

I know what Trevor is going to say next. 'But how do I know Carlson was telling me the truth?'

Trevor shrugs.

'Oh no,' I breathe. 'Oh Jem, you stupid, stupid woman.'

Trevor says, 'Don't go condemning yourself just yet. You can only ever do what you think is right in the moment. Moments change.'

'I appreciate you trying to make me feel better, Trevor. I

really do. But let's face it: I've royally screwed up. I've made a terrible mistake. I thought I was running for my life and I was running from the damn FBI.'

'You don't know that for sure.'

'I do,' I snap back. 'And you do too.' I open the passenger door. 'I need to make this right before they put together a nationwide manhunt. Oh Trevor, you might have been harbouring a fugitive this whole time.'

'Let's not jump to any conclusions.'

I shake my head. 'That's exactly what I've been doing.' I climb out. 'I've already jumped to the worst possible conclusion based solely on a phone call from a stranger. I already knew I was crazy but I didn't know I was this crazy. Go home, Trevor. Take Merlin home. Have a good laugh at my expense because once I'm over the humiliation, once I can walk okay again, I'm going to have a good laugh at myself. But not right now. Not for a good long while.'

Trevor leans across the seats so he's closer to me. 'Why don't I drive you round the block and drop you off outside?'

'No, thanks. You've done more than enough already. I don't want to waste any more of your time. And I need to have a few moments to myself. I need to get my thoughts in order before I walk in there.'

His furry eyebrows arch. 'Your call, Jem. You know what's best for you. And don't worry about my time because if nothing else it's been an interesting morning.'

He smiles at me. I can't smile back.

'See ya round,' I say, and head off to face my judgement.

I don't move with any kind of speed. I'm dragging my feet. Not because they're sore but because I'm so embarrassed, so ashamed, I don't want to reach my destination. Looking back, I can't believe I ever listened to Carlson, whoever he is. I'm trying to remember exactly what he said and what I said to him and it's all a blur, all fuzzy. He must have been convincing. I didn't doubt his sincerity. Maybe I'm easily led. Maybe I'm too quick to believe what I'm told, too passive in my own thought process.

Have I always been like this?

No, definitely not. I never used to feel incomplete. I never used to hate myself.

I turn round to see that Trevor is still parked, still waiting for me. A ceaseless guardian.

I put my hands on my hips.

He gestures with his hands, wondering what I'm doing.

Go, I mouth.

He frowns. Shakes his head.

I shrug in defiance. If he's not going to go, I'm not going anywhere either.

Fine, he mouths back. Then something else I can't read. I expect something along the lines of have it your way, but probably a little less cordial.

He pulls away from the kerb, rolls past me. He gives me a nod and I nod back.

Then he's gone. At least Merlin will have stopped growling now.

As I near the police department I sigh, shake my head at my rash actions, my poor judgement. What got into me?

Time to put it right. Time to find out what is really going on.

When I'm closer, I see the big SUV out front and Wilks standing near it. She's talking on a cell phone. She's too far away for me to hear what she's saying and she hasn't looked in my direction, so she doesn't realise I'm approaching. I was terrified of her less than an hour ago and now I can't understand why. She looks like a decent woman, a strong authority figure. She bears no resemblance to a killer working for a drug cartel. She looks, surprise surprise, like an FBI agent.

Oh, Jem, wait until Leo hears about this.

Leo, the criminal, laundering money for a cartel. Can it be true? Even if what Wilks told me earlier is correct, that he's being pressured into it, I still can't bring myself to believe it. How could I not have known? How could he have kept such a secret from me?

I guess I'll find out more in a few minutes once I've had a good telling off about what happened earlier. I hope Messer didn't have a heart attack after chasing me through the woods. He's a big guy, after all. I don't imagine he ever spent much time on a treadmill.

I'm about to call out to Wilks when I hear a vehicle behind me. I glance back, expecting to see Trevor returning. Instead I see a plain grey sedan, which pulls up fast alongside me.

The window is already down, and the man behind the wheel is looking my way.

'I'm Carlson,' he says. 'You need to come with me. Right now.'

9:31 a.m.

After all the surprises of this morning I guess I should have been expecting another. Carlson looks to be in his late forties. He's African-American, with his curly dark hair thin and buzzed short and a shadow of stubble despite the early hour. He wears a suit, white shirt and tie. In many ways he's cut from the same cloth as Wilks and Messer. On the surface an FBI agent, but I'm not so easily fooled a second time.

'Get away from me,' I say, backing off, surprise at his sudden appearance becoming concern.

'Please, you have to get in. You have to come with me right now. I need to get you out of here while I still can. That's not a lot of time. Please, Jem, get in the car.'

'Where's your badge? Where's your credentials?'

'There's no time. You'll have to trust me.'

'Fat chance. I trusted you before and it got me nowhere. Look at me, I've been through hell.'

He says, 'I saved your life. Let me save it again.'

'From who?'

'The two people who knocked on your door this morning, Wilks and Messer. They're still out there and still looking for you.'

'You mean the same Wilks and Messer who are at the police station at this very moment?'

He nods. 'They're dangerous.'

'Are they? Are they really? They're so dangerous that they're hanging out with the local law enforcement. How does that work? I'm dying to know why criminals, cartel killers, are doing that.'

'It's complicated,' Carlson answers.

'That's pathetic.'

I'm walking now, stepping away along the sidewalk. Carlson is persistent, rolling his car alongside me, keeping pace.

'There's so much I have to tell you,' he continues. 'About them, about Leo, about you. I can't do it at the side of the road in thirty seconds. Come with me. I'll explain everything. I'll answer all of your questions. If you don't believe me, if you don't trust me, then I will drive you back and you can go see the police. But please, we must hurry.'

'No chance.' I'm shaking my head. 'The last thing I need to do is hurry. Hurrying is what started this mess. I did it once. There's no way I'm making that mistake again. I'm going to do things by the book. You want to talk to me, you can come with me into the police department. Let's all of us talk this through together. How does that sound?'

He hesitates, then says, 'I can't do that.'

'I had a funny feeling you might say that, Agent Carlson . . . or whatever your name is.'

'I am Carlson,' he insists. 'I'm trying to help you, Jem. I'm trying to help Leo too. Please. Just trust me. All I want to do is keep you alive.'

86

'An hour ago you were a voice on the phone telling me to run for my life. Now you're a stranger in a car asking me to get in. Are you nuts? Leave me alone.'

'Please,' he says, almost pathetically, begging.

There's something sincere in his eyes that makes me doubt myself, that makes me consider believing him. I pause, hesitate.

He stops the car and releases the door for me, taking my hesitation as consent to come with him, a stranger in a car.

'No way.' I back off again. 'I don't care who you say you are or what you say you want. I don't know you. I don't trust you. I don't trust a single thing you've told me.'

He tries one last time. A simple plea. So much said in one short word: 'Don't.'

I turn.

I'm gone.

9:33 a.m.

Wilks isn't out front any longer – she must have entered the building at some point during my encounter with Carlson – so I walk uninterrupted across the short parking area, past the black Explorer that seemed so frightening earlier and then by an officer's blue and white. I'm more aware than ever of my hurt feet and I'm not quite walking, not quite hobbling. A kind of shuffle, trying to keep my weight off the parts of my soles that are most painful. I'm on the balls of my feet more than my heels, wincing with every awkward step.

Never run barefoot through a forest, trust me. Especially not after you've scuttled across a tiled roof. In short: always wear shoes. Shoes are great. Shoes need more love.

The precinct is a single-storey building with a flat roof and a dull, featureless exterior. A functional place. No budget left over to put a friendly face on things. I push open the door, which seems ridiculously, unnecessarily heavy when I don't have a secure footing. A little brass bell chimes as I step into the lobby. The scent of pine air freshener hits me, strong and potent. I picture one of those tree-shaped things you can get for cars, but a giant one. It must be hidden somewhere because I can't see it.

'Is Rusty about?' I ask the pencil-thin guy who looks up to greet me with small, questioning eyes.

He has a moustache of sparse blond hair that twitches before he speaks. 'Who's asking?'

'Jem Talhoffer,' I reply.

'What should I say it's about?'

I shrug because I'm not sure exactly how to explain this morning's events, so I simply say, 'She'll know when you tell her I'm here.'

He looks sceptical, like I'm trying to trick him and embarrass him in front of his boss. Some practical joke he doesn't quite understand, yet fears nonetheless. Maybe Rusty doesn't like to be interrupted without a damn good reason.

'Please,' I add. 'Tell Rusty that Jem needs to see her immediately.'

The moustache twitches but he says nothing further. He pushes himself up from his desk and hikes up his trousers. He gives me one last sceptical look but scurries off to find Rusty.

I have nothing to do but stand and wait and try to compose my thoughts, to work out what I'm going to say, what excuses I'm going to make, because speaking the truth, even to myself in my own mind, sounds ridiculous.

A stranger on the phone told me to run, so I ran.

Oh, how I wish I worked in marketing or politics so I could find a way of spinning that into something that sounds a little less crazy.

Maybe that's the way to go.

I had a bout of temporary insanity.

Then again, maybe not.

No more time to consider because I'm aware that the moustache guy is heading back towards me and behind him, trailing a little way, is the town police chief, Rusty, and behind her are Wilks and Messer.

'Where you been, Jem?' Rusty asks, nearing. 'I got a couple of folks here awful worried about you.'

Rusty is almost as wide as she is tall, and she's not tall. She has that squat, robust build. She waddles a little when she walks but is never out of breath. We've crossed paths a few times and she's always been friendly and always fair. I don't trust many people these days, if anyone, but I know Rusty takes no crap and gives none out either.

'Nice to see you again too,' I reply, my mask slipping instinctively back into place. 'How's Alice?'

She rolls her eyes. 'Little shit has only gone and got herself a tattoo.'

'That doesn't sound so bad.'

Rusty shakes her head. 'On her face.'

'Oh,' I say. 'Maybe it'll wash off?'

A hint of a smile from Rusty.

Wilks and Messer are silent behind her. Neither has so much as blinked.

Rusty says, 'Why don't we all sit down in my office? Talk this through.'

I nod. 'Sure.'

The thin guy with the moustache looks lost – he's not in the loop – and I step around him to follow Rusty into her office.

There are only two seats for visitors, so Wilks props herself against the windowsill after I sit down and Messer takes the other chair. I'm uncomfortable so close to both of them, confined as we are in Rusty's small office. It feels warm with body heat, and humid with perspiration. I'm the only one who seems to notice.

She's the last of us to sit down, settling into her big leather chair behind a desk that overflows with paperwork. Interspaced between the piles of documents and forms are picture frames of various dimensions. I can't see what's on them from this side of the desk. Family, no doubt, although she doesn't wear a wedding band. Maybe pets.

'If you don't mind me saying so,' Rusty begins, 'you look like hell, Jem. I barely recognise you.'

'I feel worse than I look, I assure you.'

'Would you like some aspirin?'

'I'm okay for now.'

Rusty leans a little forward. 'I've got some gin in my desk drawer if you want it. I know it's a little early for happy hour but I won't make any judgement. I'm sure you could use it.'

I shake my head.

She sits back again. 'Agents Wilks and Messer here have been telling me about their little visit to your house earlier this a.m.'

'I'm sure they have,' I say, trying not to sound too meek, too pathetic.

'Why'd you run?' Messer asks.

Rusty isn't happy with this directness of approach. 'I think what Special Agent Blunt meant to say – I mean beyond him saying nothing at all at this particular juncture – was what spooked you so bad, Jem? Why'd you get scared like that?'

Messer is similarly unhappy with the chastisement. 'Were you trying to warn Leo?'

Rusty's palm finds the desk surface. 'How's about you go fetch us all a nice cool cup of extra special delicious tap water?'

Messer doesn't move.

Rusty's eyes shoot laser beams at Messer. 'If I phrased that as a question then please accept my sincere apologies.' She clicks her fingers and points a meaty thumb at the door. 'Water. Now.'

The muscles in Messer's thick jaw flex so hard I'm surprised he doesn't crack his own teeth but he says nothing. He stands, slow. He leaves, slower.

Rusty sighs and looks at Wilks. 'Do you want to put a muzzle on your boy or do you want me to do it? Because trust me when I say you don't want me to have to do it for you.'

Wilks gestures in apology. 'Won't happen again.'

Rusty nods. 'Damn right it won't happen again. They stopped teaching you fancy schamsy FBI agents manners at the academy?'

Wilks shrugs in response. It's not a question that needs an answer.

Rusty turns her attention back to me. 'Just tell me in your own words what happened.'

I take a deep breath and explain about the phone call, Carlson. I try to tell it as well as I can but there are gaps in my memory. I'm not certain exactly what he told me. I can recall my fear, however. That I do remember.

Rusty listens, a frown of concentration on her brow the entire time.

After I'm done, she seeks some clarifications: 'This Carlson told you he was FBI?'

'Yes.'

'He told you that the two people in your living room worked for a cartel?'

'Yes,' I say, then I'm suddenly not sure. 'He might have implied it.'

'How would he imply such a thing?'

I think back, trying to recall every sentence, every word. The more I try, the blurrier it all becomes. 'I seem to remember he said something like they were business associates.'

'Business associates?'

I nod. 'I'm pretty sure that's what he said. He told me that he

92

was the only one working on my husband's case, that no one else knew anything about what he's supposedly been doing for the cartel except the cartel.'

'So,' Rusty says, 'might he have led you to infer that Special Agents Wilks and Messer were representatives of this cartel?'

'He must have done.'

Rusty is silent, thinking. I glance at Wilks. She's just as silent, just as much in thought.

'What does this mean to you?' Rusty asks her.

Wilks says, 'There's no one at the Bureau named Carlson that I know personally. I'll check, obviously, but I doubt very much that whoever this person is will turn out to be FBI. My guess is he knows Leo somehow. In all likelihood he's one of the business associates he warned you about.'

I say, 'Why did he call me? Why did he tell me you were dangerous?'

Wilks says, 'Again, I can only speculate at this point, but if he knows your husband then he could very well be involved in the money-laundering operation as well. Evidently, he doesn't want you talking to us. I'm not sure how but it's conceivable he learned of our investigation.'

Rusty says, 'You folk at the Bureau have sprung a leak?'

Wilks shrugs. 'It's not unheard of when cartels are concerned.'

I nod. It makes sense: Carlson is one of the very people he's tried to warn me about, all the while trying to make me think he can help me. A good trick because it worked.

I say, 'That's why he wanted me to go with him, to make sure I couldn't talk to you.'

Wilks is confused. 'Say what?'

'He didn't want me to come here.'

Rusty says, 'He told you on the phone not to go to the authorities?'

I shake my head. 'No, he stopped me on the street. He wanted me to get in his car. Begged me, really. Like Wilks said, he doesn't want me talking.'

Wilks is on her feet now. She points. 'Carlson was here in town? Outside?'

I nod.

'When?'

'A few minutes ago. How long have I been here? Just before I came in through the door.'

'Licence?' Wilks barks.

The intensity of her tone takes me back. I hesitate. 'I ... I don't know. I wasn't paying attention. I—'

'What car was he driving?'

'I don't know. A sedan. Grey, maybe.'

Wilks is out of the office within a second.

I watch her go, peering between the blind slats hanging on the inside of the windowed walls of Rusty's office. I hear her shout the news to Messer and they both rush out of the exit, almost knocking over the moustache guy in the process. He's even more confused now.

Slowly, I swivel my head back round to see that Rusty's laser beam eyes are fixed my way and I feel like the smallest person in the world.

'Guess I should have mentioned that part earlier.'

Rusty nods. 'Little bit.'

9:40 a.m.

No one ever wants to feel anxious but it's a totally normal part of life as a human being. We're all going to have anxiety in the face of severe stresses from time to time. Thing is: the cause should be clear. When there's no cause there should be no anxious feelings.

If only things were that simple.

With anxiety there are no little stresses and there are no small fears. Every stress is extreme. Even the most minor problem can trigger crippling feelings of hopelessness. Everyday obstacles can be terrifying to overcome. Even today most people don't understand anxiety because everyone worries at times and everyone can be occasionally anxious. That's natural. It's even a good thing. We would be dangerously reckless without any fear. The difference between feeling anxious and anxiety is that the latter is chronic. There might not be any good reason to feel afraid. You might be afraid of something that shouldn't be scary. You know you shouldn't be anxious but you are anyway. You can't control it.

There are plenty of reasons why you might develop anxiety, from a side effect of long-term illness to traumatic experiences to an imbalance in serotonin and noradrenalin. Your genes might make you pre-disposed. You might have taken too many drugs. You might have endured a trauma so severe you just can't get over it.

In that way, I'm lucky. I know what caused this condition. There are people out there with no answers. They have anxiety and they don't even know why.

I guess I should be grateful for this small mercy.

Rusty is making me some coffee. She doesn't have one of her troopers do it for her and I'm not sure if this is a special consideration for me or just the way she does things. If I were a police chief I'd have my men scurrying around after my every beck and call. I didn't tell her that I'm not thirsty. I don't even like coffee all that much. Give me a matcha tea and we're talking.

She seems to take her time, so I wonder if she made it as an excuse to leave the office, to talk to someone or check on something. I don't know what to do while I'm on my own so I just sit in the uncomfortable chair and wait for her to return and hope she comes back before Wilks and Messer. I'm not frightened of them now but I don't want to be scolded for not telling them about Carlson sooner. It's not my fault, is it? Surely I'm owed a little consideration given the atypical morning I've had.

I realise my breathing is quick and shallow.

I can feel the beat of my heart inside my chest. It's pounding at an irregular rhythm. I can feel my pulse in my shoulders and in my ears. I hear the fluttering beats of my heart and can almost see it jumping around, unable to stay in place. There's an awful sensation in my neck, as though my heart is trying to squeeze its way up my throat.

I tell myself it's just palpitations. I'm panicking.

I'm safe now, I tell myself.

I'm safe.

When Rusty returns my heart rate has slowed back down again and she hands me a white plastic cup with rings of corrugation around it to give it some strength but I still have to be careful not to grip it too hard. The coffee is spewing out clouds of steam and blowing on the surface doesn't stop me burning the tip of my tongue when I take a sip. Rusty has a big ceramic mug, evidently her own as it has 'Me boss, you not' emblazoned upon it. She must have an asbestos mouth the way she slurps the steaming coffee without any hesitation.

'So,' Rusty says. 'How do you end up a yoga teacher?'

'There's not much else I enjoy doing.'

'Did you go to school for it?'

'Not exactly. In fact, I studied accounting at college.'

'No kidding? Yoga is a long way from decimal places.'

I nod. I agree. I don't want to talk about it now.

'So,' Rusty says again, but in a different tone. 'What do you think?'

I put the coffee down on her desk. 'I don't believe it.'

She takes her seat. 'You think your husband walks on water?'

'Oh, he certainly thinks he does. But I don't think he could hide that kind of secret from me. I mean, I would have known something was up. I would have noticed him not sleeping or being irritable or stressed and scared out of his mind. He's been none of those things. He's Leo, a wine merchant. Nothing more. It must be some mistake.'

'Some folk are better at hiding what's going on inside them than the rest of us.'

This resonates with me and my issues but I'm different, I'm not well. There's nothing wrong with Leo. He's normal.

I say, 'Leo's not like that. He wears his emotions on his sleeve. Always has.'

Rusty slurps some coffee.

'Whatever Wilks and Messer think they know is wrong. They've got the wrong guy. Maybe this Carlson is the real money launderer. Maybe that's why he called me this morning. Has anyone stopped to find out? Have they?'

Rusty says, 'You'll recall that until very recently no one but you, Jemima, knew anything about any Carlson.' Her tone is wonderful in its subtle yet still obvious condescension. She seems to then regret it because she says, 'But you've been put through the wringer so you shouldn't beat yourself up about that.'

I don't know I'm beaten. 'Don't worry, I'm not.'

Rusty huffs and slurps some more coffee.

'Drink up,' she says. 'Don't let it get cold.'

Wilks and Messer aren't gone long yet they return with weary faces. Messer makes a point of looking at me a single time, then not again. I imagine Wilks had a word with him, to rein in his frustration. At least temporarily, at least until they're out of Rusty's uncompromising reach.

Wilks says, to Rusty, not me, 'If he was out there he's long gone by now.'

'He was here,' I insist.

'And he's long gone,' Wilks says again.

Rusty says to her, 'Tell me what you need.'

Wilks is shaking her head, unsure of her next move. 'Time,' she says after a moment. 'That's all I need right now. I have to make a lot of calls. Dig around ... This thing is getting too loud, too fast. I gotta roll back, try and put the lid back on it. This Carlson development changes everything. I need to be careful exactly who I speak to and what I reveal.'

Rusty says, 'What can I do to assist?'

'For now, nada. I appreciate your cooperation but I think this is as far as we go together. I mean no disrespect when I say there's nothing you can conceivably do.'

Rusty turns down the corners of her mouth. 'Well, whatever works for you works for me. You sure you don't want me to put an officer outside the Talhoffer residence, see if Carlson shows up?'

Wilks shakes her head. 'I don't think we'll hear from him again like that. Besides, should any of Leo's associates swing by they're going to know he's blown. That'll reset the entire investigation and put him in extreme danger.'

'Please don't do that,' I say.

Rusty nods at Wilks. No surveillance.

Wilks leans across her desk, offering a hand that Rusty shakes.

It's like everyone has forgotten about me.

So I say, 'What about me?'

'You're free to go,' Wilks says.

I turn up my palms. 'Just like that?'

Wilks looks at me like I'm speaking in a foreign language.

'After all that's happened this morning, it's over?'

My voice is getting louder.

'Yeah,' she says. 'You can have your day back.'

'I can have my day back,' I say.

'Yeah,' she says again. 'We'll need to speak to you again, obviously. But not now, not today. We need to find out who this Carlson is before we do anything else.'

Rusty gestures to me. 'Go home, Jem. Take a bath. Clean your feet. Have a glass of wine. Have two. Relax. Start working on how you're going to tell this tale at your next steamed kale party.'

I nod. 'What about Leo?'

Wilks says, 'What time does he land in Europe?'

'Just after six,' I say. 'P.m.'

Wilks and Messer exchange looks. They gesture. Counter gesture. A whole conversation without words.

'We'll be in touch before then,' Wilks tells me. 'But for a few hours at least, we're done. Leo can wait until he gets back.'

It all feels anticlimactic. I'm told my husband is a money launderer, I run for my life because a stranger named Carlson is trying to manipulate me for reasons no one yet understands . . . and now it's finished. All over. Done.

I stand. I'm awkward. I don't know what to do with my hands.

I say, 'Guess this is goodbye then,' and head to the door. 'It's been fun.'

I put weight on where I shouldn't. I yelp. I have to grab Wilks' arm for support, so I don't stumble.

She says, 'Do you need a ride home?'

I look at my dirty, bloody feet. The thought of walking another inch is too much to bear.

I say, 'Sure, I'd love a ride home,' with no idea how much I will come to regret it.

Growing up in the big city, I felt like a true New Yorker, yet I didn't know myself then. I thought I needed the bustle of city living. I was so used to buildings everywhere; I thought of wide-open spaces and nature as alien environments. Quietness meant boredom. Peace meant frustration.

Travelling changed all that.

I lost my parents when I was still at college and I went off the rails for a time. It was hard to care about quantitative analysis, auditing and microeconomics. I dropped out and fell in with the wrong crowd, trying to cope with grief through drugs and alcohol and bad decisions. After one hangover too many and one more existential crisis than I could handle, I packed up my things and bought the first ticket to the first destination available.

I went to South America doing the usual tourist stuff: following the Inca trail, taking pictures with Christ the Redeemer, hiking open-mouthed around the Galapagos and watching the sunset on Easter Island. My mom and dad left me quite a lot of money and I stretched every last cent as far as it would go.

My inheritance couldn't last for ever and after the carefree adventures of those first few years funds were becoming an issue, so I worked to pay for my travels. I spent a lot of time tending bar. I did a lot of waitressing. I picked fruit. I made jewellery and sold it on market stalls. I taught English as a foreign language. I was a tour guide. At one point I thought I might be a writer. I began keeping a journal of my adventures with the intention of turning them into one great travelogue some day. But I'm no wordsmith. I found myself elaborating too much to make my trips seem more interesting instead of achingly pedestrian sightseeing excursions. I mean, I had a blast, but who wants to read about a wayward soul on one long vacation? I had nothing meaningful to say about the places I visited. There were no grand revelations. No insights. I didn't see or do anything new. So, I made fun nights out seem seedy, interesting people I met became nefarious characters, dull journeys became dangerous expeditions.

I abandoned the journal eventually. I loved making up stories but I needed to focus on something more productive.

I spent my entire twenties on the move. Or perhaps 'on the run' would be a better description. Running from my old life, my mistakes, my grief.

I'll resist slipping into cliché to say I found myself, but I did discover more about Jem than I ever knew before.

Life accelerated at lightning pace.

First I set my sights on Europe.

Then in Rome I met Leo and before long we were back in the States.

After years on the move without a thought to the future I was married and the future was all I could think about.

Leo called me one day to say he'd found the perfect town to move out to, the perfect place to start a family.

'How did you end up here?' I asked him when we first pulled up outside the only bar.

'Long story,' he said in reply, and I never did press him for specifics.

We walked around in a kind of awe that day, so used to the big city and big city noise and big city people. It was unreal that strangers would say hello as they passed, that drivers would slow their cars to let us cross the street when there were no stop signs to tell them to do so. It felt as if we had travelled back in time to a more civilised age.

'I love it,' I said. 'It's perfect. It's just what we need.'

Leo smiled that matinee idol smile of his. 'Good, because I've already made an offer on a house just outside of town.'

'You didn't.'

'Hey, you're the one with the plan,' he said. 'I'm just implementing it.'

He told me he'd seen the 'For Sale' sign and had to go for it, scared that someone else would swoop in and steal our dream home out from under us before he could get me up to view it.

Thankfully, it really was our dream house. We'd spent so long planning and looking that I had an image in my head – a blueprint – of exactly what I wanted, what we needed. The property Leo had found ticked every box I had and more that I didn't even know about.

Moving in turned out to be a blast.

'We should have hired a removal firm,' Leo said, out of breath after ferrying in yet another box.

I wiped my forehead with a sleeve. 'Where's the fun in that?'

'You think this is fun?'

'Maybe we can play a game while we break our backs?'

'Breaking our backs isn't enough of a game?'

'We could see who breaks theirs first. Whoever wins, loses.'

'I fancy my chances.'

He flared out his elbows to make himself look larger and more powerful. He strutted for a moment with an intense look on his face: a silverback surveying his domain.

I rolled my eyes. 'I've seen how you bend over when you lift a box from the floor. You have precisely zero chance, mister.' I held out my fists, side by side as if they were clutching a breadstick that I then snapped.

'I hate to be the one to tell you this,' Leo said, 'but your victory would be short-lived. We'd both lose. I break my back and you'll have to look after me. I could be bedridden for months. You'd have to dress me. Wash me. You'd even have to—'

'Don't say it,' I implored him. 'For the love of all that is pure in this world let's not go there. Let's not even get close to going there.'

I was wearing a pair of denim shorts and one of Leo's shirts that hung off me like some kind of old-world cape. It provided plenty of ventilation but moving boxes and furniture was strenuous work and I was covered in a film of sweat. Leo was soaked. He looked as though there'd been a miniature rain cloud following him around like in one of those cartoons. His T-shirt wasn't so much stuck to him as glued to his skin and I couldn't resist tweaking one of his protruding nipples.

He recoiled.

'What was that?' he yelped, batting my fingers away.

'It was right there. It was calling to me.'

'Calling to you?'

'It was looking right at me,' I assured him. '"Tweak me, tweak me."'

'You speak nipple now?'

'You betcha, bud. Three lessons a week for four years. Not to brag, but I can speak classical and ecclesiastical.'

'I've never respected you more.'

I think we were giddy making this first proper step towards our future. It felt like we were building something real.

It hadn't been easy but we felt victorious at that moment. I had conducted a military-like campaign, harassing the realtor several times a day until the offer was accepted, bombarding the owners with kindness, with flowers and hampers, hand-written cards and homemade candles. I couldn't let it slip through our fingers. I fought for it like I'd never fought for anything before.

It would be our home.

It was all part of the plan.

9:54 a.m.

I'm in the rear of the SUV for the journey back. There's plenty of room – more than enough – for little old me, all alone. The interior of the Explorer is so big I kind of feel like a tiny kid again. The idea is helped by the fact that Wilks and Messer aren't talkers. The silence reminds me of riding in the back with my parents in the front. Messer drives, big hands almost stationary on the steering wheel, at two and ten. A smooth, steady ride. A steady speed. I try and relax but I can't get comfortable. The seats are too firm, the leather too slippery. I keep fidgeting. I can't keep still.

'Won't be long,' Wilks says, noting my restlessness.

She's doing something on her phone. Texting or emailing or whatever. She's not looking at me but she can feel my unease. It's a clumsy attempt to calm me down yet I appreciate whatever I can get. Just don't actually *tell* me to calm down. That's a guaranteed way of sending me berserk.

I'm anxious to get home again, although until I can speak to Leo and we can sort out this mess and until I know the truth, going home isn't going to solve anything. It's a bandage, at best. Only the wound won't close beneath it.

Why do I get the feeling everyone just wants me out of the way?

I peer between the seats to look at the clock on the dash. It's almost ten a.m. This whole mess started only a couple of hours ago. It feels like so much more time has gone by yet there are so many hours left until I can speak to Leo. I imagine him on the plane, relaxing in his seat, unaware the FBI are asking about him. Again, I think back over the last few weeks, thinking about his behaviour, looking for signs of duress. None. I don't remember anything out of the ordinary.

He couldn't have hidden this from me.

I know my husband, don't I?

'Hey,' I say, leaning forward, 'can I get my phone back?'

Messer glances at Wilks, who stops using her own phone for the moment it takes to say, 'Don't have it.'

I frown. 'Wait, what? You guys took it from the kitchen table, right? It wasn't there when I went back for it.'

'Maybe it fell off the table,' Wilks suggests. 'Slid under something.'

'I can't see how that would happen.'

She shrugs without looking at me. 'It'll be in the house somewhere, I'm sure.'

I'm annoyed at the thought my phone isn't where it's supposed to be. If it's missing, how am I supposed to get in touch with Leo? I'm not sure I even know his number. I don't think I know anyone's any more. The days of memorising phone numbers are long gone. It could be written down somewhere, I suppose. Or perhaps it will come back to me when I need it.

The roads are quiet. We see less than half a dozen vehicles on the way out of town and fewer on the highway. Wilks and

Messer don't say anything to each other and nothing further to me. I'm surprised they aren't asking me more questions. Surely they need to know more about Leo, about Carlson? They can't be done with what little I've told them.

Can they?

Messer slows the SUV to a crawl as we approach the intersection. I see a pickup coming the other way and for a moment I hope it's Trevor so I can wave at him as he passes, but we turn off before it reaches us. I swivel round in the back seat to peer through the rear windshield to see the pickup is a different model to Trevor's and a different shade of red.

The single-lane road that leads to the house has an incline and Messer takes it slow. I can hear gravel crunching beneath the tyres as I look out into the woods, remembering fleeing through them, desperate, terrified of the two people I'm now alone with in a vehicle going back to the same place I ran from earlier.

Quite the turnaround.

Messer parks the Explorer right outside and activates the handbrake. For a long moment neither says anything, nor do they act with any consideration and get out to open the door for me.

The engine ticks as it cools. I reach for the door release but the door stays shut.

Locked.

'Can you let me out?'

Wilks says, 'Sure,' and Messer thumbs a button.

I'm out first, taking it slow and easing myself on to my sore feet. The drive is covered in sharp gravel that may as well be caltrops and I find myself balancing on the outer edges of my feet, one palm on the SUV to help spread my weight.

'Thanks for the ride,' I say. 'Guess I'll wait for that call.'

Wilks and Messer watch as I round the vehicle, moving at a snail's pace, half-leaning on the bodywork until I have the narrowest possible stretch of gravel to traverse. I'm shaking my head to myself at their lack of manners. I can do this on my own, sure, but it would have been nice to have at least had an offer of help. This isn't easy and none of it would have happened had they not shown up earlier.

I'm aware of Wilks and Messer talking to each other in hushed voices. I can't hear a word they're saying but I can see their lips moving. I wonder what they're saying.

I wonder why they waited until I got out before saying it.

I brave the caltrops, wincing and trying not to yelp, and make it to the doormat. The coarse fibres feel amazing against my soles in comparison to the gravel. I can't wait to get my feet cleaned up, disinfected and put dressings on. I can't wait to take that shower I needed two hours ago before all the excitement began. With trepidation, I lower my nose towards my armpit. I don't get anywhere near it.

Jeez, I reek so bad.

I turn back. Wilks and Messer are still there, still sat in their seats, neither looking like they're ready to set off to wherever the local FBI field office is located, or back to NYC or wherever else they're based.

The SUV's engine's still off, I notice.

The front door has a deadbolt and I don't have my keys. Why didn't I think about that before? Good thing Wilks and Messer haven't gone yet.

'Door's locked,' I call to them.

Wilks says something to Messer, who nods. Both agents climb out of the SUV.

Messer heads to the trunk, while Wilks says, 'What did you say?'

I point to the door. 'Don't have my keys.'

'Ah,' Wilks responds, digging into one of her trouser pockets. 'Got them here.'

'Phew,' I breathe. 'I was worried I'd have to smash a window.'

Wilks approaches. 'Wouldn't want you to do that.'

'Is it a crime if it's my house?'

'Is what a crime?'

'Breaking in.'

Wilks is deadpan. 'It's your house.'

Messer has the trunk open. He takes something out.

'Here.' Wilks inserts the key into the lock. 'Allow me.'

She turns the key and pushes open the door, holding it open for me as if she's suddenly developed a sense of charity. I hobble inside.

Messer's big feet make loud crunches on the driveway as he comes over. He's carrying a sports bag.

Wilks says, 'May we come inside?'

I look at her for elaboration.

'It's a long drive back,' she explains. 'I could do with making some calls first. Reception's dicey on the roads up here.'

'Ain't that the truth,' I say. 'Sure. Come in and knock your-selves out.'

I step aside to allow them past, almost missing the glance Wilks and Messer share as I allow them into my home for the second time.

10:03 a.m.

I lead Wilks and Messer into the living room, trying to ignore the lingering sense of unease. This is some literal déjà vu, I think, offering them seats. They sit down. Messer puts the sports bag down on the floor next to his chair.

'Can I get you guys anything?'

Wilks shakes her head for both of them. 'We're both fine, thank you.'

'Okay. I'm going to take a shower and sort out my feet.' I glance around the room. 'If you see a cell phone lurking about the place, please let me know.'

Wilks nods. 'Will do.'

I hobble back out into the hallway. The downstairs bathroom is a water closet only, so I make my way to the staircase.

They ascend before me as a mountain.

At the foot of the mountain, I stare down at my feet, then back to the stairs.

This just isn't going to work the conventional way.

I regress back to infanthood and crawl up the stairs as might

111

an overgrown baby. It's pretty easy, I discover, and I can move at a decent speed. Better yet, my battered soles don't have to support any of my weight, least of all one at a time. At the top, I stand back up, albeit with reluctance. If not for feeling silly I was tempted to carry on crawling all the way to the bathroom.

We have a walk-in shower, thank goodness, and it's no trouble for me to get inside the cubicle once I've gone through the ordeal of undressing. The hot water feels so good I don't want to get out. I give my feet several good washes, sat down on the shower floor because it's too awkward to balance on one leg to clean the other foot. I wash out all the dirt from the cuts, prise free all the debris embedded in my skin, scrub away the crusted smears of blood. I grimace and wince the entire time yet it's also immensely satisfying.

The water that swirls around the plughole is a whirlpool of black and red. The shower is a rainfall design and, stood directly under it, the rest of the world tends to cease to exist.

Which is how I like it.

The effect isn't quite as powerful today when so much has happened already and there is still so much unresolved. So many questions without an answer.

Leo. A cartel. Money laundering.

Can it be true?

It feels like a lifetime ago since we met in Rome, which was supposed to be just another stage in my endless journey. I wasn't planning to stay there for any length of time. I figured I would hang out for a few weeks. A couple of months tops. See the sights. Learn to make pasta. Hopefully come away knowing a smattering of Italian once I had earned enough money to buy the next plane ticket.

I wasn't looking for a husband, or even romance. I wasn't looking for anyone or anything at all. I rarely thought more than a week ahead at any time. My life was divided up into moments. There was no plan. I was quite happy to live a nomadic lifestyle. I had no real needs. In fact, I never questioned my lifestyle. I just lived.

But I didn't account for meeting Leo.

I had several boyfriends while travelling but nothing that I would call a real relationship since my college days. My need to keep moving, my relentless restlessness, ensured that I never grew too close to anyone for long. Maybe that was why I never settled down in any of the destinations. Maybe I was too scared to open myself to someone. Maybe I was always running from myself.

Given I had worked in a lot of restaurants and cafés by the time I arrived in Rome I expected I would do the same there once I had found a kindly owner or manager who didn't mind that I couldn't speak the language. That part was easy enough – Italians are some of the loveliest and most welcoming people I've ever come across – but staying employed wasn't so simple. It was summer in Rome and it was a hell of tourists. The pressure to serve them all fast and accurately was too much for my limited Italian and, I'm embarrassed to say now, lazy work ethic.

I was fired before the end of my shift.

Which really put the pressure on to find something else fast because I had a shared room in a hostel I had used the last of my cash to rent.

I spend so much time standing in the shower I'm as pruned as I would be after a long bath when I finally step out and grab a towel.

Dry and dressed in a robe, I take the first aid kit from the medicine cabinet and sit down on the edge of the bathtub to apply a liberal amount of antiseptic salve to my soles, before wrapping my feet in tight gauze.

I do a pretty good job, if I do say so myself. At least until I decide to give my toenails a trim while I'm here and cut my big toe with the nail-trimming scissors. They're so sharp it didn't take much to produce a fat little blob of blood. Just a nick that barely stings but it makes me so angry I want to scream.

I toss the scissors and the waterproof grooming bag I took them from across the room. I clench my teeth and my fists. I feel my pulse thundering at my temples.

The anger subsides eventually. I regain my calm and tidy up, collecting the spilled contents of the grooming bag and setting it back in its place next to the sink.

I must have done a good job with my feet because I can walk again. I'm not going to be breaking any records on the treadmill any time soon but I can take proper steps. A little awkward, sure, yet it's a huge improvement over the hobbling and shuffling I've been forced to do since running through the woods. The gauze wrapped around my feet acts a little like slippers. It's almost comfy.

I return to the medicine cabinet to put back the first aid kit and grab a couple of paracetamol ... and stop. I stare at the many bottles of medication lined up. Diazepam and Tramadol. Prozac and Lithium. If I were on my own I would take something stronger than paracetamol, that's for sure. But I need to stay alert. I can't spend the rest of the day in a numbed stupor. I need to be coherent by the time Leo lands and I don't know how long Wilks and Messer are going to be hanging around.

It occurs to me I've been so long in the bathroom that Wilks and Messer could have finished their phone calls or whatever they needed to do and be gone already. Maybe they shouted up the stairs that they were leaving and I couldn't hear them.

If I weren't so tired I would check, but I'm yawning as I go to our bedroom and sit on the bed to towel my hair. Then, I find

114

myself slumped against the headboard because supporting my own weight is too much effort.

Before I know it, I'm lying down.

My eyelids are so heavy.

I just need to close them for a minute.

Just a minute ...

11:45 a.m.

Rusty is tired because Rusty is always tired. It's not her weight, she knows. No one is more tired than those super-fit people with their skin so thin and drawn it looks like it might slide right off them. No, she's always tired because tiredness is inherent to adulthood in this day and age. The human body was not designed for the stresses of modern living. It was built to survive the wild, to hunt and gather, not to fight through this unforgiving wasteland that we once called civilisation.

In this quiet apocalypse we're all tired, all zombies.

Worse, we don't even know it.

'You ever concern yourself with the human condition?' she asks Sabrowski, who enters her office with a neat binder of documents midway through Rusty's wayward thought process.

Just asking is asking for trouble, she knows. Asking for her faith in her officer, nay humanity, to be shaken once more.

'Is that like a virus?' he asks, frowning in confusion.

She sighs and nods in reply, because why not? It's her own

fault for inviting him into her ponderings in the first place. Might as well roll with it.

'Yeah,' she answers, 'and the worst part is it kills you stone dead. Guaranteed. Once you have it, you're doomed.'

The concept of inevitable doom slows Sabrowski down a step and he's hesitant to place the binder down on her desk in case it might expedite his demise.

'Are they fixing on coming up with a cure?'

His tone is both hopeful that Rusty will dispel this new dread she has instilled in him and yet fearful she cannot.

She leans back in her chair and drums her fingers on her desk. 'I guess some super-smart folk are working their asses off to find one. Might even be a whole lab dedicated to that very pursuit. But, way I see it, some things aren't worth curing even if they can be.'

Rusty sees she has stoked the fires of Sabrowski's imagination because his sparse moustache is twitching in a way she's never witnessed before.

'Vaccination, then?' he suggests in a thin voice. 'Cause you can't trust them. They got arsenic and all kinds of stuff inside to keep you sick so you keep on paying.'

'Apples contain arsenic.'

'Then I won't eat apples no more.'

Rusty pushes both palms down on the desk and leans forward again, closing the distance between herself and her officer so she can stare right up at Sabrowski and he can't fail to recognise her scepticism.

'Officer Sabrowski, kindly inform me of the last time you actually ate a piece of fruit.'

He thinks. 'I had maple syrup on my pancakes this morning.'

'Maple syrup isn't— You know what, forget it. Get back to work, Officer.'

He gestures to the binder. 'I don't have nothing to do now.'

Rusty throws the closest pen at him. 'Then find something.'

He's quick enough to flinch out of the way of the pen because she throws so many. He's no cat but he's built up a decent amount of muscle memory on account of all the practice she's given him.

Sabrowski collects the pen from the floor and slots it back into the desk tidy before exiting. He's well-trained in that way.

Rusty slides the binder closer and scoops it up to check the printouts inside. She isn't too good with computers. From the very first time she sat down with one and realised her chunky fingers were going to struggle typing with anything approaching accuracy she pretty much gave up on the idea. She can get by because she has to as the chief of police, but she gets Sabrowski and Zeke and whoever else is in earshot to do most of the work when it comes to technology. Better for all concerned that way.

So, it was Sabrowski who dug into Leo Talhoffer's background on her behalf, and when he finished he printed out all the relevant information and assembled it in the binder Rusty now reads through. She appreciates his efforts even if he could have used the hole puncher a little more carefully so half of the documents didn't spill out when she held it a certain way.

To make sure he knows this, Rusty yells at him through the internal window. Only a little bit, however, because he's been so thorough in his research.

A while later, he fetches her a cup of her good coffee by way of apology. She didn't even have to ask and is quite touched by the gesture.

'You've got a good heart deep down,' she tells him as he presents the cup. 'Maybe the rest of you will catch up one day.'

Rusty sips and leans back and reads through all the information on the focus of everyone's attention.

Leo Talhoffer is thirty-six years old and has the sort of blond-haired, blue-eyed, perfect-teeth look to him that gets Rusty's back up on general principle. Some people are born with a winning hand and people like Rusty didn't even get a seat at the table.

She's seen him around town now and again – Rusty's seen everyone around town now and again – but she's never exchanged words with the man and never seen him up close.

She reads that he had humble beginnings all the way to Brown and did well for himself, majoring in Business. Funny, then, that he seemed to drift in and out of dead-end jobs during the rest of his twenties, a few months here, a few months there. Never made it a year in any one place yet all the while having the time and resources for plenty of overseas travel. Some people just get an easy ride in life, Rusty is sure just from looking at those perfect WASP features.

The sommelier business was probably started with family money too, and grew fast every year until now, when Leo is turning over a mighty fine chunk of change. Not yacht-buying profits, but enough to make Rusty re-evaluate her life choices as a government employee. She can't afford a paddling pool.

Maxed-out credit cards, though. Not a great deal in his personal bank account and his business account is in the red.

Rusty finds this interesting.

What's also interesting is there are no large transfers that give her reason to look twice. His accounts look normal. He's spending too much, but who isn't? We need to buy as much stuff as possible to distract ourselves from the apocalypse all around us, to convince ourselves that the relentless tiredness is a choice, that being a zombie is worthwhile.

Rusty puts the folder down, careful to make sure all the unholed documents aren't going to fall out again. She pushes her chair back so she can swivel it ninety degrees and set her heels up on her desk. Then, she thinks.

She didn't find what she expected to find. It's still early days and despite Sabrowski's fine work she only has the abridged biography of Leo Talhoffer. It'll take time until she has the complete picture of the man and his life. But still . . .

On a hunch, she shouts for Sabrowski to return.

'Coffee okay?' he asks, worried and tense in readiness to duck another pen.

Rusty says, 'If it walks like a duck and quacks like a duck . . .'

Sabrowski is as confused as he is concerned.

'Rest assured this might be the single greatest cup of coffee the world has ever known.' She gestures to the cup. 'Civilisation has peaked right here, right now.'

Sabrowski beams. 'Really?'

'Not even close,' Rusty says, and Sabrowski's light dims so fast she feels a stab of guilt. 'But it's a commendable effort, Officer, and one you should be proud to call your very own doing. However, it is not this B-plus cup of java that I have summoned you inside these hallowed halls to discuss.'

'It isn't?'

Rusty shakes her head. She stabs at the binder with a rigid finger.

'Did I miss something out?'

'On the contrary. Again, you did some fine work, Sabrowski. Mighty fine. You did such good work it makes me wonder why you're so bad at your job the rest of the time.'

Sabrowski's skinny shoulders sag.

'Lighten up, Officer. I'm just giving you a gentle ribbing.' Rusty scoops up the binder and slides it across her desk. She would throw it to him only half the pages would fly out in the process. 'But now I want you to do it all over again … albeit with a single caveat.'

'Ma'am?'

3:59 p.m.

It's dark when I open my eyes.

Not full dark, not night, but it's much later in the day than when I closed my eyes, much later than I intended. I've been asleep for hours in that deep, trance-like slumber of the truly exhausted. Only I don't feel in the least bit refreshed. My eyes are sore and my throat is dry and I'm groggy like it's first thing in the morning and I've woken up far too early. It's an effort to push myself up and a worse struggle to get off the bed.

For a brief moment I think it is morning and I dreamt Leo leaving and the knock at the door and Wilks and Messer and Carlson and Rusty. In that moment I believe the morning's events have all been one horribly realistic nightmare.

That delicious delusion ends the instant my feet find the floorboards and I feel the unforgiving sting of reality.

Why is reality always painful?

I retie my robe. It came loose as I slept.

The house is quiet. I hear only ambient noise, my own breathing and my own thoughts. Wilks and Messer must be long gone by now having done everything they needed to do. Perhaps they left while I was in the shower, or if they left a little later maybe they called up to say they were going and I was so fast asleep I didn't rouse.

I feel relief that they are no longer here, because I want to be alone, but there is a creeping sense of worry too as I think about Carlson. Whoever he is he's still out there and I'm all alone.

Wilks and Messer wouldn't have left me here by myself if there was any danger. Carlson might be in custody now thanks to a coordinated dragnet of federal and local officers. Or he might be downstairs right now, having broken in after he watched from the treeline as Wilks and Messer left.

Don't be paranoid, I tell myself.

If only my anxiety listened to reason I wouldn't have anxiety issues in the first place.

On the landing, I notice the door to Leo's office is closed. Did I close it earlier before I climbed out of the window? I almost smile, almost laugh. It all seems so silly now. Did I really flee from my own house because a voice on the phone told me to do so?

I descend the stairs, relieved to be able to do so standing up, although it does hurt a little. The gauze around my feet is doing a tremendous job but I'm still unsteady, still cautious of placing too much weight on the wrong parts of my soles. I use the banister for support and it helps me to take the edge off the pain.

I don't hear anything, which leads me to believe there's no Carlson waiting to ambush me on the ground floor. He could be stationary, of course, but if he was really here why didn't he just take advantage of the fact I was asleep upstairs?

He needs information. He could be searching the house, taking advantage of my slumber to do so. I look back over my shoulder. I can't see the door to the office but I picture him in there, perhaps hacking Leo's computer or rummaging through documents. Has he heard me get up?

I take a breath and hold it tight and try to silence those thoughts. They're not about Carlson, they're about me. They're doubting me. They're the voice inside my head that will never trust me, that will never be satisfied with anything I do.

They wake me up, at least, and my thoughts switch to Leo. He'll still be in the air over the Atlantic, I think. What do I say to him when he calls after he lands? I feel ill-informed and unequipped to deal with whatever comes next. Wilks and Messer may have been light on the advice, but before I speak to Leo I intend to think things through. I want to run my marriage through a mental microscope and see what I've been missing for however long this money-laundering thing has been going on.

Assuming it isn't all one big mistake.

I'm still clutching to that hope, but it's feeling more unrealistic the more I think about it. The FBI wouldn't show up at my door unless they were sure, unless there was some compelling evidence, some proof. And there's Carlson. Whoever he is, his involvement reinforces the case against Leo. If it weren't true, why would Carlson call me, try and get me to go with him? If what Wilks and Messer claim is untrue then Leo is just a sommelier. No one calls a wine merchant's wife first thing in the morning to play some twisted practical joke that just happens to match up with what two FBI agents in her home are saying.

Oh, Leo, you should have told me.

I'm almost at the bottom of the stairs and feel relieved I made it down without falling, without so much as slipping. It's rare that I give myself any credit but I take a disproportionate sense of pride in this small accomplishment.

The front door lies a few feet away. There are semi-transparent blocks framing the upper edge, and from the boost in height provided by the stairs I can see through them. There's a porch light outside that comes on automatically when it gets dark and illuminates the driveway and I see a dark ripple outside.

A vehicle.

The big Ford Explorer still parked on the driveway.

I find Wilks in the living area but not Messer.

Wilks has her back to me. She's stood up, talking on her cell phone.

'... I don't know what to say about that. It's not how we planned it. But problems can be fixed. That's why we're here, after all.'

There's a pause, and for some reason I resist the urge to speak, to demand to know why she's still in my house. I say nothing. I want to listen.

'No, the police chief is a neutral observer. She's not a problem.'

I frown. Why would Rusty be anyone's problem, least of all the FBI's?

'That's factually incorrect,' Wilks says, the volume of her voice a little higher, a little more intense. 'We have this under control. There won't be any further missteps. The wife isn't—'

Wilks cuts herself off because she's seen my reflection in a picture frame.

'I'll call you back,' she says to the person on the other end of the line.

She turns to face me. For a moment her face is blank and expressionless.

Then she smiles as if she's forgotten her manners.

'How did you sleep?' she says.

I rub my eyes. 'Who were you talking to?'

'A colleague,' she answers. 'At the Bureau.'

'What time is it?'

'About sixteen hundred hours.'

I say, 'Why are you still here?'

'We would have had to come back,' she explains without explaining at all. 'Didn't make sense to drive all that way only to do it again.'

I frown. 'This is not okay. You can't just camp out in my house all afternoon without permission.'

She nods. 'You're right, I'm sorry. I would have asked but you were asleep. I didn't want to wake you after all you've been through. I made the wrong call. I see that now.'

I shrug to say I'm over it – I'm not – but while she's here anyway I might as well exploit that. There's so much I need to know, after all.

'Have you caught Carlson?'

She shakes her head. 'Not yet. But we're working on it.'

'Do you know who he is yet?'

'We're working on it,' she says again.

Turns out Wilks doesn't have much for me to exploit.

'Where's Messer?' I ask.

'He's taking care of a few things.'

I shift my feet. 'Look, I don't want to be funny. I know I said you guys could come in before, I know you didn't want to wake me up. I appreciate that. But I'd kind of like some space to myself now. I need to get my head together, you know?'

Wilks says, 'I understand.'

'I've slept but it hasn't helped. I'm still tired. I need to rest and eat and think. I've got so much to think about. I need to relax more than anything else and I just can't do that with you two here.'

'I understand,' Wilks says, 'but since we're here there's a few more questions I need answering.'

'Can it wait?'

She shakes her head. 'Not really. Not given the involvement of this Carlson individual.'

'What do you want to ask me? I told you everything I know earlier, which is nothing. I didn't think of anything else while I was asleep, I promise.'

'I'm sure,' Wilks says. 'But we've found out more in the meantime. You might recall we asked you about information your husband might have regarding his associates.'

'Yeah, yeah. You said it might be on an external hard drive or something like that.'

'That's right,' she says. 'Do you think you might recognise one that doesn't belong to your husband, that you've never seen before?'

'If I've never seen it before then how could I possibly recognise it?'

Wilks says, 'As an odd one out. Would you know that you hadn't seen one before if we found it in your husband's possessions?'

'No, I don't think so. I'm not good with technology.'

Wilks considers.

'Hey,' I say, 'what do you mean when you say if you found it in Leo's things?'

Wilks doesn't answer.

I remember the closed office door. 'Is that where Messer is? Is he in Leo's office?'

Wilks can't answer quick enough before I add: 'He's been searching for hard drives while I've been asleep?'

'We need to find out just who Leo's business associates are before they realise we're on to them.'

'You told me before you know who they are.' I'm backing out of the room as I speak, heading for the stairs. 'And either way it doesn't give you the right to snoop around my home without my consent. How dare you. *Hey*,' I shout up to Messer, 'get out of my husband's office.'

Wilks is following me. 'Why don't you try calming down?'

Of all the wrong things to say.

I spin a fast one-eighty, getting my face into hers. 'Get out of my house. Get out right now and don't come back until you have a warrant.'

4:06 p.m.

Wilks makes no move to do anything of the sort. She stands before me mere inches away and doesn't react except to calmly wipe away a little of my saliva from her cheek. This only infuriates me further, but what else can I do?

I ignore her for the moment and begin climbing the stairs, clutching the banister for support, moving faster than I should because I'm so angry at this intrusion, this betrayal. How dare they? After all I've been through, how dare they do this as well?

I call down to Wilks without looking at her. 'Whatever else is going on, this is not okay. This is not okay.'

Wilks is silent and I know she's watching me from the bottom of the stairs.

Messer, reacting to the commotion, is on the landing by the time I reach it. He stands in my way, blocking my route to Leo's office. He fills the width of the landing so I try to push past.

I might as well be trying to shift a boulder.

'*Get out of my way,*' I yell at him.

He does, but in his own time, stepping back with one foot so he's parallel to the wall and I march through the space he's left.

I gasp when I see the state of Leo's office.

The floor is strewn with papers. Every drawer has been emptied, every file and folder has been stripped of documents. It'll take all day to put right. Maybe longer.

'What the hell have you done this for?' I'm so angry I could scream and I'm doing everything I can to maintain a last modicum of calm. 'Get out of my house,' I say at Messer and, leaning over the banister, I yell down to Wilks: '*Get. Out.*'

Wilks says back up at me, 'We're not going anywhere just yet, I'm afraid. We don't need a warrant, Mrs Talhoffer, not when it comes to matters of national security. The law is very firmly on our side with this one.'

I'm heading back down the stairs now, still awkward in my movements but quick now I've already been down and up in the last few minutes. Messer doesn't try and get in my way this time. He just stands and watches.

'Why?' I ask Wilks. 'What are you talking about? How is a drug cartel a matter of national security?'

Wilks waits for me at the bottom. 'I'm afraid I can't share the specifics with you at this current juncture due to the aforementioned national security concerns.'

I glare at her. 'Oh, so you're afraid you can't share the specifics with me at this current juncture?'

She nods as if she doesn't detect my obvious sarcasm.

'Well,' I continue, 'doesn't that just make everything peachy?'

'I don't think I follow,' Wilks says, deadpan.

I summon some resolve, some restraint. 'I'm asking you to leave. This is my home. You have no right to be here. Please.'

'We still have some things we need to—'

'Are you going to leave?'

Wilks shakes her head.

'I want it to be noted that you are refusing my very reasonable request to vacate my property.'

Wilks nods. 'Noted.'

'Can you at least tell me how long you're going to be?'

Wilks glances at Messer, still at the top of the stairs.

Messer says, 'An hour, maybe.'

Wilks' gaze falls back on me. 'An hour, maybe.'

I sigh, because that's all I have left. 'First money laundering, now matters of national security. What's it going to be next?'

I'm not expecting an answer and Wilks doesn't supply one. I would storm out of the hallway and into the kitchen but I can't walk well enough for storming. Instead, I have to express my anger and dissatisfaction with a modest speed and light step. It fails to have the same impact. I'm committed, though. I give it my best.

I pour myself a glass of water in the kitchen. All of a sudden, I'm aware of how parched my throat is, how long it's been since I drank anything. I don't consider a few sips of Rusty's scorching coffee to count as hydration. The glass is drained in seconds and I pour another and sit with it at the table, the table where I left my phone earlier.

I take a look underneath. Nothing. I look around the kitchen. It's not here. There's nowhere it could have slid out of sight.

Aside from Carlson's call earlier I don't remember the last time I used the house phone. It's attached to the kitchen wall near the hallway. It has one of those long curly wires that once seemed so useful, so essential. I pick up the receiver and pause with my finger over the keypad as I try and recall my own number. For a few seconds my mind is blank – I haven't had to remember it for years – but then it comes back to me, flashing loud and clear in my thoughts. I press the buttons. It's been so

131

long since I did so it comes as a surprise how nice it feels to have that tactile feedback from actual, real buttons instead of tapping a glass screen. Maybe progress isn't all it's cracked up to be, as Trevor noted.

It takes so long to start ringing that there's a brief moment in which I think I've dialled incorrectly, that I don't remember my own cell number. As soon as it rings I lower the receiver to better listen for the sound of my cell's ringtone. I can't hear it at all. Out of battery? No: even if it's here, I won't hear it because it'll still be on silent mode from class this morning. Sometimes I can go days without realising I haven't switched it back to normal. I don't get a whole lot of calls or messages to make me notice.

I'm holding the receiver to my chest and concentrating hard to listen out for any sound of vibration, any rattle, so I almost don't realise it when the dial tone ceases, when someone else's voice answers my phone.

'Hello?'

I raise the receiver, shocked but ready to demand to know who has my phone, when the voice speaks again.

'Who is this?'

The voice is female. I recognise it.

Wilks.

Wilks has my phone.

I set the receiver back, hanging up. My heart is racing.

She told me in the car she didn't have my phone. She said it must still be at the house. She said it must have fallen off the table.

Why does she have my phone?

Why did she lie to me?

What else is she lying about?

4:09 p.m.

I slide back into my seat at the kitchen table. I sip some water. I try to control my breathing. Messer is upstairs, tearing apart Leo's office looking for information. Wilks is in the living room with my phone in her possession after claiming she didn't have it. They wouldn't leave when I asked them to leave.

There's a horrible feeling of doubt, of dread, creeping up my spine.

I'm starting to feel like I've made a terrible mistake coming back here, but it doesn't make sense. Wilks and Messer are FBI agents. They were in Rusty's office. They have to be who they say they are. Don't they?

That doesn't change the fact Wilks has my phone and hasn't given it back to me. There's no good reason she should have my phone. No reason to lie.

I look down at myself. I'm still in my robe and suddenly it feels so light, so thin, so weak. I make my way upstairs yet again so I can change into proper clothes for the first time today. I put on underwear, a pair of jeans, a sweater. No socks, though, because I don't want any extra compression on my sore soles. I pull my hair back and tie it into a ponytail.

Downstairs again, I put on some sneakers. This takes a little work because the gauze makes my feet fat. I compensate for this by first loosening the laces. It still takes some effort to get my feet inside without aggravating a cut or scrape and my teeth are clenched the whole time.

With the dressings bulking out my feet the sneakers are a tight fit but I'm not complaining. Standing up in shoes for the first time in hours feels like the height of decadence.

I feel complete, finally. More capable.

I'm alone in the hallway. I take my car keys from the bowl by the front door.

I've never picked them up so slowly before. I'm trying to be quiet, hoping to be silent.

I'm not, because from behind me Wilks says, 'What are you doing?'

I've thought ahead. I expected this could happen. I'm ready.

'Need some milk,' I say. 'We're out.'

'You can't go anywhere,' she tells me. 'It's not safe.'

I face her. 'Why isn't it safe?'

'Until we have identified the man who calls himself Carlson then we have to work on the assumption he's a threat.'

I say, 'But he could have killed me before I walked into the police precinct, couldn't he? Yet he didn't.'

'It's not safe,' Wilks says again.

Yes, it's beginning to feel like that – but not out there, in here.

'I'll risk it,' I say, breezy of tone.

Wilks is coming forward. 'I can't allow that.'

I don't ask her if she's going to stop me because she's said as much and I can see it in her eyes I'm not going anywhere. I try and keep my expression even, pretending I don't know what I

134

know. I don't have the landline programmed into my cell – does anyone any more? – so she won't know I just called.

'Great,' I hiss, sounding frustrated and irritated but hopefully not scared. I drop the keys back in the bowl, making sure she can see. 'Happy now?'

The display seems to win her over. She sort of shrugs, sort of nods. She returns to the living area.

What now, Jem? What now?

How did I end up exactly where I started?

If this is a nightmare, please wake up. I promise never to eat cheese before bed ever again.

I don't wake up. It's no nightmare because it's real. Somehow, I've repeated the exact same mistakes. I have two people in my house, two people who are lying to me, two people with guns who are preventing me from leaving. I'm a prisoner in my own home and I invited my captors inside twice.

Stay calm, I tell myself. Blame can come later. Self-loathing can wait.

I tried running away last time and it's only brought me full circle. This time, I need a different approach. Keep acting ignorant, play naive. I tell myself that whatever I do, don't let them know that I know.

If only I could listen to my own advice.

I head to the kitchen so I'm close to the back door, because even if my plan is to stay put until I know more, I still want to have an escape route nearby. I ran through the woods barefoot once. I can do so again in sneakers.

What do I know? Next to nothing. That needs to change.

This is all about Leo, his business, money laundering and cartels and national security ... if what Wilks and Messer claim is true. But they've lied to me. I can't trust a word they've said. But what little Carlson has told me reinforces some of what they've said. Which parts? Leo and Leo's business. He mentioned nothing about a cartel or national security or even money laundering. He told me that only he was investigating Leo and that only Leo's business associates knew what Leo was doing.

So, what has Leo been doing?

Is it possible Wilks and Messer are in fact FBI agents but also business associates of Leo? Is the cartel story just a smoke-screen for something else? And that something is a matter of national security?

I have no more time to ponder this because Wilks enters the kitchen. At first glance I figure she has grown suspicious of me or wants to ask me some questions, but it's neither. She strides towards me.

She's holding a cell phone out in her palm, only it's not her phone.

It's mine.

'Answer it,' Wilks orders me.

My phone is vibrating.

'Say nothing about us.'

Her tone is intense, frightening.

On the screen of my phone the caller ID displays the name 'Leo'.

4:15 p.m.

Wilks is close to me. Far too close. I have nowhere to go. I don't have any space left that I can call personal. The kitchen table is behind me, its edge pressing into my lower back as I instinctively try and lean away from her.

She now has the phone edges clutched in her fingertips, held up at me. Leo's name glows before my face. He's pulling a face because he hates having his picture taken.

There's no time to think about why he's calling or even how he's calling because Wilks is so close, so frightening. Her face is a stark contrast to Leo's. Wilks has such an intensity in her expression that I can barely look at her. Her green eyes are ablaze and unblinking.

'You're going to answer the phone,' Wilks instructs me in a tone somewhere between growl and whisper. 'You're going to answer it and you're going to act like everything is normal. You're going to act like everything is fine. It's just another day for you. Say nothing about us. Nothing about this morning. Do you understand?'

The phone continues to buzz. Leo's goofy face looks right at me.

'I . . .'

Wilks barks into my face, '*Do you understand?*'

I flinch. I nod. 'Yes.'

'*Messer*,' Wilks yells. 'Get down here, now.' She turns her attention back to me. 'I'm going to put it on speakerphone so don't think you can pass on any messages and get away with it. I'll know. You'll only make it worse for yourself and even worse for Leo.'

'I . . . I won't,' I stammer.

I'm shaking. I'm so scared.

The phone is still vibrating. It'll go to voicemail soon, in seconds.

Wilks says, 'Are you ready?'

I nod. I think I nod.

Wilks turns the phone and uses a thumb to tap the answer button, then hits speakerphone. She holds it back out to me.

I clear my throat. 'Hey . . . you.'

'Heya back,' Leo says, his tone breezy, missing the significance of my breaking voice, because why would he think anything was wrong? 'Flight's grounded.'

'Dammit,' I manage to say. 'How come?'

'Oh, I don't know. Something about insufficient crew. I kind of switch off during those announcements. They make too many of them so you have to zone out to save your sanity. At least, I do. Then, when they make one you actually need to pay attention to your mind is a mile away. They're supposed to have moved me to another flight but it was overbooked. If I had known I'd be waiting this long I would have called sooner. Anyway, I'm rambling. How are you? How's your day?'

'Yeah . . .'

Leo laughs a little. 'Your day is "yeah"?'

'Yeah,' I say, forcing a laugh of my own.

Wilks is glaring at me because I'm not doing a good enough job.

I try harder. 'You know, my day is ... yeah. Whatever.'

'Oh,' Leo says back. 'That kind of day. I'm having one of those too.'

Messer arrives. Wilks raises a finger to shush him, then mouths *Leo*. Messer edges closer.

Leo says, 'You okay, babe? You sound distracted.'

Wilks eyeballs me, gesturing for me to convince him things are fine. If I haven't so far, what can I possibly do, possibly say, to cover for this moment, this fear?

'I'm ... I'm okay. I'm just tired.'

'Huh. You seemed pretty perky when I left. Are you sure you're okay?'

I'm not sure Wilks has blinked once. I can feel her rage bubbling under the surface, waiting to erupt in my direction. She terrifies me.

And just like that I know exactly what to say to Leo.

'I didn't sleep too well.'

There's a pause, a silence, and Wilks' barely contained rage worsens. I hold my nerve because this is going to work.

Leo says, 'Didn't you tell me you'd slept like a baby?'

'I didn't want to worry you before you left.'

'Ah, babe,' he says. 'You should have told me you were feeling down.'

Yes, I don't say. You should have told me about the money laundering too but I guess we keep secrets from each other now.

'I'm much better,' I tell him. 'I just need a nap to catch up and everything will work itself out.'

'Good,' he says. 'I'm glad you're feeling better.'

Wilks is nodding along, now pleased with my act as she hears Leo's tone relax.

'Have you eaten?' Leo asks.

'Made some more avocado on toast since you stole half of my breakfast.'

This makes him laugh. 'You snooze you lose.'

Wilks mouths something at me but I don't quite get it. I'm no lip reader. I have to shake my head at her and she urges Messer closer and hands him the phone.

'Am I on speaker?' Leo asks.

'I'm too lazy to hold the phone to my ear.'

'That's because you burn too much energy at yoga. Maybe save some for your husband, okay?'

Wilks has dug out a notebook and pen and written *Coming home?*

I swallow. I clear my throat again. I don't want to ask this because I don't want to hear the answer because I don't want Wilks and Messer to know.

Wilks thrusts the notebook at me. She stabs at the words with a finger, the rage returning. I can't resist it any longer.

I say, and I hate myself for saying it, 'Are you coming home?'

Wilks and Messer are listening intently for the answer.

Leo exhales. He clicks his tongue. 'I've been here for hours because I was told I would be on the next flight and now I'm kind of committed to the cause. If I come back the whole day will have been wasted and I'll only have to come back tomorrow. Jennifer – why are ticket agents always named Jennifer? – has promised me she's doing everything she can, but who knows if she is? They just want you to keep calm, don't they? They'll tell you anything if they think it will avoid a scene. I might stick it out here a little longer or I might call it quits and get a refund and make that scene Jennifer is trying to avoid. Maybe I'll swim to England instead. I could use the exercise. What do you think? Should I go for the open-water butterfly record?'

'Good idea,' I say, too distracted by the threat posed by Wilks and Messer to realise Leo is joking.

He, in turn, knows something is wrong. 'What's with you, Jem? You're not just tired, are you?'

Wilks is staring at me hard, so much menace in her gaze I can't speak to give Leo the reassurance Wilks wants me to provide. Messer steps closer.

Leo says, 'Jem?'

I swallow. There's no saliva in my mouth. I'm trying to speak but my larynx isn't working.

Wilks mouths *Tell him you're fine*.

'Jem?' Leo says again. 'What's wrong with you?'

'Sorry, sorry,' I say, clearing my throat and able to speak again. 'I'm so tired I can barely keep my eyes open.'

'Take that nap. What are you waiting for?'

I can hear the frustration creeping into his voice.

Wilks mouths *Tell him to come home*.

My eyes widen. My pulse races. My breathing quickens. I shake my head. I'm not doing that. I'm not luring Leo here.

Without making a sound, Wilks growls *Tell him*.

She inches closer to me. Messer does the same, and I'm flanked by these two scary people with so much danger in their eyes promising retribution if I refuse.

'Leo,' I say. 'Come home.'

I'm so ashamed of myself. I've betrayed Leo to save myself.

I'm a coward.

He says, 'Does someone miss her husband?'

Wilks is nodding for me to agree.

'Yeah,' is all I can say. It doesn't sound convincing. I'm too frightened to sound genuine.

141

'Jem, are you absolutely sure you're okay? In fact, I don't know why I'm asking. I can hear that something is wrong so please tell me what's going on. Have you taken something? Is that why you're so distracted? If so, has something happened? What's triggered this? We can talk it through. I don't want you hiding these moments from me. I keep telling you that. It's not healthy. It doesn't help you.'

Wilks and Messer couldn't be any closer to me.

My eyes are moist. 'I promise I'm fine. I'm just tired. I was drifting off when you called.'

Somehow it sounds genuine. A plausible excuse.

Leo exhales, relieved. 'Okay, okay. I'm sorry. I don't mean to put pressure on you. It's just because I know you bottle things up. Do you promise me you're okay?'

'Yes,' I say, blinking tears.

'Good. Great. I'm glad. And while normally I would wait it out here for a while in the hope Jennifer works her magic, I'm going to come home right now. No, don't say anything. Even if you're fine, even if you're only tired, I want to see you. I want to be with you. Take that nap and I'll wake you up with a green tea and a kiss. How does that sound?'

'Perfect,' I say, wiping my eyes.

Wilks and Messer are relieved. They're pleased that Leo is coming to them. Messer hands me the phone and they step away from me to whisper among themselves. I can't hear them and nor can I read their lips but I know what they're saying, what they're doing.

They're working out how best to ambush Leo when he comes home.

For a moment, neither Wilks nor Messer is looking at me.

'Don't come home,' I yell at Leo. 'There are two people here who say they're FBI but I don't believe them.' I turn away as I say this, presenting my back to Wilks and Messer and making it harder for Wilks to snatch the phone from my hand, which she rushes to do. 'They want you to come here. They're after something. I'm scared, Leo. I'm—' Wilks can't get to the phone as I bend over the table so she grabs my arms to pull them away from the protection of my torso – '*Get off me*' – so that Messer can tear the phone free from my grip – '*Help me, Leo, help—*'

Messer hangs up the phone.

For an instant all three of us are frozen in a chaotic tableau of bent limbs and contorted torsos.

Then my phone starts buzzing.

Leo calling back.

Wilks untangles herself and takes the phone from Messer, throws it on the kitchen floor, and smashes it beneath her heel.

Wilks roars in a primal display of the rage that's been building up.

I'm silent. Terrified. Cowering.

'You don't know what you've done,' Wilks hisses at me.

One of Messer's hands shoots out and grabs my upper arm. His hands are so big his fingers almost reach his thumb. I try and pull away but he's so strong. I'm helpless.

'This could have been so easy,' Wilks continues. 'This could all have been over by now. I've tried my best. I've tried to keep this civil despite your frequent provocations. And this is how you repay the decency I've shown you?'

I manage to say, 'Who are you?'

Wilks sighs. She pinches the skin between her eyes with a thumb and forefinger. 'It doesn't matter now, does it? Nothing matters for you any more.'

What does that mean?

She looks to Messer, who shrugs back at her.

Wilks nods and tells him, 'Take her upstairs.'

'Why?' I demand, voice breaking. 'What's upstairs?'

Wilks says, 'What's upstairs, Mrs – Jem – is the inevitable conclusion of your interference.'

Messer says to me, 'Let's go.'

'No, I'm not going anywhere.'

Messer is still holding on to my arm and he squeezes me tighter, applying so much pressure to his grip I can feel the circulation cut off and pins and needles in my fingers.

I hit him. It makes no difference. He drags me out of the kitchen with almost no effort.

'Try not to make a mess,' Wilks tells him.

4:23 p.m.

I fight the entire way.

I scream. I struggle. I punch and kick Messer with everything I have, not caring about hurting myself in the process, and he barely reacts. He doesn't even try to defend himself because there's no need. I do everything I can to slow him but he's relentless. Slow and unstoppable. I grab the living-room doorframe as we pass, clutching hard with my free hand, digging what little nails I possess into the wood. It works for all of a second. Messer tightens his grip on me and heaves me away. One of my nails catches and rips in half.

The pain is horrific. Blood patters the flooring.

For all Messer's unconquerable strength, getting me up the stairs is far from easy. I let myself become a deadweight. I grab every banister post. I try to wrap my legs around them. I'm not heavy enough, not strong enough, to stop him but I slow him. I make him tired.

Messer is breathing hard trying to carry up an uncompliant mass of moving weight. He's red-faced and sweating. A strong man but not a fit one.

At the top of the stairs, he pulls me to my feet and I hit him in the face while he's concentrating on controlling me. It's a solid punch to his cheek that must hurt him more than the others, must have an effect, because he responds by punching me back.

His free fist collides with my abdomen, sending a shockwave of pain through my insides. My eyes fill with water. I gasp, breathless, all of my fight emptying out of me in a sudden, agonising moment.

I collapse to my knees and have no strength to resist as he drags me across the landing to the bathroom.

He flings me inside and I fall flat on my stomach, unable to push myself up. I'm gasping for air, my mouth hanging open, tears wetting my cheeks, my vision a blur. I'm in so much pain I can barely think.

Messer says, 'You brought this on yourself.'

I manage to roll on to my back in a monumental effort. I see a distorted image of Messer in the doorway, removing his jacket and tie. He has sweat stains under his armpits and at his sternum. His face is shimmering.

Without his jacket, I see the leather shoulder rig he's wearing and the pistol holstered under his left arm.

I'm dead.

I know I'm dead.

He's going to shoot me and there's nothing I can do to stop it.

He lays his jacket and tie over the washbasin. He doesn't unfasten the strap securing the gun in the holster, he doesn't draw the weapon and kill me. He unbuttons his collar and then his cuffs. He rolls up his sleeves.

I'm still writhing and can only watch but I can breathe again in short, painful wheezes as my paralysed diaphragm slowly relaxes.

Messer peers down at me, a groove of consideration between his eyebrows. He purses his lips and looks around the room. I follow his eyes, trying to decipher his intentions. His gaze fixes on the towel rail. He steps over me to fetch a bath towel, then stands over me with one big foot either side of my waist.

He holds opposite corners of the towel and twists it into a thick rope.

Now I understand his intentions.

He's going to strangle me to death.

He leans down over me to hook the towel behind my head but I'm not going to lie here and let him. I've recovered enough from the punch to the guts to thrash, to grab at the towel, to wriggle out of the way.

Messer is big and clumsy, awkward in the small space with me taking up most of the floor. He loses his balance trying to maintain his position over me and stumbles. He has to grab the washbasin to stop himself from falling.

It's enough of a window of opportunity for me to slither out from under him, start to rise.

He's spun round by the time I'm on my feet and snatches my ponytail in a fist as I make a break for the doorway.

A tug on my hair is enough to pull me right off my feet and I go back down, hairs ripping from my scalp as my ass strikes the floor first and Messer loses his grip. But that grip slows my fall enough so the back of my skull doesn't whip against the tiles.

Above me is Messer's fist, many strands of my hair protruding through the gaps between his fingers, coming straight down at my face.

I jerk my head to one side and his downward punch misses me and hits the floor tiles instead.

Bones crack.

Messer cries out.

147

His exclamation of pain energises me, giving me hope, switching my mind-set from flight to fight.

I roll on to my side, grab his foot and shin and sink my teeth into his calf.

Messer wails.

He tries to pull me away with his one good hand. It's his left, and I'm biting his left calf. He can't get the leverage to shift me.

Instead, he kicks me, driving his right foot into the small of my back.

I spit out Messer's blood as I slither between his legs, avoiding another kick, then a stomp he aims at my ankle.

I scramble away from him as much as I can until I'm blocked by the toilet and push myself up to my butt. I'm breathing as hard as him now. My heart has never beat so hard.

I'm exhausted. The run through the woods has nothing on this.

Messer's chest heaves. His shirt is soaked with sweat. His right hand is swollen. I expect he's broken several bones by punching the floor. He's looking down at his calf, pulling up his trouser hem to see the damage my teeth have done. When he looks back at me his face is red with pain and rage.

'You want me to use the gun?' he says. 'Fine, I'll use the gun.'

'Can't beat a ninety-pound girl without it?'

I'm not ninety pounds. I'm nowhere near ninety, but it's provocation. It works. His ego can't take the insult, the implicit emasculation.

'I don't need the gun,' he says.

He picks up the towel, once again twisting it into a rope, but it takes him longer this time with his broken right hand. Messer grips both ends of the twisted towel in his left fist so it becomes something between a whip and a club.

'But you're going to wish I did.'

4:27 p.m.

I have nowhere to go. The cool ceramic toilet bowl is pressed against my spine. To my left is the walk-in shower, the bathtub next to it along the wall. To my right is the pedestal washbasin. I'm trapped with Messer's giant form between me and the exit.

I look around the room. I need a weapon. Please, let me find a weapon.

Messer has two. The gun in the shoulder rig and his towel in his left hand. At least I only need contend with the latter.

He takes a step closer. The knuckles of his good hand are almost as white as the towel he's gripping. He raises it above his head.

I'm out of options. All I can do is cover my face with my arms as the towel races down, thumping against me, the energy of the blow as sudden and frightening as it is painful.

My teeth slam together. I don't feel pain so much as dizziness and nausea. My whole head is buzzing. My ears ring with an incessant whine yet other sounds seem distant.

I feel like I'm separating. I feel as if the whole that is me is

149

reverting back to component parts, physical and mental. Those distant sounds fade to nothingness. Colours leach to grey.

I'm curled up into a ball, foetal, instinctual.

Another hit and I'll be unconscious.

I can do nothing to stop it. I'm too dazed.

All I can do is lie on the cool tiles and wait for it to be over.

I wait.

I keep waiting.

For an instant, I think I'm already unconscious. I think I'm dying.

Then I blink the ocean from my eyes and peer between my fingers to see Messer is not standing over me but in the doorway, looking outwards. At what, I don't know. I'm aware of his voice, shouting maybe, but he's so far away it's like he's whispering in a storm.

Whatever he's doing, whomever he's *whispering* at, is taking up all of his attention. For how long, I don't know.

I'm too weak to move. Too scared. Yet I'm no quitter. My body is unresponsive. My senses are scrambled. But my mind is still there, still me, at the centre of it all. I need to fight my way out of this prison.

Move, Jem, I will myself. *Move.*

Live.

Messer steps out of the bathroom, shouting more whispers into the unseen tempest.

The doorway is clear, open. Calling out to me with promises of escape, of freedom.

False promises, because I'll never make it. Messer is outside that doorway, whether on the landing or the stairs or even downstairs. I can only escape this bathroom, which is no escape at all.

I can't run from this when I can't stand.

Here, in this bathroom, is where I live or where I die.

Where I fight.

I uncoil myself out of the foetal ball, dragging the unresponsive shell in which I exist along with my fingertips. My ripped nail is bloody and raw yet I feel no pain from it because there's too much pain elsewhere, too many other priorities.

But seeing the tiny wound gives me an idea.

I swivel my head and see where a little waterproof pouch sits on a shelf of the dainty unit that stands next to the washbasin. I bought the unit from a thrift store in town because it is a tacky piece of furniture to accent the otherwise clinical bathroom. It holds cosmetics, spare hand towels, the first aid kit I used earlier, and has space for the shaving kit Leo has taken with him.

I crawl towards the unit, towards that little waterproof bag.

A slow, painful crawl. Each inch is hell.

But I make it.

I lift one hand to reach for the bag and get nowhere close to it. I'm too dazed, too uncoordinated to extend my arm fully.

So I tip the dainty unit over. Items scatter across the tiles. Some fall on me.

I reach for the waterproof bag, dragging it through the mess.

The zip is difficult to work. My fingers have a fraction of their dexterity.

My hand shakes as I pull and yank the zipper, opening it almost one small plastic tooth at a time until I can turn it upside down and shake out the contents. A nail file falls out first, followed by nail clippers, a bottle of cuticle oil, and finally what I want: the pair of stainless-steel scissors that cut my toe.

The scissors are only small because they're designed to trim nails but the blades are heavy duty and extra sharp for that purpose. A precision-made expensive item that I bought to add a little luxury to my grooming routine.

151

I realise I can hear Messer outside on the landing.

'I'm handling it,' he yells down to Wilks. 'You sort out that.'

I don't know what it is Wilks needs to sort out and I don't care.

I care that my hearing is better, my vision clearer, my muscles stronger.

I care that Messer is coming back, to handle it.

Me.

My grip is tight around the scissors' handle. The closed blades protrude from the bottom of my fist. I hide them under the free palm of my left hand.

The instant I see Messer coming back through the doorway, I let myself go slack. I half-close my eyes. I groan. I whimper.

'Where were we?' Messer is saying.

He ignores the fallen unit, the mess. He's convinced enough by my playacting to come right up to me. He squats down, grimacing from the pain in his calf, bracing himself against the sink to ease that pain. His right hand dangles useless at his side.

'I don't enjoy this,' he tells me.

His tone is different, his voice quiet. Maybe he thinks I'm unconscious.

'If it were up to me it wouldn't have got this far.'

Maybe he's confessing to me because he thinks I can't hear him.

'But it's not up to me.'

He adjusts his footing and goes down to one knee so he no longer needs to brace against the sink, then he wraps the twisted towel around my neck. It's not easy for him because he can't grip with the broken right hand. He has to take both ends of the towel in his left only. He begins to twist the towel, tightening its grip on my throat, constricting my airway.

152

'Shush,' he whispers. 'This won't hurt. Just drift away. Drift away . . .'

I grab Messer's forearm for purchase, taking him by surprise, and haul myself up enough to stab him with the scissor blades in his neck.

4:32 p.m.

Messer doesn't scream but he does go white. He throws himself away from me, going to his feet briefly and stumbling backwards until he collides with the wall which he then slides down, stopping when he's propped up against it, legs splayed before him. He doesn't scream, but he gasps, he keens. He stares at me with wide eyes. His good left hand is covering the wound, the scissors protruding between his fingers. He's in shock. He doesn't know what to do.

There's only a little blood. I don't know if it's a fatal wound and neither does Messer. Either way it's serious.

I stand. I use the bathtub for support and then the washbasin for more.

I approach him.

I think about reaching for his gun but decide against it. If I get that close to him he's going to grab me. I have to go past him to exit the bathroom but I don't have to get close.

His mouth opens to say something but no sound comes out.

I step over his legs.

I'm unsteady on my feet. Not only are they sore from the run across the hard forest floor, I'm also suffering from all the blows to the head. I can see fine, I can hear fine, but I'm wobbly. My balance isn't right. I'm drunk without the buzz. Which is no one's kind of fun.

Something breaking startles me when I step out on to the landing.

It comes from downstairs. Maybe glass. Maybe a mirror.

Then come more sounds. Thumps and bangs. Grunts.

What is going on down there?

I shuffle to the top of the staircase, peer over. My heart is still racing. I'm trembling with adrenalin.

I see the front door is open. Wide open. I can feel cooling air blowing inside. It makes me more aware of the sweat on my skin, the blood. I grip the banister hard and begin to descend. I don't know where Wilks is and I don't know why the door is open but this is my chance. I have to seize it.

I'll have to run again. The Explorer is blocking my Prius just like it did this morning. At least this time I'm wearing shoes. Even with sore feet I'll run all the way to town, to Rusty, if that's what it takes.

What do I tell her? The two FBI agents are trying to kill me so I stabbed one in the neck?

It sounds ludicrous, but the credibility of my story seems the least of my concerns at this moment.

I can only manage one step at a time and I need to have both feet securely on that step and a secure hold of the banister before I can attempt the next one. It's agonisingly slow progress. This time it's not my feet slowing me down. I can barely feel them. It's the fizzing, buzzing sensation inside my head making my body hard to control.

The closer I get to the bottom of the staircase the more I

hear of the commotion downstairs. At the top, it sounded like it was coming from the living area, yet now it seems as though it's originating in the kitchen.

A vase is broken in the hall, lying in pieces on the red oak floor where it's fallen from a sideboard. A framed watercolour painting is askew on the wall. I could have done both as Messer dragged me along yet I know I didn't do either. Someone else did.

The sounds coming from the kitchen become clearer, more intense. There are grunts among the gasps, growls and grimaces.

Two people are fighting.

I know Wilks is downstairs, but who is the other person?

'Leo,' I call out.

He must have been driving home when he called, then sped the rest of the way to come to his wife's aid. Any joy that he is near takes second place to fear for him. Wilks is dangerous. She has a gun. Leo is just a regular guy. I don't think he's ever been in a fight before in his life. It's one of the many things I like about him.

It can't be Leo, can it? He was at the airport when he called.

I lean around the end of the banister to look back through the hallway. The dizziness intensifies as I do and I almost lose my grip and fall.

I see a snapshot of the kitchen: Wilks, face twisted in a grimace, wrestling with a man who isn't Leo.

It's Carlson, or at least the man who calls himself Carlson.

The man who warned me about Wilks and Messer, who tried to help me. How I wish I had listened to him and got into his car.

He's losing the struggle against Wilks. Carlson is naturally bigger, stronger, but Wilks knows what she's doing and has him bent backwards over the island, fighting to keep a knife in

Wilks' hand away from his face. Wilks is winning. The knife is inching closer. It's one of my good samurai knives, taken from the rack.

Carlson sees me in his peripheral vision. He glances my way.

Wilks doesn't see me. All of her focus is on Carlson, on killing Carlson.

The front door is open behind me. All I have to do is walk through it and keep going. No one is in a position to stop me. Messer is upstairs in the bathroom, paralysed by shock. Wilks has no idea where I am, what I'm doing.

All I have to do is go.

And leave Carlson to die.

The same Carlson who was on my side all along, who was right about Wilks and Messer, who warned me.

The same Carlson who has just come here. Who has come here for me.

I can't do it. I can't leave him.

I can't save myself if it means leaving him to die.

I don't hurry along the hallway because I can't hurry. I can't do anything at speed. I'm still drunk without the buzz, still unsteady, still weak.

Carlson sees I'm coming. It gives him a surge of hope, of energy. He fights back harder so Wilks is forced to fight back harder too. It keeps her attention on Carlson. Wilks doesn't know I'm coming.

My short, shuffling steps are silent on the hard flooring. I'm looking around as I get closer, looking for some kind of weapon. There's no good sneaking up on Wilks empty-handed.

There are no convenient wrought-iron pans lying nearby for me to hit Wilks with, no knife block within reach. There is, however, a wine rack. I can use a good bottle of merlot as a club.

Carlson, however, has a better idea.

4:34 p.m.

Rusty quit smoking way back. She still buys a pouch of tobacco from the store every couple of weeks. She never finishes it and ends up throwing at least half away. Dries out too quick, even sealed in a little tin decorated with an image of a fish. A pike she painted herself. She doesn't fish, has never fished, but pikes are famously aggressive and she likes that. The pike is a reminder for her to be more aggressive sometimes because sometimes that's what the job needs her to be and that isn't who she is or has ever been.

'Feels like rain, doesn't it?'

Earnest isn't looking up from his newspaper. Barely ever does. Must read slow as shit otherwise the paper wouldn't last him the morning, let alone all afternoon too. Could be for show, of course. An attempt to appear erudite.

'I only feel rain when it's hitting me on the top of my head,' Rusty says back.

She's not a fan of small talk. All talk should matter. All interactions between sentient beings do matter and should be treated accordingly and with reverence. But if you voice such opinions you find no one talks to you at all so Rusty keeps her lips locked.

Earnest mutters more about the weather as Rusty counts out the price of the tobacco from the change in her pocket. Earnest doesn't have to ask for the money any more than Rusty has to ask how much it costs. She slides the coins across the counter so he doesn't have to reach too far. Earnest had polio as a kid.

He slides the coins off the counter without looking up from his paper. Hits buttons on the register without looking up. Drops them into the right slots while he turns a page.

Rusty says, 'So, what's going on in the world?'

Earnest huffs. 'Damned if I know, but it's not looking too good out there.'

'Let me know when things are getting better, will you?'

'We're doomed, Rust.' Earnest licks a thumb and turns a page. 'Best get used to the idea. Sands of time ran out for humanity long ago. The End of Days is coming whether we like it or not.'

Rusty heads for the door. 'See you, Ernie.'

Earnest calls back, 'Keep keeping us safe.'

Rusty wonders who exactly she keeps safe as she makes her way back to her vehicle. She might feel better about herself if she thought she made any kind of difference instead of just ticking boxes by giving motorists a hard time.

Home is a short drive away that takes longer than it should because Rusty can never quite bring herself to apply enough pressure to the accelerator.

Engine off, she sits behind the wheel and stares at the house and the glow at the windows. It's a warm light but it's deceptive, she decides. Almost a trick.

A warm glow can disguise even the coldest of homes.

There's an incline to the driveway that becomes a little steeper every day. Must do because it takes more energy to climb than it did yesterday, than the day before that.

Rusty lays her forehead against the door for a second, or a minute. She's not sure. Time is relative and maybe this is why.

The key goes into the lock. The door opens.

The screaming begins.

Obscenities, Rusty can handle. Words are just words. Just sounds to which we attach meaning. Even the worst curse could be birdsong if only we let it. She's been called every name out there, heard every insult. Not just in English either. She's bullet-proof when it comes to such things. She's Kevlar. So, she stands in the hallway and takes the barrage from her mother and tries not to react. She's learned that the less she reacts, the sooner it's over.

The swearing and the cussing doesn't bother her. It's that it has no end. No solution. There is no possible retort, no way to stop it, and that's the real heartache. Her mother won't calm down because she is calm. As calm as a person in her situation can be calm.

Doctors have their fancy names for it in the same way they have fancy names for most things but Rusty doesn't need a doctor to explain to her what is happening. It's obvious. It's inevitable.

Her mother is old.

It affects people in different ways and her mother has gone from a polite, almost meek woman to a monster. Not quite overnight, but the process was so fast it was all over just as soon as it began.

Now, all Rusty hears from her mother is how much she is hated, how fat she is, how she is a disappointment, a failure, ugly, useless, a mistake.

Rusty doesn't know if Mom has always felt like this and only

160

now, her mind gone, speaks the truth. When it's real bad Rusty sometimes has to get out of bed to change the pillowcase for a dry one.

'Thanks, Mom,' Rusty says. 'I'm glad to be home too.'

Mom has tired herself out or her focus has switched to something else. A favourite ad on the TV, perhaps. Rusty doesn't hang around long enough to find out why she has a reprieve. She takes it and runs.

With Alice moving in with her piece-of-shit boyfriend it's just Rusty and Mom. Rusty would have Alice move back in a heartbeat, despite all the money she stole, but at the same time she wouldn't want her to endure the abuse. In that way Rusty is glad the piece-of-shit boyfriend came along when he did, before Mom lost the ability to control what came out of her mouth.

Rusty heads to the kitchen to put dinner in the microwave and carries it upstairs to her bedroom so she can eat it alone and without the need to wipe her mother's saliva from her face every few mouthfuls. Mom can't make it up the stairs these days so Rusty is safe for now. Maybe in a couple of hours Rusty will brave going back down to do some housework. Mom should have fallen asleep by then.

Rusty thumbs on the old TV in her room and perches on the bed to blow on her lasagne. It smells good but she thinks they've changed the recipe. Consistency isn't the same. Sauce used to be thick, now it's a little runny. Watered-down. There should be a law that forces them to make such things clear on the packaging.

When she's done she sneaks downstairs past the living room to put the plastic tray in the trash and the fork in the sink. She won't risk washing up until the morning because she's hopeful Mom has fallen asleep already, and why chance waking her again?

On the way back Rusty sees that she was wrong: Mom is wide awake and looking straight at her. There's so much malice in her eyes, so much hate.

Mom says, 'I should have had you aborted.'

Obscenities, Rusty can handle.

4:36 p.m.

As I near, I realise that Carlson is alternating glances between me and the kitchen floor. A pointed movement, which he repeats, and I follow his eyes to see a gun lying at the foot of the refrigerator. I don't know guns so all I see is a boxy automatic pistol. Black metal and plastic. Ugly. Maybe Carlson's, maybe Wilks' own. It doesn't matter. I've never shot one, but how hard can it be? Point and shoot.

I force myself forward those last few steps, seeing Carlson weakening under the relentless pressure of Wilks, knowing he's running out of time. I bend over to scoop the pistol from the floor. I have to do so with slow, careful motions to maintain my balance.

The gun is warm in my palm. It feels awkward and unfamiliar and I have to fight the instinct to drop it, to get it away from me.

I'm so close now that Wilks is aware of me an instant before I say, 'Let him go.'

Wilks is surprised I'm here, hesitant because I'm armed. She looks past me to the hallway, no doubt hoping to see Messer coming to her aid. Wilks doesn't know Messer is incapacitated.

Wilks says, 'Put the gun down, Jem.'

I say, 'Let him go,' for the second time.

Wilks doesn't.

I take careful aim at Wilks' face.

'Do it,' I say.

She still doesn't but relaxes enough in her efforts to stab Carlson that Carlson can wriggle out from under her. Carlson sinks to the floor, exhausted. He's no fighter.

Wilks turns to face me. She doesn't seem scared of me or the gun in my hand. She seems annoyed at this intrusion, annoyed Messer hasn't killed me.

I make sure to keep my gaze fixed on hers as I say, 'Drop the knife.'

She hesitates for a second, then does as she's told. The knife clangs and clatters on the kitchen floor tiles. Wilks shows her palms.

'Don't do anything stupid,' she says.

'Too late for that,' I reply. 'I was beyond stupid to believe anything you told me.'

'We can work this out.'

'How? How can we possibly work this out?'

Wilks doesn't answer.

'Exactly,' I say, then to Carlson: 'Are you okay?'

I'm trying not to look at him because I don't want to take my gaze from Wilks, even for a second. I'm certain she'll launch herself at me given the slimmest opportunity. I don't want to trust my poor reactions and poor aim to save me if I don't have to.

I can just about see Carlson nod in response to my question. It's not a good sign that he's sat slumped on the floor with the island the only thing keeping him from lying down. I can't maintain my aim at Wilks and haul Carlson to his feet at the same time.

'Call for help,' I say to him. 'Call for backup or call the cops. Dial 911. Get someone. Get the police chief. Get Rusty.'

He doesn't react.

Wilks says, 'He's not going to call anyone, are you?'

Carlson doesn't answer her. He's also not calling for help.

'He's not your friend,' Wilks says. 'He's not on your side.'

'He hasn't tried to kill me,' I say back. 'So he's on my side a hell of a lot more than you and Messer.'

Wilks asks, 'Where is Messer?'

Carlson says, 'Shoot her.'

His voice is low, weak. He must have taken a hell of a beating. I'm not sure I hear him correctly.

'What?'

'Shoot her,' Carlson says again.

I'm shocked. I glance at him in surprise, for confirmation. Reassurance. I don't notice Wilks edging closer.

'She's a killer,' Carlson says. 'She'll kill you the second you lower your guard.'

Wilks says nothing. We've gone past the point where she could argue otherwise. She fooled me before. She's fooled me twice in fact. She knows she can't again.

I don't shoot her.

I can't. I knew I wouldn't be able to from the moment I picked up the gun. Upstairs and fighting for my life there was no time to think about what I was doing. Now I have too much time to think. I don't want to kill anyone. I don't want to be a murderer. And I would be. Right now, it's not self-defence. At this moment, I'm not fighting for my life. I kill Wilks, I'm as bad as her.

165

Rusty can deal with her. She can stand trial. I'll happily testify against her.

'Shoot her,' Carlson says for a third time.

He's getting up now, using the island for support. My few seconds of thought have given him time to get his breath back. He has several red marks on his face, plus cuts to one eyebrow and his lip. Blood leaks from his head too. There's a wound on the top of his skull.

'Call the police,' I tell him.

'Give me the gun,' he says when he's fully standing.

I want him to have the gun because I don't want the responsibility of it, of deciding whether to use it or not. But I hesitate. Doubt creeps in. I don't want to give up the only means I have of defending myself.

Besides, I know he's going to use it to kill Wilks. I hand the gun to Carlson and I'm complicit in Wilks' execution.

'Please,' Carlson says.

Wilks says, 'You can't trust him.'

'That's right,' I tell her. 'I don't trust anyone right now, myself included. So the answer is no, I'm keeping the gun.'

'Then shoot her,' Carlson demands.

I shake my head. 'No one's getting shot.'

Wilks is relieved. 'You made the right decision, Jem.'

'Only because I'd rather see you rot behind bars, you piece of shit.'

The intensity in my voice surprises me as well as the two others. Wilks keeps her hands up, palms facing me.

I say, 'Why won't you call the police, Carlson?'

Wilks says, 'Yeah, why won't you call the police, Carlson?'

Carlson says, 'If you're not going to shoot her, Mrs Talhoffer, we need to get going.'

'Answer the question,' I insist. 'Or I'm going nowhere.'

He doesn't answer because we've taken too long to reach this point. I've only been in the kitchen a few minutes but it's been long enough. I get a second's warning because Wilks' eyes widen and she makes a move, grabbing Carlson.

She makes a move because behind me in the hallway is Messer.

He must have shaken off his shock a lot sooner than I expected or perhaps he was imitating me and faking passivity in the first place. Either way, he's made it down the stairs. His broken right hand hangs useless at his side. The scissors are still in his neck. In Messer's left hand is his gun.

The gun is pointing my way.

4:39 p.m.

I shoot first.

I'm no gunslinger but Messer is wounded and unsteady on his feet and there is a colleague in close proximity he doesn't want to hit. He has the same slow, shuffling gait as I have. Mine from blunt force trauma to the head, his because of the scissors sticking out of his neck.

I shoot first and nothing happens.

Just a click.

Safety, of course. Guns have safeties. Where is it? I run my fingers over the weapon, searching for a catch or a lever or something. I find one, I work it.

The magazine comes free.

Thankfully, it doesn't fall to the floor because my other hand is right there and it drops into my palm and I push it back inside the grip without delay.

'It's a Glock,' Carlson says through gritted teeth, fighting with Wilks.

He says this as if it explains the problem I'm having and also solves it at the same time. It does neither.

Wilks has Carlson around the throat, choking him, trying to drag him further into the kitchen, away from me so they're both out of the line of fire.

Messer is shuffling closer, gun raised and pointed at me, trying to get a shot. Wilks and Carlson are still close, still in the vicinity, but for how much longer?

Carlson, his face beet red as Wilks chokes him, is trying to speak, trying to tell me what to do to make the gun work. He can't get enough air through his constricted throat to make words.

'*What do I do?*' I yell at him.

Messer, closer and closer.

Carlson releases his hands from Wilks' arm around his neck and makes a pistol shape with his fingers. With his other hand, he grips the top of that imaginary gun and slides that hand back towards his wrist. He does this several times in rapid succession and I get the message.

I grab the top of the pistol and slide it back. Something happens. Something clicks.

A gunshot.

So incredibly loud, terrifying.

I gasp. Splinters of wood from the doorframe pepper me. I jolt behind the interior wall before the next bullet comes my way.

Metal pings as the round goes into the refrigerator.

I'm shielded from Messer but that doesn't stop him shooting, maybe hoping for a bullet to go through the wall I'm hiding behind.

Several shots sound in rapid succession. I'm frozen, cowering, as glass breaks and plaster clouds in the air.

Wilks and Carlson are on the floor now, still fighting, still

169

wrestling. Carlson is on his back and Wilks is on top of him. Carlson is losing, weakening. Wilks has him where she wants him, where she can choke him better, easier.

'What about the safety?' I shout to Carlson. 'Where is it? What do I do?'

Carlson, his hands now back on Wilks' forearm, shakes his head. His face is no longer red, but purple.

I don't understand why I don't have to work a safety but I have to trust Carlson knows what he's talking about. What other choice do I have?

I summon every iota of courage, of desperation, and step out of cover.

I point the gun at Messer and pull the trigger.

The noise is incredible, frightening, shocking. The recoil jerks my hand upwards. I'm weak anyway and unprepared to resist such force.

Messer's still coming. I missed him. I aimed too high.

I adjust my aim and pull the trigger again.

This bullet hits.

His right shoulder jerks and I see a hole in his shirt, blood.

The realisation I've shot a man hits me with almost physical power. I'm stunned by what I've done. A slight adjustment to where I pointed and he could be dead.

Messer shoots back but he has a pair of scissors in his neck, a broken right hand, and now a bullet in his left shoulder. He can't keep the gun steady, let alone pointed my way. The bullet hits the floorboards at my feet instead of me. It still makes me jump.

Messer is coming closer and I miss again because he's swaying as he stumbles forward, rebounding off each wall in the hallway, from one to the other.

I try to track him as he goes back and forth, missing once more.

He shoots at me mid-sway, the bullet striking the ceiling above me.

I feel debris in my hair.

I take a breath, this time not trying to track him but keeping my aim steady at the midpoint of the hallway, waiting for him to sway into the line of fire, and I squeeze the trigger.

I don't see where the bullet hits, but the reaction is instantaneous.

Messer drops to his knees and tips over backwards.

'*I got him*,' I call out to Carlson.

No response, and I spin round to see Carlson is blue-faced and almost unconscious. He's lying on his back on top of Wilks, who has Carlson tight and immobile in a chokehold.

No doubt that position aids its effectiveness but it also means that Wilks has trapped herself beneath Carlson.

'That's enough,' I say, stepping into Wilks' view and pointing the Glock at her.

Wilks needs no further convincing. She releases the chokehold and Carlson takes an almighty lungful of air. The blue begins to fade from his skin. He coughs and splutters for a long time.

'Get up,' I tell Wilks.

She rises. She's slow, tired from her fight with Carlson.

'Are you okay?' I ask Carlson, who is still on the floor.

He doesn't speak – maybe he can't – but he answers with a raised thumb.

Messer groans behind me. It's a quiet, wheezing sound. There's enough distance between me and Wilks to risk a glance over my shoulder. Messer is prostrate on the hallway floor, wriggling in small, slow movements.

I gesture with the gun to the house phone.

'Take the receiver,' I order Wilks.

She makes no move to do so.

'Do it.'

She just stands there as if she hasn't heard me or can't understand me.

'Call Rusty or I'll put a bullet in you.'

'No, you won't.'

'Messer's hurt,' I tell her. 'He's hurt bad and he needs medical attention.'

Wilks doesn't react.

She's called my bluff. We both know I'm not going to shoot her. I wish I were a stronger person. I wish I could just pull the trigger and kill her. But I can't. I'm not a killer.

I'll never be a killer.

Wilks says, 'You need to let me go, Jem.'

'And why exactly would I even consider doing that?'

'Because I'm the only one who can get you out of this.'

'How does that work?'

She says, 'I'm the only one who knows who Leo really is.'

'What does that mean? I know who Leo is.'

'Do you?' she asks me.

I don't answer. I'm silent. I tell myself not to listen to her, that this is another deception, another trick. Yet ... something tells me there's some truth in what she says. Today has already proved I don't know my husband as well as I thought. There's a side to him he's kept hidden from me and I had absolutely no idea. How long has he been keeping secrets from me? How many years?

Since I've known him?

I say, 'Who is he? Who is Leo?'

Wilks' mouth forms a small, tight smile. Pleased to have hooked me.

I'm staring at her so hard, so eager for the answer, that I don't notice how close she's come to me.

'Leo is not who you think he is,' Wilks tells me, inching closer.

I'm desperate to know more, to know who my husband is.

'His name isn't even Leo.'

I'm overwhelmed with surprise, with loss. My eyes moisten. Wilks launches herself at me.

I can't react in time. The gun goes off as she collides with me but the muzzle has already been pushed away. She's so close, so strong, and grabs the housing of the Glock.

She tears it from my grip and smiles, triumphant, because it's over. But, like me, she's been ignoring Carlson, figuring him out of action. He's not.

Carlson, having used the island for a second time to pull himself from the floor, charges into Wilks from behind, who drops the gun.

Carlson is still weak and his attempt to wrestle Wilks fails. Wilks deflects him away and turns for me because I'm going for the Glock.

She tries to grab me and overreaches, slips.

She loses balance.

I shove her. Hard.

She falls and hits her head on the island on her way down.

Wilks lies motionless on the floor tiles. Blood trickles from her scalp, bright on the white tiles, glistening on the black. She's still and silent.

God, what have I done?

I realise I'm panting and shaking yet I'm fixed to the spot. Wilks looks almost peaceful. She looks as though she's sleeping. I want to touch her and see if she's still breathing but I can't bring myself to risk shattering the illusion and face what I've done.

'I . . . I think I might have killed her.'

'Hopefully,' Carlson says, his voice a rasping croak.

'I didn't mean to. I ...'

Carlson retrieves the gun. 'I know, but also you really need to just shoot people when you have the chance.'

I'm about to respond when I notice movement behind Carlson, in the hallway.

'*Watch out.*'

Messer, gun back in hand, shoots from the floor.

I wrench Carlson out of the line of fire as bullets come our way, hitting the table, the wall, the window.

Wild shots, fired blind.

Then nothing.

Maybe Messer has run out of bullets?

I don't find out because Carlson leans out to return fire. Two quick shots and Messer doesn't shoot again. He doesn't do anything again.

'Is he—?'

'Yes,' Carlson says. 'Let's go.'

4:43 p.m.

I grab Carlson and he grabs hold of me. We're both injured, both weak and exhausted. He needs my help and I need his. We head along the hallway, stepping over and around Messer, and I do everything possible not to look at the corpse on my flooring. I don't know if this is guilt or squeamishness and I'm not going to hang around to analyse myself right now.

'Here,' Carlson says, pushing car keys into my hand. 'You'll have to drive. I can barely stay conscious.'

I have my own keys, my own car is on the drive, but Carlson's sedan is blocking it. I see as we near that the doors are unlocked and I open up the back and help Carlson on to the seat. He flops down on it like it's a bed and he's had a heavy night. I slam the door shut and get behind the wheel.

'Don't go to the police,' Carlson says from the back seat.

'What? Why?'

'We can't trust law enforcement.'

'Why not?'

'Someone's been working with Wilks and Messer.' It takes him several breaths to get the words out. 'Right now, I don't know who that person is. There could be many people involved. We can't trust anyone right now.'

I try not to think of what that means because I will slip into despair. Instead I take a breath and insert the key. The starter motor whines and the engine comes to life. I work the transmission into reverse, accelerate backwards off the driveway. I manage a fast three-point turn and I drive us away.

To where, I have no idea, because it's kind of hard to know where to go when you have nowhere to go.

My head throbs. There's a persistent ache that permeates my entire skull, interrupted every so often by waves of nauseating agony. Those waves are brief, but they rock my whole being and leave a high-pitched tinnitus whine in my ears that is its own kind of hell.

I want all the aspirin in the world.

I'm glad to be alive, I realise. It's maybe the first time I've ever considered the inherent benefit of existing over not. It's hard to admit it but I feel okay, almost good. Like I've won ... I don't know what. Something.

Life. I've won life.

I can't rationalise that thought, that idea. I've been through hell today. I should be balling my eyes out right now. I should be shaking. Instead, am I happy?

At the intersection, instead of going right towards town, I go left. I never go left. Left is the country, the interstate, the rest of America. Left is the unknown. Left is fear.

The road seems to stretch for ever. The forests either side are infinite. I feel small and insignificant and vulnerable. Carlson is silent in the back, massaging his throat.

I see flashes of the bathroom, stabbing Messer, shooting

him, thinking I'm going to die. I feel both disembodied to that experience and trapped inside it.

I roar at the top of my lungs and thump the horn, letting the dual assault of sound overwhelm those thoughts, those flashbacks, and force them away through sheer violence of noise.

For a brief moment, I'm at peace. In that peace, I need answers.

'*What the hell is going on?*' I shout over my shoulder at Carlson.

He's wide-eyed from the roaring, the banging of the horn. He thinks I'm nuts. I don't care. I have every right to be a little nuts.

'People have tried to kill me. I want to know why.'

My voice is a bullhorn in a library. I'm surprised by my own ferocity. Where did that come from?

Who is this person?

Carlson says, 'Calm down.'

'Don't you dare tell me to calm down, buddy. Don't you dare tell me to calm down when I've stabbed and shot a man.' I'm glaring at him in the rear-view. 'When I've been shot *at.*'

Carlson's voice is a raspy whisper. 'I know you've been through a lot, Mrs Talhoffer. I know you're confused. I promise, I'm going to do my best to help you understand.'

'Jem,' I hiss. 'My name is Jem.'

'Okay,' Carlson says, 'Jem.'

I thump the horn again. I roar again.

It feels good to unleash some of the incredible tension inside me.

Carlson grimaces at the noise. 'Please, try and remain ... relaxed.'

'I'm not very relaxed on my best days,' I say back. 'And this is pretty far from one of those. So start talking, Carlson. Start talking or I'll stop this car and leave you at the side of the road before going to Rusty. I'm not kidding.'

'I believe you.' He sits up, struggling to do so, but he grabs hold of the passenger seat to assist. 'I do.'

'I hear words but I don't hear answers.'

Carlson says, 'I'll tell you what I know, which I'm afraid won't give you all the answers you want because I don't know all the answers. This has accelerated so fast that I'm still working things out myself. Wilks and Messer were clearly one step ahead of me, which is why they knocked on your door before I was able to reach out to you first. As you already know, this is about Leo.'

'They said he was a money launderer working for a cartel.'

'Do you believe it?'

I shake my head. 'I've never believed it.'

'You're right not to believe it, and also wrong at the same time,' Carlson explains without explaining. 'The money laundering, the cartel, they're window dressing. It's a diversion, a distraction. A cover story.'

I'm losing what little patience I had. 'Get to the point, Carlson.'

'Your husband isn't just a money launderer, he's an information launderer. He's not washing dirty money for the cartel. He's taking dirty information and making it clean.'

'You're telling me a lot without telling me anything at all.'

'I work for the government, Jem. Just like Wilks. Just like Messer. Just like Leo.'

'What do you mean Leo works for the government? He's a sommelier. He's a wine merchant.'

Carlson nods. 'He is, and he's very good at it, but he's also my informant.'

I'm shaking my head. 'Now I know you're talking nonsense. Leo isn't an undercover agent.'

'He's not,' Carlson says. 'But that label is out of date even when it's more appropriate. Once we're off the road, once we're safe, I'll help you understand.'

I wince, blinking, momentarily feeling a wave of dizziness ripple through my brain. When it passes, I have to jerk the steering wheel to keep on the road.

'We need to go to Rusty,' I say. 'She can help us. She'll understand. She's not involved in this. She can't be.'

Carlson is not convinced. 'Can you trust her?'

'Of course I can trust her. Why wouldn't I?'

'Are you saying that you know her, really know her? I mean, you've known her well for years, know her personality inside and out, know her financial position. I mean: do you know all of her secrets? Do you know what keeps her awake at night? Do you know what she regrets, what she aspires towards? Do you know how many sugars she puts into her coffee?'

I frown. 'No, of course I don't know all of that. How could I possibly know all of that? That doesn't mean I don't trust her. She's the chief of police.'

Carlson doesn't respond. He doesn't need to because he's right. I don't know Rusty, so how can I trust her? Is the fact that she's the chief a good enough reason? Does that make her pure and righteous and incorruptible?

I say, 'So, where do we go instead? We can't just drive around for ever.'

'We need somewhere to lie low. I need to make calls. We need to think very carefully how we proceed because we don't know how far this thing goes. We already know that they're willing to kill to keep a lid on it.'

I'm quiet, thinking.

Carlson says, 'Do you have anywhere else to go?'

'Leo has some warehouse space,' I say, 'where he stores wine. That's not too far. About an hours' drive. Between here and the city.'

Carlson shakes his head. 'That's too far away. We can't

afford to be on the move all that time.' Carlson coughs and clears his throat. It hurts him to talk. 'Plus, they're bound to know about it. I would be very surprised if they didn't. So, they could have it under surveillance.'

'Maybe you should make a suggestion instead of dismissing every one of mine.'

'I'm not trying to be dismissive of you, Jem. I'm trying to avoid getting my ass kicked again. I'm trying to avoid killing anyone else. So, to that end, do you have anywhere we can go that isn't connected to you on paper, that doesn't involve law enforcement, that no one but you would know about?'

I think for a minute, staring out at the long, winding road, the trees. We pass a handful of vehicles. Most of them flash by in a blur. I'm not paying attention to them. One, however, gets my attention because a German Shepherd has its head out of the open passenger window, enjoying the evening air in its face.

The dog reminds me of another dog, and that dog reminds me of its owner.

'Yes,' I say. 'I know where we can go.'

6:01 p.m.

Trevor's cabin is hard to find, which I guess is the point. He gave me his address when he dropped me off in town this morning but that proves to be of little use. He lives about five miles out of town, deep in the forest at the end of a narrow dirt track that Carlson's sedan can barely handle. Again, I guess this is the point. Trevor wants to be left alone. He doesn't want visitors.

He strikes me as the kind of man who owns a lot of guns and the kind of gun owner who doesn't like strange cars rolling up unannounced on his property.

'Let's stop a ways from the cabin,' I tell Carlson. 'Let me walk up the rest of the way by myself.'

'Why?'

'Because I don't want to get shot for trespassing after all I've been through today.'

'You told me he was nice to you. You said he was a kind, sweet old man.'

'True, I did tell you that,' I say, feeling unsure of myself now. 'I've only met him the one time, though. He was just like I told you: kind, sweet. He gave me a ride. But that was then. A lot has happened since this morning. Now, I'm kind of on edge and expecting the worst. Which I think is understandable.'

Carlson is sat upright now he's shaken off the worst of his fight with Wilks. I imagine he's still in pain, however, like I am. My awful headache won't quit.

'Exactly what else can you tell me about this Trevor?' Carlson asks. 'Besides the fact he's kind and old.'

'Well,' I say, 'he lives on his own far away from anyone else because he's not a big fan of the modern world. What can you extrapolate from that?'

Carlson nods. 'Good point. You go first.'

'You could try saying it in such a way that I don't think of myself as your human shield.'

Carlson offers me an apologetic look.

I stop the car maybe a hundred feet from Trevor's cabin after pulling it round. I want to be able to get away fast should the need arise. The track twists one last time before it reaches the building so there is a stretch of trees between where I park and the cabin itself. I can just about see the timbered walls through the foliage. I wonder if Trevor can see us in return. I picture him at a window, rifle in hand, taking aim with Merlin at his ankles, growling at the intruders.

Stop being paranoid, Jem. Trevor is one of the good guys. Maybe the only good guy.

But good guys can have itchy trigger fingers, especially the ones who don't own cell phones and live by themselves.

'Wish me luck,' I say to Carlson.

'You'll be fine,' he reassures me with a bare minimum of comfort.

I'm sure I will, and I'm worried I won't be. You're not

paranoid if they really are out to get you, and if today's events have taught me anything, it's that they really are out to get me. I open the car door and put my feet down on the dirt track.

'Sit tight,' I say to him.

The dirt track isn't easy to traverse, even in shoes. It's rutted and changes from firm to squishy underfoot with no warning. My sneakers are coated in mud by the time I reach Trevor's cabin. There's an expanse of open space before it – a driveway of sorts – with a pile of firewood under a shelter and a pile of logs collected from the woods waiting to be split next to a stump and axe. Trevor's pickup is parked in front of the cabin so I know he's home.

I'm not sure if I should knock on the door or call out a greeting first. If he's seen me then it doesn't matter. I don't want to startle him though, and I don't want to give Merlin a reason to be any more aggressive towards me.

I do both. I knock on the front door and call out, 'Trevor, it's Jem.'

There's no response, and I hear no footsteps on the other side of the door, no barks either.

'It's Jem,' I call again, 'from this morning. You kindly gave me a lift to the police department. I'm sorry to say I need your help once more. Bet you're wishing right now you never stopped your truck.'

I try and make it sound breezy and I have no idea how successful I am.

No response.

Maybe he's not home. The pickup's here, but he could be out collecting firewood or hunting or just taking Merlin for a walk.

What to do?

I can't see Carlson's car through the trees, and for a horrible moment I think he's driven off and abandoned me. I would have heard the engine though, so he's still there even if I can't see him. I shake my head and shrug in case he can see me.

What to do?

There are a couple of windows flanking the front door. I cup my hands and peer through one. There's a net curtain so I fail to make out anything significant of the interior. Maybe that's a sofa. Maybe that's a staircase. I don't see any movement.

I think back. I think back to when I ran out on to the road and flagged down Trevor's truck. I think back to when he drove me away and I saw Messer coming out of the trees behind us. Was he close enough to see the licence plate?

My pulse quickens. Is Trevor dead?

Did Messer pass on Trevor's details to co-conspirators?

I peer back through the window, this time trying to focus on the floor, looking for a corpse. I see nothing. He could still be alive. He could be injured.

I try the front door in the vain hope it's unlocked. I thump it with my fist, increasingly fearful.

'Trevor,' I shout, 'can you hear me?'

'Yeah, I can hear you,' he replies. 'They can hear you all the way up in Canada. You got quite the set of lungs on you.'

He's behind me, Merlin at his side. They're emerging from the dirt track. Carlson is with them. He has his hands up because Trevor has a rifle pointed at the back of his head. Trevor is frogmarching him.

Carlson calls out to me, 'He didn't believe me when I said I was on your side.'

'He's got a shifty look about him,' Trevor says.

'Because I'm black?' Carlson says.

Trevor seems confused. He says to Carlson, 'Are you? I didn't 'realise,' and then to me, 'I figured he might have coerced you to come this ways.'

'It's okay, he's okay,' I say, stepping towards them. 'He helped me. He's on my side, I swear.'

Trevor seems disappointed. 'Put your palms down, son. You have yourself a stay of execution.'

Carlson lowers his hands. 'He snuck up on me.'

'But I didn't shoot you, did I?'

'And I'm supposed to be grateful for that?'

Trevor nods. 'Mighty grateful, I should say.'

'Thank you,' Carlson says, making no attempt to hide his sarcasm.

I'm not sure if Trevor hears it or just doesn't care.

'You should be more aware of your surroundings,' he says to Carlson. 'In fact, we might deduce that I've done you a favour by demonstrating the disadvantages of assuming safety in a non-recce'd theatre.'

Carlson is confused. 'You've done ... what?'

Trevor doesn't answer. He leaves Carlson standing in his confusion and approaches me. 'You don't look so good, Jem. I'm guessing things didn't work out as intended with Rusty.'

I sigh as I nod my agreement. 'Something of an understatement, Trevor. Don't suppose we can lie low in your cabin for a short while? I know it's a lot to ask. I wouldn't if I had any other choice.'

'Long as you know it's a little light on the creature comforts you might have come to rely on.'

'It's got a roof. It's got walls. That's more than enough for me right now.'

'Then you're welcome to come inside and take a load off.' He unlocks the front door. 'But before you come in it's my duty to advise you both not, under any circumstances, to sit on the red chair.'

'I can live with that,' I tell him. 'Why, is that yours?'

He shakes his head. 'The red chair is Merlin's and he's not one for sharing.'

I manage to smile. 'Why am I not surprised to hear that?'

6:06 p.m.

Trevor's cabin seems larger inside than I expected from its exterior dimensions. It's pretty much one huge room with a staircase at the far end that leads up to a mezzanine level where Trevor sleeps. I work this out for myself but he's still quick to tell me.

There's a kitchen in one corner of the cabin, a dining table in the other and a living area taking up the rest of the space. Everything that Trevor needs and nothing he doesn't. Despite the space and the modest furniture and appliances there's not a lot of room to manoeuvre because there are stacks and stacks of books. They're everywhere: along every inch of wall, under the dining table, on top of the dining table, next to the sofa; the coffee table is what looks like a door cut in half and rested on top of a dense pile of books.

'I like to read,' Trevor says.

'Never would have guessed.'

Dog-eared paperbacks for the most part, although I can't see a single work of fiction. There are biographies and books on science, politics and current affairs.

187

'I put the ones that make me mad under the coffee table,' he says. 'That way I won't read them again by mistake.'

'Sounds like a good system.'

Merlin is so quick leaping up to his red armchair that Trevor need not have warned us outside, although it's not a strong leap. The little dog only half-makes it and has to scramble up the rest of the way with skinny back legs kicking out for purchase. I'm suddenly aware that Merlin is probably the same age as Trevor. In dog years, I mean. Merlin spends a moment sniffing the chair before flopping down and watching us with his beady black eyes.

Trevor settles into his own chair next to Merlin's, and together they have a certain charm: a couple of old guys hanging out together.

'Make yourselves comfortable.'

There's a tatty leather sofa covered in a tatty patchwork blanket. I take a seat and almost get swallowed whole. The sofa cushions are as soft as ice cream.

Carlson says to Trevor, 'Is there a restroom I can use?'

'Course there is, son. I said there might be a lack of creature comforts not essential amenities.'

Carlson looks apologetic. 'Where is it?'

Trevor gestures with his chin. 'Out back.'

'As in outside?'

Trevor nods.

Carlson is horrified. 'A latrine?'

Trevor squares up in his chair. 'Is that not a good enough depository for your waste materials, Mr Agent Man? Cause if not, why don't you try holding it in instead for the entire time you're here? See how that works out for you.'

Carlson shows his palms. 'No, no. It'll be fine, thank you.'

He mutters apologies as he makes his way outside to find the latrine.

Trevor has a mischievous glint in his eye.

'It's fully functional,' he tells me. 'Installed it all myself. I just like seeing him squirm.'

I smile.

He chuckles to himself and scratches Merlin behind the ear.

'So,' Trevor begins, 'what kind of bother have you got yourself in now?'

Trevor already knows a good chunk so it takes only a couple of minutes to summarise the rest of the day's events since he dropped me off in town. I tell him about Carlson trying to warn me, I tell him about Rusty, I tell him about going back home with Wilks and Messer … This time, however, I tell him everything that Wilks and Messer said about Leo, about the money laundering.

'I'm sorry I kept that from you earlier,' I say, 'but I was embarrassed. I wasn't ready to believe it, let alone be judged.'

'Thing about me's worth knowing is that I don't judge anyone.'

'Thanks, Trevor.'

Carlson returns.

'Except,' Trevor continues, 'employees of the corrupt federal government.'

Carlson has no idea how best to respond, so he doesn't. He takes a seat next to me on the sofa.

Trevor eyeballs him. 'Did I invite you to sit down?'

Carlson moves to stand again, so I intervene. 'He's joking. He's just screwing with you.'

Trevor chuckles to himself.

'Hilarious,' Carlson says. 'Great sense of humour. Really appropriate to the circumstances.'

'Talking of circumstances,' Trevor responds, 'what exactly is your story, Mr Agent Man?'

'The name's Carlson.'

'A short story is it? Right you are, Mr Agent Man.'

'I'm helping out Jem,' Carlson explains, trying again. 'I mean, I'm trying to help her out but I've been doing a pretty lousy job of it so far.'

'Don't beat yourself up,' I tell him. 'I'm not a good recipient of advice. I always think I know best even when I clearly don't. The rest of the time I don't want to admit I don't know best so either way I'm screwed.'

'Even still, I should have contacted you sooner. Or, failing that, found a better way to convince you to trust me.'

I ask Carlson, 'Why didn't you tell me on the phone Leo was working for you?'

'Standard operational procedure when dealing with an informant,' he explains. 'Above all else is secrecy, security. Leo's safety is always my top priority. He's put himself in tremendous danger by giving up information on his employers. These are very powerful people, very influential people. I can't overstate how long their reach is and just by mentioning Leo's name I put him at risk so I don't do that lightly.' He pauses. 'I needed an excuse to call you, to warn you and to warn Leo while hiding our connection. I had no choice, Jem. I had to pretend Leo's name had just come my way in case anyone was listening, in case anyone came asking questions.'

I nod. I think I understand.

'Had you told me on the phone my husband was an informant for the FBI I probably would have laughed.'

'There's that too. Leo, even though he works for me, for the Bureau, is not on our regular system. Standard security protocols in action in case of moles. Only a handful of people know he exists in this context. But I have alerts nonetheless, as I do with other informants. So, if people start asking questions about them, it flags. I notice. Nine times out of ten when this

190

happens with an asset it's entirely innocent. They've got themselves a parking ticket. Maybe a DUI.'

'What about the other time?'

Carlson says, 'That's where things get prickly. Every once in a while someone is interested in an informant because they're an informant. Now that someone might not know the asset in question works, or has worked, for the FBI, but the fact they're interested in that asset poses a security risk, as I'm sure you can imagine. In that scenario it's the duty of the agent responsible for the asset – in Leo's case, me – to investigate those asking questions. What do they want to know? Why do they want to know it? What are the consequences of their questions? You get the idea. In the case of your husband, I've never had to deal with this situation before. So, I'm thorough. The request for information came from within the FBI, so I—'

'You told me Wilks and Messer weren't from the FBI.'

'I did,' Carlson says, 'because that's correct. But the request for information about Leo was from the FBI. My first thoughts were he was a suspect in a crime. A federal crime, naturally, given the FBI's interest. But what I found was that there was no active investigation in which your husband was a person of interest or even a potential witness.'

'What does that mean? I'm so confused.'

'So was I. Very confused. Perplexed, even. I—'

'The request was made by the FBI on someone else's behalf,' Trevor says.

Carlson nods. 'That's right. We need to call them the third party because I don't know exactly who they are.'

I say, 'And if you were to guess?'

'I think what Wilks and Messer said to you when they came to your house could be the truth.'

I exhale for a long moment. 'You're saying that Leo really has evidence that could bring down a drug cartel?'

'I'm saying it's possible. I'm saying it would explain the direct involvement of Wilks and Messer. Some of these cartels have unparalleled levels of influence.'

'Enough influence to convince the FBI to help them? That can't be true.'

Trevor shrugs. 'All it takes is one bad apple. Isn't that right, Mr Agent Man?'

'I'm afraid so,' Carlson agrees. 'Much as I would like to believe no one working for the FBI could be bribed or coerced to supply information to a drug cartel, I just can't say it's impossible.'

Trevor huffs. 'Federal government can't ever be trusted.'

'So let me get this straight,' I say. 'Leo's been laundering money for a drug cartel, and that drug cartel used the FBI to find out information on him? What information?'

Carlson looks at me like it's obvious. Maybe it is.

'They must have been suspicious,' he says. 'Perhaps they thought they had a rat in their organisation and were fishing out wide and Leo was just one of many in the net, or they might have suspected him in particular for some other reason. Regardless, they used their sources to see what we had on Leo.'

'Cue Wilks and Messer knocking on my door,' I say.

Carlson nods. 'That's how it looks to me.'

'God,' I say. 'And now at least one of them is dead, and the cartel are going to know for sure Leo has been betraying them.'

Carlson nods again. 'I'm afraid so, Jem. But I'm going to do everything I can to keep you and Leo safe. I swear it.'

I say, 'Thank you,' but I don't believe he can.

I don't believe anyone can.

Endometriosis.

It's a mouthful, right? A complicated word for a relatively simple-to-understand condition. The lining of my uterus doesn't only grow in the uterus, but on my ovaries too. I have no outward symptoms, unlike many sufferers. I've rarely ever had what I would call a heavy period. No pain during sex. The only downside to it, and it's a pretty major one, is that I can't get pregnant.

When endometriosis affects different areas, such as tissue growing on the outside of the womb, then surgery can sometimes offer a solution.

In my case, there's no treatment.

'Now we know,' Leo said that day on the sidewalk outside the doctor's office. 'Now we have an answer.'

'What good is an answer without a solution?'

He said nothing.

Instead, he held me. He kissed the top of my head while my arms hung limp at my sides.

I heard the crinkle of paper because he was holding an inch-thick wad of leaflets about the condition, on how to cope, about support groups, about drugs, about surgery, about what to do next, about donors, about surrogates, about adoption. The doctor gave them to me but I couldn't bring myself to take them. Leo did instead.

I thought then that I wouldn't read them. What would be the point?

'We still have options,' Leo said. 'This doesn't have to be the end of the road.'

'We had a plan,' I said.

'I know,' he said.

'We have the house,' I said.

'I know,' he said.

It was a glorious, sunny afternoon. A magnificent blue sky dotted with cotton-wool clouds.

Why did it have to be such a perfect day? Why couldn't it be freezing cold? Why couldn't there be a rainstorm, or wind blowing so hard it stung my eyes?

That was the kind of day I wanted. Not this. Anything but this.

Pedestrians were walking back and forth. Some young, some old. Everything in between. My gaze was drawn to families, to mothers and fathers with children. I looked to couples holding hands and imagined them in the future plastering their social media accounts with the announcement of their first child to a barrage of likes.

I hated them.

I'd never hated anyone so much.

I was wrong. There was someone I hated more.

'My immune system,' I said, voicing my thoughts. 'Of all the reasons ... I've caused this. It's me turning against me.'

Leo said, 'It's not your fault. You know that, right? You can't think of this as something that is your own fault.'

'How can I not, Leo? How can I not?'

He didn't answer.

'It's a three-bedroom house,' I said. 'Three.'

'I know.'

'We don't need all that space just for the two of us.'

'We make one an office. One becomes the spare room.'

'Spare room?' There was more sarcasm in my voice than I was proud of. 'Who exactly is going to come to stay with us?'

'Making friends is part of the plan.'

'The plan,' I told him, 'is over.'

'One part of the plan,' he said. 'One setback. A significant one, obviously. But everything else is the same, isn't it? We still have each other. That's all we started with. That's all we've had so far. It's been enough, hasn't it?'

'Until you replace me with a woman who can actually function like one.'

Even under my unfair provocation he remained calm. Even when I was challenging him, he only cared about me.

To my shame I didn't for a second think about how it was affecting him.

'That's not going to happen,' he said. 'We're a team.'

He always said the right thing. Maybe he always knew what I wanted to hear. It could have been that he understood me better than I did myself, or perhaps he would say the right thing because he was such a kind, decent human being. But I still didn't believe him. I didn't know it then but all the stress of failing to conceive had been filling up my capacity to handle it and now there was no doubt it was my fault we couldn't have a baby the limit had been reached and exceeded.

195

But even without this threshold crossed, I didn't believe his reassurances. They were just words.

I knew at that moment he would one day leave me.

The only question was: when?

6:13 p.m.

I spend a while taking in what's been told to me. Leo: sommelier, money launderer and informant. I can't deny the plausibility of this explanation but I'm not ready to believe it wholesale. Not without proof. This is all conjecture at this stage. Wilks and Messer didn't just turn up and shoot me. They could have done. I could easily be dead right now but they were asking me questions. They were talking about information.

'What did Wilks and Messer want?' I ask. 'What information were they trying to find?'

'Proof,' Trevor says. 'Isn't that right, Mr Agent Man?'

Carlson nods, albeit with some reluctance. 'And I'm guessing any evidence Leo had collected on the cartel that could hurt them.'

Trevor and Carlson talk for a while and I'm silent. I'm listening, then I'm not hearing them at all. I'm not processing anything, I'm not coming to terms with anything. I'm numb. I'm just so numb. Despite all that has happened I guess I was hoping it was some kind of mistake. Something that could be explained away, resolved. Fixed.

I can't see any way out for me, for Leo.

For us.

I say, 'We need to find Leo. I don't know how but we have to before he gets back to the house looking for me.'

'He won't,' Carlson says.

This enrages me. 'Of course he will. He's my husband. He thinks I'm danger.'

'If he does then he'll be smart about it. He won't put himself at needless risk. I've worked with him for a long time. He knows how to stay safe.'

Needless risk . . . I try to let it go. 'Then what do we do?'

'We can't do anything tonight except keep our heads down. Leo will do the same. We all lie low and attempt to sync up tomorrow. Then, I'll bring him in and keep him safe. You too.'

The thought of waiting a whole night before I can see Leo again is devastating. Trevor sees the absolute sense of hopelessness in my face.

'How's about some coffee?' he suggests. 'Don't know about you two, but I could use a cup.'

I don't like coffee but I still want some.

Carlson says, 'Yeah, why not?'

Trevor nods at Carlson, only he doesn't get out of his chair.

Carlson gets the hint. 'You want me to make it?'

Trevor shrugs. 'That depends on whether you think it's decent to take a man's hospitality and contribute nothing in return. Unless, that is, you're of the belief that—'

Carlson stands. 'I'll make it.'

'See,' Trevor says, 'I knew you weren't as ill-mannered as you're apt to make out.'

Carlson is rolling his eyes as he trudges off to the kitchen area of the cabin. Trevor winks at me. He enjoys tormenting Carlson far too much, and even though I've too much to think about to find it all that funny, Trevor's schoolboy humour, coming from an old man, has a certain infectious charm about it.

Carlson looks lost as he tries to find a drip machine.

Trevor shakes his head and stands. 'Park your ass down, Mr Agent Man. I'm not trusting a Fed to make coffee.'

Carlson drops back down on the sofa next to me and whispers, 'Of all the people you had to know ...'

Merlin opens one eye to growl at Carlson, as if he understood every word.

I say, 'He's a sweetheart. If it weren't for him I would already be dead.'

When Trevor returns with the coffee he's carrying three enamel mugs. He hands one to me and I thank him. He then places the second one down for Carlson on the coffee table at the furthest possible point so Carlson has to sit forward and reach out to take it.

Merlin growls again as Carlson's hand nears him.

'That's because he can smell weakness,' Trevor says, sitting back in his chair. 'He growls at threats, naturally, but he really growls at the weak. He's letting you know exactly what he thinks of you. He's letting you know you're for his belly just as soon as he decides it's dinner time.'

Merlin is the size of a breadbin.

Carlson says, 'I think I'll be okay.'

'Thing about a small dog,' Trevor continues, 'is that you underestimate them. You're not scared of them like you should be because you think he can't really hurt you that bad if he bites you. Well, that's not the real issue, is it? It's the fact that when he bites you he don't let go. Then what? You can't prise his jaws open because they're a vice, so you try hitting him, right? Which brings us back round to my original statement. You underestimate the small dog because he's small. Now you're finding out that small dog is all muscle and bone. There ain't no fleshy parts to him. Everywhere you hit you're hurting your hand a damn sight more than it's hurting him. You're just wearing yourself out, getting tired, making the wound worse. Then where are you? You've burned precious energy, precious hydration. And that little dog just keeps on holding and all the while he's getting fluids on account of your blood leaking out of you and into his mouth. And that wound ain't closing. How long before it gets infected? How long before you got sepsis?' Trevor sits back, finished. 'Don't underestimate the small dog.'

I exhale. 'I bet you were great fun at parties, Trevor.'

He shoots me a look. 'I was a riot, I assure you. I could tell you stories that would turn your hair white.'

'I believe you,' I say. 'But maybe another time.'

'For the best. Reminiscing is a dangerous pastime. Before you know it, you're—' He stops himself. He shakes his head, deciding against continuing with whatever thought process he was voicing. He takes a glug of coffee.

Carlson, mug now in hand, goes to do the same. 'Sweetened with rat poison, I suppose?'

'Don't be silly,' Trevor says back. Then, as Carlson is about to drink, 'Battery acid.'

Carlson looks him dead in the eye and sips.

'Finally,' Trevor says, 'some backbone.'

I cough after swallowing some. 'You could clean engines with that.'

Trevor is pleased. 'Thank you.'

'Will Leo go to prison?' I ask.

Carlson rocks his head from side to side. 'I really wouldn't want to say.'

'Try.'

'His deal as my informant only goes so far. If he's willingly committed other crimes without my knowledge then he could face charges.'

'Why do you say it like that? There's no "if". Of course he hasn't. They'll have forced him from the start. He would never do anything illegal willingly, let alone work for a cartel. There's an explanation for all of this. I know there is.' After a short pause I ask, 'How do I get out of this mess? How do I get Leo out of it?'

Carlson doesn't answer. He doesn't know. Trevor is also out of suggestions. I stare into the enamel mug, into the coffee.

'The only thing I can tell you with any certainty,' Carlson says after a long silence, 'is that until we find out how deep the conspiracy goes, I'm afraid we're entirely on our own.'

6:21 p.m.

Trevor insists on making us some food, which he prepares by heating up three tins of beans on his stove and adding some kind of meat chunks to those beans. He doesn't explain where the meat has come from and I figure it's better not to ask. I can only manage a couple of mouthfuls because my stomach is sore from when Messer punched me and even a little food makes me nauseous. Trevor isn't offended. He gives my leftovers to Merlin, who makes short work of them. When the little dog's finished, the plate looks clean enough to eat off.

It's not late, but after dinner Trevor announces it's time for bed. Carlson is still hurt and worn out from his fight with Wilks and falls asleep on the sofa. I'm not sure if this was his intention or not but I can't blame him for being exhausted.

I move off the sofa to give him more room and settle into Trevor's chair. I've felt drained in one way or another for the last nine hours yet I'm not tired so it's no surprise when Carlson is snoring away yet I'm staring at the ceiling.

Trevor tries to sneak back downstairs not long after he climbed up to his mezzanine bedroom. I hear him do his best to be silent but fail miscrably, knocking into furniture and books on his way to the refrigerator, his footsteps audible. I appreciate his efforts not to wake me and don't have the heart to tell him otherwise.

After the pit stop in the kitchen, he heads outside.

I give it a couple of minutes and follow.

I find Trevor on the porch. He's sipping from a can of beer, looking out to the trees and the bright silver moonlight streaming through the foliage.

'Beautiful,' I say as I join him.

He nods. Sips.

'Thank you again for sheltering us.'

He nods. Sips.

His silence makes me feel awkward. I guess he wants to be left alone so I retreat back towards the front door.

I'm about to push it open when I hear him say, 'You shouldn't trust him.'

I turn back. 'Carlson?'

Trevor nods. Sips.

I shake my head. 'I should have trusted him outside the police precinct. I could have skipped the headaches from getting beaten half to death.' I step closer. 'Carlson saved my life.'

'But why did he?'

'Because Wilks and Messer were trying to kill me. He intervened. What's with you?'

Trevor exhales. 'I'm just thinking out loud here.'

'You're free to speak your mind, Trevor. Especially on your own property. Especially when you're providing me with a roof over my head.'

Trevor takes a moment to gather his thoughts and find the right words to express them. He fails. He shrugs and shakes his head.

'Go on,' I assure him. 'I want to hear what you have to say. I'll tell you now, though, whatever it is I think you're wrong. Dead wrong. If it wasn't for Carlson I'd be a corpse right now, strangled and beaten to death in my own bathroom. It's as simple as that.'

'Is it?'

'Talk to me, Trevor.'

He faces me. 'Correct me if I'm wrong, but this FBI agent calls you up at the exact time you have a couple of bad guys in your living room?'

I nod.

'He tells you to run so you run.'

I nod again.

'Then he's waiting near the police HQ and tells you to get in his car. You don't.'

'All correct so far. All innocent so far.'

'Then he shows up at your house when those other two goons are trying to kill you?'

'Yes,' I say. 'I don't get what you're trying to tell me.'

'This man you don't know keeps showing up when bad things are happening to you.'

'Yeah, thank goodness he does. Thank goodness he didn't give up on me.'

Trevor waves a hand, dismissive. 'Seems awful convenient to my ears.'

'You don't like him because he works for the government.'

'That's exactly right. I don't like him because he works for the government. They're all – all – a bunch of crooks. But that's not what I'm talking about here. That's not what I'm saying. My personal opinions on the federal government and its determination to infringe upon my freedoms are irrelevant right here, Jem. Take the government out of the equation. Take his so-called job in the government out of the equation. What are you left with? A person that always shows up at the worst possible time. That's not a friend. That's a ghoul.'

I lay a hand on Trevor's shoulder. 'I say this with the greatest possible respect, but maybe you've been out here by yourself too long. Maybe you don't trust anyone. Is that close to the truth?'

'Trust is earned.'

I nod. 'I agree. And Carlson has earned my trust, Trevor. He's earned it tenfold. Just like you have.'

He turns away. If it weren't so dark and his skin weren't so tanned I might detect a blush.

'How long have you lived here?'

He shrugs as if he's never really thought about it. 'Half my life, I guess.'

'Why?' I ask.

'What do you mean, why? Why not?'

'I think you know what I mean. Why do you live out here by yourself, away from everyone else?'

'That's simple,' he explains. 'The more I know people the less I like them.'

'You say that as though everyone's bad.'

'Aren't they?'

'I don't think they are. I hope they're not.'

'There you go then,' he says. 'You haven't met enough of them yet to know they're not worth knowing.'

'I don't want to believe that. People are good. Most people, at heart, are decent, aren't they? We do the right thing. We try to, at least. Most of the time we try to be good people.'

'How many good people have you met today?'

'That's different.'

'How is it different?'

'Because those people aren't good people. They're not normal. They're not like everyone else.'

'What if they are like everyone else? What if everyone else could be just like them given the right push?'

'You really think that all it takes for a good person to do bad is the right push?'

He nods. 'Yes, I do. I've seen it my whole life.'

'Half your life,' I can't help but add.

'Half my life,' he agrees with some reluctance. 'But that was plenty of time. It was more than enough time to know people are inherently selfish. Doing good is not a natural state for humans. We do what's best for us. Doing good is usually an accident.'

'Oh, Trevor, what happened to you?'

He's annoyed with my sympathy. 'Don't go feeling sorry for me, Jem. I'm glad my eyes were opened.'

We look at the moon for a little while before something occurs to me.

'You know,' I begin, 'I can prove you're wrong.'

He huffs. 'Now, how exactly are you going to do that?'

'I'm glad you asked,' I say, feeling smug. 'Because you've actually proved it for me.'

He eyes me, suspicious.

'You've proved yourself wrong, Trevor. You proved yourself wrong when you stopped your truck for me this morning, when you saved me. If you were right, then you wouldn't have done that, would you?'

He doesn't answer.

'You're a good person, Trevor,' I insist. 'You're not selfish. All I've done is ruin your day and you've asked for nothing in return.'

He's thinking, hard. Desperate for a counter point.

'Just admit you're wrong,' I say. 'It'll make you feel better.'

He holds up a finger. He's thought of something. 'Maybe I saw a rich lady and figured she would give me a reward for helping her. So, you see, I'm not so good after all.'

I roll my eyes. 'Trevor, is that really the best you can come up with?'

He grumbles. 'Give me my reward and I'll think of something better.'

I laugh. It feels good to laugh.

I wasn't sure I'd ever laugh again.

10:28 p.m.

I try to sleep but I can't. How can I possibly sleep? There are so many unanswered questions in my mind that to ignore one is to shift the focus on to a hundred more. It's not helped by the fact that Trevor's sofa is perhaps the most uncomfortable sofa ever designed by man. A medieval torturer would have given anything to own such a device. There's an irony in that torture, because the sofa is soft and I sink into it. Problem is, I don't stop sinking. Any position I try I end up like a log dropped in a lake.

It's cold too. No surprise that Trevor doesn't have central heating. He's upstairs, snoring quite happily. That isn't helping either, although Carlson isn't suffering in the same way I am. He's sat upright, his jacket over him as a makeshift blanket. His head is lolled to the side, mouth hanging open, a content rumbling emanating from him. There's little I'm envious about with men, but their ability to sleep no matter where, no matter what, is something I'd give anything to possess.

I wonder where Leo is, whether he's able to sleep right now. Or is he awake, like me, thinking of me like I am him?

I hope he's okay, if only in this moment. He must be worried sick about me and going through his own kind of hell. There's something eminently capable about him that's meant I've never been worried about him before, never been concerned that he'd ever get himself into a situation he couldn't handle. Is that based in fact or in my own needs? Does my anxious nature need an opposite so that's one less thing to worry about? Could it be that I lie to myself, believing my husband to be this strong, resourceful, unflappable man because that's what I need?

Like I said: ignore one question and a hundred more take its place.

My heart is racing again. More palpitations.

I concentrate on breathing to calm myself down.

It works after a time but I'm left feeling frustrated and angry at myself for being like this.

I didn't walk out of the doctor's office that day and suddenly suffer from anxiety. Instead, I cried every day for weeks. I couldn't get out of bed. I suffered under the weight of incredible sadness but I pretended I was fine. I wanted to be fine. I wanted to be strong enough so that this one setback wouldn't dictate my entire life. I didn't want infertility to define me as a person.

I should have got help. I shouldn't have lied to Leo about how useless I felt, about how much of a failure as a woman I saw myself.

That sadness never left. The trauma of hearing the doctor tell me about my ineffective ovaries and hostile uterus never went away. I spent too many nights wide awake and staring at the ceiling while Leo snored next to me. I ignored the feeling of my heart leaping around inside my chest. I pretended it was just a headrush when I became so dizzy I almost collapsed.

I took the avoidance approach, which is just about the worst thing you can do. I was worried people would ask about children: were we trying, were we planning to, were we expecting? I couldn't bear the thought of those questions. I didn't want to have to answer them, to decide whether to lie and pretend everything was fine or tell the awful truth. So, I stopped seeing anyone. I turned down lunch and coffee and drinks and parties and barbecues and everything else that might involve conversation either with friends or even strangers, who can be worse. They don't know you and so they don't know the right thing to say from the wrong thing.

Of course, this avoidance just reinforces the need to avoid. By doing so you tell yourself that you are right to be afraid and that only makes the anxiety worse. Once you're in that negative feedback loop then there's no conceivable way out again.

In the early days I thought I was losing my mind. I thought I was dying. When you dwell alone in your anxious mind for too long then every thought becomes an enemy. Pessimism becomes the default state, interrupted only by abject dread.

I didn't want to get treatment. I couldn't bear the idea of even seeing another doctor after the pain of the last time, but I did it for Leo. I tried cognitive behavioural therapy. I took antidepressants. CBT didn't work because no matter how hard I tried to change the way I think any change in thought wasn't going to make me fertile. No reworked state of mind was going to overcome my shrunken eggs and hostile womb. I knew it was a waste of time after the first session but I kept at it for Leo, to show him that I was trying. I wanted him to know I wanted to be better. I didn't tell him that it was impossible.

I sit up. I'm not going to sleep any time soon so there's little point lounging on the sofa and doing nothing. If I'm going to be restless I may as well get a little exercise, a little air.

My sneakers are on the floor next to Trevor's book-stack coffee table. Carlson's shoes are nearby. They're good shoes, robust and comfortable. Brown brogues made from supple leather, with a wooden heel and lace holes ringed with brass. I didn't notice earlier but they are quite lovely. I pick one up for a closer look. The quality is obvious. The craftsmanship is exquisite. These are expensive items of footwear.

I put the brogue back in place and work on my sneakers over the dressings. My feet are still sore and it takes a minute to get the sneakers on without antagonising my wounds too much.

I stand.

In the quiet, I hear my knees creak and crack. Did they always do that or am I getting old?

I tread with careful, quiet steps, making my way to the front door. I ease it open, expecting it to make an ungodly noise. It doesn't. It's silent. I should have known that Trevor would be fastidious in his maintenance.

Outside, my breath clouds in the night air. The temperature has dropped through the floor and I shiver. Moonlight paints the cabin silver. There's no other sound but those I make myself. I stand on the porch, enjoying the peace, the tranquillity. I hug myself, rubbing my arms to generate a little warmth. I'm not dressed for this. I should go back inside.

I don't.

The trees are dark where the moonlight doesn't reach. My pulse quickens as I remember my desperate run through the woods this morning, pursued by Messer. That thought inspires others.

Messer, trying to kill me in my bathroom.

Messer, stabbed in the neck.

Messer, shot dead by Carlson.

I'm crossing the driveway before I realise what I'm doing. I feel compelled. Drawn by something.

There's nothing out here, though.

Except Carlson's car, parked around the bend in the track where I left it to facilitate a swift exit should it be needed. Moonlight gleams from the bodywork. For some reason I approach it. There's nothing remarkable about the vehicle. A plain sedan. The kind of car a government agent drives.

Why do I find it so intriguing?

There's a memory, a thought. Something half-formed and incomplete. An image. A smell, maybe. When I drove it earlier I saw ... I heard ... I felt ...

Nothing. I can't summon the memory and I can't dismiss it either.

I let my subconscious guide me. I approach the car, the sneakers protecting my tender feet from the cold, hard ground.

I run my fingertips along the bodywork, the paint chilly and a little damp against my skin. The car is unlocked, which is a surprise yet not a surprise. Trevor forcibly ejected Carlson from it earlier and Carlson hasn't gone back to it. He only left the cabin to use the latrine.

My fingers find their way under the door release. I squeeze.

It clunks open.

What are you doing, Jem?

I don't know.

I keep doing it.

I slide on to the driver's seat and ease the door shut after me. It's a little less cold inside the vehicle, but my breath still clouds. The keys aren't in the ignition so any half-fantasy I had about just driving away is over before it began. Carlson must have taken them with him as Trevor ordered him out of the car. I place my hands on the wheel anyway. I sit for a moment, thinking.

I look around the interior. It's dark, of course, but there's enough moonlight for me to see with my natural night vision.

The interior is empty. No personal effects. No change in the cup holder between seats. No gum wrapper in the footwell.

What about the glove compartment?

I lean across and work the release. It falls open.

There's something inside.

A piece of paper. White. Folded.

I open it up.

I gasp.

10:36 p.m.

Blowing a smoke ring is hard enough but blowing a perfect smoke ring is only for the most patient, the most dedicated of smokers. You have to care for the aesthetic of smoke. That care has to be as deep as it is loyal, for it is only with persistence that the most aesthetic smoke ring can be realised.

Rusty is a dedicated smoker.

Not to pat herself on the back, but she achieved the perfect smoke ring way back. She hasn't quite managed to blow a small ring through a larger ring yet she knows she's getting close. She's the patient smoker, the persistent smoker. Rusty cares about the aesthetic of smoke.

Smoke rings in the moonlight. That's true beauty.

Rusty rocks on her back porch with nothing but the smoke and the moon to keep her company. The rocking chair is a huge, old piece of furniture she picked up at a yard sale, sold so cheap she felt like she was stealing it. The seller assured her they were happy to part with the chair. They were clearing the house as fast as possible. Rusty didn't ask why. Didn't want to know about a stranger's problems any more than the stranger wanted to share them.

Some mysteries are best left unsolved.

The night is conducive to thought. When most of the town is silent and all is still for miles around, what else is there to do but think? These quiet nights are the worst for a restless mind because the only sound comes from within yourself. That sound can't be ignored. Can't be escaped.

She thinks about the two government ogres who dropped a pebble into the town's pond this morning. She still doesn't know – *really* know – what a skinny yoga teacher and her husband have done to warrant the attention of federal agents. Rusty isn't deemed important enough to understand the goings-on of her citizens.

In government, we trust.

Something wasn't right about Wilks and Messer.

She's not sure exactly what it is because it's a feeling. A hunch. An innate scepticism that makes her question everything. Rusty believes nothing at face value because time and time again she's learned that faces lie easier than words ever can.

Because of the unusual appearance of a pair of suited and booted Feds in her town, Rusty can't relax. She feels not only out of the loop but out of control too. Could one of her citizens really be laundering money for cartels right under her nose? Possible, sure, because Rusty knows she can't know everything. But she doesn't want to believe it. She doesn't want the perfect tranquillity of this little slice of paradise to prove disingenuous.

So, she made a call. A call to a friend who might be able to circumvent the hierarchy that looks down on her and doesn't like to share.

'Hot Mama,' her friend said upon answering the call, 'when you going to come visit me?'

'When you live somewhere I want to visit.'

'You cut me with your words, Hot Mama.'

'Please don't call me that.'

Her friend told her, 'Come see me and you can make me stop.'

'I don't roll like that no more,' Rusty said. 'I'm back to a more biblical way of living.'

'Even if I believed you to be serious,' her friend replied, 'you know I can change your mind.'

'I'm afraid this is a strictly professional call.'

'I have money.'

'Could you be serious for nineteen seconds, please?'

'What's got you so riled?'

Rusty explained and asked her friend to do some digging for her. Whether that will pay off or not, she doesn't know. Rusty doesn't like not knowing.

'Just you and me against the world,' Rusty tells the moon.

She blows another smoke ring and listens to the silence.

The house is only quiet, only calm, during the night. So that's when Rusty prefers to be awake. She needs that silence. Dead tired every morning is a small price to pay for these moments of serenity.

Plus, kind of hard to get away with smoking marijuana otherwise.

Not as the police chief in a small town.

Folk get funny about that.

Rusty never busts anyone for smoking weed because that would make her a hypocrite, but she has to maintain the illusion that she would. Teenagers have to believe there's a price to pay for breaking the law, even if the law is stupid. Plus, she has her officers to think about. She's pretty sure Zeke spends every waking moment he isn't on duty getting red-eyed, which is fine by her. But he can't know it's fine with her. Authority is an illusion. One that only maintains if all tiers believe in its absolute inflexibility. The second that inflexibility is questioned, the illusion vanishes.

Then, anarchy.

Rusty blows another smoke ring and wonders which of her thoughts are her own and which are the manifestations of the grass in her mind. She explores her mind with a detective's tenacity, interviewing it, interrogating it for answers until her mind exists as two separate entities: co-existing, communi- cating, debating and arguing. Each thought is countered by an alternative thought until two sides of a rapid-fire discourse are battling to be heard above the other and she doesn't know which is which.

Does that mean there is now a third mind listening to the other two in conversation?

Is Rusty a spectator to herself?

And if she is, can the two other minds inhabiting the same space hear her?

Yes, one says.

No, says the other.

Rusty slaps her cheeks, bringing those minds back together in one. She exhales and slows her racing heart. She places the joint on the lip of a nearby ashtray.

Maybe that's enough serenity for one night.

Her flip phone vibrates, startling her.

It's Sabrowski calling.

What the devil does he think he's doing calling her in the middle of the night? Rusty lets it ring. She's too stoned to talk to her trooper, even to chastise him for this unprecedented discourtesy.

The vibrating stops in time and Rusty wonders if perhaps it was Sabrowski's skinny butt making the call by mistake. That's something that doesn't happen with a flip phone, she thinks with a delightful smugness.

Then the phone vibrates a second time. Sabrowski again.

Not an ass-dial after all.

Rusty is intrigued and scared in equal measure.

She opens up her phone, and says, 'This is the chief.'

Sabrowski's voice is thinner than he is. 'Sorry to call so late, Rust, but there's ... We got a bad one here. You'd better ... There's a corpse. We need you ... I—'

'Where, Officer?'

'The Talhoffer residence.'

10:41 p.m.

The folded piece of paper I take from Carlson's glovebox is a computer printout of a picture, a face. Colour. Decent quality but nowhere near photograph resolution.

The face is Leo's.

Why does Carlson have a computer printout of my husband's face?

I don't know, but I know one thing: if he has an association with Leo, if he knows Leo, then there's no legitimate reason to have such a picture. Is there?

I imagine Carlson sitting in his car. Maybe in town. Maybe along the highway. Maybe at the intersection. He has the piece of paper unfolded on the dash or passenger seat or in his lap. He glances at it every now and again when he sees a man pass by, checking if that man matches the face in the picture.

Leo doesn't work for Carlson.

Carlson doesn't know Leo at all.

Oh God, not Carlson too.

I'm breathing so hard the windows are beginning to steam

up. I re-fold the paper and go to put it back inside the glovebox. I stop midway, open it up again to take a closer look.

The photograph is of Leo's face but it's no passport-style headshot. It's a zoomed-in section of a larger picture. Behind Leo in the background are red bricks, which makes me think that it was taken somewhere in town. That can't be the case. Leo's hair is different, longer than it's been in years, since before we moved here. He's younger. Tanned. I stare at Leo's face, at the red bricks behind him. I know this picture. I know I do. Come on, Jem, think. Remember.

Rome.

That's where it was taken. Ten years ago, in Rome. Where I met Leo. I took this picture. He's sat on a bench in a square. I'd known him all of three days at this point, when he was still little more than a handsome stranger who asked what I was reading.

As far as I know the photograph is at my house, in an album. It's a proper old-school one. I took it with Leo's Nikon. That camera is at the house too, in its case and gathering dust as it has been for years now.

How did Carlson get the photo?

I put the sheet back where I found it. I close the glove compartment. I climb out of the car and into the moonlight. It seems colder now. The woods seem darker. There's no beauty in this night, only danger.

I need to get out of here.

But I'm going nowhere on foot. I've learned that mistake the hard way. Even wearing sneakers I'm not running through the woods. Not even if I was wearing Carlson's good shoes.

Carlson's good shoes.

Of course. How could I not have noticed before?

High quality. Excellent craftsmanship. Expensive. Too expensive for a government salary.

If only I knew how to hotwire a car I could drive off right away. I've seen them crossing wires in movies and the engine magically whirring into life but it's not going to be that easy. I wouldn't even know how to get the steering column off in the first place, let alone what wires I need to cross.

I need Carlson's car keys.

They're back in Trevor's cabin. They're with Carlson.

I make my way back along the track. I'm slower crossing the driveway this time because I'm trying to be even quieter and I'm apprehensive about this course of action. I'm doubting myself with every slow, short step.

Maybe there's a reasonable explanation for the picture in Carlson's glovebox. Maybe he's sweet on Leo.

Keep it together, Jem. Don't talk yourself out of this.

As I open the front door and it's soundless, I'm even more grateful for Trevor's fastidious maintenance. I slip inside, gaze on Carlson's sleeping form, upright on the sofa. He looks harmless. He looks trustworthy.

Should I confront him? Demand to know what he's doing with a photograph of my husband?

No, I don't want to back him into a corner. I can't know how he'll react.

If he's cornered, he might be dangerous.

I think of Trevor.

I don't want to leave him here with Carlson, but I don't see any other option. I'm not going to creep upstairs and somehow wake him up and warn him without waking up Merlin in the process. Hard to sneak back out with an angry dog barking.

Trevor has a gun, I remember. A rifle. He can defend himself should he need to do so. I don't think he *will* need to, because Carlson will no doubt come straight after me once he realises what's happened.

I don't close the door again. I leave it ajar so I can make a hasty exit should I need to do so.

Carlson's head is lolled to one side and his mouth is open as it was a few minutes ago. I'm nervous regardless. I creep across the floorboards, wincing at any noise they make, my soft footsteps seeming like angry stomps.

I approach the coffee table. Carlson's things are resting on the cut-down door next to where he's sleeping. His phone is there. His wallet too.

And his car keys.

I control my breathing as I near, one slow footstep at a time. It takes an eternity to pass the sofa and reach the coffee table. I stand still for a moment, looking down at Carlson.

Is he fast asleep?

Is he faking?

I swallow. I edge closer. I reach out a hand towards his things. They're in a neat little pile. Phone on the bottom, then wallet. Car keys resting on the top. I swallow again. My fingertips inch towards them.

Carlson stirs.

The breath catches in my throat.

I yank my hand back, but his eyes remain closed. His breathing remains regular. It takes me a few seconds to calm down, to control my anxiety. I try again. I reach out, my gaze on Carlson's face the entire time my fingers are approaching the keys.

I touch them. My fingers close on them like a pincer.

I know they're going to make a noise when I lift them up. They're going to clink. It's going to be a quiet sound, but will it be enough to wake up Carlson? He could be a light sleeper. He might not even be asleep.

He's set a trap for you, Jem.

He's left the keys here to test you.

He wants to see if you believe his story. He wants to know if he can rely on you. He wants to know if you're the kind of problem he can do without.

I try to silence the voice inside my head. That endless, lingering doubt that sabotages all of my decisions, my actions, is no good to me at the best of times, least of all now.

I focus.

I try to focus.

You can do it, Jem.

I lift the keys.

The metallic clink is soft, I know it is, but in the silence of Trevor's cabin it's a chorus of steel drums. I wince. I grimace. I try and keep my grip consistent and move them towards me at a steady pace.

I don't blink the entire time. My eyes remain open and my focus is on Carlson's face, looking for trembling eyelids, looking for any kind of reaction at all.

There is none.

I swallow and close my hand around the keys as I back away. I still can't blink until I reach the door because I'm still expecting Carlson to spring up from the sofa in some terrifying surprise attack. But he doesn't.

He's not faking. There's no test. He really is asleep.

Outside, I don't notice the cold. I pull the door shut and back away across the drive. I don't dare turn round until I reach the turn in the track, when the trees are shielding me. I hurry the last stretch to Carlson's car, pulling open the driver's door and sliding behind the wheel.

I glance into the rear-view: no one.

I'm shaking so much I can't get the key into the ignition on the first try, or even the third.

I close my eyes, take a deep breath and try and find a way to calm down. The more I think, however, the more I shake.

Leo.

I think of Leo. I picture his smiling face. I remember the warmth of his embrace and the happiness and peace I only have when I'm with him. It works.

My fingers regain their dexterity and the key slides in and I turn it.

The starter motor whines but the engine fails to start.

'Oh no, don't do this to me.'

Is it the cold? Is it something else? I've no idea. I'm no mechanic.

I try again, the starter motor whining so much I'm sure I'm waking up the entire forest. The engine remains silent.

I glance into the rear-view: again, no one.

I look at the dashboard. No engine warning light is glowing. There's fuel in the tank. The oil gauge shows plenty. Everything looks fine. I can see no obvious reason for the unresponsive engine.

Maybe Carlson sabotaged the vehicle to ensure I couldn't escape.

Oh God, *this* is the test.

In my head I can see him stirring on the sofa, hearing the whine of the starter motor and leaping up, rushing to the door, sprinting across the driveway with his gun, about to round the bend in the track at any moment.

I try the ignition again. The engine starts up.

I glance into the rear-view: someone.

10:50 p.m.

A dark silhouette against the backdrop of trees. A hint of detail in silver moonlight. A man, nearing. I'm paralysed with fear, but only for a moment.

Not Carlson. Trevor.

He approaches the car, me.

'What are you doing?' I ask.

Trevor grumbles. 'What am I doing? What are *you* doing?'

'No time for that,' I tell him. 'We need to get out of here. Jump in.'

He's confused. Of course he's confused. 'And why exactly do we need to do that?'

'You were right about Carlson,' I say. 'Something's wrong with him. He doesn't know Leo like he claimed he did. I don't have time to explain. Just get in. Please.'

'What's happened?'

'Trevor, there's no time. Get in the car. We need to go before he wakes up.'

Trevor shakes his head. 'I'm not leaving my home. If

something's wrong then we'd best go back and find out what it is.'

I gesture for Trevor to get in. 'Please, Trevor. Get in the car or I'm going to have to leave you here.'

He says, 'You mean, like you were all set to do before I showed up and spoiled your plan?'

'I didn't want to leave you, I swear. But I'm scared, Trevor. I couldn't tell you what I was doing without alerting Carlson. It's me he's interested in, not you.'

Trevor thinks for a moment, then says, 'You show up at my cabin with this man, you assure me he can be trusted, and now you're scared of him? Jem, you don't make a whole lot of sense.'

'Believe me, I understand that. But that doesn't mean I'm wrong. Trevor, I've had a hell of a day so far. People have tried to kill me. I still don't understand why and I don't know who I can trust. I don't know anything except that I need to get out of here right now. I don't want to leave you here with Carlson. I swear I wouldn't have just driven off if I thought there was a way of waking you without alerting him, but I had no other option. I don't want to leave you now, so don't make me. Get in the car. Come with me. I'll do my best to explain and if after that point you don't want to stay with me, I'll pull right over and let you out. Or take you to town or wherever else. But that's then. That's ten minutes from now. Now, I'm going. So, for once in your life, just trust someone else. Just get in the damn car.'

Trevor does.

'Thank you,' I say, and put the transmission in drive.

Trevor is looking back through the rear windshield the entire time it takes me to negotiate the winding dirt track.

'Merlin will be fine,' I tell him. 'Carlson isn't interested in a dog. As soon as he realises we're gone he's going to take your truck and come after us. He's not going to give Merlin a second thought. We need to be long gone by the time Carlson knows it.'

'I understand,' Trevor says, trying to pretend he's not worried. 'I'm more concerned with Carlson running himself off the road. My truck pulls to the left like an SOB.'

Once we're on the highway I lean across Trevor and open the glovebox. I shove the folded piece of paper into Trevor's hands.

'Who's this pretty boy?' he asks.

'That's Leo,' I tell him. 'That's my husband.'

'Bit young for you, don't you think?'

'Firstly, that's an old photograph. Secondly, even if it weren't, any age difference is none of your business. Where's your manners?'

'Sorry,' he says. 'What's got into you?'

'I'm in no mood to be judged, Trevor.'

'You said it was an old photograph.'

'That's not the point,' I snap. 'Anyway, what's Carlson doing with a photograph of Leo if he knows Leo?'

Trevor doesn't answer.

'He wouldn't need it, would he?'

'To show people?' Trevor offers.

I shake my head. 'Then it wouldn't be an old photograph. It's not like Leo has changed a great deal over the past decade but if you needed to show someone a picture of anyone you'd used a recent one, wouldn't you? I know I would.'

'I would too,' Trevor agrees with a nod. 'Not that I have pictures of anyone to show anyone.'

'Not even an ex-girlfriend?'

'No.'

'Not even Merlin?'

'Why would I need a picture of my dog? I see him every moment of every day.'

I want to tell Trevor that Merlin won't be around for ever, but I can't bring myself to tell him that perhaps having photographs of Merlin will help when he's gone. I'm not sure if Trevor is wilfully ignorant or just doesn't want to admit it. Either way, I don't press on that matter.

'Trevor,' I say, 'why are you up anyway, and why are you dressed?'

He shrugs. 'Was taking a leak if you must know.'

'You get dressed to take a leak?'

'No, I sleep in my clothes so when I have to get up in the night to take a leak I don't need to get dressed to use the latrine. Gets kind of cold at night up here, in case you hadn't noticed.'

He pauses, then says, 'You know, you could have just told me Carlson had a picture of your husband. Would have been quicker than that fancy speech you gave me about trust.'

'Yeah.' I'm loath to admit he's right. 'I just worked that out myself.'

'Good speech, though.'

I smile at Trevor. He smiles back.

'Where we going now?' he says.

'I have absolutely no idea.'

We're heading back towards town because Trevor's cabin lies to its north and I happened to turn that way from the track that leads to his cabin. Doing so makes me nervous, but as I don't know what I'm doing and I don't know where I'm going, any direction has to be as good as another.

'There,' I say, leaning forward.

Trevor says, 'What am I looking at?'

I gesture over the steering wheel. 'Near the stop sign.'

A payphone.

I hadn't noticed how rare they had become, or maybe always were. I don't remember the last time I needed to use one. I don't remember the last time I used one at all. But they still exist as relics of an earlier, simpler time.

A better time.

'Wait here,' I tell Trevor as I encourage him to hand over coins.

'Where else am I going to go?' he remarks.

I feed in quarters. I don't know how many to use. I don't know how this thing works but it does. I punch in Leo's cell phone number.

It rings and rings and rings and rings.

'This is Leo, leave a message after the tone.'

I wait for the tone, then say, 'Leo, baby, I don't know what's going on but you're in real trouble. People have tried to kill me today. God, I ... I'm so confused. I'm so lost. Don't trust anyone. Don't trust anyone named Wilks or Carlson. Don't go to the house. Stay away from town. I don't have my cell. I'm calling you from a payphone. I've been looking for one all day. Why are they so hard to find? Baby, I'm trying to get to the bottom of this. I don't want to say any more on the phone. They could be listening. I'll call again when I can. God, I hope you're okay. In fact, you probably should—'

The call disconnects. Out of credit.

I consider adding more coins but I've said everything I need to say. I'm sure he knows all of it by now anyway. I'm sure he knows exactly what's going on. He has to know.

And I have to find him.

12:00 a.m.

Corpses are funny things. They look so lifelike, which is kind of ironic. People are more used to seeing bodies in movies than they are real ones so it can be a shock to witness the full, unfiltered spectacle. Some people just can't handle it the first time. And then there's those whose corpses go out the hard way ...

'How's Zeke?' Rusty asks.

Sabrowski shrugs. 'I think he's just about done throwing up by now.'

'Please assure me he made it outside before making a mess of my crime scene?'

He says, 'Might be a couple of spots of vomit on the front step.'

Rusty sighs. Not much can be done about it now seeing as she left her time machine in her other shirt. Messer's corpse is one big, ugly mess in the hallway.

Rusty says, 'What can you tell me?'

'He did not die peacefully in his sleep.'

The medical examiner is not in a good mood because he lives

230

three towns over and was fast asleep when the call came in, so Rusty doesn't tell him to cut the BS. It's late for her too. Late for everyone. No one wants to be here.

Rusty looks at Messer.

'Least of all him,' she says to herself.

Sabrowski looks to her because he heard something but nothing specific. Rusty shakes her head at him to say, forget it.

'Is that a grease stain on your collar, Officer?'

There isn't one, but Sabrowski tries to rub it clean regardless as Rusty moves on. She keeps blinking because she's doused her eyes in drops about sixteen thousand times since she received his call. She's convinced they're still redder than a Bloody Mary and knows that's probably just the paranoia, but she's a stoned police chief at a crime scene and has every right to be paranoid.

She's sure he's looking at her funny. She fakes a yawn. Tired folk look a lot like high folk.

'How are you feeling?' Rusty asks Wilks to stop her thinking about the knowing curiosity in the officer's beady eyes.

Wilks has ice cubes in a towel, and that towel held against her skull. 'I've had worse.'

Rusty's eyebrows arch. 'You have? Then might I recommend you try and do your job without getting your ass whooped in the process?'

Wilks is silent.

Rusty feels bad. It's not her nature to kick a person when she's down but Rusty's tired and stoned and paranoid and her blood sugar is low. A saint could get irritable given such provocation.

She opens her mouth to apologise, but Wilks is already turning, already heading off to make a call or check something out or to have a moment to herself.

'What are your thoughts, Officer?'

Sabrowski isn't paying attention so gives her a dumbfounded expression when she looks to him for an answer.

'What are your thoughts?' she says again. 'What do you think happened here?'

'Someone shot the big dude on the floor. Not when he was on the floor, I mean. They shot him before. That's why he's on the floor.'

'Thank you for the clarification, Officer.'

The medical examiner, tired and irritable like Rusty, shoots her a little grin because they're kindred sarcastic SOBs. She winks at him in return.

Rusty's phone rings. She sees the caller ID and steps outside to take it, making sure to avoid the yellow splats of Zeke's stomach contents on the doorstep.

'This is Rusty.'

It's her friend on the West Coast, working late but not as late as it is here.

Rusty listens.

'You're kidding?' she says when her friend has finished.

Sabrowski knows something is up given Rusty's expression but he's not privy to any of the conversation and is eager for enlightenment when Rusty hangs up. Rusty ignores him.

She finds Wilks in the kitchen, getting some more ice for her head. She stands before her for a moment, trying to find the words.

'What is it?' she asks.

'What is it?' Rusty echoes. 'It's more what it's not, Agent Wilks.'

'I'm not sure what you're getting at.'

'I have this friend,' she explains. 'From way back. Like, the Dark Ages back. Bet you have friends like that too, don't

232

you? You've been through something together and you end up with a fierce bond that survives distance, that even survives decades. The kind of friend you can call up out of the blue and they'll drop everything to help you. You have friends like that?'

Wilks says nothing.

'I have,' Rusty continues. 'She's been in the military, in law enforcement. She's done all sorts of work she can't tell me about and met all sorts of people in the process. She's done so much for so many that she could get a meeting with the President quicker than you or I could see our bank managers. This friend of mine, this connected friend of mine, I called her earlier today, you see. After you and your newly dead associate left my office. I called her because something wasn't quite right and I couldn't quite put my finger on it. I tell her about the two FBI agents who came to see me this morning when no one from the Bureau has so much as pissed up the wall of my building since I've been chief. I tell this good friend of mine that something isn't right, that although you've got the badges and the suits and the holier-than-thou expressions, something's missing. I don't know what that something is, but if she could ask around and check out a couple of Feds by the name of Wilks and Messer and let me know what she finds I would be mightily appreciative.' Rusty pauses. 'Care to guess what she found?'

Wilks is silent.

'That's exactly right,' Rusty says. 'She found nothing. She found nothing about a pair of FBI agents named Wilks and Messer because Wilks and Messer aren't FBI. Which is all kinds of confusing to a simple girl like myself.' She pushes her thumbs against her temples to emphasise the point. 'So, Not-So-Special Agent Wilks, you want to tell me who you really are

233

and what you're really doing in my town before I arrest you for impersonating a federal agent?'

'We should probably talk about this in private.'

Rusty nods. 'Now why did I have a funny feeling you were going to say those exact words?'

12:05 a.m.

Aside from a quick pit stop in an all-night coffee shop – or was it a diner? – we stay on the move. Keeping mobile feels safer than the alternative. Trevor isn't saying much and neither am I. There's too much to think about and the silences are intense. I long simply to have a conversation about something boring and mundane like the weather to ease the anxiety but small talk is beyond either of us right now.

It's not long before we need to stop at a gas station because the needle is threateningly close to the red line and the last thing I want to do is run out of fuel. Trevor stays in Carlson's car while I go inside to pay.

There's a kind of awkwardness I feel doing this. I know I've done nothing wrong, that I have only acted in self-defence, but I still feel like a criminal, like a fugitive. I suppose I am because I've failed to report a crime or left the scene of a crime or what-ever. I've no idea what laws apply here nor which ones I may have broken and may be currently breaking. Ignorance is no defence, I know, but there's too much else on my mind right now.

I pick up some water and some snacks because I don't know how long it will be before we will get to eat again. I spend a while browsing the aisles because I barely touched the grilled cheese sandwich I ordered earlier. Seeing all the treats on offer is making me hungry. Of course, my restless, anxious mind won't let me decide what I want. Actually, I know what I want. I want a nice, freshly made meal, prepared in my own kitchen with my own utensils and using vegetables I've grown, and I want to sit down at my own table and eat it with Leo and chat about our crazy day and laugh that it's all over.

Such a simple fantasy, so far out of reach that I wonder if it will ever happen like that again.

Where are you, Leo?

What are you doing right now?

I spend so long browsing that the attendant behind the register is looking at me like I'm a nervous shoplifter. As soon as I notice this I feel anxious to the point of panic, as if I'm guilty until proven innocent. I knock some snacks off their hook and on to the floor in my sudden clumsiness.

They're back on the shelf soon enough despite my butterfingers and I grab a bag of tortilla chips and a couple of bottles of vitamin-infused water and take them to the counter.

As I pocket my change I say, 'Do you happen to have a payphone here?'

The young attendant looks at me like I'm crazy. 'A payphone?'

'Yeah, you know. A phone that you pay to use.'

'You don't have a cell phone?'

'I have a cell phone but I don't have it on me. Which is exactly the reason why I need a payphone.'

'Ah,' she says, illuminated.

'So . . .'

'So?'

'Do you have a payphone?'

She shakes her head. 'Of course not.'

'Of course not,' I say back.

Trevor says 'What kept you?' when I return to the car.

I slide on to the seat, shaking my head. I pass him the tortilla chips and a bottle of the water which he eyes with suspicion and then proceeds to drop into the footwell as he turns his attention to the chips.

'Didn't they have the spicy ones?'

'I . . . I don't know. I was in a daze, Trevor. I'm sorry.'

He grunts to say it doesn't matter.

'We need a plan,' he tells me.

I crack open my bottle of water. 'That's kind of the cause of the daze.'

Trevor tears the bag apart. 'You don't want to go to the police?'

'No,' I say, firm and resolute. 'I don't know who is working for the FBI and who isn't and who is working for a cartel and who isn't. I don't know who in authority is on my side and who is against me. I go to Rusty and I may as well put a flashing sign on my head to alert the next Wilks and Messer or Carlson for that matter to come for me.'

Trevor grunts approval. 'I did say you can't trust government types.'

Clouds smother the moon.

He crunches on chips and stares out of the windshield. I watch his reflection, fascinated by the intensity of his gaze and the deliberation behind his silver-blue eyes.

'It's impossible,' he says between chews. 'So don't bother.'

'What's impossible?'

His gaze remains on the outside world. 'Reading my mind. Isn't going to happen, so quit trying. Got myself a microchip

237

implant to stop the government using gamma rays to analyse my thoughts.'

I almost – *almost* – take the bait.

He smiles to himself, pleased enough that I nearly humiliated myself.

'You're a mystery, Trevor,' I reply. 'One I'm determined to solve.'

'Might be a better use of your time to solve the mystery of who wants you dead and why they're looking for your husband.'

'Noted.'

I give it a go. Fail.

Trevor sucks salt from his fingers. 'If I might make a suggestion ...'

I swallow. Nod with vigour. 'Please, I'm all ears.'

'What do these people want?'

'As far as I'm concerned I can't believe what anyone's told me so far today. Leo's a money launderer, he's a thief ... he has cartel information, he's an FBI informant.'

'Okay.' He pauses, tries again. 'What do they have in common?'

'They're looking for Leo.'

'Why?'

'Because he's a money launderer or a thief or a secret bus driver.'

Trevor nods. 'There you go then.'

'There I go what?'

'That's what you need to find out. Which is it? What is Leo? Then, when you know that, you'll be able to work out what they actually want with him.'

'That sounds great in theory, Trevor, but how am I supposed to find out in the first place?'

He shrugs. Munches on chips. 'He's your husband, not mine. You should know him better than anyone.'

'Right now I feel like I don't know him at all. Whatever he is, whatever he's been doing, he's kept it a secret from me for a long time.' I shake my head. 'I feel like an idiot. I feel like I've been duped into believing he's something he's not.'

'You don't know what he's kept secret from you so don't judge yourself too harshly.'

'Judging myself too harshly is kind of my MO. If there's one person in all this I trust least of all it's me.'

'That's TV talk.'

'TV talk?'

'Yeah,' he says with vigour. 'TV talk. The nonsense they go on about on TV nowadays. Everyone's got this problem and that condition and no one ever has just a bad day because everyone's got to be depressed instead. You know why that is?'

I roll my eyes. 'I'm sure you're going to tell me.'

'Damn straight I am. Everyone's got to have something wrong with them because there's no profit in a bad day. A snake oil salesman can't sell you snake oil if there's nothing wrong with you. And people lap it up. They lap it up because it gives them an excuse. They are absolved of responsibility for their actions because there's this wrong with them or that wrong with them. How did folks get by in the past if they were all suffering undiagnosed and untreated? Civilisation should have ground to a halt long before now.'

My cheeks are warm with rushing blood. 'Just because you have no direct experience of something doesn't mean it doesn't exist.'

'Sometimes a bad day is just a bad day.'

'You're being incredibly insensitive right now.'

He huffs. 'Insensitive ...'

'Yeah, insensitive.'

'To who?'

239

'Me, for one. And to a lot of other people too. You may have been blessed with a hardy, healthy brain but that's not the case for everyone. The brain is an organ like any other. Sometimes, things go wrong. Someone has a bad heart, you don't tell them there's nothing wrong with their heart because your own heart is fine, do you?' He doesn't answer quick enough for my righteous fury. 'Do you?'

He mumbles something that I take as a sign of concession.

'Show a little sympathy for those less fortunate than yourself, please.'

'I'm just saying that sometimes a bad day is just a bad day.'

'Yeah, sometimes it is,' I agree. 'Today, for example. Today has been a really bad day.'

He presents the bag of tortilla chips my way. 'Take a handful. They'll make you feel better.'

I shake my head. 'I don't eat PUFAs.'

'What the hell is a PUFA when it's at home?'

'Polyunsaturated fatty acid,' I say.

Trevor's expression tells me he doesn't pay a lot of attention to nutrition.

'Vegetable oil,' I explain. 'Well, they call it vegetable oil, but it's seed oil really. PUFAs go rancid really quick. They cause huge amounts of oxidative stress in the body, triggering inflammation that can lead to a whole host of problems ranging from heart disease to diabetes.'

Trevor is wide-eyed. 'You're saying all sorts of things but I'm not hearing any of it.'

'Poison, Trevor,' I say. 'Those chips are fried in poison.'

Now his mouth is wide open like his eyes.

'Screw it,' I say, reaching my hand into the bag. 'Diabetes is the least of my concerns right now.'

Trevor smiles. 'There you go. Always an upside.'

I crunch for a little while. They really are all kinds of delicious.

'Got it,' I say.

Trevor's eyebrows arch like two bushy caterpillars. 'Diabetes? That was fast.'

'Ha, ha,' I say with a sneer. 'No, not diabetes. I've got a plan.'

Trevor brushes salt from his fingertips. 'Let's hear it.'

'We're going to give Leo an audit.'

'We are?'

I nod. 'Whatever they want, whatever the truth is, we know it's related to Leo's wine business. Whether it's being used as a cover to launder money or whatever, it's his business that is enabling it.'

'If you say so.'

'So, let's go take a peek in Leo's books.'

'Why?'

'Because numbers don't lie.'

'I don't understand.'

'You will,' I say. 'Now take this bag off me before I eat the lot.'

Trevor does, and peers inside. 'You've made a pretty good dent in them already. Not sure there's enough left to—'

'Not the time, Trevor. Not the time.'

Trevor can't sit still. He's restless, fidgeting. I can see that he's working up to say something and I'm happy to let him give me more time to think things through.

Eventually, Trevor says, 'Jem, I'm—'

'No need to apologise for all the TV talk stuff,' I interrupt. 'I've already forgiven you.'

He grumbles. 'Actually, I was going to say that I'll drive us if you're feeling tired.'

I shoot a sideways look. He's got a little wry smile on his face.

'Don't change, Trevor,' I tell him. 'Don't ever change.'

But I need to change. I need to stop believing what people tell me.

As Trevor said: I can only trust myself. I can't take anyone else's word for anything. I need to get to the bottom of this myself.

Then, only then, will I know who's been telling me the truth.

12:17 a.m.

There's a lot of road to traverse before we get to Leo's warehouse and hence a lot of time to think, to worry. There are so many things on my mind to be concerned with that it's a surprise when the one that demands immediate attention is a grumpy old dog.

'I'm worried about Merlin,' I tell Trevor.

Trevor isn't.

'Don't be,' he tells me. 'That hound is one self-reliant little beast. Every now and again he'll wander off into the woods and I won't see him for a week and he comes back looking no different to how he looked when he set off. I don't know how he does it, but he can take care of himself. If I drop down dead of a heart attack right now he's going to be A-okay. He won't even miss me.'

I give him a light punch on the arm. 'Don't say that.'

'Why not? He's a dog.'

'Not that,' I say. 'Don't say that about dropping down dead.'

'Why not?' Trevor says again. 'I'm an old man, older than I

243

ever expected to get. Every second I'm vertical is a victory, way I see it. But I ain't winning this fight. No sucker ever does and only true suckers don't accept it.'

'I'm not sure if you're purely pragmatic or a nihilist.'

'Maybe I'm neither. You consider that? Maybe I'm just me.'

I stop the car when I see another payphone, this one at a rest area off the highway. I call Leo's cell, and just like before I get his voicemail. I don't leave a message.

Maybe he's out of battery, I think.

I feed in more coins, calling home. I'm not sure why but there's a feeling. Is it hope? Is it delusion?

Three rings and a woman says, 'Talhoffer residence, who's calling?'

I say, 'Who's this?'

'Jem?' she asks.

'Who is this?' I ask again.

'Jem, this is Rusty. The chief of police.'

I wasn't expecting her to answer. I'm not sure who I was expecting to answer if not Leo, but now it makes sense it would be Rusty. Who else would it be?

I take a breath. 'I expect you've got a few questions you would like to ask me.'

'If there was an award for understatement you've just took gold.'

'I'm scared, Rusty. I'm really scared.'

'I think you should come home, Jem. Or to my office if you prefer. I'm good with either. But you need to come see me. Sooner the better.'

'I can't do that,' I tell her.

'Why can't you?'

'People are trying to kill me, Rusty.'

'That's why you need to turn yourself in. I can protect you.

No one's coming through me to get to you, I can promise you that.'

I'm looking around in case there's cruisers creeping up on me. 'I tried coming to you already, remember? And now I'm here.'

There's a pause before Rusty says, 'Why don't you tell me what happened?'

'Wilks and Messer,' I begin, 'they're not who they say they are. They tried to kill me.'

'Go on,' she says.

'They're looking for something of Leo's. When they took me back home they were looking for it and I ... Leo called. I warned him. They tried to ... Messer's dead.'

'I know he's dead, Jem,' Rusty says in a flat monotone. 'I'm looking at his corpse right now. And it's a real ugly corpse. He's got several bullets in him and a pair of scissors sticking out of his neck. Makes me a little queasy, I'm not embarrassed to say. In all my years in uniform I've never seen anything like it.'

'Is Wilks alive?'

There's a silence. She's not sure how to respond.

'She is,' she says. 'She's here with me.'

'And that's exactly why I can't come back. She'll kill me.'

'Wilks is on your side,' Rusty says.

I laugh. A bitter, sarcastic laugh. 'Then she has you fooled like she fooled me.'

'Let's all sit down and talk this through. You can tell me your side of the story. You can explain your side of the story and I'll listen. I promise I'll listen. I'm a good listener, Jem. Real good.'

'They tried to kill me,' I tell her. 'Carlson saved me.'

'Carlson,' Rusty says.

'Yes, Carlson.'

'Where is he now? With you?'

'He was,' I tell her. 'But he lied to me too. He's ... I don't know where he is now. He's out there somewhere. You need to find him before he finds me.'

Rusty says, 'I'm doing everything I can to help you, Jem. But you need to help me too. You need to turn yourself in before this gets any more out of control. There's a dead man in your house, Jem. There's a dead man in your house and you're on the run. You've fled the scene of a crime. That's not okay.'

'I'm not on the run,' I tell her. 'I mean, I'm not on the run from you.'

Rusty's tone becomes grave, serious. 'You're an accessory to murder, Jem, and every second you're out there and not here makes it look worse for you and makes it harder for me to help you.'

Are they looking for me right now? Has Rusty sent out an APB or whatever it's called? I take a deep breath and try to silence those questions. Worrying, despite being my number one skill, isn't going to help me now.

'*I've done nothing wrong,*' I yell down the phone.

'I want to believe you,' Rusty says. 'But you need to turn yourself in if you want me to help you because at this moment it's your word versus Wilks', and who would you pay more attention to if you were me?'

She's right and I know it, and hate it. I hate that I can't do anything about it right now. Yet if I turn myself in, tell my side of the story, I lose control. I trap myself. I give all the power to Wilks.

'Whatever she has told you is a lie. She's not a good guy, Rusty. She might be an FBI agent but she's dirty. She's corrupt. She's trying to turn you against me.'

Rusty says, 'She doesn't work for the FBI, Jem. She's from National Security.'

'Is she? Well, she was FBI this morning. I wonder what she'll be tomorrow.'

'There are national security concerns at work here. Sensitive matters. She's explained why she couldn't tell you the full story earlier today and I've been thorough in checking out her claims. They're legitimate, I assure you.'

'Messer tried to kill me, Rusty. He was going to strangle me to death. I'm not making it up.'

'How is Carlson involved?'

She says 'Carlson' in a way that makes me think she doesn't believe he even exists.

'Carlson is the one who saved me from Wilks and Messer. I'd be dead if it weren't for him.'

'So he's been helping you? Is that right?'

I hesitate. 'No. I mean, he was. But ... I ran from him. I can't trust him. He's not who he says he is either. He told me he knows Leo but it was a lie.'

'Uh huh,' Rusty says.

I realise I'm sounding paranoid, erratic. Insane. I can't make Rusty understand over the phone. It's my word against Wilks', and she's a stone-cold liar. She's a professional liar. Whether she's FBI, NSA, both or neither, she knows what she's doing. She's got this all worked out.

I'm making it up as I go along.

'I'll prove it,' I tell her. 'I'll prove all of this.'

'I believe you,' she says in return. 'Just come find me and I'll listen with open ears. They're like jugs, Jem, and they know truth when they hear it. I swear I will give you every chance to tell me what happened, your way.'

'I know you will, Rusty. I know you'll listen to my every word and I also know it won't make a single bit of difference unless I can back up my claims with proof.'

'Jem, please listen—'

'No, Rusty, you listen. I'm not coming in. I'm not going to sit down and talk it through because you've already made your mind up. I can't change it, can I?'

'I'll try to understand. Why don't we start from there and see where we end up?'

'I'm going to get proof, Rusty. I'm going to clear my name and I'm going to protect my husband.'

'Have you heard from Leo?'

'Not since this afternoon,' I tell her. 'Not since I warned him about Wilks and Messer.'

There's a long pause; I think Rusty is talking to Wilks or whoever and has her hand over the receiver.

Then she says, 'Do you know where Leo is now?'

'No, I have no idea. He was at the airport when I spoke to him. He was supposed to be on a plane to England but it was grounded. He—'

'Jem,' Rusty says in a soft tone, 'Leo wasn't booked on any flight to England.'

'What are you talking about? I don't understand.'

She's silent for a moment. I grow uneasy, thinking about what she might say next. Is this a trick?

'Jem,' Rusty says, gentle, sympathetic. 'I told you I'm thorough, didn't I? Well, I've checked flight records. I've spoken to airliners. I've spoken to the staff at every airport in driving distance. Leo was booked on no flight. No flight has been grounded. All the planes to England left on time and Leo was on none of them because he wasn't booked to be on any in the first place.'

I stare out into the night. 'But he said—'

'He lied to you, Jem. Your husband's been lying to you for a very long time.'

'What are you talking about?'

'I'm afraid I can't say any more over the phone. You're going to have to come in if you want the truth.'

'Nice try,' I say, and hang up.

12:32 a.m.

I've never enjoyed driving at night. It's too easy to get focused on the darkness, the isolation. If I have to, I keep the radio on so that song lyrics push my thoughts away and I don't feel the overwhelming urge to look over my shoulder to check that no one is hiding in the back. Trevor is driving now, so I'm slumped in the passenger seat, tired but unable to sleep. He's keeping quiet so as not to disturb me. He's such a sweet man. The only person who hasn't lied to me, hasn't tried to trick me. I have no idea how I'll ever be able to repay him for all he's done.

I will, though. Somehow. When – if – this is finally over.

I'm trying to find a solution to a problem that didn't exist yesterday. I'm trying to find an answer to a question I'm not sure how to ask.

Was Rusty lying about Leo, or has Leo been lying to me?

I don't want to believe that Rusty can't be trusted any more than I want to believe that I can't trust Leo.

I talk it through with Trevor. I tell him everything Rusty said, all my thoughts and worries, and he is quiet for a long moment after I've finished. He looks both contemplative and wise and I want his input. I want to hear his opinion. I can't trust myself at the best of times and I need someone calm, someone sane.

'Well?' I say. 'What do you think?'

'I'm not sure my opinion holds any weight here.'

'It does, Trevor. That's why I want you to tell me what you think. Rusty could be lying to me, couldn't she? She could be trying to get me to turn myself in by telling me what she thinks will lure me into custody.'

He exhales a big lungful of air, shaking his head the entire time. 'The chief has always struck me as a righteous woman. In the traditional sense, I mean.'

'Sure,' I say. 'She's straight as an arrow.'

'But I've never had any reason to see her at work, so to speak.'

'You're saying she thinks I'm a criminal, maybe even a murderer, so she's not going to be truthful with me?'

'It's a possibility, sure. What does your gut tell you? It usually knows best.'

'My gut? My gut tells me that this whole situation is so messed up it can't be real and I just need to wake up and everything will be okay again.'

'On second thoughts maybe don't listen to your gut.'

'Come on, Trevor, I'm lost in the wilderness here. I need an outside perspective. I need some guidance or I'm never going to find my way home again. Literally.'

'Then I think Rusty would tell you the truth as best as she knows it.'

'So, you're saying she could be mistaken?'

He grunts. 'Don't go putting words into my mouth. Only you know your husband, Jem. I'm just along for the ride.'

'I'm sorry,' I say. 'I shouldn't be looking to you for answers. That's not fair. You should be tucked up in bed right now.'

'He's your husband,' Trevor says. 'You love him. Up until this morning everything was right as rain. You don't want your whole world turned upside down again when it's been turned upside down already. I can't even begin to tell you how sorry I am.'

'Technically,' I say, 'if it's been turned upside down and gets turned upside down a second time, then it would be put right way up again.'

He makes a noise, a low growl of discontent from the bottom of his throat.

'Sorry,' I say.

'You don't need to apologise every five seconds.'

'I can't help it.'

'Are you Canadian?'

I put my head into my hands.

'Ah, come on,' Trevor says. 'Being Canadian isn't that bad.'

I rub at my eyes. 'Is this what my life is going to be like now? Never being able to trust a single thing anyone says to me?'

'I'd like to tell you otherwise,' he says.

'But you can't?'

He shakes his head. 'I won't. I won't because you're in a hole, Jem, and there are people dangling ropes into that hole and promising to haul you out. But, pick the wrong rope and they can just as easily let go of it when you're halfways up. Don't trust anything you can't see with your own eyes, that you can't touch with your own hands. The only way you're going to get through this is by trusting yourself.'

We drive in silence for a while.

My pulse spikes whenever I see a set of headlights behind or ahead. Light is my enemy. Darkness is my friend.

Leo's warehouse isn't far now. I've been there once before, years ago when he first acquired it. He was an entrepreneur, proud of his achievements, and I was proud of him. I think I still am.

I hope I still will be at the end.

The warehouse is nestled in a business park on the outskirts of NYC. I'm not sure of the address but I remember how to get there. I can picture the building. I can picture the buildings nearby. I've told Trevor to drive towards the city and I'll direct him from there.

'I don't have much call to go to the big city usually,' he told me.

'We're not going to NYC, Trevor.'

'Have even less reason to go there.'

'When was the last time you left the state?'

'Probably before you were born.'

If nothing else I'm unravelling the mystery that is Trevor.

The highway is a ghost road at this time of night. Just the occasional haulage truck. Every regular person is in bed. I miss my bed so much. I want to be engulfed in my duvet.

I'm wary of Rusty's troopers scouring the highways looking for me. God, I'm a fugitive. They think I'm a criminal. Am I? I'm sure I've broken some laws. I'm sure Wilks has ensured Rusty believes I've broken others. I see no cruisers. I hear no sirens. If they're out looking for me then it's not this far south.

It's approaching one in the morning by the time we reach the business park. There's a traffic island before the in-road and I can't quite remember if the soulless piece of modern art at the centre of the island has always been there. Either way, it's hideous. A barely formed lump of metal representing something I cannot possibly comprehend. I'm sure Trevor thinks the same. I don't ask him, though. I'm too focused on what we might find.

The business park is dead at this hour. I'm sure there is some activity in some of the large buildings, but for the most part it's quiet and there are no signs of life. I don't see a single person. Good. I don't want to be seen if it can be helped.

Leo's unit is harder to find than I expected. In my head I could picture it well, but I didn't account for the number of meandering roads that lead me through a myriad of twists and turns, and I get lost.

'Haven't we driven by here before?'

'Yes, Trevor. Well observed.'

Did we go right here, or left? Are we going down the same road or do the units just look similar?

At last, I find where I'm supposed to be going. I recognise a big square building that used to house a start-up tech firm but now I see it's been converted into storage units. Unbeatable prices, apparently.

Two units further on is Leo's warehouse.

'There it is,' I say to Trevor after we've passed.

'Then why didn't you tell me before I'd driven straight by it?'

'In case.'

'In case of what?'

'They might be watching it?'

'Who might be watching it?'

I frown his way. 'Wilks. Carlson. Rusty. Whoever . . .'

'How would they have beat us here?'

'I don't know,' I snap. 'I'm being cautious. Even if no one got here first, I don't want to park outside and advertise the fact that we're here.'

'Hmm. Smart thinking.'

'I have my moments.'

Finding a place to park isn't quite as easy as I would have liked. I don't want to be right outside Leo's unit and I don't want to be a significant distance away either because on foot we'll be exposed and if we need to get out of here with haste, we won't be able to. I'm the Goldilocks of parking requirements.

I tell Trevor to pull on to a strip of open space before the offices of some financial firm. There's gaudy signage that makes me think they provide quick loans to poor people in return for exorbitant interest rates. I feel zero guilt for trespassing on their property.

We're far enough away that no CCTV cameras will get a shot of us. There's bound to be a security guard in front of monitors somewhere. I don't want to give him a reason to come investigate what we're up to.

Trevor turns off the engine, and the only sound I can hear is my breathing.

Trevor says, 'Are you ready?'

'No, but let's do it anyway.'

12:57 a.m.

The night is cold. I can feel it on my exposed skin and for some reason it doesn't bother me. I'm impervious to its touch. I walk slow because Trevor walks slow. He's an old man, after all. I feel bad for making him walk any distance, least of all on a cold night like this. He makes no complaints about either. I look at him, wondering why he's even with me on this wild adventure. He's known me less than a day. We're strangers. For all he knows I could be a criminal. I could, in fact, be crazy.

He notices me looking. 'What is it?'

'Why are you here, Trevor? Why are you backing me up? You don't know me. You have no skin in this game.'

'I would argue otherwise, young lady,' he says back. 'The moment I stopped my truck to let you in I became responsible for you.'

'Are you talking about chivalry?'

'That sounds a little too European for my liking. I prefer to think of it as good old-fashioned American decency.'

'Whatever it is, I'm glad of it. I don't think I could do this on my own.'

'There you go again with that TV talk self-doubt nonsense. You are doing this on your own. I'm just a bystander.'

'I'm not sure the authorities will see it like that if I'm charged with a felony. I think they might consider you an active participant. Aiding and abetting a fugitive or whatever.'

'You're a fugitive?'

'Rusty says so. I did stab a guy with a pair of scissors, and shoot him.'

'Self-defence. No jury in the land would find you guilty of any crime in that. We may be circling the moral drain but we haven't entered the sewer quite yet. Besides, if they want to throw me behind bars and give me three squares a day on the government's dime then I'll say thank you very much.'

'I don't believe that last part for a second,' I tell him. 'You're trying to make me feel better, and I appreciate it.'

He grumbles to himself. 'I'm doing nothing of the sort.'

I gesture. 'Here we are.'

There's space for maybe half a dozen cars in front of Leo's warehouse, set back from the sidewalk by a narrow grass verge topped with flowers. I wonder who tends them, whether they're the responsibility of the business park or the individual companies. Does Leo pay someone to do it? If I don't know such a simple thing about his life, his business, how can I be surprised by everything that's happened today? Rusty told me that Leo's been lying to me for a very long time but what if I've simply failed to see what's obvious?

Is my husband a stranger and I've never noticed?

I take a breath, trying to settle my anxiety.

'What's wrong?' Trevor asks.

'TV talk stuff.'

'Sometimes a bad day—'

'Yeah, yeah, I know.'

I feel exposed approaching the unit. The space for cars is small yet feels a mile wide. There's plenty of ambient light from street lamps and the units themselves, but the shadows are dense and plentiful. There are numerous places for someone to hide. I try and reassure myself that what Trevor said is right: neither Wilks nor Carlson could conceivably have got here ahead of us.

But what if there are more enemies I don't yet know about?

Both Wilks and Carlson could have backup. Either could have arranged for that backup to be waiting for us.

I look up towards the warehouse roof.

Perfect spot for a sniper.

I shake my head. What do I know about snipers?

Nothing, it seems, because no shots ring out. Even moving at Trevor's snail's pace, we make it across the empty asphalt alive. If not for the very real danger I know I'm in I could laugh at the ridiculousness of thinking there could be a sniper on the roof.

'Didn't want to say it beforehand,' Trevor says, 'but I was a little scared there might have been a sniper on the roof.'

I bat him on the arm with the back of my hand. '*I know, right?*'

There's a large rolling metal door for vehicles on the front of the building and a regular entrance to one side of it. There could be others on the side or round back, but if there are, I didn't use them.

'You've said nothing about keys,' Trevor says as we near the entrance.

'That's because I don't have any.'

'Then how are we supposed to—'

I point. 'Key code.'

'And you're sure you know it? You said you haven't been here in years.'

'Of course I know it, Trevor. The code's my birthday.'

There's an electronic entry system and I tap the keys with my six-digit birthday date.

Nothing happens.

Trevor's mouth opens.

'Yes,' I say before he can say it. 'Leo's changed the code. Maybe it's his birthday.'

I try it. Nothing happens.

'What are we going to do now?'

I give Trevor a sly look. 'We're going to break in.'

'How?' he says.

'I ... I have no idea, but how hard can it be? It's not like burglars are geniuses, are they? If they were, they wouldn't be burglars.'

'True enough, I suppose. But they at least know what they're doing.'

'Don't stamp on my dreams, Trevor. Give me a little positivity, okay? Some encouragement. I could use a little boost right about now.'

'You want me to encourage you to be a thief?'

'We're not going to steal anything. We're just going to break in.'

'I believe in you,' he says, deadpan.

'Is that really the best you can do?'

'Maybe I could use some encouragement too.'

I sigh. 'You don't have to look so pleased with yourself.'

He nods. 'I don't, but I want to. How's the breaking in going?'

'I'm still working out the details. Don't suppose you saw a crowbar in Carlson's car, did you?'

He shakes his head. 'I did not.' He gestures. 'There's going to be an alarm, you know.'

'Yeah. I'm really hoping it's the same code as the alarm at home.'

'And if it's not?'

'Then we'll be sprinting back to the car.'

'Not sure if you've noticed but my running days are well and truly behind me.'

'Good point,' I say. 'In which case I'll run back to the car and come pick you up.'

He grunts, pleased. 'Much better plan.'

I examine the door. It's made of frosted glass, so I stride back out across the parking spaces and scale the little grass verge to where the flowers grow. The flowerbed has a border composed of bricks. Half-bricks, to be exact.

I prise one out from the soil. It's a good fit for my palm. A good heft to it.

Trevor is watching me with a quizzical expression as I return to him. He looks at the half-brick in my hand. 'What are you going to do with that?'

'This,' I say, and throw it at the frosted glass door.

It bounces off the pane, straight back at me. I leap out of its path.

'Safety glass,' Trevor says. 'I could have warned you if you had—'

He stops. He stops because I'm murdering him with my eyes.

He reaches down and picks up the brick. It's not easy for him and he winces as he stands back upright again.

He throws the half-brick up a few inches into the air, catching it again.

'You know, this can't break safety glass but I bet you a shiny nickel there's some windows on this building somewhere.'

There's a glint in his eye. 'And them windows will be good old regular glass. Good old regular breakable glass.'

'There you go,' I say. 'That's the kind of encouragement I was talking about.' I take the brick from him. 'Let's go make a mess.'

12:59 a.m.

Rusty is dead tired after leaving the crime scene. The weed hasn't helped, of course. Thanks to lots of fine coffee and generous squirts of eye drops no one seems to have noticed the town police chief is stoned. Only a little, because nothing counteracts marijuana's aptitude for mellowing her out like having to hide that fact on official business. She should have just ignored the call from Sabrowski, she tells herself. Only there was that gnawing sense of doom she couldn't ignore. Maybe that was the marijuana talking – a little old-school paranoia – but she hasn't been herself since the two government folk strode into her office with all sorts of crazy talk.

She peers at her eyes in the rear-view and decides to give them both another squirt of wash. After blinking away the excess, she pushes open the driver's door and shuffles out of the seat of her cruiser.

Rusty has parked near to the diner, but not too near. She doesn't want to walk any further than she has to, but she wanted to be far enough away to take a minute to compose herself without being watched.

The diner's lights look far too bright for Rusty's liking, she notes as she nears.

Inside, they're even worse. She squints and frowns, resisting the urge to put on her sunglasses or use a hand like a sun visor. There are no eye drops powerful enough to disguise that level of intemperance.

She wonders why it's an all-night establishment when so few customers seem to require its services. There are a couple of truckers sitting on their lonesome – not locals – and a college-age young woman who looks drunk as a skunk.

Rusty approaches the only waitress working this shift.

'Hey Dana, how's your evening treating you?'

'Is it still evening when it's after midnight?'

'Great question,' Rusty says. 'Answers on a postcard.'

'On a what?'

'Forget it,' Rusty says. 'Just something they used to say on kids' TV back in the day.'

'Which day?'

Rusty keeps her lips tight for a moment. 'You called?'

'Sure did,' Dana says, ushering Rusty out of earshot of the young woman, whose drunkenness makes her curiosity obvious. 'Had a little encounter an hour ago that I figured you'd want to know about.'

'I'm listening.'

'It was quiet like it is now. You always get the same kinds of people come in here in the middle of the night and I've been doing this piece-of-shit job long enough so I know them all.'

'I bet you do.'

'I don't mean by name,' Dana explains. 'I mean the kind of people they are.'

'I know what you meant. Continue, please.'

'So, given what I just said, I noticed right away when these two, a man and a woman, came in and sat down. He orders a bacon burger and she wants a grilled cheese, but the way her lips are all tight like this' – Dana demonstrates – 'as she orders tells me she doesn't really want it. Like she's under duress.'

'He was forcing her?'

'No, no, not like that. You know, she's too good for it.'

Rusty pinches the skin between her eyebrows. 'You called about a grilled cheese sandwich?'

Dana doesn't appreciate Rusty's lack of patience. 'No, I did not. I'm just giving you some background colour.'

'It's late, Dana. I'm tired. Could you do me a favour and skip the colour? I'm only here personally because right now my department is stretched thin. Like, crêpe thin. Keep the colour in your head, though. Maybe it'll come in handy afterwards.'

'Fine,' Dana says, sharp of tone. 'That skinny officer of yours, Sabrowski, came in for his usual. Sat right there by the door like he always does and tries not to watch me any more than would be considered gentlemanly. So, this woman asks me to do her a favour because she doesn't want him to see them leave for some reason or another. I tell her to give me a hundred per cent tip and I'll see what I can do.'

Must have happened right before Sabrowski was told to haul his ass back to work.

'And you did it?' Rusty asks once Dana has finished.

Dana nods. 'I most certainly did. I gave your boy a little extra attention and he didn't see them go. He didn't see anything but little ole me.'

'Why would you do that?'

'Why wouldn't I?'

264

Rusty doesn't answer. 'Tell me why you decided to contact me.'

'Because I knew she had done something if she wanted to slip away unnoticed,' Dana explains. 'I didn't know what, of course. I figured she hadn't paid her taxes or whatever.'

'That's not a matter for the police, Dana.'

'I apologise for not being a professor of law, but like I said that was at first. I didn't have a whole lot of time to consider the rights and wrongs of what I was doing. It was only when I was talking to that skinny trooper of yours and he had to rush off because there had been a shooting—'

'Sabrowski discussed the details with you?'

Dana backtracks. 'No, not exactly. I inferred.'

'You inferred?'

'A waitress can't infer?'

Rusty says, 'So, you put two and two together that the woman who asked you to distract him was involved in the aforementioned shooting?'

'I most certainly did,' Dana says, shoulders squared with pride.

'And then you called me nearly an hour later?'

The shoulders loosen a little. 'Well, I wasn't wholly sure.'

'I see.'

Dana's hands find her hip bones. 'Am I in trouble?'

'For aiding and abetting a fugitive?'

Dana doesn't detect the sarcasm. 'Am I?'

Rusty lets her off easy. 'No, Dana, you're not in trouble because by some cosmic miracle you have me as a town police chief and not some hardass. But you really shouldn't have helped her.'

Dana pouts.

'You did the right thing by calling, though,' Rusty adds. 'Did they do anything else while they were here? Did they speak to anyone? Anyone sit down with them?'

'Kept to themselves but I believe she may have used the payphone.'

Rusty's eyebrows arch. 'That one on the wall by the restrooms?'

'That's the only one we got,' Dana says. 'I forgot it's even there.'

'Has anyone else used it since?'

'Nuh, uh, and I don't remember the last time anyone used it before her.'

Rusty nods. 'Did you happen to see the vehicle they were driving?'

'I did, but all pickups look the same to me.'

'Of course they do,' Rusty says. 'Colour?'

Dana shrugs. 'Blue, black, red, brown ... I didn't pay attention.'

Rusty gestures to the lot outside and the highway beyond. 'Did you happen to see which way they turned when they exited?'

Dana thinks.

'Did they turn left or did they turn right?'

'I believe,' Dana says, 'that they turned right.'

'How sure are you?'

'Sure enough to say so.'

Rusty asks, 'What about the man she was with? Did he say anything?'

'He said my coffee was the best he'd ever tasted.'

'Did he say anything not related to your coffee?'

Dana thinks, lips pressed together. 'No. I don't believe he did.'

'Can you describe him to me? White? Black?'

'He was white. Old, but normal.'

Leo's not old but he could be in disguise, Rusty thinks.

'Did you get a name? Leo, perhaps?'

Dana shakes her head. 'Perhaps he was using a false name.'

'Did he give you any name?'

'No.'

'Then how would you know if he was using a false name or not?'

Dana frowns. 'I believe that's your job, not mine.'

Rusty shows Dana a photograph of Leo. A printout that she unfolds from her pocket. 'He look anything like this?'

Dana plucks the printout from Rusty's fingers and gives it a long look. Rusty leaves her to it while she inserts coins into the payphone and hits redial, memorising the number that comes up on the little screen.

'Well?' Rusty asks, returning to Dana.

'Not even a little bit.'

'Seemed to take you a while to be sure about that.'

Dana shakes her head. 'But you'd have to be dead from the waist down not to appreciate such a fine specimen.'

'Uh huh,' Rusty says as she takes the printout back. 'If you think of anything else please give me a call. And if they happen to come back, don't make any more deals.'

Dana waits until Rusty is near the door before calling out, 'That would depend on how much they pay me.'

Rusty leaves the diner, feeling the icy pinch of the night air when she steps outside. Rusty, who is prone to perspiring, appreciates a refreshing breeze. She makes the most of it as she gazes at the highway, silent and black at this hour.

Right is south. South is NYC and all the airports. Could be that Jem Talhoffer is aiming to hide in the big city or attempting to flee by plane? The latter would seem a foolish option, but fugitives have been known to make worse mistakes. On the run is constant pressure, relentless tension. No one operates well under those conditions. The scared are also the dumb.

Only something tells Rusty that Jem Talhoffer isn't dumb.

And who is her travelling companion if it isn't Carlson? Could be an innocent bystander she's pulled into her schemes. Which makes sense. She's less obvious as one half of a pair. Or maybe he's more involved? Rusty isn't sure. But if they came to the diner together and left together that suggests they're more than strangers.

Rusty calls in the new information and tells Zeke, 'Get me the address this number belongs to.'

She hears Zeke tapping keys.

'Warehouse outside of NYC,' he says, then gives her the address.

'That's what I thought,' Rusty says, flipping shut her phone.

She's used a flip phone since for ever. Smartphones scare her with all those fiddly apps. Touchscreens terrify her. She's seen Sabrowski's skinny fingers dance like a pianist's on those things and Rusty knows she's never going to be able to do the same in a million years. She doesn't want to spend all that money just so all her messages come out as gobbledygook on account of her tapping three letters at once. So, the flip phone it is, despite her troopers taunting her at every opportunity. She gets her own back on a frequent basis every time they go into a panic because their batteries are low. Boys and toys.

Pulling out of the lot, she almost heads right, almost heads to the warehouse, but who is she kidding?

She's tired. She's beat. She should be in bed.

Someone else can check it out.

1:07 a.m.

It's not quite as simple as I thought to get in, because there are no windows reachable from the ground. There are, however, some that are accessible after I've clambered up on top of a dumpster round the back of Leo's warehouse. Trevor watches me with no attempt to hide the apprehension in his expression. He winces and sucks air between his teeth.

'You're not helping,' I tell him once I've got something resembling secure footing.

'I don't think I'm trying to.'

'Just pretend, Trevor. Pretend I'm Spider-Man.'

'Who?'

'Jesus, Trevor, where have you been for the last few decades?'

'Not taking the Lord's name in vain, that's where I've been.'

I'm suitably chastised. 'Sorry.'

'That sorry I'll accept.'

Dumpsters are not designed for someone to stand on, I'm discovering. The wheels don't help. Neither does the rounded lid that's not only hard to balance on but also feels as if it might collapse in on itself at any moment. Somehow, I'm managing. I have one palm braced against the wall for support and the other clutching the half-brick. The window is about in line with my shoulders and it looks like a regular window that should collapse without too much effort.

'Do you think they have security patrols around here?' I call down to Trevor.

'If they have, they've failed to notice a couple of people who clearly don't belong here acting suspicious so I wouldn't worry about them.'

'Good point,' I say. 'Here goes nothing.'

I'm holding the brick with my fingertips and I sort of punch the window with it – an exploratory punch with little force because I'm nervous and unsure how much strength I need to utilise.

Crack.

The brick goes straight through, along with my hand.

'Nice job,' Trevor calls to me.

I have to be careful withdrawing my hand because it's surrounded by shards of glass ready to slit my wrist. A few pieces fall away but I'm uninjured. Not so much as a graze. Maybe burglary is my lost calling.

A few more careful hits with the brick and the window pane is nothing but glittering pieces. I knock out the whole thing and spend some extra time clearing out any remnants on the lower strip of the frame so I don't slice and dice myself when I climb through.

I'm not sure what to do with the brick so I toss it towards Trevor and say, 'Catch.'

He may be slow on his feet but Trevor snatches it out of the air one-handed without so much as a blink.

'What am I supposed to do with this?' he asks.

I shrug. 'I don't know. Keep it. It's a souvenir.'

He says nothing but looks at me with one of his wide-eyed, head-shaking looks. I ignore it. I'm on a roll. I place my hands on the window frame, hike up one foot so it joins them, and push and pull my way through the gap where the window pane used to be so I drop down on the other side feet first.

Glass crunches underfoot.

I'm in an empty room. A featureless cube with nothing but a broken window to give it any character. Part of the office space that flanks the main warehouse. Unused because Leo has no staff. He pays contractors as and when he needs to bring in wine and ship it out again. As I understand his business, that's not something that happens on a regular basis. It tends to be substantial shipments now and again. He couldn't afford to pay proper employees and there wouldn't be enough work to justify them even if he could.

No alarm has sounded.

I'm not sure why. A little luck, perhaps. There's just enough light from outside for me to see. I'm not sure if that will be the case further into the building. I don't want to turn on the interior lights and advertise I'm here.

I cross the room and open the door, stepping out on to a metal walkway that overlooks the main warehouse space.

There are transparent sections to the roof above so I can still see enough to know as I look down that something is very wrong.

The walkway continues to the right and there are more doors to more offices. Left, there are steep, narrow stairs that lead to the warehouse floor. I descend and find a door to open so I can let Trevor inside.

'Hey,' I call to him, trying a couple of times to get the right volume. I don't want to shout loud enough for anyone else

271

to hear and end up making just enough noise to get Trevor's attention.

'Well done,' he says, nearing.

'Anything to report?'

He shakes his head. 'Didn't hear or see anything.'

I say, 'Good,' and stand aside to allow him to pass.

I close the door behind Trevor, who takes a few paces into the warehouse to look around. He pivots on the spot, looking high and low to get the full picture.

'Where's all the wine?' he says.

'I wish I could answer that.'

The warehouse is empty.

There are several rows of industrial-scale shelving units and not a single bottle of wine on any of them.

'Didn't you say your husband is a wine merchant?'

'I did,' I say. 'He is. Was.'

Trevor looks at me for answers.

'If I knew, I would tell you. But I don't. I don't know why the warehouse is empty. I don't know where all the wine is. I don't know what the hell's going on.'

'Does he have another property?' Trevor is reaching and we both know it. 'Perhaps he moved his stock elsewhere.'

'I very much doubt it, Trevor. Why would he need this place if he has another? And if he has another warehouse with all his wine in there, why hasn't he told me about it?'

Trevor shrugs. 'I have no idea. Could be that business has been bad and he didn't want to worry you.'

I'm silent. I don't know what to say. I stare at the empty shelving units, enough for dozens of cases of wine, hundreds and hundreds of bottles. Why are they empty?

'Hey,' Trevor says, seeing how anxious I am. 'There might still be a good reason for all this.'

'I don't see how.' I approach the stairs. 'But whatever the answer, we're not going to find it down here among empty shelves.' I ascend. 'How are your knees?'

Trevor grumbles as he heads towards me. 'Better than the respect you show to your elders.' He climbs up. 'Did you disable the alarm?'

'There isn't one.'

Trevor points to motion sensors high on the walls. 'Yeah, there is. Why is it off?'

'Huh,' I breathe. 'Well, it's not like there's anything to steal.'

The weight of what I don't know about Leo is taking a huge toll. I'm still holding on to hope that there is some explanation for all of this, some innocent misunderstanding that has spiralled out of control. It's feeling like a fool's hope right now more than ever.

I realise I'm rubbing my palms together.

My hands and fingers are tingling. Pins and needles, anxiety addition. If I can generate enough friction, enough heat, maybe they won't—

'*Dammit.*'

Trevor asks, 'What's wrong?'

My hands have seized up. My fingers are paralysed, half-curled. Tendons bulge out through the skin of the back of my hands. I can feel the hypertensive muscles in my wrists and all the way up to my elbows.

Not really painful, but frustrating.

Infuriating.

'I just have to wait it out,' I tell Trevor.

'Can't you just relax your hands?'

'*No.*'

It comes out more as a snarl than a word. A guttural, primitive response. I don't need Trevor's belittlement right now adding to my problems. I'm pre-emptively angry with him as I expect some dismissive retort but I'm surprised that he doesn't respond like that. His brow is furrowed and his eyes are narrow as they stare at my hands. He can see that this is something real. Even he can't pretend a physical symptom is all in my mind.

To my surprise, my fingers begin to relax. My forearms loosen.

'That was quick,' I say. 'Usually lasts much longer.'

'What was different this time?'

'I turned my anger on to you instead of me. Seems to have done the trick quite nicely.'

'Happy to help.'

A *fool's hope*, I think.

Even if Leo isn't a money launderer, even if he hasn't been an informant for the FBI, there has been too much deception, too many lies, for us to go back to our normal life.

If the person you care about the most in this world can hide so much from you, what does that say about your relationship?

'Well, *what do you think?*'

I *wasn't sure what to think. The warehouse seemed huge to me. It seemed cavernous. I couldn't imagine why we needed so much space. Twelve thousand square feet, he told me.*

Leo *said, 'Don't keep me in suspense.'*

He *was giving me a tour of the empty building and seemed like an excited schoolboy showing off a new toy. He was looking for similar levels of excitement from me but I found it hard to care in the same way.*

'The *shelving units are part of the lease.*'

'It's *almost too good to be true.*'

There *was nothing to see, no reason for the tour, but I was happy he was happy. The business was growing. He wasn't just recommending wine but selling it too, sourcing it himself and importing it and delivering it to restaurants and hotels.*

He *needed space.*

I *was craning my neck to look at the ceiling high above.* 'It's *just so ... big.*'

'We have to dream big,' he told me. 'We're committed now, so why limit ourselves? Why put a glass ceiling above our heads before we've found out how far we can grow? Don't you want us to grow?'

'Yeah, yeah,' I said. 'But we're risking so much. The lease is a killer of an outlay. It's such a commitment.'

My words were not putting him off in the slightest. If anything I was making him more animated and enthusiastic because he was determined for me to see this his way.

'This is who we are, Jem. We're entrepreneurs. Risking is what we do. No one gets rich without taking chances.'

'I like the way I said "risks" and you say "chances" to make them seem less dangerous.'

'What's the worst that can happen?'

My eyebrows pinched closer. 'You know exactly what can happen. Everything is on the line.'

'Bet big to win big.'

I rubbed his arm. 'I thought you were the sensible one and I was the hot head?'

He smiled that perfect smile of his. 'I guess you rubbed off on me.'

I gave him a look.

He showed his palms. 'Accidental innuendo, I swear.'

'Then why do you look so pleased with yourself?'

He gestured to the warehouse, empty now but in his imagination filled to bursting with possibilities.

'I'm pleased with this, with us. With how far we've come.'

I glanced around at the cavernous space. 'Is this not too much, too fast?'

He didn't answer.

I said, 'How much is enough?'

The question took him back. Not because he saw it as a

challenge but because he hadn't thought about it before. He hadn't stopped to question his ambitions, and that worried me. I needed to know he was reliable if this was going to work out.

'I'll know when we get there,' he said.

'That's not an answer. That's not even close.'

I was annoyed then. Not only had I not received the reassurance I sought but I was also questioning the sense of this entire endeavour.

'I grew up poor,' Leo said. 'You know that. Nothing has ever been easy for me. But I never used that as an excuse. I did everything I could to pull myself out of that poverty. Did I always do the smart thing? No. Did I never make a mistake? Of course not. I made plenty. I don't want sympathy any more than I want praise.'

'Yeah, yeah. Stop beating around the bush. How much money is enough?'

He looked me square in the eye, intense and unblinking.

'What I mean is, I'm always going to want more. When I was a kid I was happy with enough money to buy a new comic book instead of stealing it from the store. Ten years ago I was happy to pay the rent on time. What I mean is that we change, don't we? Whatever we have will one day not seem like enough. I'm not trying to dodge your question. In fact, I think I'm being as honest as I possibly can be. However well this works out and however much money we make it's not going to be enough one day in the future and then I'm going to want more. For me, for us.'

I think about my travelling years and chipping steadily away at my inheritance until I was penniless. I didn't appreciate the comfortable life my parents had raised me into until it was gone. I wanted to be comfortable again. I had to trust him.

'I trust you,' I said.

He smiled. 'Rome seems a long time ago, doesn't it?'

'A lifetime ago.'

He took my shoulders and massaged them. 'We can do this. I wouldn't say it if I didn't believe it.'

1:15 a.m.

As well as the empty room I broke into, there's a meeting room, a kitchen, restrooms and a main office hub. Only the latter shows any signs of life. The other rooms seem as though they have never been used. Or at least used so infrequently as to barely count. With just Leo running things, I'm not surprised the meeting room hasn't seen any use. Much of his work is done abroad or on the road. If he's not away he's with me.

I'm telling myself a lot of things, I realise. I'm trying to fill in the gaps and explain away what might otherwise add to a picture of a man I know less and less.

The office hub has room for a couple of workstations and Leo's office is separated off behind a glass wall. There's no lock on the door and I push it open. It's a little square space with a desk, filing cabinet, computer and a whiteboard hanging from one wall. Leo's chair is one of those incredibly expensive ergonomic mesh things. I take a seat while Trevor goes round making sure the blinds are all down.

'Squint your eyes,' he says.

I'm so distracted thinking about Leo that I don't understand what Trevor's doing until the lights come on and blind me in a flash of stinging fluorescence.

I grimace, squeezing my eyelids shut. 'Trevor . . .'

'What?' he says. 'I did warn you.'

'What are you doing? Turn those off.'

'What exactly are we going to find in the dark?'

'I have an awful feeling there's nothing to find.'

Trevor grunts. 'Don't you go giving up so easily. We've come this far. Let's not get defeatist.'

I nod, exhale. 'Yeah, you're right. I just need to focus. Got to summon some of that Trevor-trademarked can-do attitude.'

'That's my girl.'

'What are we here for? What are we looking for? I want to know who is telling the truth about Leo: Wilks or Carlson. Or, I want to prove neither of them are. Although given the distinct lack of wine in this wine warehouse I'm going to jump the gun and say something's rotten in Denmark.'

Trevor nods. 'I think we can call that a given right now.'

I look at Trevor's old jeans, his old tattoos, his old face. 'I'm going to take a wild guess and say you're not one for computers?'

'You people today, you think everything revolves around technology. You forget—'

'What did I just say?'

He grumbles something.

'There you go,' I say, pointing, 'you take the filing cabinet.'

'What am I looking for?'

'Anything that mentions Rome.'

'What does "anything" mean exactly?'

'Anything.'

He frowns at me.

'We're flailing in the dark, Trevor. This morning, Messer mentioned Rome, and Carlson's picture of Leo was taken in Rome too. That can't be a coincidence. So I'm guessing that there's an invoice or some other paperwork pertaining to Rome. There has to be a trail when money's involved.'

'I thought the whole point of money laundering was to hide it.'

'Not exactly. It's to legitimise that money, isn't it? You're making dirty money clean so it doesn't have to be hidden.'

'And how does that work?'

'Like I have even the remotest idea how money laundering works,' I say. 'But I'll take it as a compliment that you thought I might understand it.'

He shrugs. 'Well, it could be the family business.'

'Not funny.'

'I think it is.'

'Have you found anything mentioning Rome yet?'

He gets down to work.

I tap a key on the keyboard to wake the computer out of sleep. I'm greeted with a log-in screen. I make a few attempts at guessing Leo's password: favourite baseball team, basketball team, soccer team. Nothing works, which is not surprising. He no doubt has some alphanumeric password that is impossible to guess.

I give up, and I suppose this is one secret that is so common, so benign, that I shouldn't have any issue with it. Leo doesn't know the password to my laptop, so I have no right to be annoyed here. Only, it's yet another secret on top of all those other secrets. How many more things about him don't I know? How many other secrets will be revealed before this is all over?

Just thinking about the possibilities makes me livid.

That anger is intense but lasts mere seconds because I glance at the photograph that sits on Leo's desk. It's a proper photograph, taken on real film and developed by professionals. A solid silver frame houses it because the picture is special – I gave it to my husband as a present. It shows us together, smiling and happy. He has one arm around me and I'm leaning into him, my head resting against his chest. We're both tanned and more than a little inebriated because we'd just been to dinner at a busy little bistro and eaten so much food we had to loosen our belts. Leo's caught the sun too much on the right side of his face and it looks a bit red. He still looks like a movie star, more so than usual even. The setting sun paints us in perfect orange-pink light. An elderly couple passed us and told us we were a beautiful couple. Leo asked them if they would take a picture of us and they were happy to do so, almost fighting with each other to use Leo's top-of-the-range Nikon. The old woman won, if I remember correctly. She said something to us in rapid-fire Italian that we didn't understand and we looked at each other in confusion. When we got the reel of film developed, we saw that she had taken the shot at the exact moment we'd looked at each other and not at her. I was annoyed at first, but Leo liked the picture for the exact reason I disliked it: because it showed us as we were, a couple of goofballs pulling funny faces, instead of nicely posed. In our element, he said, the dual expressions of confusion perfectly captured. In time, I learned to love that shot of us.

In Rome.

I say to Trevor, 'You can probably stop looking right about now.'

'Say again?'

But I don't. Instead I pick up the frame. It's deceptively heavy. I turn it over and use my nails to open up the back. Not easy, because they're always short, always bitten down to the quick as a relief for my anxiety. I manage it after a short struggle.

Something falls out on to the desk.

Tiny, square, thin and plastic.

A micro SD card.

'What's that?' Trevor asks.

'If I were to guess,' I say with a measured amount of understatement, 'I think I've found what everyone's really after.'

Trevor stares at the micro SD card as though he has no idea what it is.

He says, 'I have no idea what that is.'

'You know what a hard drive is? Those things they have in computers to store data?' He nods. 'Same thing, only smaller. Think of every book you've ever read in your life. They could all fit on here with room for a thousand more.'

Trevor looks at me like I've discovered fire. 'So, what's on it?'

'That's kind of the question, isn't it? Whatever Leo's been doing, whoever he's been doing it for, is on here. That's my guess, anyway. Can't exactly tell anything more right now.'

'How do we get to peek inside?'

I look around the computer on Leo's desk, checking the ports. 'There's no micro SD slot. We need a reader thing.' Trevor has no idea what I'm talking about and I try and explain with my hands. 'A little device that we plug the micro SD card into, and then that little device plugs into the computer.'

'Why don't they make the computer with that little device in it in the first place?'

I search the desk drawers in case there's a reader lurking in one. 'You tell me, Trevor, you tell me.'

'Greed,' he tells me. 'That's why. It's all about their greed impinging upon our freedoms. This is what happens when society forgets its core values and instead of worshipping a power higher than itself it puts its devotion on material gain, expecting a better return. Then, what you find is—'

'I wasn't expecting an answer,' I tell him.

'Consider it an unintended bonus.'

'Uh huh.'

There's no micro USB reader in any drawer. We search the office together, carefully, but still nothing.

'I don't know where we can find a reader so late at night,' I say. 'Even if we hadn't left Carlson there, I'm guessing there isn't a reader gathering dust in your cabin.'

'I have no reader,' Trevor says. 'Because I am an actual reader, as a lot more folk should be.'

I don't comment. 'I have one at home. We probably have more than one scattered about. But, kind of off limits at this moment.'

'Why would you need more than one reader?'

'You just ... you just sort of collect these things, Trevor. No one sets out to have more than one. It's like USB chargers. Before you know it you're—'

I stop. Trevor is wide-eyed with confusion.

'Forget it,' I say.

I hold the micro SD card between my index finger and thumb and stare at it as if it might provide me with some guidance, some answers.

I'm disappointed, but not surprised, when it does not.

'So, what we going to do?'

'We could break into a store,' I suggest. 'Steal one.'

'You're not serious.'

'Why not? It's not like it'll be our first time breaking the law tonight. We broke into here, didn't we? We're already criminals.'

'That's different.'

'How is it different?'

'Because this is your husband's building, which makes it

your building. You can't be a criminal breaking into your own property because it's already yours.'

'Okay,' I concede, 'I'll give you that one.' I pocket the SD card. 'What about stealing?'

'Can't steal what's already yours.'

'Yeah, yeah,' I say.

Someone else says, 'I'm going to need that back.'

I jump. Turn.

In the space beyond Leo's office is a man. Handsome. Tall. Unruly blond hair. Matinee idol smile.

Leo.

1:17 a.m.

There's only one bar in town and Rusty knows every regular who frequents it. They're all trying their worst to help the owner pay off her mortgage. It has a certain dive-bar charm about it, like perhaps it's one of those ironic things. A theme bar, maybe. Heidi is a city gal who came upstate after making some money in real estate or something – Rusty can't quite recall – and started again in the way certain people are apt to do. Kind of like Jem Talhoffer in that respect, only Heidi is far more social, far more a local in every sense. Heidi's lost the big-city lilt to her voice and dresses like she's never sipped a Martini in her life.

She's no fugitive, either.

Heidi is alone tending bar tonight because there's only one employee and he's only needed at the weekend when folk might actually have more than a couple of beers. The rest of the week is quiet, with just the regulars to serve, and regulars in this part of the world nurse their drinks like they are newborns. Rusty has seen some sit with the same beer the whole night, until it's flat and room temperature and it didn't even start out as a good brew icy cold from the draught.

Rusty has never heard Heidi complain or make attempts to encourage her patrons to drink up, drink faster or simply drink more. Heidi isn't the sort. She had almost enough to buy the property outright, so the mortgage they're doing their worst to pay off must be tiny. Besides, Heidi didn't leave Manhattan for this town in an attempt to strike it rich. She came here for a simpler, quieter life.

There's a certain bar stool that Rusty thinks of as her own because it's the only one with all four legs of the same length. The rest of them are all skewed, all of them rock, and a woman of Rusty's dimensions prefers to have a solid base on which to perch, especially if there are going to be a couple of intoxicating beverages involved.

Tonight, there might be more than a couple.

The sudden need to go to work and pretend not to be stoned has left Rusty tired but wired. She needs a little something to detangle.

'What happened to you?' Heidi says as she lays her elbows down on the bar top until they come to rest before Rusty. 'You look like someone chewed you up and spat you out again because they don't like the way you taste.'

Rusty grunts.

'Mom or daughter?' Heidi enquires.

'Neither,' is Rusty's reply, although it could easily be either or both. 'But if you want these lips to loosen up then you need to apply some of your special grease.'

Heidi salutes. 'Yes, ma'am.'

She fixes a gin and tonic, which Rusty watches being prepared and notes there's about a one-to-one ratio in the highball Heidi sets before her.

Heidi, elbows back on the bar top, watches as Rusty takes a long sip.

'Tastes different,' Rusty says.

'Thought you could use a strong one.'

Rusty peers into her glass for answers. 'No, not that. Something else isn't the same.'

Heidi shrugs. 'When you discover the secret of perfect consistency, in gin or life in general, you let me know. Until then be grateful for what you're given.'

Rusty sips again. 'Oh, I'm grateful.'

'Don't keep me in suspense.'

Rusty makes a pistol with her fingers and says, 'Pew, pew.'

Heidi's big green eyes sparkle. 'You're kidding me.'

'Wish I was. But no, I've got a corpse to deal with. Only just this minute left the crime scene.'

'What happened?'

Rusty could stare into Heidi's eyes all night long. 'You'll appreciate if I can't go into specifics.'

Quick, Heidi says, 'Sure. Juicy generalities will suffice.'

'But what I can say is that the suspect is a resident of this fair town and they're currently on the loose.'

'Shouldn't you be out searching for them?'

Rusty frowns. 'I'm a police chief, not a bloodhound.'

Heidi apologises with raised palms. 'I'm guessing this is not an armed-and-dangerous-and-on-the-run situation.' She ducks comically low, as if the fugitive is about to storm into the bar and start blasting.

'Not even close,' Rusty says. 'I fully expect this to be taken off my hands come morning. Hence' – she gestures to the gin – 'I can afford to take my foot off the gas at this juncture.'

'What if it's left up to you to resolve?'

'Excellent question,' Rusty says, thinking that every officer on duty is out there looking for Jem, for Carlson, and no one's caught a whiff of either. Then there's Wilks, who, after much protestation, dragged herself off to a hospital to get her head checked out.

Rusty exhales.

She says, 'Between you and me I'm not all that sure. I don't like to admit it but I'm fairly certain I'm way out of my depth right now and I can't even swim.'

Heidi isn't having it. 'That's the tiredness talking, the stress. You're the police chief for a reason, Rust. You're a badass.'

'I've got a bad back, you mean.'

Heidi shrugs. 'Well, it's attached to your ass so let's split the difference.'

'Deal.'

Rusty smiles. Heidi always cheers her up.

A regular at the far end of the bar gestures for Heidi's attention and she sidles away to serve him. Rusty cannot hear what they're saying but there are plenty of smiles passing back and forth. If not for the wide expanse of polished cedar between them it could be a date, such is the flirtation. Genuine chemistry or all part of the service? The regular is a trucker, a big loveable lump with a nice smile. Could be Heidi's type, couldn't he? It's not like she moved upstate and became a nun. She has needs like any other woman.

Rusty has emptied her glass by the time Heidi returns from serving the trucker.

'Thirsty lady,' Heidi says.

Rusty nods with her gaze elsewhere.

Heidi is confused by the shutdown in interaction. 'So,' she says to end the silence. 'Did they do it?'

Rusty looks up. 'Did who do what?'

Heidi's fingers form a pistol of her own. 'The pew pew,' she says. 'Did the suspect do it?'

'Way too early for forensics but there's a witness.'

Heidi's elbows are back on the bar and her eyes are sparkling again. 'Intriguing.'

'Why did you say it like that?'

'Because you don't believe the witness,' Heidi says. 'It's written all over that long face of yours.'

'You mean round face.'

Heidi tuts. 'Now why do you have to go and put yourself down like that?'

Rusty's gaze roams the bar. 'Could be if I do it then it won't matter so much when others do the same.'

Heidi retrieves Rusty's empty glass and gives it a shake so the ice cubes rattle. 'Think I overdid it with this one because you've skipped the happy phase and gone straight to the woe-is-me phase.'

'Nice try but we both know your spirits are half water.'

'Ouch.' Heidi reels back, palms on her chest. 'I take it back. You've jumped all the way to the mean phase. What did I ever do to you?'

Rusty makes sure not to look in the trucker's direction. 'I'm kidding.'

'I know.'

'I know.'

Heidi says, 'You didn't answer my question.'

'You might need to refresh my memory.'

'I said you don't believe your witness.'

'That's not a question.'

Heidi leans across the bar so she's inches from Rusty's face. 'And that, Madam Police Chief, is not an answer.'

'If it walks like a duck and quacks like a duck ... '

Heidi says, 'How long are you going to keep teasing me for?'

'Put it like this,' Rusty says, resisting the urge to lean closer too. 'The way this day has played out so far, I don't believe a single thing anyone has told me.'

Rusty lays cash down on the bar to pay for the drink and to give Heidi a good tip. Rusty always tips her well. Too well, probably, but she has little else to do with her pay cheque.

'Where you running off to so soon? I've got things to tell you as well.'

Rusty doesn't look back. 'Sorry, Heidi, but turns out there's a little bit of bloodhound in me after all.'

1:28 a.m.

I'm so surprised to see Leo that I don't move. I just stare. I don't even stand up from the chair. Trevor stays silent. He doesn't need to be introduced to realise this is Leo standing before us.

My husband says, 'Aren't you going to give me a hug?'

I blink.

The surprise fades and I leap from the seat and throw my arms around him. I squeeze him so hard I can feel his ribs compress under the pressure I apply. He feels so warm to the touch, so reassuring, I don't want to let go. Because while I hold on to him I can ignore the rest of the night, the day. I don't have to face it.

'I'm going to need to breathe at some point, you know.'

I release him. 'What is going on?'

'No "so good to see you, Leo"? No "I've missed you so much, Leo"?'

'I think your lady wife deserves a few answers,' Trevor says.

'And who might you be?'

'A concerned citizen.'

'Well, sir, you don't need to be concerned any longer. Thank you for everything you've done for Jem but I'm here now. I'm going to take care of everything.'

Trevor is not so easily reassured.

I say, 'Leo, please. I've been through hell today. I'm relieved to see you and I'm so glad you're okay. I'm not okay. You can take care of me but not right now. Now, you need to tell me what's going on. You need to tell me why people tried to kill me.'

'It's complicated.'

My eyes moisten as my voice grows louder. 'No, don't say that. Don't you *dare* say that to me. You know. Maybe you don't know everything. Maybe you wish you knew more. But you know something. I've been told you launder money for a drug cartel, that you wash their dirty money through your books but also that you're an informant for the FBI and the cartel have found out.' Leo is silent as I keep going. 'Which is it? How much of that is true? None of it? All of it? I deserve to know. I need to know. Why did this lead to a dead man in my house? Which of those is the reason I can't go home?'

Leo looks over my head to Trevor. 'I can't talk about this right now.'

I shake my head with vigour. 'No, you don't get to do that either. Right now, Trevor is someone I trust more than I trust you because all he's done today is be kind to me. You don't get to shut him out. Whatever you tell me I'll just tell him anyway. He deserves to know what he's been helping me for.'

'You're not leaving me a lot of choice, are you?' Leo says, but he's not after an answer. 'Okay, if you trust him, I suppose I should try to trust him as well. You're my wife and you deserve to know why you're in danger, why I'm in danger. Why' – he points to Trevor – 'he's in danger too.'

'I'm still waiting.'

Leo takes a breath. 'It's true.'

'You're a money launderer?'

He frowns. 'That's really not a very accurate term for what I do.'

'Are you an informant too?'

He nods.

I exhale. Relieved. I've been hanging on to the hope that he wasn't only a criminal. I knew there had to be more.

'Is this a new thing?' I ask, tentative, afraid of the truth. 'Or have you always been like this?'

Leo is hesitant. I can see he's hesitating to tell me the truth because of the effect it will have on me.

'Oh my God, you've been lying to me for our whole marriage, haven't you? Our entire relationship is a lie.'

'The only lie is what I do for a living,' Leo says. 'Everything else is real. Jem, what we have is real.'

I say nothing. I'm devastated. This is only one half of the puzzle. It doesn't explain what's happened today. It doesn't explain Wilks and Messer. It doesn't explain Carlson.

'Why did people come to our house this morning? Why did they try and kill me? They were looking for something, information.'

He nods. 'Information I've been compiling on the cartel. All the transactions I've done for them, all the money I've cleaned. Amounts. Dates. Account numbers. Offshore companies. Contacts. Everything. I've been working my way into the cartel's confidence for years now. Finally, I'm in a position where I'm trusted with large sums of money and with that comes access to their top lieutenants and I get to see who they've been paying off. '

'Messer said you had enough information to bring down the entire cartel.'

'Maybe,' he says. 'Hopefully. I mean, I don't know for sure. It's impossible to know what is enough. But I've tried. I've done what I could.'

'Wilks and Messer had FBI badges,' I say. 'The police chief, Rusty, thought they were the real deal. Later, she told me they were National Security. How can that be the case?'

'They work for the government. They're connected to more powerful people in the pockets of the cartel, people who could be exposed by the evidence I have. It's not inconceivable that they could supply credentials of the kind of quality that could fool a small-town police chief.'

'Then who is Carlson?' I ask Leo.

A deep groove appears between his eyebrows. 'I'm confused. Why are you talking about someone named Carlson?'

'Because Carlson called me this morning a few minutes after Wilks and Messer showed up. He tried to warn me. Then again later when I went to see the police. He said he knew you. He's the one who told me you were an informant for the FBI. He said you worked for him. He . . . he saved me when Wilks and Messer were going to kill me. We escaped together, but he had a photograph of you in his glovebox. It freaked me out. I couldn't trust him then. That's when me and Trevor came here.'

Leo is quiet. 'I don't know anyone by that name.'

I feel the familiar coolness in my face. Like all the blood has been pulled out of the skin.

My eyes feel dry.

The earth tilts one way, and then the other.

It rotates.

Faster and faster.

Everything becomes a blur because everything is spinning. I reach out with my arms in a desperate attempt to keep my balance. I wobble. I stumble.

'Oh God . . . '

I sink down to my knees. I press my palms against my eyes to blind myself so I don't have to watch the world spin faster and faster around my axis. The dizziness does not go away. I can't see but I'm still nauseous because of course the earth is not spinning around me. It's a symptom of my anxiety. My screwed-up brain is trying to cope with the stress of the day and it's failing.

Leo rushes to comfort me but I wave my hand in his general direction to tell him *no*.

There's nothing he can do.

I don't know how long the vertigo lasts but I'm drenched with sweat when I'm finally brave enough to open my eyes again.

I'm deathly pale. Weak. Tired.

Angry.

Leo says, 'Are you okay?'

'Of course I'm not okay.'

1:34 a.m.

I walk away. Out of Leo's office and through the larger office space and down the stairs to the dark warehouse floor. Trevor and Leo follow. I don't know what I'm doing but my emotions are all over the place because I should be so pleased to see him, to be near him, yet I can't forget how hurt I am, how angry and betrayed. Should I let it go? For now, at least.

No, I decide. I refuse to do so.

'How could you live this double life and I had no idea?'

Leo says, 'Because I had to. The less you knew about my work, the safer you'd be. I lied to protect you.'

'Great job with that,' Trevor says.

'I did everything I could to keep you safe, Jem. If you believe nothing else, believe that. You know I'd never do anything to hurt you. You must know that.'

I do. But, 'How could you have lied to me about who you are all this time?'

'I lied, yes, but about what I do for a living. I lied about one thing. That's it. That's all.'

'That's enough,' I tell him. 'That's too much. Any lie is too much.'

'I never lied about who I am.'

'But you did,' I insist. 'Even if that's the only lie you told me, you lied about who you are. Because the Leo I thought I knew would never lie to me. That Leo was a lie.'

He says nothing. What can he say? Nothing is going to change that fact. I either have to accept my husband isn't who I thought he was, or . . .

I can't think of the 'or' right now. It's too much even to consider.

He hugs me. He kisses me. I don't respond.

I feel cold. I feel alone.

'I'm sorry,' he says behind me. 'I'm so sorry. Once this is over, I'm through. I thought I could do this and have a normal life. I thought the two never had to cross. I was wrong. I made a mistake. I'm not going to make another, so I'm out. I'll quit.'

'You'd do that?'

'Of course,' he says. 'I care about my work but it's nothing compared to you.'

His words make me feel better. Just a little, but I'll take it. I'll take whatever positivity I can get at this moment.

'How do we end this?' I ask, eager to do just that. 'Drive to FBI headquarters and hand in the SD card?'

'I wish it was so simple. The whole reason I haven't done so already is because that's putting it back in the path of the people like Wilks and Messer and those far higher up. Once it's in the system, the evidence is out of my hands. Things get lost. Things get changed. What was once proof can end up inconclusive, inaccurate, falsified. What then? The traitors go free and I've put my life on the line for nothing.' He gestures to me, to the scrapes on my arm and the scabs on my face. 'All this is for nothing.'

'You can analyse the reports yourself?' Trevor asks. 'You can identify the dirty agents from what's on that little plastic square?'

Leo nods. 'I can.'

'Then why haven't you? Why has it been sitting on your desk like a worm wriggling on a hook all this time?'

'That's an oversimplification. It's not a case of reading a spreadsheet and looking for whose name is filled in under the "bad guy" heading. I've had to investigate. I've had to research. I've been working on this for a long time now. I'm sorry if I haven't worked fast enough for your liking, sir. I've been doing my best.'

Trevor mutters to himself.

'Feel free to take a step back, friend,' Leo continues. 'As I said: I appreciate what you've done for my wife, but maybe it's time for you to go home to your own.'

'I don't have a wife.'

'My point is, this is where we part ways.'

Trevor is silent for a moment. 'I'll be on my way if Jem here wants me to be. Not because her two-face of a husband tells me to go.'

I say, 'I'm so grateful for everything you've done for me, Trevor. I really am. You're maybe the nicest person I've ever known in my life. I haven't even known you a day, yet you've risked your life to help me. I don't have the first idea how to thank you for that.'

'You've thanked me plenty,' he says. 'Don't need to do it again.'

Leo says, 'We really need to get out of here. I was hoping you'd come, hoping I could find you. If I can think of this, so can they. We need to make a move before anyone else gets here.'

'Too late,' Wilks says from behind us.

1:38 a.m.

She's waiting in the shadows in the darkness. How long she's been there, I don't know. Long enough for us to let our guards down, at least. When she steps forward into a swathe of moonlight the bruising and discolouration on her scalp are obvious. Little strips of medical tape keep the wound closed. It must hurt like hell.

Good. I want her to hurt. I want her to suffer.

She's holding a gun. Could be the same one she held before or it could be a new one. Regardless, it glimmers in the moonlight, held steady in Wilks' iron-firm grip.

Her face is serious and determined. Intense.

I freeze. Leo and Trevor are either side of me.

The muzzle is a hole of pure black pointed our way.

'Good to see you again, Leo. You're looking well, as always.'

Leo says nothing in response.

I glance at him. 'You know each other?'

Wilks feigns surprise. 'I guess he forgot to mention that part.'

Leo is silent.

Trevor says, 'Why don't you put that firearm away. You point it long enough it's bound to go off.'

'What a tragedy that would be.'

Trevor nods. 'I'm guessing it would be else why haven't you shot us all yet? You still want that information, don't you? And you've been through far too much today trying to get it for your efforts to amount to nothing should a negligent discharge occur and put an end to your chances of finding it.'

Wilks considers.

'I'm not saying for you to put it away. I'm suggesting you point it at the floor until you decide to use it or not. That's all. You can do that, can't you?'

'I'd try and be quiet if I were you.' Wilks aims the gun at Trevor. 'Because right now you don't know a thing about what's going on here and you should really try and keep it that way for your own sake. Don't force me to think of you as more than just a poor old fool in the wrong time at the wrong place.'

'I beg to differ, ma'am.'

'How so?'

'Maybe I'm exactly where I need to be exactly when I need to be there.'

'Don't go getting any ideas,' Wilks says. 'I don't want to have to hurt you, so keep your mouth shut and maybe you get out of here alive. You can go back to your miserable existence.'

'Leave him alone,' I say.

Wilks turns her attention to me. 'It's a pleasure to see you again, Mrs Talhoffer. How have you been?'

'Truth be told I've not had the best day.'

She nods. 'I bet. I'm sorry about that. This whole thing has spiralled out of control. If I could go back and do things differently, I would. But here we are.'

Leo speaks, finally. 'What do you want?'

'You know what I want, Leo. You've always known. I want what's mine. You give me the information, I walk away. You and Jem get to walk away. Whoever this old guy is gets to walk away too. Sound like a fair deal?'

'I don't have it.'

'Sure you don't.'

'It's safe,' Leo says. 'I can take you to it. Let these two go and we can head there right now.'

'I think we'll all head there together. I don't want to be the one to break up the band.'

'No,' Leo insists. 'Just you and me go.'

'I'm not a patient woman, Leo. I didn't want it to come to this. I offered you a fair price. Too fair, probably. I gave you every chance to avoid this and you refused me every time. What did you think was going to be the next step? Did you really think we were going to go away? Did you really think this wouldn't happen? It's just business, Leo. It's not personal. I don't have a single problem with you or your lovely wife. Had things played out a little differently I could imagine us having a barbecue together, laughing and joking and sipping beer while burgers sizzle.'

I say, 'I'm having a hard time believing that.'

'Well,' Wilks says. 'Perhaps I'm being overly optimistic about your husband's capacity for friendship.'

'Who are you?' I ask. 'Why do you know Leo?'

'Oh yeah, in all this excitement I'd forgotten he hasn't told you. Leo and me, we work together. Worked, I mean. Can't see us being too cosy after this. Can you?'

'I know you're NSA too.'

Wilks laughs a little. A coarse, cruel sound. She looks to Leo. 'Too? Is that what you told her?'

Leo doesn't answer.

I say to Wilks, 'You're not National Security?'

'I am,' she replies. 'Your husband isn't.'

'Not directly,' I say. 'He's an informant. That's why you know each other.'

Wilks is frowning and glancing between me and Leo. 'Is that what he told you?'

I don't answer.

'Is that what you told her, Leo?'

He doesn't answer.

Wilks says, 'I'm sorry to be the one to break it to you but your husband is not, and never has been, any kind of informant. What he is is a money launderer. But he's not only that, are you, Leo? He's also a thief.' There's a glimmer in Wilks' eyes. She's enjoying this. 'But mostly he's a pathological liar, and I'm thinking you're starting to work that last part out for yourself by now.'

1:42 a.m.

Leo isn't an informant working to bring down a drug cartel.

Leo is a liar.

Leo is a thief.

I don't want to believe it but as I look at Leo he can't meet my gaze and I know that everything he told me just minutes ago was false. He doesn't work for the FBI or National Security. There's no evidence. There are no reports. It was all an elaborate story to cover his actions. Another deception to hide the other deceptions.

Inside, I'm in pieces. Outside, I don't react. I'm hiding my true reaction so I have the focus of will to say: 'I don't believe you.'

Wilks turns down the corners of her mouth. 'I don't care what you believe. I'm not interested in convincing you of the truth. I just want the money Leo stole from me.'

'Money?' I ask Leo.

He doesn't want to answer, so Trevor does on his behalf: 'Your hubby ripped off the cartel, Jem. He stole from them.

304

Maybe once, maybe a thousand times. He hasn't been compiling evidence against them, he's been hoarding their money.'

'Pretty much,' Wilks says. 'Except it's my money too. And Messer's, the poor bastard.'

Leo finds his voice. 'I expect you'll be keeping his share for yourself.'

'Don't say it like that,' Wilks says. 'So, I took a little money? So, I stole from drug dealers? Pocket change to them but not to me. Life's not fair and it's expensive too. All I took was enough to get by without worrying all the time. I wasn't greedy. Not at first. But once you take a little it's easier to take a little more and a little more. And all those tiny pieces add up to a lot and before you know it you've gone too far. When you're in over your head you can't back out again. And when you understand that and accept your predicament it's actually quite liberating. Because then you let go of all the previous restraints you had. Then you understand that you have no limits.' She pauses. 'Isn't that what happened to you, Leo?'

He's silent.

'You should be thanking me,' she says. 'I could have sent you to prison for the rest of your life but I gave you an opportunity. You carry on doing what you were doing for the cartel and I help keep you free from a nine-by-nine. In return for a small percentage, naturally.' She says to me: 'Problem was, I didn't realise your husband was taking a percentage of his own.'

'I didn't steal from you,' Leo tells her.

'Doesn't matter. You got greedy and ruined everything. Thing about a cartel you forget is that even though they've trusted you to do something for them it doesn't mean they trust you. Doesn't matter how good you are, they'll assume you're going to steal because that's what they'd do in your place. So, sooner or later they're going to check up on you. They're going

305

to go through everything you've done for them and realise you've been stealing from them.'

I say, 'And now you want to steal it all?'

'Although I don't like to think of it as stealing, so much as making better use of idle resources. I can take early retirement in five years. I figure it might be nice to spend that retirement on a big schooner sailing around the South Pacific without a care in the world.'

'Sounds nice,' I say without inflection.

'Oh, it will be. I have the boat already picked out.' Wilks shrugs. She doesn't care that she's a thief or that people know it.

'You think someone might notice if you suddenly buy a boat you can't afford on your government pension?'

'Don't sweat the details, Jem. I'm going to sit on the money until I'm long gone, until everyone who matters has forgotten I ever existed. That was Leo's plan too, wasn't it, Leo?'

Leo is silent again. I hope he's working on a different kind of plan. Some strategy to get us out of this nightmare. Whatever he's done can wait until there's no longer a gun pointed at us. Marriage problems, trust issues, kind of take a back seat in such situations.

Trevor says, 'How is money stored on one of those little hard drives?'

I think I know. 'Accounts? Investments? Real estate? Stocks? Numbers on spreadsheets?'

Wilks says, 'Something like that. Come on, Leo. You know you have no choice. Don't make me hurt the person you care most about in this world.'

'You so much as breathe on her and you get nothing. I'll take you to it. Just you and me.'

There's an intensity in Leo's tone that demands attention.

Wilks frowns. 'I think you're forgetting which of us has the gun. I think you're also forgetting which of us has a loved one in the room.' Wilks points the gun at me. 'I shoot her in the guts and you'll be begging me to bring her along.'

'You can have the information,' Leo continues. 'Go sell it. Get rich. I don't care. But if at any point I think, even for a second, that anything has happened to Jem, I will die before I give it up. So, you have to ask yourself: how much do I want it? Because you need to convince me you want it so bad you won't dare risk pissing me off.'

'Okay, take it easy,' Wilks says. 'This is about priorities, Leo. I have mine. You have yours. They're not mutually exclusive.'

Leo, without a gun, commands the room.

'Good,' he says. 'That's what I wanted to hear.'

As confident and powerful as he is in this moment, I have no idea how he's going to get us out of this. I have the information Wilks wants in my pocket. Leo knows this. Trevor knows this. The only person who doesn't know this is Wilks. Whatever Leo promises her is moot without the micro SD card in my possession.

There's a compelling urge inside me to take it out of my pocket and throw it to Wilks. That's what she wants. If she doesn't get it, who knows what she might do? I can end this right now.

Leo must sense this because he makes a gesture with his closest hand: a short horizontal swipe of his fingers. Over in an instant so Wilks doesn't notice.

Leo's meaning is obvious: no.

I want this over as soon as possible. I want this over now.

I have the information in my pocket. Take it and go.

It takes all my willpower not to say it. Wilks wouldn't just take it and go, would she? She would take it and kill us all. She can't escape with valuable secrets if we're around to tell the tale.

There has to be another way.

I have to trust Leo. He knows what he's doing.

Or does he?

There's little evidence of that so far.

He's the one who's got us into this hell in the first place. All this is his fault.

It's always been up to me to fix it.

'I have the information in my pocket. Take it and go.'

This time I say it for real.

1:45 a.m.

'What are you doing?' Leo demands.

I ignore him. I'm looking straight at Wilks.

Wilks says, 'Take it out. Let's see it.'

She's sceptical, which makes sense. Why would I have it and not Leo? Which makes me wonder why I do have it and Leo doesn't. I'm not going to get an answer here, now.

I reach for my pocket.

'Slow,' Wilks says. 'Nice and slow.' She glances to Trevor. 'Don't want to provoke a negligent discharge, do we?'

Trevor stays silent.

Taking it slow, I push fingers into a pocket of my jeans.

'Don't,' Leo says.

My fingers close and grip and I begin to withdraw them.

'She'll kill us,' Leo says.

'Don't listen to him,' Wilks says. 'We all want this to be over. This is the only way that's going to happen.'

Fingers clear of my pocket, I make a fist. Wilks gestures for

309

me to come closer. She's not prepared to come closer to us herself. I stay where I am.

'Come on, Jem. Give me the information and we can all go back to our lives. That's what you want to do, isn't it? Go back to your life and pretend this never happened.'

'Can't quite do that, can I?' I reply. 'Not with a corpse in my hallway.'

'You didn't kill Messer,' Wilks says. 'When the crime scene report comes back the evidence will exonerate you. You've done nothing wrong.'

'Then why do I feel like everything I could have done wrong today, I have?'

Wilks doesn't answer, but says, 'Give me the information.'

'Don't,' Leo says again.

I ignore him. I step towards Wilks, one slow step at a time.

'That's it,' Wilks encourages. 'Just a few more steps.'

I raise my fist, pull back my elbow, and throw.

I throw above Wilks, and a muted *clink*, *clink*, *tap* sounds far behind her.

Wilks' face hardens. 'What have you done?'

1:47 a.m.

I shrug, playing innocent. 'I've given you the information. Only, you'll have to go find it if you want it.'

Wilks' arm extends my way, the gun in her hand aimed at my face. 'I should kill you.'

'Kill me,' I say, 'and you have to kill those two too. Three gunshots, at a minimum. Bang. Bang. Bang. Loud. Obvious. And that's assuming you can shoot. That's assuming we all go down and stay down. Either way, gunshots are hard to miss and ignore even in this area. I'm sure you noticed plenty of businesses are still operating. I'm sure you know they've got private security patrols.' I'm making that part up, but hopefully she doesn't know for sure they don't. 'So, are you really prepared to risk it? Because after you've fired that gun you're going to have to crawl around on your hands and knees for however long it takes you to find a piece of plastic the size of a thumbnail.'

Wilks says nothing.

'The one point in your favour is that this warehouse is pretty empty, but that's still a whole lot of floor space to cover. All those shelves to look under. God, maybe it fell down that drain. There's two questions you need to ask yourself: how long do you think it will take to find, and how long will it take for the police to show?'

Wilks is raging in silence.

'My bad,' I continue. 'It's three questions.'

I don't elaborate.

Wilks has no choice but to ask, 'What's the third?'

'Is there a password?'

Wilks steps towards me. 'Well, is there?'

'Only one way to find out.'

She's so angry she's making herself sweat. There are little beads of perspiration along her hairline. It's an impotent fury because despite the gun in her hand she is no longer in charge.

Somehow, I'm the most powerful person in the room.

Wilks' jaw muscles are flexing so hard she's going to start cracking teeth soon. 'Okay.'

It comes out more of a hiss than a word. I'm sure she's never hated anyone in her life like she hates me right now.

'Okay?' I echo.

'You win.'

'I win? I'm not sure I've ever won anything before.'

She nods. 'Yes, you win, Jem. Because you've bought your-selves a reprieve. But that's all, because no one is leaving here until I have that information. And if I don't get it, none of you leave here. If I don't get it, I'll put a bullet in each of your heads and be gone before anyone even thinks to respond to the noise. Now, get on your hands and knees and find it for me.'

Trevor says, 'Don't you ever get tired of being an a-hole?'

Wilks waves the gun in Leo's and Trevor's direction. 'You two as well. Get looking for my information.'

'I have bad knees,' Trevor says.

'Knees are no good without a head.'

Trevor shrugs. 'Depends whose heads we're talking about here.'

Wilks isn't amused. 'Get busy looking or get busy dying.'

She doesn't yet realise her mistake and I'm certainly not going to be the one to tell her. I guessed she would order me to look for the lost SD card while she kept the gun trained on Leo and Trevor.

Instead, Wilks has put us all to work.

Due, no doubt, to Trevor's provocation generating a reaction, a response. Had she taken the time to think things through Wilks might have understood it wasn't the best thing to do. It's not the smart thing to do because she now has three of us in different places to watch at the same time.

Impossible.

Thanks to Trevor, my idea is working even better than I could have hoped.

Trevor is down on one knee, scouring the floor for the micro SD card. He's not making a huge effort to find it, but he couldn't even if he tried. Leo is nearby, on his stomach and reaching beneath one of the metal shelving units.

He whispers to me, 'Why did you offer her the information?'

'We didn't have a lot of options,' I whisper back.

Wilks is closer to Trevor, a little out of range to hear us. She's pacing back and forth, restless and anxious. She knows the longer this goes on the worse it is for her. There's not much she can do about it. My suggestion that uncommonly observant private security guards will be aware the second a gun goes off in their business park must be playing on her mind.

I've bought us time.

The longer this goes on, however, the more chance of Wilks growing some sense.

We need to do something before we reach that stage.

'She could have killed us all,' Leo whispers. 'You shouldn't have done that.'

I try to whisper back but it's not easy to control the volume of my voice given such provocation. 'Don't blame me for how I act in a mess you created.' He's silent. 'Let's figure out how to get out of this mess before Wilks realises I've fooled her.'

'Excuse me, what? How have you fooled her?'

I gesture to what we're doing. 'There's nothing to find.'

Leo is lost.

I tap my pocket. 'I've still got the information on me.'

'What did you throw?'

'A button.'

Leo's first reaction is surprise. He hadn't even considered this as a possibility. Maybe I should be insulted by his lack of faith in me, but that's for later. If there is a later. After surprise comes relief, then confusion. 'Why didn't you tell me?'

'Because your reaction needed to be genuine if Wilks was going to buy it.'

He smiles a little despite the situation. 'When did you get so good at this?'

I exhale. 'I've been going through a crash course all day long. Thanks to you.'

His smile fades.

'Move away from me,' I tell him. 'The further all three of us are apart the harder it is for Wilks to keep track of us. Whoever spots an opening has to take it, whatever it is.'

He nods and is about to reply when Wilks notices us whispering.

'Hey, stop talking.' She comes closer. 'Find those accounts. I don't have all night.'

Trevor says, 'Then perhaps you should look yourself.'

'Shut up, granddad.'

Leo does as I suggested and starts searching elsewhere, increasing the gap between us while keeping his distance from Trevor too. Pretty soon I see that Wilks is really struggling to keep track of all of us. She's having to constantly move, constantly turning her head. She's getting frustrated, angry. I've witnessed her temper and see the signs of it spiralling out of control. If we don't do something fast she's going to herd us back together.

'Found it,' I call out to her.

She hurries over to me. 'Where?'

'Under that shelving unit,' I answer, pointing. 'But my arms aren't long enough to reach it.'

In an ideal world she would try herself but she's not dumb enough to do that. She does follow my finger with her gaze however, and in that moment of distraction I grab the gun with both hands.

I'm nowhere near strong enough to wrestle it from her grip but that isn't my plan – just to keep her occupied long enough for Leo to reach us.

I'm weaker than I thought, or Wilks is stronger, because I hang on to the gun for the briefest of moments. She rips it free from my hands and shoves me away with so much force I hit the floor hard enough to cry out in pain.

Leo gets to Wilks a split-second later and charges into her, catapulting her back into the metal shelving unit, which tips and almost falls with the impact.

The gun is knocked from Wilks' hand and clatters on the floor near to me, but before I can reach out my hand it skids beneath another unit.

Leo is fit and in shape but Wilks is fast and skilled. She beats off his clumsy attempts to wrestle her and headbutts him, producing a gush of blood from his nose that splatters on the floor near me. Leo, dazed, tries to fight back until a second headbutt knocks him unconscious.

'Nice try,' Wilks says as she wipes Leo's blood from her forehead.

1:53 a.m.

But it's not over yet because Trevor, slow yet fearless, grabs Wilks from behind, wrapping his arms around her in a bear hug. Trevor's not a small man. He may be old yet he's old like a mountain, weathered and strong. Wilks can't break that grip. She tries, grunting and roaring.

I shake Leo. He's groaning and otherwise unresponsive. He's going to wake up far too late to help.

The gun. I have to find it.

I spin around on the spot, staring into the darkness, trying to think, trying to remember. Was the sound of it clattering on the floor close? Was it far?

I remember. I saw the gun slide under a unit, but which one? There are so many. They all look alike.

Wilks is powering backwards, forcing Trevor to do so as well, straining his hold, his balance. They collide into a shelving unit, Trevor taking the impact and cushioning it for Wilks. Trevor still doesn't let go. I see the pain in his face and the determination to keep fighting despite it.

His determination powers my own. I charge the shelving unit that I think stands over the gun.

I throw myself against it, pushing, yelling.

It tilts.

Falls.

A thunderous boom reverberates through the warehouse. So loud and unexpected that Wilks and Trevor stop fighting, if only for a second.

I scan the floor by the shelving unit. No gun.

I back up. Yell. Charge. Push.

The next set of shelves tilts and falls, clangs and bangs and clatters on the floor.

Wilks and Trevor continue wrestling.

I'm panting, sweating, sore and grimacing from two hard collisions with metal shelving units. I back up further for the next one to compensate.

I charge.

It doesn't tilt in the same way as the first two. I'm slower, weaker.

I yell louder, push harder.

The tilt comes, slow at first.

I roar.

It falls.

I'm so weakened from the exertion I almost fall over with it.

There, on the dusty floor, hidden until an instant ago, is the gun.

Twenty-four hours earlier the mere sight of it would have scared me. I would have wanted nothing to do with it. Now, I have no fear of the weapon. It's just a tool, a necessary tool to save the life of Trevor, my husband, and myself.

I scoop it up off the floor without hesitation, turn to face Wilks.

She's on the floor now, having shaken free of Trevor's hold. Trevor's on his back, fighting to stop Wilks hitting him, strangling him . . . killing him.

'*Get off him.*' I scream.

Wilks can't fail to hear me, but she pays no attention. I'm no one. I'm no threat. I'm nothing to fear.

I point the gun at the ceiling and squeeze the trigger.

Bang.

That gets Wilks' undivided attention.

'Get off him,' I repeat. 'Now.'

Wilks obeys. She releases Trevor and climbs to her feet, hands rising.

'Stay calm,' she tells me. 'Don't do anything rash.'

I laugh at her. 'Calm? You're telling me to stay calm and you don't even have the good manners to do it in a sarcastic tone. Because, guess what, I'm not calm.'

Wilks' hands rise further.

'I'm about the furthest possible point I can be from calm. I haven't been calm since the moment you knocked on my door.'

'We can work this out,' Wilks says. 'I'll split the money.'

'No way. We're going to call the police and you're going to be arrested and then charged and eventually convicted on multiple counts of attempted murder. Treason too, I'm guessing.'

Trevor grunts as he hauls himself to his knees. 'At the very least.'

I glance his way. 'Are you okay?'

He isn't. He's exhausted and hurt and old.

'Never felt better,' he says.

I smile. 'Please tell me we're going to stay friends after this, Trevor.'

'People who get to spend any time with me eventually find me disagreeable.'

'Just say yes,' I tell him. 'You don't have to mean it. Just say yes for me.'

He nods. 'Yes.'

'Thank you.' I turn my attention back to Wilks. 'Bet you're regretting ever showing up at my door, aren't you?'

Wilks is silent. Cowed. Beaten.

'Trevor,' I say, 'could you do me the kind favour of heading to Leo's office and calling Rusty?'

Trevor hesitates. 'It would be my pleasure, only I don't think I can make it up those steps right now.'

'Oh, yeah, of course. Come here and take this gun. Watch Special Agent Asshole for me, will you?'

Trevor nods. 'That I can do.'

'And shoot her if she so much as looks at you funny.'

'That I'd like to do.'

He shuffles over, even slower than before. Limping. Bloody and tired.

'Oh, Trevor,' I say. 'I'm so sorry I've put you through all of this.'

He grumbles his unhappiness with my expression of sympathy and snatches the gun from my hand. 'Go call Rusty.'

I check on Leo first.

'I'm okay,' he says. His voice sounds weak. 'I'll be fine in a few minutes. Help me up.'

'I need to call Rusty. I need to—'

'Please,' he says, taking hold of me to brace against. 'Help me up.'

I do. Not easy as he's weak, but we manage it. He exhales. Takes a moment to find his balance.

'You good?' I ask.

He nods and lets go of me. 'See? All better.'

'I'll be back in a minute,' I tell him, heading for the stairs.

'Sure,' he says back.

He approaches Trevor as I reach the steps and hurry up them.

Leo reaches a hand out to Trevor. 'Let me check the gun is loaded.'

'It's loaded,' Trevor tells him. 'Your wife fired it a moment ago.'

'Please,' he says. 'We don't want any more surprises.'

I slow as I reach the top of the steps. 'The gun is loaded, Leo. Don't worry.'

He nods, then looks to Wilks and yells, 'Watch out, she's—'

My gaze snaps to Wilks. So does Trevor's own.

Wilks is standing still, hands raised as before.

It's a distraction.

Leo disarms Trevor, taking the gun.

'What are you doing?' I shout down to him.

'What I have to do,' Leo shouts back.

Leo fires a single shot that hits Wilks in the head and she drops straight down, no bones, all water.

A mist of blood floats lazily in the air where Wilks had stood, the fine vapour glistening in the moonlight.

1:59 a.m.

The business park gives Rusty a post-apocalyptic vibe. It's built-up as an apparent outpost of commerce, of civilisation and progress, but it's also a wasteland that is dead and empty of life in the middle of the night. If real actual zombies rush from the shadows to swarm her cruiser she won't be the least bit surprised. Can't call them zombies, though, can you? Some kind of rule. She doesn't understand why not, why it's a thing. A zombie's a zombie.

It's way past her bedtime and she's yawning, yet Rusty feels alert, as though she is both awake and asleep at the same time. The latter has a good portion to do with firing up the lights and doing her best to push the accelerator pedal through the footwell. She's gripped by some exhilarating urgency she can't explain. What's she trying to do anyway? Catch a fugitive on her lonesome? Madness. She doesn't even remember the last time she slapped cuffs on anyone. Besides, there's no guarantee Jem Talhoffer headed to the warehouse with an old man in tow. In fact, it has to be lottery-level odds if she did and Rusty hasn't so much as won a balloon at a fair in her time. It would make more sense for a scared Jem to head to the big city and lose herself in the millions of other lost souls. She'd be so hard to find there she would be as good as invisible.

That's what Rusty would do if she ever had to run.

She can't imagine she would ever need to, but she's fantasised many times about doing just that. Hitting the road. Leaving her life behind with no plan as to where she would head, just an endless horizon of possibilities and the past behind her.

Rusty's pretty sure no one would even notice she'd gone.

Positive no one would miss her even if they did.

That's night driving for you, she tells herself, combined with the residual paranoia caused by marijuana in her system. She's usually asleep well before this stage. She couldn't sleep now, even high. She's too alert, too switched on. This is the buzz she's read about, heard about. This is what some law enforcement officers live to feel. The rush of hunting down dangerous criminals and bringing them to justice is supposed to be what it's all about.

Rusty finds it a little unsettling. She's not used to it.

Isn't small-town life supposed to be a quiet life?

She told Heidi she felt out of her depth, and while a good part of that was to encourage some sympathy from the Emerald-Eyed Maiden, there was plenty of truth there too. Rusty doesn't have to do much other than keep the wheels turning in the precinct, which means banging Sabrowski and Zeke about the head every so often to make sure they are doing what they are paid to do. And that usually involves booking folk for driving too fast on the highways and mediating domestic altercations.

Whatever ambition Rusty might have once had was reined

in when her girl came along, stopped once and for all when her deadbeat husband walked out on them both, and then stomped all over when her mom got old and had to move in.

Rusty isn't bitter about any of that because that's life and you have to play the hand you're given. She's happy enough as the chief of a town where nothing ever happens.

Except that town is now the scene of a murder.

So, no smoking away the night on her porch from now on.

She keeps the vehicle rolling at a slow speed with the windows down so she can listen to the night. She's not sure what she might hear but better to be able to hear whatever it might be than not. She passes many large buildings, wide and low. If not for the quiet rumble of her cruiser would there be any other sound?

She slows to a crawl when she reaches the unit. An ugly, blocky building so nondescript she could have driven right past it and not even realised.

Unlike much of the business park it doesn't quite fit the post-apocalyptic landscape. It doesn't quite fit because there's lights on inside.

More than that, Rusty is almost sure she glimpses a figure at one of the windows.

No zombies here. Only the living.

Her heart thumps, hard and quick.

This is the buzz.

Breathing fast, Rusty pulls the cruiser up outside the warehouse.

Call for backup? No, she can't be positive she saw anyone inside. She doesn't want to make a fool of herself.

Seeing things again, Chief?

Shut up, Sabrowski.

Rusty stops the cruiser, uses the rear-view mirror to look

herself dead in the eye to summon courage, to reassure herself. It doesn't work but she gets out of the car anyway.

She heads towards the building, alone.

2:00 a.m.

I gasp, horrified. My hands are on the railing, knuckles white.

'What have you done?'

'I'm sorry, Jem,' Leo says. 'I didn't want you to see that.'

My eyes are moist. My legs are weak. 'What have you—'

'Come down, baby,' Leo says. 'We need to go.'

I can't move. If I let go of the railing I'm going to tumble down the stairs. 'Why?' is all I can say. 'Why?'

'She's a killer, Jem. She would have killed every one of us and not raised her heart rate one beat. Come down, come to me.'

He holds out a hand to me and I can't breathe.

Trevor says, 'You didn't need to kill her. She was disarmed.'

'You don't understand the full facts, Trevor. Trust me, I did the right thing.'

'Then you'll be willing to give me that gun?'

'Not possible,' Leo says. 'This stays with me.'

Trevor grunts. 'Figured you might say that.'

'You just killed her,' I find myself saying. 'You didn't even flinch.'

Leo approaches me, ascending the steps. 'I'm protecting you. I know this is a lot for you to take in, but this is how it has to be. We can't be weak. We have to be as strong as our enemies.'

I retreat from him. 'I ... I need to call Rusty.'

'I'm afraid that's not a good idea.'

'Why not?'

'Use your head, Jem. There's a dead body in here.'

'You just a second ago said it was the right thing to do.'

'It was. It is. The law might not agree, however.'

'What does that mean?'

'It means we need to go. It means we don't call the police. We don't call anyone. We just go.'

'Go where?'

'Away from here. Lie low. Wait for things to calm down while I figure out our next move.'

'Figure what out? What next move is there?' My voice is anxious, desperate. 'We need to go to the police. We need to stop this.'

'Jem, get smart. We'll all go to prison for this, even the old man. You're accomplices to everything I've done. We're on our own.'

I'm shaking my head. I can't believe it. I don't want to believe it. I want this over.

Leo points to Wilks. 'That's a bad woman dead on the floor. A thief. A murderer. A woman who would have killed us all to get that money back. Come tomorrow they'll paint her as a hero who died trying to recover stolen intelligence and you'll pay for her death. We all will.'

'No ...'

'That's how the government works. That's how it always works. We have no villains any more, only dead heroes.'

327

Trevor says, 'The federal government can never be trusted, on that we can agree.'

'Rusty,' I say. 'Rusty is different. She's not part of the federal government. She's a small-town police chief. She'll do the right thing. She'll protect us.'

'Maybe,' Leo says. 'Maybe that will ultimately be the right course of action. But not right now. Not in the aftermath of a life-and-death situation like this. We need to stop. Think. We only get one shot at making the right decision. We don't get it right we never get a chance to correct it.'

I'm silent.

'Come with me,' he insists. 'We need to get some rest. There's nothing we can do tonight.'

'Do you promise?' I ask. 'If I still want to go to Rusty in the morning, you'll do it?'

He nods. 'If that's what we agree is best then yes, I'll come with you.'

I search his eyes and see truth. I hope it's not simply the truth I want to see. I can't know. I have to believe him.

I have to trust him one last time.

2:03 a.m.

Rusty is out of her depth but she keeps swimming anyway.

There's a riptide trying to drag her down into inescapable black depths of doubt, of self-loathing. But she remembers she's carrying a buoyancy aid and she unsnaps her holster, feeling a different kind of unease because she can't remember the last time she did so on duty. She knows how to use her pistol – she cleans and shoots it often enough – but that's not the same. Hard to get the blood pumping putting holes in paper targets. The cold night feels colder than it did. Her damp skin sucks the chill from the air and deposits it into her bones. Each exhalation sends a dense cloud of white vapour into the dark.

Why are her footsteps so loud? Try as she might she can't seem to lessen the thunderous boom, challenged only by the throbbing pulse in her ears.

There are no vehicles parked in the narrow lot in front of Leo's unit and she wonders if that means she really did mis-see the figure at the window. No, she saw what she saw. Her back is bad and her knees aren't great and she wheezes under the slightest exertion but her eyesight is good and true.

For once, she thinks, trust in yourself.

She remembers Heidi's words, repeating them in her mind for reassurance.

You're a badass.

A quick nudge informs her the main entrance into the unit isn't going to open and there is no obvious other way in from the front, so Rusty edges around the exterior to an alleyway that runs along one flank.

Shapes.

Shapes in the darkness. Not whole. Not formed. A swirling pattern of disjointed limbs, disembodied heads. One rippling body connecting those disparate pieces. Her first thought is paranoia: she's seeing things, a monster. A nightmare made real, made substantial. But no, it's not her mind playing tricks.

Shadows on the wall. Multiple people. She can't be sure who they are.

Maybe a man and maybe a woman.

Rusty's pulse quickens.

She hurries across the asphalt, pistol out from the holster before she's aware she's drawing it, closing the distance at a decent pace despite her lack of fitness. She's energised by urgency. If she takes her time, they'll be gone. She knows she's making noise, knows her footfalls are heavy and audible and there's nothing she can do about it.

The shadows retreat from her view as those creating them move further away from her.

She sees their silhouettes, dark and featureless yet distinct and unmistakable at the far end of the alleyway.

'Hey,' she calls to them. 'Stop.'

She intended to say more, but she's out of breath and her heart is hammering.

There's a moment of silence, of pause, and though she cannot see their faces, she knows they've stopped and looked back her way. Rusty's silhouette must be as clear to them as theirs is to her.

'*Police*,' she calls in case they don't already know. 'Stay where you are.'

They do stop, which is surprising to her. She was all set to run after them, as ineffective as that would no doubt prove. She hears nothing. They say nothing to her but they could be whispering among themselves. Rusty's breathing so fast and hard she would struggle to hear them at this distance even if they were screaming to her. She swipes sweat from her eyes, takes a step forward. The gun feels heavy in her grip, slippery in her damp palm.

She feels something in the air. There's a tingle in her spine.

Is this still the buzz she's heard about, read about?

Or something else?

The latter, she discovers, when light flashes brighter than the stars, than the moon, than daylight, and then she feels a strange, dull sensation in the centre of her chest.

She staggers backwards a short step, knees buckling under unseen pressure. She doesn't realise she's dropped her pistol until she hears metal banging and scraping on the concrete before her. So close all she needs to do is squat and retrieve it but she knows that such an extravagance of movement is beyond her.

'You shot me,' she says to no one. 'You shot me.'

She reaches for her radio to call for help, for the backup she should have already called, but her hand is weighed down by something, something heavy. Invisible forces pin her entire arm to her side.

Rusty's held in a vice, trapped. Immobile.

She doesn't know if the darkness is the night or if her eyelids have drawn a veil over her sight. She's aware she no longer has control of her body, if she still resides inside it at all.

Rusty's falling, she realises, she's falling . . .

2:07 a.m.

'No,' I scream the moment I see Rusty go down. I'm screaming with horror and fury, grabbing at Leo, at the gun, before he can shoot again. His right arm is outstretched before him, the muzzle of the pistol hot and smoking.

Then I'm hitting him, attacking him, but only in my mind. In reality, I can't move. I haven't moved. I can barely breathe.

'How could you?' I manage to ask.

'I didn't mean to hit her,' Leo answers in a quiet voice, rotating his head to look at me. 'I just wanted to get her to back off. A warning shot, that's all I intended. It's dark. I . . . '

His eyes are wide with surprise and alarm, sheening in the sodium light. He looks terrified and about to cry and I don't know what to do or how to react.

'She's still moving,' Trevor says. 'We have to help her.'

His old face is cracked and creased, he's shocked and horrified like myself and Leo, but Trevor is frozen by the paralysis of what has happened. Then he swallows, steps forward. At least he tries to, but he's old and slow and Leo moves to intercept.

'No one is doing anything,' Leo says, stepping between Trevor and where Rusty lies, moving before me. 'We need to leave. Now. We can't hang around. There's been a gunshot.'

'Get out of my way,' Trevor tells him in a tone that is both whisper and growl.

Leo doesn't back down. 'I can't do that.'

'Go if you want to,' Trevor says. 'I'll take care of Rusty. And don't worry, I'll tell them you didn't mean to shoot her.'

Leo is silent.

Trevor says, 'Get out of my way.'

Leo shakes his head. 'I can't do that.'

I see his grip tighten on the pistol and I'm stepping between them before this can become any uglier, resting one hand on each of them. They're each knotted balls of tension. Right now I don't know what either of them is capable of doing and I don't want to find out.

'Please,' I say, 'let me call an ambulance. Then we can go.'

Leo shakes his head. 'She will have called it in before she confronted us. Backup will already be on the way. Every second we're talking about this they're getting closer.'

Trevor says, 'You don't know that.'

'I do. I know exactly how these things work.'

'How can you be so cold?' I say to Leo.

'Because you're my priority,' he tells me. 'Not some cop.'

'She's not "some cop",' I hiss at him. 'Her name's Rusty and you shot her.'

'She would have killed us,' he answers. 'Or put us in prison for the rest of our lives, which is worse.'

Now it's me who says, 'You don't know that.'

His eyes are wide, angry. 'I won't be put in a cage, Jem, and I won't allow anyone to put you inside one either. I'm your husband, I love you, and I will do anything – *anything* – to protect you. If I have to shoot at some cop then that's what I'm going to do.'

'I don't want your protection. I just want to go home.'

'Get it through your skull, we're never going home again. Not you. Not me. Not us.'

He grabs me by the arm and pulls me away. I'm too weak, too overwhelmed, to resist.

Trevor is stationary.

'You too, old man,' Leo tells him.

Trevor doesn't move.

Leo raises the gun and is about to say something further, to order or demand, but Trevor sighs and shakes his head and does as he's been told. What choice does he have? What choice do I have?

I look at Rusty, lying on the cold ground, alone in the dark. Is she alive? Is she moving? I can't tell.

Leo ushers us to where his vehicle is parked on a street behind his unit. I note he makes us walk ahead of him, steering and guiding us instead of leading us.

Is my husband kidnapping me?

'Get in the car.'

It's a vehicle I haven't seen before. I don't know how long he's had it and I don't know if Leo owns it or rented it or stole it and I don't ask. If I did ask him, would he tell me the truth? Would I even believe him if he was honest with me? I'm shaking my head as I tug open the passenger door after Leo thumbs the key-fob and the car unlocks with a loud *thunk*. Trevor does the same with one of the back doors, but Leo shakes his head.

'You're driving,' he tells him.

Trevor frowns. 'I am?'

Leo opens the driver's door for him and says, 'Get behind the wheel and do exactly what I tell you to do.'

Trevor does so, and Leo slides on to the back seat behind him.

'Where are we heading?' Trevor asks him.

'North,' is Leo's answer.

I'm momentarily hopeful. 'Back home?'

He breaks into a laugh, short and bitter, and my shoulders sag. 'Don't be ridiculous. No, we're not going home, Jem. What did I tell you? We're never going home again. Never. Ever. Again.'

My voice is weak: 'Then where?'

'To the coast. There's a place we need to reach where we can lie low.'

'What kind of place?'

'A house.'

'Whose house?'

I'm turned in my seat to look directly at him but Leo is not looking at me in return. Instead, his gaze is focused on the night on the other side of the windshield. Is it regret I see in his eyes or is that regret only there because I want to see it?

I'm so sorry, Rusty. I'm so sorry.

3:11 a.m.

The house sits on a spur of land facing the ocean. The Atlantic is black like the night above it, with waves breaking in crests of shining silver in the moonlight. White sand stretches in a straight line south from the house until the night swallows all. Far away from any other living souls I expected quiet, stillness, but the ocean is noisy and never rests. It roars with every breaking swell and I feel its animosity. The ocean does not want us here. The ocean does not like us.

I'm leading, although I'm being led. Leo is behind us, marching Trevor and me along the dunes. The sandy ground is uneven and treacherous in the darkness. I lose my footing often but I'm agile enough not to fall or turn an ankle. Trevor is less able and I reach out to grab his arm and help his balance on several occasions and each time this angers him and he shoos away my help.

Then he falls.

On his hands and knees he's immobile. He's hurt, but it's his ego that hurts the most and he can't look at me as I help him back to his feet. Leo doesn't help. Leo keeps his distance at all

337

times, as though we might attack him. Perhaps Trevor would, given the opportunity.

Trevor limps and puts a hand to my shoulder for support. In turn, I reach an arm around him and he nods thanks he's too embarrassed to say aloud and I nod in silent acknowledgement of that thanks, yet it's unnecessary. I would do anything for this sweet old man who has done so much for me.

Please don't hurt him, I plead in silence to Leo.

My eyes are damp and it's not the cold sea air that causes me to wipe them with my free sleeve. Trevor notices and says nothing and I'm glad.

'Almost there,' Leo says from behind.

A needless comment because the house is obvious and so is our proximity to it. Almost there, yet so far from the end. Can everything be resolved now? Can anything be repaired?

I don't see how. I don't see an end that puts things right.

My husband is walking behind me and I cannot hope to understand his intentions because I don't know him any longer. I know who he was, not who he is now.

Did I ever know him?

I realise Trevor is supporting me as much as I am supporting him. Our pains are different but our suffering is equal.

'What are you talking about?' Leo demands to know.

Neither Trevor nor I had spoken. Leo's paranoid.

'Nothing,' I tell him.

'You're whispering to each other.'

I don't look back. 'Why, Leo? Why would we whisper?'

He doesn't answer.

'Why would you worry if we did whisper?'

Again, no answer but the roar of the breaking waves.

We're not welcome here.

The house is small and old, but it is not rundown. The wind

and salt have assailed it without mercy and it wears little scars as testaments to its endurance. Paint is chipped and faded. Wood is warped. The porch steps creak and whine underfoot.

'Use these,' Leo says, pushing keys into my hand.

I stare into his eyes, once baby blue yet now changed to a glacial shade devoid of warmth.

'What happened to you?' I ask him.

'I'm trying to keep us alive, Jem. Please don't forget that.'

'Yet I feel we've already died.'

'Don't be so melodramatic,' he says back. 'This isn't the time for one of your episodes.'

My eyes dampen again. His mocking words slice through my resolve. 'My episodes?'

'I'm sorry. I didn't mean it like that. I know this is stressful. I ... Please, let's just get in the house. I'm going to make right, I promise.'

'How, Leo? How can you possibly make this right?'

He's angry my unshakable faith in him has gone.

'What are we doing here?' I ask.

'You know why,' Leo replies. 'We need to hide. We need to lie low. This is the safest place.'

'For you, or for us?'

'I'm doing this for us, Jem. Why can't you see that? You realise I could just have gone, don't you? I could have left you and never come back. If I was acting purely in my own interests I would just have run. In fact, that's what ...'

He trails off, and I see that he almost said too much.

'What?' I demand. 'In fact what?'

'Forget it. I'm tired. I'm stressed.'

'Forget what, Leo? What were you about to tell me? You're saying you could have left me like I'm supposed to be grateful that you didn't abandon your wife? Oh, thank you so much, dearest husband, for not abandoning your wife to the people trying to kill her.'

'Jem—'

I'm not done. 'The people, lest we forget, that are your associates. The people, lest we forget, who would never have come after me if it weren't for you. The people you were running away from. The people I . . .'

This time it's me who trails off, but not because I'm scared of saying too much but because I now understand the truth.

'My God,' I say. 'That's what.'

Leo is silent. He knows I know.

'That's what you were going to say, isn't it? The people you were running away from.'

Leo struggles to hold my gaze.

'This morning. That's what you were doing, isn't it? You told me you were going away on business when in fact you were running away. You knew you had been found out, didn't you? You knew Wilks and Messer would come for what was rightfully theirs.' It takes an enormous amount of self-restraint to get the next words out. 'You left me. You abandoned me.'

'But I came back,' is all he can say.

'You left me,' I say again. 'You knew they were coming and you left me behind.'

'I came back.' He's blurry through the tears.

'You didn't even warn me.'

'I came back for you.'

'Stop saying that,' I yell at him. 'You have no right to say that to me. I could have been killed. I nearly was killed. You knew the danger I was in and you didn't say a thing. But why would you? If you warned me then you wouldn't get a head start.'

Trevor says, 'You're a coward. You're the worst kind of coward.'

340

Leo, enraged, raises the pistol to strike Trevor with it.

I push myself between Leo and Trevor.

For a moment, I'm not sure what will happen.

'Everyone calm down,' Leo says, lowering the gun. 'What's done is done. If either of you wants to get out of this mess then we do it my way. Now, before we go inside, does anyone have a problem with that?'

Trevor says nothing.

I look at the gun in my husband's hand and say, 'No.'

'Good,' he says, cold and sharp. 'So just open the damn door.'

I do. I wipe my eyes and steady my fingers and unlock the door that opens into a deep blackness where all hope is absent.

I'm hesitant to enter this abyss, as is Trevor. Leo has to shove us across the threshold.

'What kept you?' Carlson asks from within the black.

3:16 a.m.

Carlson has his gun aimed our way. We're all taken by surprise except I shouldn't be surprised by Carlson's appearance here. He's already shown himself to be determined and resourceful. I realise I don't care any more. I'm done with this.

I just want it over, whatever that means.

'Everything okay out there?' Carlson asks. 'Sounded like you weren't all getting on so well.' He looks at me and my red eyes and tear-stained cheeks. 'But I'm glad to see it's all been resolved so . . . amicably.'

Carlson lowers the gun. I tense at this, ready to spring into action one final time, but I feel Leo's hand around my arm.

'It's okay,' he says. 'It's okay.'

I'm not sure what he means. Does he have some plan? Does he have some way of getting us out of this? Yes, is the answer. Yet my eyes widen at how simply, how easily, it's brought to fruition.

Leo releases my arm and approaches Carlson.

They shake hands.

'You did it,' Carlson says.

Leo nods. 'Thanks for your assistance.'

'All part of the service.'

I'm open-mouthed witnessing the exchange. I thought it was all lies, about Rome, about Carlson. Didn't Wilks say Leo was making it all up?

He returns to me and says, 'Give me the SD card.'

'Why?'

'Just do it, Jem,' he tells me. 'Give it to me so this can be done.'

'You're going to give it to Carlson,' I say. 'But why?'

'I couldn't do all this on my own,' Leo tells me. 'The money's no good if it's in my name, if I'm connected to it. That's where Carlson helps out. He invests it on my behalf.'

He steps forward. 'For a modest percentage of the profits, of course.'

I'm reluctant, but I know I have no choice. My life isn't even my own any more. I pass the micro SD card to Leo, who then hands it to Carlson.

'I'll get right to work,' Carlson says, opening the front door and letting in a blast of cold sea air. 'Message me when you're out of the country.'

Then he's gone into the night.

Leo heads to the kitchen and opens the fridge while I just stand still, not knowing what to do, what to say, what to think. Trevor rests a comforting hand on my back that provides no comfort.

I hear Leo twist open a bottle of beer, which he swigs as he returns to us. He seems pleased with himself, victorious. He doesn't like the look on my face and tries to ignore it while he enjoys his celebratory beer.

'I'll make all of this up to you, Jem,' Leo tells me when he's finished. 'I don't know how I will, but if you give me the chance,

I'll spend the rest of my life trying. If you have even a flicker of love left for me, say you'll give me that chance. It's not a promise. I don't expect you to see me now how you used to see me, but just say you'll try. Say you'll allow me to be your husband again one day.'

I can't talk, but I nod. I can try. I can do that, can't I?

'Thank you,' Leo says. 'We can start again. Wouldn't you like to start again?'

I nod. I do want to. I wish everything could be reset, to go back to the way it was before this nightmare began.

'It's not going to be easy,' he continues, 'I understand that. But I also need you to understand one thing. I need you to understand that this has to be a fresh start.'

I nod.

'It has to be just you and me, Jem. We have to go away together, alone. Where no one knows us and no one knows what we've been through. Do you understand that?'

I nod once again, although it's a tentative nod. It all seems so obvious I'm growing concerned that I don't fully understand what he's saying.

I don't, it turns out.

'Good,' he says. 'I want you to remember this conversation. I want you to remember every word. It's really important that you do.'

'Why?' I ask, now scared. 'Why is it so important?'

'Close your eyes, Jem,' he tells me. 'Don't watch.'

I'm confused, yet only for an instant. I know exactly what he's going to do.

'*No,*' I scream.

Too late.

He shoots Trevor.

344

3:19 a.m.

A single shot to the chest.

Trevor falls straight down, legs collapsing, and I'm pushing away Leo's attempts to stop me as I rush to Trevor's side, half-sliding, half-falling to my knees. I don't know what to do. I press my palms over the wound. I'm crying. I'm screaming.

Trevor's eyes are closed. He's not moving. He's not reacting.

Dear, sweet Trevor. The best man I ever knew.

He's dead.

'It had to be done,' Leo says, behind me. 'It has to be just you and me, Jem.' I feel his hand on my back. He's trying to comfort me. 'This is how it has to be from now on, the two of us. Only the two of us.'

He takes my shoulders, strong fingers pressing into my skin, my flesh. He helps me to my feet, holds me, pulls me closer to him as he speaks, as he pleads. I hear some words, I miss others. His breath, sour with dehydration and beer, is hot on my face. His saliva flecks my cheeks.

345

'Are you listening to me, Jem? Do you understand what I'm telling you?'

I nod because I know that's expected of me. I'm the dutiful little terrified wife. He's talking, explaining, justifying. He's arguing with me but I'm not arguing back. I couldn't if I wanted to. My ears are ringing from the sound of the gunshot, a relentless tinnitus whine interrupted with Leo's words and the awful memory of Trevor's last gasp for air.

Leo, my husband, unrecognisable before me. A blur through bleary eyes. I'm crying for Trevor, for me, and for this man I no longer understand.

I'm wrong, I realise. I do understand him. Finally. How could I have been so ignorant to what must have been obvious? Was I blind? Did I allow myself to be fooled? Did I so want Leo to be perfect that I ignored any sign that he was not? Have I lied to myself all this time? Whatever the answer, now I know him, now I understand who he is, in this moment.

'You're a monster,' I say.

He makes a sound somewhere between a sigh of frustration and a roar of disbelief. It is a fitting sound, guttural, bestial.

'I've done this for us,' he insists. 'For you.'

He's squeezing my shoulders with such strength, such urgency, that I know I will have bruises yet somehow I feel no pain, only pressure, only his force of will. I can picture the little fingerprint smudges of black and purple that will be left behind. I see them with such clarity, such intensity, that I no longer see Leo before me. I see only the future evidence of this moment.

'Are you listening to me?' he yells, and the force of his breath, his saliva on my face, in my eyes, obliterates that image and I regain focus on him, on the anger that creases his face, on the stress that reddens his eyes, on the distorted refraction of the Leo I once knew.

346

Where is the sweet man I fell in love with? Where are his easy smile and entrancing blue eyes? I don't recognise this person.

I nod again, and again. I keep nodding because it's all I can do. I can make no sound, speak no words. I'm a prisoner inside myself, caged by fear and barred by loss.

His grip on my shoulders softens and his frantic, heavy breathing slows. His face, so pinched and creased in frustration, smooths back to something resembling the Leo I once knew.

'Oh Jem,' he says, wrenching me into an embrace.

I cannot return the hug. My arms are limp at my sides, immobile. He's trying to comfort me but I feel so small, so weak and insignificant. For a moment I just want it to be over. I want him to keep squeezing, to use his strength to crush the life out of me because I no longer want this life, my life.

'I don't expect you to be okay with what I've done,' he continues. 'I know it will take time but I also know that you will, eventually, understand that I had no choice. I'll be patient, I promise. I'll make things right. Just give me some time, please. Allow me to try. Can you do that? Can you do that for your husband?'

I nod into his chest.

'Yes,' I manage to say.

The effort it takes to respond is enormous.

The effort it takes to lie is immense.

There is a silence, and I try not to tense. I can't see his face so I don't know if he believes me, if he even heard. Does he detect the lie? Does he know me more than I know him?

He exhales. 'That's all I ask.'

He believes me.

He releases me from the embrace. Steps back.

'I'm so sorry I had to put you through all of this,' he says, using a thumb to wipe away my tears with such delicate intimacy that I don't want him to stop. I don't want him to stop because then reality will return and he will be a murderer again.

Don't stop, I mouth in silence. *Don't stop.*

But he does. He's wiped the tears clean from my eyes, my cheeks, leaving the skin tight and irritated. He smiles then because he sees I'm smiling too. Only it's the smile he wants to see instead of any smile I could possibly feel. When did you last make me smile, Leo? I wish I knew, I wish I could remember, because whatever this night brings, whatever happens next, Leo will never make me feel like that again. He'll never make me smile again.

'It's going to be okay,' he tells me. 'It's going to be okay.'

He's stroking my cheek and I rest it in his palm.

'I'm going to make it up to you, I swear it,' he tells me. 'It's hard, I know. And it's not going to get any easier any time soon. But it will, when we're far away from here. And that's what we need, Jem. We need to be far away where no one knows us and no one knows how we got there or why we left. We'd never get far if anyone else knew what happened here, what happened today. It has to be just us. It has—'

He stops because he cries out in pain.

He cries out because I've sunk my teeth into his hand.

'*Bastard*,' I scream when he tears his hand away.

I leap to my feet as he stumbles away, shocked and pained.

Blood is smeared around my mouth. It stains my lips and my teeth.

I attack him, this murderer I married. This monster. He's slow to react, still hurt and shocked from the bite. I land a couple of punches, cutting his lip, knocking him backwards, but he's resilient, strong. The effect is only temporary and he's ready for me when I go for the gun. I can't prise it from his grip.

'What are you doing?' he yells at me.

I don't answer. I don't know. I just want this over. I just want this to stop.

He grabs a fistful of my hair and wrenches my head back. All my balance goes, all my stability. I have to release the gun to stay on my feet. He shoves me away and I trip, fall.

I scramble to my feet, rage and adrenalin overriding pain.

I'm about to charge him again when the hammer of the gun clicks back and I'm staring down the muzzle.

Leo says, 'Stop.'

I recognise the seriousness of his tone, the message delivered in that one short word. If I go for him, he'll shoot. He's not bluffing.

I don't care. I don't care any more.

I charge.

He shoots.

But I don't die. Instead, I scream.

I'm on my knees before I realise I've fallen. I'm grabbing my left arm before I understand I've been hit. There's so much pain, so much blood.

'You shot me.'

Leo steps closer. 'It's a flesh wound, and I had to.'

'You shot me,' I say again.

'You didn't leave me any choice.'

I peel away my palm. There's a shallow groove carved through my flesh, leaking bright blood. Just seeing the wound makes me light-headed.

'It didn't go in,' Leo says. 'You're lucky I'm such a good shot.'

I don't feel lucky. I feel nauseous and cold and weak. I feel betrayed and distraught.

'You're my wife,' I hear Leo saying, 'and I'll do anything to protect you. I've done everything to protect you. But I will hurt you if you leave me no other choice. I will hurt you if you put us at risk. I won't let you end what we have on account of a stranger you only just met. I'm your husband. You need to remember that. Everything I've ever done is for you.'

I grimace. My teeth are clenched and my eyes squeezed shut.

'I'll get a first aid kit and take care of the wound,' he tells me, sympathy creeping into his tone. 'And then, we're going. We're going and never coming back. I need to know you understand that, Jem. I need to know you accept it.'

Teeth still clenched and eyes still shut, I nod.

'Good,' Leo says. 'I'll be back in a minute.'

I hear footsteps as he leaves the room.

My teeth stop clenching and my eyes snap open.

I run.

3:25 a.m.

Out through the front door, down the porch steps and on to the beach.

So fast I flail with my arms to stay vertical and avoid crashing face-first into the sand. I know my lead will be short. I know Leo is fast and fit and uninjured. I have mere seconds and I cannot waste even a fraction of one.

The dunes are to my right, prickly with long grasses that sway and rustle in ceaseless synchronicity. The ocean is to my left, black and violent, roiling and foaming. Between lies endless sand, beautiful and glowing silver in the moonlight. I run along that infinite beach, not knowing where it will take me or where I need to go, but I'm not thinking, I'm not planning. My desperation requires only distance, my fear can only be satisfied with separation from the house, from Leo.

I think I can run away from him.

I think I can run away from everything.

My body knows otherwise. I've been through so much and

rested so little since that knock at the door that I'm fatiguing after mere yards. My legs are weighted with lead and I struggle to lift them, to extend them. My chest is so constricted no inhalation feels like anything close to enough air.

The wind surging in from the Atlantic buffets me as I run, trying to stop me, trying to push me over. The sand, loose beneath my feet, conspires with the ocean, with Leo, threatening to trip me up, to swallow me whole.

I'm alone. I'm so alone.

I'm running into darkness, running into nowhere, running from the only man I've ever loved, the only man who has ever loved me in return.

I hear his voice pushing through the wind, calling for me.

I'm expecting to feel the searing pain of a bullet in my back at any moment yet Leo doesn't shoot me. Maybe he's too far away. Maybe he's out of range. Maybe he'll let me go.

I glance back even though I shouldn't. I see him leaping from the porch, chasing, gun clutched in one hand. Long limbs powering him to frightening speed.

He won't let me go.

I keep running, fighting through the exhaustion, through pain in my feet, my arm, fighting the wind and the sand. I'm losing pace. I can feel myself slowing and I can feel Leo catching up to me with a terrifying inevitability.

I can't outrun him.

I can't escape.

Then, I can hear him. He's so close I can hear him despite the roar of the ocean. I hear his rapid, urgent breaths. He sounds like an animal, a beast.

His fingers reach my hair. Their proximity sickens me as much as terrifies me. He fails to grab hold.

I try to run faster, to tap into some last reserve of energy. I fail. That well is empty, dry. I've turned to it too many times already and it can no longer save me.

Leo reaches again, this attempt finding enough strands of hair to grasp at, tug at, unbalancing me.

Only for a second, but that's all it takes.

I stumble.

It's enough for him to make up the last of the distance.

He tackles me from behind, arms around my waist.

I fall, hitting the beach elbows-first before the rest of me crashes down after them. Air exits my lungs in a painful blast and my eyes close the instant before my face whips against the sand and I'm dazed and disorientated, sliding, rolling laterally, Leo holding on to me, on top of me, under me, on top of me again as we tumble over and over.

We roll from dry sand on to wet sand and into seawater that's so cold it takes my breath away with even more ferocity than the fall and I scream without sound.

I come to a stop on my back, Leo on top of me, pinning me with his weight to the beach as a wave breaks against me and icy black seawater rushes over my head. Some gets into my eyes, my mouth. I cough. I gag. I retch.

I blink my eyes clear to see Leo pushing himself to his knees, either side of my abdomen, but no further. There's no gun in his hand. He must have lost it in the fall.

Leo, sitting atop me, looks down and there is so much sadness and regret in his eyes I almost don't recognise him because for that instant he looks like the Leo I once knew, the Leo I married.

'I'm sorry, Jem,' he says, 'but this has to stop. I didn't want this, I promise. Anything but this.'

To make himself heard over the raging wind and breaking waves he's shouting, yelling the words at me, yet the voice that reaches my ears is quiet and almost soft, almost gentle.

'I don't know how else to fix this.'

He places both palms on my shoulders and pushes down.

The wet sand beneath me gives way under the pressure and I sink into it. Only a little – an inch or two – but it's enough for the seawater at my ears to rise up and cover my face in a freezing shroud that stings my eyes and slips into my nostrils and mouth.

I gasp and cough and yank my head up enough to clear my lips and nose and manage to suck in air before the next wave comes and I'm underwater, unable to see even with my eyes open, unable to breathe, trying to hold my breath and not inhale the black ocean hungry for my life.

I'm gripping at his wrists, trying to pull his hands away from my shoulders. Those hands are immobile. He's too strong, or I'm too weak, or both.

I'm aware of Leo's voice, somehow far away, disembodied and muted by seawater and my own soundless screams.

The wave withdraws and I gasp and cough.

'Let go, Jem,' Leo yells in his faraway whisper. 'Let it happen. Let it be over. Go to sleep, baby. Just go to sleep.'

He raises himself higher on his knees so he can lean forward further, so he can apply more pressure on my shoulders.

I sink deeper into the sand. I can no longer force my head forward enough to clear my face from the seawater. It sloshes around my lips, sluicing down my nostrils, icy, thick and coarse with salt and sand.

Every breath is accompanied by a gag, a retch, a cough. I'm drowning and choking at the same time.

'I'm sorry,' he says as he continues murdering me.

Another wave hits us hard and I don't get the chance to suck in even half a breath before my head is beneath the ocean once more and I grow faint in the airlessness, but I'm no longer cold.

Darkness blacker than the ocean, than the night, encroaches on my vision and I feel no fear. I begin to welcome this blackness because it means release from all the hopelessness, all the pain.

Go to sleep, baby. Just go to sleep.

Yes, that's what I want.

I stop fighting. My grip loosens on Leo's wrists. I'm so tired. I'm ready to sleep. I'm ready for this to end.

The surge of another incoming wave buffets me back to a wakefulness I don't want, jabbing at me, at my ribs, hard, painful.

Too hard.

I release one of my hands from Leo's wrist, fumbling with numb fingers to feel something solid and angular against my side.

Leo's gun, washed into me by a merciful ocean not as hungry as I thought.

I have so little dexterity it feels like many seconds go by before I manage to take it in my grip, finger slipping through the trigger guard, and I elevate my arm so that as the seawater pulls back, my hand and the gun rise above the retreating wave and the weapon is pointing up at Leo.

'Don't,' my husband begs.

I do.

8:01 a.m.

Jem Talhoffer looks exhausted.

No, she looks beyond exhausted, so physically and mentally drained that the fatigue has transcended mortal experience and has become spiritual, as if her very soul is tired. Rusty struggles to think if there is even a word for such a state. If there is in fact such a word, she can't think of it now. Maybe when she's next sat on her porch with just the night, her thoughts and her weed for company she might just work out the proper way of describing such exhaustion.

Rusty has walked the scene. Shuffled the scene. She can't move fast. She never could, of course, but now she's a slow-motion version of her previous self. Like she's walking on the moon or into a hurricane. It helps if she doesn't move, but breathing is the worst part and the only thing she can't stop herself doing. Each inhalation is a red-hot poker stabbing into her sternum. Each exhalation is that same burning spur of metal yanked back out again.

Why couldn't she have been shot in the belly? she thinks. Probably wouldn't have even felt it.

She's still alive thanks only to her body armour, she knows. Tightly woven layers of Kevlar to be precise. Bullet didn't even get halfway through. The vest didn't do a whole lot to stop the blunt force trauma dropping into her chest like a pebble in a duckpond, however.

She toughs it out in front of the local law enforcement who were first to the house, followed closely by the EMTs. They found Jem sitting on the porch, wrapped in an old blanket, with lank, wet hair draped over her face. That face is bone pale and her eyes are focused on a point far, far away. She's been shot in the arm, but it's not serious. There are superficial injuries all over her. Cuts and scratches and bruises and grazes turn her flesh into a tapestry of brutality the likes of which Rusty has rarely seen. It's all going to be photographed, of course, once she's been examined at the hospital and those injuries have been treated.

'She's in no danger,' a paramedic explains, 'but she's going to be suffering for a long time.'

Rusty nods.

Two bodies have been found at the scene. One in the house itself and the other on the beach. Both men. Both shot.

Another is at Leo Talhoffer's empty warehouse.

She deals with one violent death per year at the most. Now, it's four in one night.

Formal statements can wait but Jem has talked them through her day from hell. How it happened, as it happened. From eating avocado on toast for breakfast and kissing her husband goodbye all the way to shooting him dead. Everything in between too. The two corrupt government agents, Wilks and Messer, the Good Samaritan Trevor, now

357

sadly deceased by Leo's hand. And the mystery man, Carlson. Who is he? Rusty thinks she knows. Rusty has a theory.

She spends a lot of time discussing the details with her local counterpart. There's a lot to go through and he's happy to talk.

'What do you think?' Rusty asks him.

'It's a miracle she's alive,' he tells her. 'That's one tough cookie.'

Rusty agrees.

She is not surprised when a black SUV arrives on the scene and a pair of trenchcoat-wearing government types climb out and head her way. They introduce themselves, showing National Security Agency ID and not complaining when she asks for a moment to check they are who they proclaim to be. A quick phone call and Rusty is content she isn't dealing with another Wilks and Messer situation. These two are Percival and Hirsch, as their IDs state.

Percival does the talking. She seems too young to be in charge of anything, but Rusty is at that age where anyone young looks too young. Is Percival thirty or is she some child prodigy who went to college at twelve years of age and became a government agent the day she was old enough to drive?

Percival gets straight to the point.

'We're hoping this can be handled with a degree of discretion.'

'I figured you might say something of that ilk.'

Percival is unsure of Rusty's tone. 'Is that a problem for you?'

Rusty shakes her head. 'Not at all, but I would like to know why.'

'That I can do,' Percival says in return. 'We screwed up. Hugely. Embarrassingly. We'd rather not advertise that fact.'

'I was sure you were going to hit me with the national security excuse.'

Percival shows a tight smile. 'I doubt you're the kind of

woman who'd be satisfied with being deflected. I expect you'd be insulted. I know I would be. In my experience it's the people we offend we have to worry about the most. They're the ones who will spend their spare time checking facts and asking questions.'

'I'm no one to worry about.'

'You misunderstand,' Percival says. 'I'm being straight with you as a courtesy, but I also recognise it is the most tactically assured course of action.'

'Then you won't mind telling me how you screwed up?'

'Lacy Wilks and John Messer were useful agents. Two of hundreds, if not thousands, like them. Not special. Efficient, no more. That they had any extracurricular activities going is something I've only recently become suspicious of. They were being investigated internally. Or not, when you consider large sums of cash money are involved. I vouched for them, so it's my fault. My embarrassment.'

'They fooled me too. I thought they were legit.'

'I'm going to take heat for this for years to come. I'm not angry about this and I'm not bitter. I'm disappointed in myself and I wish to keep it as the only stain on my jacket. I'm going to have to work twice as hard just to get back to where I am. If this becomes publicised we will have it shot down and any reporter discredited in a matter of days. We do it all the time. That's not what I want to happen here because even an extinguished bonfire was still lit, however temporarily.'

Percival doesn't want to advertise the stain on her jacket.

Rusty says, 'You can survive it privately.'

Percival says, 'Publicity is worse than screwing up in the first place. It will bury me.'

'I don't want to bury you.'

'Thank you.'

'No need,' Rusty says with a shrug. 'It's nice to be nice, right?'

Percival nods.

'What about the money, the information?'

'We'll seize what's obvious and keep an eye on any accounts or businesses in Leo Talhoffer's name. But between you and me, recovering money is not a priority. What might be large sums to an individual aren't even on our radar.'

'Four people have died because of that money.'

'I don't know what to say about that,' Percival says.

Rusty says, 'Neither do I.'

'People have died for less.'

Rusty nods.

'How's the wife?'

'A mess. Do you need to talk to her?'

Percival is silent for a second, then shakes her head in a short, efficient movement. 'At some point further down the road to fill in inevitable blanks, but I think she's been through enough tonight without having me quizzing her all over again, wouldn't you agree?'

'Probably.'

'Makes you think, doesn't it?' Percival looks to the middle distance. 'Never can tell who people really are. Even those closest to us.'

'Especially those closest to us.'

Percival meets her gaze. 'And what a sad truth that is.'

'Most truths are.'

Hirsch, silent and subservient until now, checks his watch with an exaggerated movement and says to Percival, 'We need to be making a move if we're going to make the debrief.'

She nods to him without looking at him, then says to Rusty, 'Thank you for making this simple.'

'No problem. I like simple.'

'I owe you one.' Percival hands Rusty a business card. 'Cash in any time.'

Rusty watches Percival and Hirsch stride back to the car. Maybe it's the suits, Rusty thinks, that makes government types walk like that. They never stroll. They never saunter. They never traipse. It's always a stride. Strong. Purposeful. As if every step is necessary, as if any direction is the correct one.

Rusty likes the way Percival walks.

Rusty carefully slides Percival's card into her wallet.

Rusty needs to go home. She needs to sleep. She needs to smoke on her porch and try and put this out of her mind for a little while. Maybe give her friend in LA another call and arrange that long-awaited visit.

Before all that, though, she's going to drive up to Trevor's cabin and pick up the little dog, Merlin. Rusty's never been big on the idea of pets but she feels that perhaps she'll take him home with her instead of to the pound and that thought takes enough shape for Rusty to begin imagining what having a pooch might be like. It would give her an excuse to get more fresh air now and again. Perhaps given enough long walks and throwing balls Rusty might shift the dread of climbing a set of stairs. Plus, she's heard that dogs are therapeutic, that they're calming, which sounds pretty good to Rusty. She needs all the calm she can get. Could be a dog might even help her mother, although Rusty isn't going to put any expectation on that. It would be unfair, even to a pet, to load it with such responsibility. Either way, she's liking the idea of a dog more with every passing moment. She might change the name, though.

Merlin just doesn't sound right to her ear.

Rusty heads to her car, which is only a short walk away yet

it takes for ever to get there with that red-hot poker stabbing at her chest.

Funny how much it hurts now when at the time she barely felt a thing.

THE NEXT DAY

'I have so little dexterity it feels like many seconds go by before I manage to take it in my grip, finger slipping through the trigger guard, and I elevate my arm so that as the seawater pulls back, my hand and the gun rise above the retreating wave and the weapon is pointing up at Leo. "Don't," my husband begs. I do.'

Jem Talhoffer wipes tears from her eyes, clearing the exhaustion of her soul. She gulps down water from the plastic cup Rusty had Sabrowski fetch for her. She didn't want coffee and Rusty tried not to get offended by this. Jem gulps the water down. Not surprising her throat is dry after telling her story.

She says, 'Like I told you at the start, Rusty, a knock at the door really can change everything. I wasn't exaggerating because nothing will ever be the same again, will it? In the space of one short day I learned my whole marriage was a lie. I found out my husband was an entirely different person to the man I believed him to be. But in a strange way that helps, doesn't it? Because it means I didn't shoot the man I loved. I killed a man I didn't even know.'

Rusty says, 'Is there anyone I can call?'

Jem shakes her head. She went to the hospital alone, was discharged alone, came to the precinct alone to make her statement.

'No one to pick you up?'

Another shake of her head.

Rusty leans forward. 'No family? No friends?'

'I don't have any family and I don't have any friends.'

'How's that happen?'

She shrugs.

'You had parents, didn't you?'

'They're dead.'

'Friends then,' Rusty says. 'You don't have to have a best bud but you must've met people in your life, haven't you?'

'I'm not good with people.'

'Huh,' Rusty says. 'You might be the first ever person I've dealt with in this job who's more of a loner than I am.'

'I don't know what you want me to say.'

Rusty turns up her palms. 'I'm merely concerned for your well-being, Jem. You've been through a hell of a time and I don't want to send you out of here with no one to look after you.'

'I don't need anyone to look after me. My injuries are all superficial.'

'You're traumatised,' Rusty says. 'Your husband's dead. The husband who tried to kill you.'

'I'm okay.'

Rusty is pleased with herself because that's the reaction she was after, and she's ready with her reply, 'Yeah, Jem, you don't seem as traumatised as I would have expected.'

Jem is silent.

'Which is probably shock, right? That's what happens to people who've undergone a trauma. They go into shock.

They're numb. Survival mechanism, I suppose. Evolution. So, I guess what we're experiencing here is Darwinism in action.'

'Darwinism,' Jem says.

Silence for a moment.

'You didn't talk about the diner,' Rusty says.

'I did. I told you we stopped by.'

'Yeah, a "pit stop" as you called it. You didn't tell me about recruiting a waitress to distract my officer.'

'I didn't think to,' Jem says after a pause. 'Didn't seem important.'

'Guess mentioning the phone call you made to the warehouse wasn't important either. That's how I found you, by the way.'

'I can't remember every last detail exactly, can I?'

'Dana mentioned you and Trevor left in a truck. Not a car. Trevor's truck by the sounds of it.'

'She's mistaken. We were in Carlson's car.'

'The car you used to drive away from Trevor's cabin and head to the warehouse.'

'Yes.'

'Then why isn't it still there? Since you left with Leo to go to the cottage?'

Silence, then, 'He must have collected it.'

'Then where's the car Leo drove you in? Since we only found Trevor's truck at the cottage.'

'Carlson must have driven the truck and then drove away in the other car.'

'And then gone to collect his own car?'

'Yes.'

'Do you see why I'm confused? Because then where is this other car?'

'How am I supposed to know?'

'Well, I do have this theory that might explain it,' Rusty

says. 'It's probably crazy. Like a "what if?" kind of thing. Wanna hear it?'

Jem Talhoffer listens.

'It's been building up all day long and all night too. Started out as a tiny seed in my thoughts that has been germinating in the dark, sprouting without my awareness and growing stronger and stronger until I couldn't ignore it no longer. Now, it's fully developed. So developed that I'm even considering it to be more than your everyday theory.'

The build-up works because Jem Talhoffer says, 'What is it?'

'You got a few minutes? You're under no obligation to stay now you've given your statement. I just want to be clear on that.'

'Sure.'

'Great,' Rusty says. 'I've been itching to share it with someone. My officers are not – how do I put this delicately? – of a particularly creative mind-set. They're not likely to appreciate any idea that requires them to think any harder than they absolutely need to. And this theory of mine requires the ability to think so far out the box that the box can no longer be a consideration. The box might as well be a dot.'

Silence, and Jem has no choice but to say 'What is it?' for the second time.

Now Rusty has her undivided attention, and that's what Rusty requires above all else. While Jem is eager to hear more, she won't be thinking of what is showing on her face. Before, Rusty couldn't read her eyes, so now she's enlarged the font.

Rusty says, 'Incredible, isn't it? You're just a regular, everyday citizen when this began. Then, you're running for your life, people want you dead, your husband is a thief. He's lied to you your whole marriage. He kills the one person who has believed you, helped you without question. You fear for your life. You don't know this Leo, this monster. You have no choice but to kill him in self-defence. Carlson gets away. The only one to survive besides you.'

Jem swallows. Nods. Tears on her cheeks.

'And no one around to contradict your story.'

Jem dries her eyes.

'Hope and expectation are two separate things though, aren't they?'

'I'm not sure I follow.'

Rusty leans forward. 'Then let me explain it to you. I hope we find Carlson, I really do. I hope we find him because according to you he killed Messer, he worked with your husband. He could be working for that mysterious third party. You're not sure. But he's clearly dangerous.'

Jem nods.

'But,' Rusty continues, 'I don't think we will find him.'

Jem says nothing.

'You ever hear the expression if it walks like a duck and quacks like a duck?'

She nods. 'Then it's probably a duck.'

'Yeah, probably.' Rusty pauses. 'Only in this case we might consider me an expert in ornithology. Because I'm looking right at something that walks like a duck and quacks like a duck. And you know what? Not a duck.'

Jem hasn't blinked in a long time.

'I've been focused on Leo all this time, Jem. I've been looking into Wilks, into Messer, into this mystery man Carlson. And all that time I never stopped, even for a second, to think about looking into you.'

'Why would you?'

'Why indeed, Jem? Why indeed? You're just a part-time yoga teacher who keeps to herself. No offence, but you're kind of boring. Aside from the fact you happened to marry a money launderer.'

'Everyone makes mistakes.'

'They do,' Rusty agrees. 'I make a dozen a day and that's me being generous. You, as far as I can tell, made only one.'

Jem waits for elaboration.

'You killed Messer.'

'Carlson killed Messer.'

'That's not what Wilks said.'

'Wilks was corrupt.'

'Why did they try and kill you?'

'I don't know,' Jem says. 'I had become a problem they didn't need.'

'Sure, but wouldn't it have made a lot more sense for them to tie you up? To restrain you and keep you around if they needed you to lure Leo into a trap, for example? That's something I just can't get my head around even if everything else makes absolute sense. There's just no way they would try and kill you in your own home, strangling or beating you to death in the bathroom. How would they have planned to get away with it? There would be a ton of evidence left behind. These were not junkies off the street but two federal agents. Why would they risk it? Why? I can't answer it.'

'Neither can I.'

'But searching for that answer made me think about everything you had told me earlier. About the knock at the door.' Rusty pauses. 'About the phone call.'

Jem doesn't react.

'And there it is, the phone. Just hanging from the wall. So, do you know what I do? I pick it up. I hear the dial tone. I tap 69 to get the number of the person who called last. I write down the number. I call them. Do you know who called you last? Carlson, right? Well, it was the Department of Motor Vehicles.'

'Maybe Carlson works at the DMV as a cover. Or just used their phone.'

'There is no Carlson, is there? You made him up. That's why I'm not going to find him. He's not real. But why make him up?'

'I'm sure you're going to tell me.'

'Because you needed a reason to run like you did. You needed an excuse. When Wilks and Messer turned up on your doorstep you freaked out. This wasn't supposed to happen. You ran. But then you changed your mind. You thought of a plan. You real-ised you could get yourself out of this mess and blame it on Leo. You came to see me, knowing that's where Wilks and Messer would have gone. You told us what happened and I admit there's a certain arrogant genius to it all. Walking into a police HQ and lying like that ... Wow, the balls on you. How can you even walk? Bet you have bruises all over your inner thighs, yeah? You go back home with Wilks and Messer. You split them up. You attack them. You catch them by surprise. Maybe it all worked out exactly as you hoped or maybe it wasn't that easy. Either way, you hurt yourself. Just enough to leave your blood behind in the bathroom, the hallway, the staircase. You make sure the house looks like a bomb went off, like you fought for your life, like someone arrived and saved you. Wilks, when she wakes up, even backs up your lie about Carlson to distract me from what's really going on. You head to Trevor's cabin, which is only a few miles away but by your own account takes you an hour. Why? Because no Carlson means no car. You feed Trevor more lies. He's a good man and wants to help you. You take his truck to the warehouse that no one is supposed to know about since it's registered offshore. Which is a hole in your version of events, because why would Leo try and run and leave behind the valu-able accounts? I can fully believe that Leo kills Wilks here as he tries to protect his wife, the wife who has manipulated him all this time, using his sommelier business to hide her schemes. Of course, it's you who convinces Leo to head to the cottage so you can engineer another attack. Carlson conveniently shows up and escapes with the money, naturally.'

Rusty takes a breath.

'But the worst part, the very worst part in all this, is that you killed Trevor. How could you do that? He just wanted to help you, Jem. I bet he insisted on going with you, didn't he? I bet you tried to sneak off from his cabin in his truck and he caught you in the act and wouldn't take no for an answer. He just wanted to help you. You killed Trevor and you killed Leo. You killed them both and you called me. Reliable Rusty. Too dumb to see the truth.'

Jem begins to cry, shaking her head in protest.

'Leo, the secret money-laundering thief working with corrupt NSA officers. Only that's not accurate, is it? That's nowhere near the truth, is it? Jem, the anxious little wife. No one would suspect there was so much more going on behind those big, dark eyes of yours. But that's the thing with secrets, isn't it? They have a will of their own. They simply must come out, sooner or later. You killed your husband. You had to, I know. But what I don't know is if that was always part of the plan or not.'

Jem Talhoffer is silent for a long time.

Rusty says, 'The government won't be coming after you for anything more than background on Leo. They're more concerned with the press finding out about their screw-up than recovering any money. They're embarrassed, not out for blood. Whatever you stole isn't worth their time.'

Rusty can't read a thing in Jem's eyes. She's not used to that and she doesn't like it one little bit.

When Jem speaks, once she's dried her eyes, she says, 'Can you prove any of that?'

Rusty shrugs. She shakes her head. 'I have a funny feeling all of the physical evidence is going to back up your story, won't it? We'll keep looking, of course, but if you were in the least bit concerned we might find anything you wouldn't have called the police from that cottage, would you? You'd have just vanished.'

'Am I under arrest?'

'No, there's nothing to charge you with. Besides, it's just a theory.'

'Then we're done.' Jem stands up. 'See you around, Rusty.'

Rusty escorts her to the door. 'I figure you'll want to move away. Maybe overseas.'

She shakes her head. 'No, I'm exactly where I want to be.'

Rusty holds open the door and Jem steps through the threshold into the new morning. The setting sun paints the buildings in orange-pink light. It's been a beautiful day.

Rusty watches her go, admiring her poise. Rusty is neither angry nor disappointed. Like she said, it's just a theory. Doesn't matter what you know, only what you can prove. Rusty is an officer of the law not a champion of justice. She'll investigate every lead, every clue. And she'll accept the end result.

Watching Jem make her way from the police department with all that sangfroid gives Rusty no confidence there will be anything to find.

Maybe because there is nothing to find.

Jem crosses the street and stops for a moment on the far kerb. Turns.

Faces Rusty.

There's no traffic. No other noise of any volume, but there's enough distance and wind between them that they would have to shout to hear each other. Jem doesn't shout. Instead she says two words that Rusty can't hear but can read well enough on Jem Talhoffer's lips.

Quack. Quack.

'Are we really strangers?'

He smiled again. 'Not any more.'

We talked for a while. We chatted about Rome and what we thought of it. I told him about the hostel where I was staying and how it was impossible to get a good night's sleep but somehow it didn't matter. I never felt tired. Each morning I couldn't wait to get out of bed and out into the city. I told him how I would wander the backstreets to seek out the dense, old neighbourhoods and take pictures of children kicking soccer balls against alley walls and women hanging sheets from windows. How I felt both an outsider and conversely at home, like I belonged there.

Leo told me how he had eaten so much pasta he had to stab another hole in his belt and I laughed as he demonstrated with exaggerated stabbing motions. I told him I would never understand how there were so many glamorous, skinny Italian women striding through the plazas to the polite applause of local men.

I told him about all the many fascinating, unique people I had met.

He told me how he fell in love a dozen times a day.

After finishing our coffees, we drank iced water and listened to a pair of locals discussing jazz. They spoke so fast we couldn't possibly understand everything they said but we didn't care. It was part of the fun. Like a game, trying to recognise enough words in their hundred-mile-per-hour conversation to piece together each one's point and counter point. It was a lively exchange, getting heated but remaining casual at the same time in the way only Italians can manage.

Leo asked, 'What are you reading?'

I held up the paperback for him to see.

'"On the Precipice",' he read. '"One woman's journey through anxiety". Sounds like a thumping good read.'

'It's a little self-indulgent,' I admitted. 'But I'm learning a lot.'

'I'll bet,' he said.

There was silence.

Comfortable enough for me. Uncomfortable for him.

I said, 'I sense you want to talk details.'

'Well, I was having fun just having a conversation but it has to end sometime, right?'

'It's good that we get on,' I told him. 'I was worried you would be hideous.'

He smiled. 'I was the same.'

'I'm pleasantly surprised.'

'Likewise.'

I said, 'How long have you been doing this?'

'A year. You?'

'A few.'

He shook his head. 'The money is amazing.'

'It will only get better. You already have the business set up?'

'That's right. Wine. Buying and selling. Good excuse to travel far and wide. Lots of foreign companies and accounts. But I'm not moving enough digits for them. They want me to clean a lot more than I can. I'm just not a numbers guy.'

'Which is where I come in.'

He sips some water. 'How did you meet them?'

'Travelling,' I told him. 'South America. You know how it goes.'

He nodded. 'They put us together for a reason.'

'When we go back we need to do everything right. I don't just mean with the business. I mean everything. Marriage. Kids. House.'

'I'm not a big fan of children.'

'Me neither, but if we look the part then that's half the battle. I'm in this for the long term. We want to hide in plain sight and the more normal we are the better. People need to look at us and think we're just like everyone else.'

Leo smiled. 'You consider everything.'

'I have to.' I smiled back. 'It's all part of the plan.'

'The plan?'

'Yes,' I said. 'We have to have a plan.'

'How do you think of all these things?'

'I've always loved making up stories,' I told him. 'It's my favourite thing in all the world.'

ACKNOWLEDGEMENTS

Writing can be a lonely profession but writers are never alone. Many people have helped with this book from the very early days when it existed only as an idea all the way through to the finished article. I am grateful to these heroes behind the scenes, sadly far too many to name – from friends and family to copy-editors and proofreaders, designers and typesetters.

However, some superheroes must be singled out. These are Philip Patterson, Ed Wood, Nithya Rae, Will Carver, Chris Whitaker and Lidia Teasca.

Finally, the author would like to draw particular attention to the support and encouragement of Liz Barnsley, who provided equal parts pom-pom waving and kicks in the rear. Both much needed.